*Praise*

# THE VEILED WEB

"Known for her brilliance at combining science, adventure, and riveting characterization, Catherine Asaro breaks new territory with a compelling story set in the world we know, at the dangerous intersection of cutting-edge technology and the age-old conflict of culture and the human heart. A romance of ideas as well as the story of a man and a woman attempting to build a bridge between two very different societies, *The Veiled Web* is a thought-provoking and entertaining tale for the dawn of a new millennium."
—Mary Jo Putney, *New York Times* bestselling author of *The Wild Child*

"Catherine Asaro has done it again with *The Veiled Web:* she's written another taut, fascinating novel, this one a timely and provocative look at both artificial intelligence and the relationship between Islam and the West. And she's done it with flair, and with all the excitement of a thriller. Highly recommended."
—Kate Elliott, author of Nebula Award finalist *King's Dragon*

"I read this book twice—the first time for the exciting plot and striking ideas on the development of artificial intelligence, the second time to savor the fine character interaction and loving detail of description."
—Charles Sheffield

"Who but Asaro could have written such a wonderfully romantic adventure about a subject like artificial intelligence?"
—Laura Resnick

*Also by Catherine Asaro*

PRIMARY INVERSION
CATCH THE LIGHTNING
THE LAST HAWK
THE RADIANT SEAS

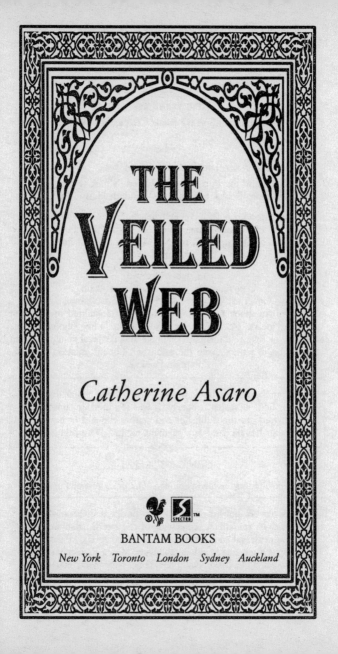

# THE VEILED WEB

Catherine Asaro

BANTAM BOOKS

*New York Toronto London Sydney Auckland*

**THE VEILED WEB**

A Bantam Spectra Book / December 1999



The translation on p. 227 comes from the *The Holy Qur'an, Text, Translation and Commentary.* Abdullah Yusuf Ali, Tahrike Tarsile Qur'an, Elmhurst, 1987, pp. 941–42, Sura "The Criterion," No. 25, verses 63–64.



ISBN 0-553-58151-1

*Published simultaneously in the United States and Canada*

---

Bantam Books are published by Bantam Books, a division of Random House, Inc. Its trademark, consisting of the words "Bantam Books" and the portrayal of a rooster, is Registered in U.S. Patent and Trademark Office and in other countries. Marca Registrada. Bantam Books, 1540 Broadway, New York, New York, 10036.

---

PRINTED IN THE UNITED STATES OF AMERICA

OPM 10 9 8 7 6 5 4 3 2

*To my mother,*
*Lucille Marie,*
*with love*

# ACKNOWLEDGMENTS

I would like to express my gratitude to the readers who gave me input on writing and research for *The Veiled Web.* Their comments greatly helped strengthen the book. Any errors that remain are mine alone.

To Michael Abdurrahman Fitzgerald, Director of the American Language Center in Marrakech, Morocco, for his gracious, gentle, and extensive insights; to author Mary Jo Putney, for her on-target wisdom; to naval veteran John Scudder, R.N. and pastor intern at the Calvary Chapel in Oceanside, California; to Sayed Hassan, president of Dar-Al-Taqwa (the House of Piety) and to the Hassan family for their gracious hospitality at the community Ramadan dinner; to the Columbia Interfaith Center in Oakland Mills; to Katherine Finch of the Ballet Theatre of Annapolis and Caryl Maxwell School of Classical Ballet.

To Larry Clough, acting program manager for the Situation Assessment and Data Fusion Division of Teknowledge Corporation; to the commander, Naval Surface Force Atlantic Fleet Public Affairs Office; to author Jamil Nasir, for his gracefully poetic insights; to Aly's Writing Group: Aly Parsons, Simcha Kuritzky, Connie Warner, Al Carroll, Paula Jordon of NASA, and Maj. Michael La Violette, USAR; to Mike Resnick, for his encouragement that I write an Internet suspense novel; to the many other people who answered my individual questions, including Maj. James Cannizzo, USAF, Jeanine Cannizzo, Alicia Cardona Tope, formerly of ABT, Mr. Sallam, Margaret Slack, and all the folks on the web.

I would like to give special thanks to my excellent editor, Anne Lesley Groell, who is everything an author could ask for in an editor; to my much appreciated agent Eleanor Wood, of Spectrum Literary Agency, for her advice and unfailing support of the book; and to the publisher and all the people at Bantam who made this book possible.

A most heartfelt thanks to my husband, John Kendall Cannizzo, and my daughter, Cathy, whose constant love and support make it all worthwhile.

*Chapter One*

# LIGHT ARISING

*July 2010*

Word came backstage that the king and queen of Spain had taken their places with the President and First Lady in the audience on the south lawn of the White House. Lucia del Mar waited offstage, in the wings, with the other members of the Martelli Dance Theatre.

And then the show began.

They first performed selections from Manuel de Falla's *Ritual Fire Dance*. A man's flamenco solo came next, followed by a lyrical Spanish ballet. Then Lucia was alone on the stage, the audience a wash of color before her, the sky a blue arch overhead. In the breezy golden afternoon, wind tickled her skin.

Even a few years ago she could never have imagined she would someday dance for presidents and royalty. To the daughter of a small desert town in New Mexico, this stage had been as far off as the stars. Now, alone before the audience, she froze.

The opening chords of Lecuona's *Malagueña* swept up from the orchestra—and she had no memory of the steps. Nothing.

But what her mind forgot, her body remembered. Without conscious thought, she spun into an arched-back turn. Her layered skirt swirled out, gold with red lace. Notes shimmered in a waterfall over her body, and her supple arms swayed above her head. As she moved, her fear evaporated. She skimmed across the stage, lost to the music and the pure, blissful joy of the dance.

One by one, the other dancers whirled onto the stage. Then *Malagueña* slowed, melting into long notes while the dancers shifted in tableaus. Lucia spun among them on her pointe shoes, performing a meld of classical ballet and flamenco. The music built and the dancers built with it, through passage after passage, their steps becoming ever faster, until it seemed *Malagueña* would lose control. Finally it did, its powerful chords soaring while the dancers exploded across the stage. With a crashing crescendo, the dance thundered to its finish.

They were done.

And the audience was silent.

In the stillness following the last note, Lucia stood rigid on the stage. They had given their all for a stratospherically select audience—and the response was utter, complete silence.

Then a tidal wave of sound surged up from the audience and swept over the stage. Suddenly people were on their feet clapping, cheering, shouting, "Brava!"

After that, Lucia's vision blurred. She felt the tears on her cheeks. Someone put roses in her arms, but the rest was a haze. Her friends later told her she had four curtain calls. Although that terrifying instant of silence, what reporters later called "an awed hush," had felt endless, it actually lasted no more than a few seconds.

What she remembered most was relief. They had done their best, and the audience appreciated it. As an artist, it was one of her most gratifying moments.

She had no idea then that it might be the last performance of her life.

Lucia walked out of the bathroom in her apartment, drying her hair with a towel. She picked up the robe on her bed and slid it on, letting the terry cloth soak up excess water on her body. She felt peaceful, pleased the performance had gone well this afternoon. More than well.

She still had a few hours before tonight's dinner. Wishing she had someone to share her success, she gazed at the photograph in a silver frame on her bureau. Her parents smiled in the faded picture: her father, a vaquero, a cowboy who worked the ranches in New Mexico, and her mother, a Spanish teacher. Homesickness brushed her heart. She had grown up in Hachita, population seventy-five, where the desert stretched in great open spaces dusted with sagebrush and mesquite, a land that belonged more to the giant tarantulas, rattlesnakes, and bandolero scorpions than to humans. Its silences embraced the sky. If she stood on a hill and gazed out over the vast land, she could hear the grumble of a truck on a road that edged the horizon. She knew the angles and steps of that desert, the crisp midnight wind, the honey scent of night-blooming flowers.

Her first dance teacher, Ellen Vásquez, lived in Deming, about an hour's drive from Hachita. Ellen had danced with the New York City Ballet and performed in Spain. She taught Lucia all she knew, in both ballet and flamenco. Lucia's dark hair and large eyes evoked the Gypsies who had created flamenco, melding their Eastern heritage with the influences of Moorish Spain. Born as a cry of pain from a people persecuted throughout their history, flamenco could also brim with audacious joy, a refusal of the human spirit to bow under adversity. It was emotion at its deepest, the passion and vigor of a wandering race.

Eight years ago, when Lucia was sixteen, her parents had begun to fear her intense focus on dance would burn her out like a candle left to flicker too late into the night. They borrowed a computer for her, hoping to expand her interests. So she learned to wander the World Wide Web.

Now, with a few hours to fill, Lucia sat at her computer and started up a program called Websparks. A large white square appeared on the screen. The border that framed the square was gorgeous, a mosaic of stylized flowers that repeated in geometric, interlocking patterns. Gold and bronze, with flashes of deep turquoise blue, the border brought to mind a grotto gilded by the sunset over the Mediterranean Sea. Centered in each corner, an eight-pointed starlight pattern radiated intricate, repeating designs. She often wondered about Webspark's maker, what sort of mind could both design such a sophisticated program and create such beautiful artwork.

A pleasant voice spoke. "Good evening, Lucia."

"Hi, Miguel," she answered, using the name she had given her copy of Websparks. The program was available with either a male or female voice. She had picked this version because it reminded her of her father, Enrique Francisco del Mar.

Websparks was a Web browser. It guided her around the Internet and World Wide Web. The Internet was a world-spanning net of computers, all in communication with one another; the Web consisted of places on the Internet she could visit, either to explore or to talk with other people, like an electronic gypsy traveling the landscapes of an electronic universe.

She liked Websparks because the program talked, not *to* her, but *with* her. Four years ago, it had hit the market like fire on a gas-soaked field. Three camps formed: those who loved the garrulous browser, those who loathed having their computer try to chat with them, and those who didn't care a whit either way but who found it entertaining to watch debates flame between the first two camps.

At first she had wondered if Websparks was an artificial intelligence. AI had long been an interest of hers, ever since she researched it at sixteen for a school project. To her disappointment, Miguel didn't qualify. He could interpret and speak several languages, using his huge database of knowledge. But he didn't "think" about what he said. He simply applied rules his human designer had given him. It was true that when she asked him to find her a good vacation spot, he knew better than to list billions of places. Instead, he asked questions such as: Which did she find more restful, beaches or mountains? But his apparent leap of understanding, that humans took vacations to rest, didn't really qualify as thinking, either. He was just applying another rule.

The problem was, Miguel had no common sense. She had to teach him all sorts of things she took for granted, such as that cinnamon toast smelled better than rotten eggs. When she asked him how he thought she should render her performance of the princess Aurora in the ballet *Sleeping Beauty,* he suggested she buy a graphics program. He interpreted "render" to mean creating computer images rather than the artistic expression of a dance. In that case she didn't try to explain. She had found that if she gave the program too many facts and rules, his response times slowed until he could no longer hold a normal conversation.

No matter what, he always spoke in the same pleasant voice. To Lucia, whose life was intricately bound up with the expression of emotion, that lack of variation showed, more than anything else, that Websparks wasn't alive. The program had no feelings. Nor was it aware of itself. It had no conscious identity. Yet despite that, Lucia always thought of Miguel as "he."

In any case, he made a marvelous Web browser. Today he brought up her Web page. At the top of the white screen, the Martelli Dance Theatre logo gleamed, the letters *MDT* cut from rubies, with a sheen of gold suggesting treasure dug up from a sunken galleon. Overlapping its lower edge, the gold silhouette of a man and a woman leapt through space, legs outstretched and arms curved over their heads. Lucia's name appeared in jeweled letters beneath the logo, with a picture of her dancing Kitri in *Don Quixote*. A menu offered links to other displays at her site: a picture gallery, film clips, a performance schedule, a bio she wrote to answer questions her fans often asked, and her favorite part, comments posted by people who visited. According to the counter, 2,023 people had come to call in the last month. Not a huge number by Web standards, but respectable.

"You have e-mail," Miguel informed her. "Twenty-seven letters and six spams."

Lucia winced. Her "spam" invariably consisted of breathless promises for fame and fortune if only she would buy whatever the spammer desired to sell her. "Delete the junk mail," she said. "I'll answer the rest when I get home tonight."

"Spam deleted," Miguel said. "Where would you like to visit this evening?"

"How about the New York City Ballet or the Dance Theatre of Harlem?"

After a pause, Miguel said, "Their pages haven't been updated since the last time you visited. Do you still want to go?"

"No, I guess not." She leaned back in her chair and stretched her arms over her head. "Find me a relaxing place. What do you think? Somewhere warm and beautiful."

"The Madrid tourism bureau has a lovely Web page. You might like that."

She smiled. "Take me to Madrid, Señor Miguel."

"It would be my pleasure, Señorita Lucia."

Lucia spent the next hour wandering the roads of an electronic Spain, traveling from town to town, alone in the golden sunlight that glowed from her screen. So her life continued as it had for the past eight years, with two—and only two—parts: dancing and the Web.

She used her shyness as an excuse for her loneliness, knowing that at least onstage she would feel neither.

The envelopes radiated elegance. The return address said, simply: THE WHITE HOUSE, WASHINGTON, D.C.

Lucia walked to the south entrance with Carl Martelli, the founder and artistic director of the Martelli Dance Theatre in Maryland. Sharon Smythe-Powell and Jason Tyler came with them, two other principal dancers in MDT.

They went through a security checkpoint and had their invitations to the state dinner verified. Then an aide greeted them, a crisp young man in a military uniform, medals gleaming on his chest and a gold braid looped on his right shoulder. He brought them into the Diplomatic Reception Room, an oval chamber with white walls, gold chairs, and wallpaper showing American landscapes. At one end, a harpist and flutist played soft music.

After they put away their wraps and coats in the cloakroom, the aide escorted them to a vaulted corridor with portraits on the walls. Reporters stood behind a red velvet rope, pointing cameras, asking questions, holding microphones. Carl paused and spoke to them, relaxed, at ease with the attention. Lucia was too disconcerted to respond, so she just smiled. That seemed to be enough, though; every time she did it cameras flashed, until all she saw were spots.

Mercifully, they soon started walking again, to a staircase down the hall. At the top of the stairs, a glittering military aide escorted Lucia along the red-carpeted Cross Hall, with Carl following. Behind them, another aide escorted Sharon, followed by Jason. Like a portal opening into an enchanted land, the doorway at the end framed a shimmering crowd in the room beyond. A chandelier hung from the ceiling high above them, tier on tier of sparkling crystal.

Lucia looked up at the aide. "Is that the East Room?" The quiver in her voice made her wince. She sounded as overwhelmed as she felt.

He smiled. "That's right. It's where First Lady Abigail Adams hung her laundry to dry."

She returned his smile, relaxing a bit. At the doorway, the aide showed two small cards to a man posted there, who then spoke over a public-address system: "Ladies and Gentlemen, Miss Lucia del Mar and Mr. Carl Martelli."

Lucia reddened at the unexpected announcement. Then they were inside the East Room, surrounded by people. As they moved forward, into the swirl of elegance, the aide announced Jason and Sharon. The East Room exuded grace: white walls hung with portraits, floor-to-ceiling windows draped in gold, and a polished parquetry floor. It looked like a ballroom, having almost no furniture except a Steinway piano with gilded American eagles for legs. While a waiter served drinks, another military aide spoke to the assembled guests, giving the room's history. Presidents' daughters had been married in it and deceased presidents had lain in state here. President Garfield's children used it for pillow fights.

Then the Marine Band started to play "Hail to the Chief." Music reverberated off the floors and high ceilings, filling the hall with vigor. The color guard entered first, four military men with perfect posture. The inner two, Army and Marine Corps officers, carried the United States and presidential flags. The outer two were Air Force and Navy. They split, two going right and two going left—and the President stepped forward with the First Lady and their honored guests, the king and queen of Spain.

Lucia stared, unable to believe she was actually here. When Carl nudged her, she glanced up with a start. Smiling, he tilted his head, indicating they were to join the receiving line.

As they waited in line, she and Carl talked with Sharon and Jason. A former debutante from Connecticut, Sharon glistened, from her beaded blue gown to the sapphires around her neck. Jason and Carl were handsome in their tuxedos, both well built from their years of dance, Carl silver-haired and distinguished, Jason with the lithe grace of youth. Lucia tried to match their confidence, but she felt like a small-town girl playing at glamour. She had worn a simple strapless gown made from white velvet and pulled her hair up in a Spanish roll, with a glittering comb added at the back. As usual, she had no jewelry except for the gold cross on its slender chain around her neck.

Snippets of a conversation too intriguing to ignore floated to her from two men near them in line.

"On the nets, they're calling it the Duke's suit," one of them was saying. "It should hit the market soon."

"What does it do?" the second man asked.

"It's a virtual-reality suit," the first said. "If you use it on the Web, it creates virtual simulations of Web sites or avatar worlds." He paused. "Quite frankly, I've heard more rumors about the missing software than the suit itself."

His companion looked intrigued. "Such as?"

"The advance demos of Duke's suit were released this month. But they're missing a software program that was supposed to come with the suit."

The second man shrugged. "So what? A lot of software goes buggy during its testing stages."

"This is more than software bugs," the first man said. "Supposedly, if you hook up the suit using the rogue software, it creates a back door that could let someone into your system, read e-mail, alter and download files, and change passwords."

His colleague spoke dryly. "Excuse my cynicism, Parkson, but wouldn't it benefit your company if this Duke's suit lost business due to those kinds of ugly rumors?"

Parkson smiled. "You don't trust my rumors?"

"I'd rather hear facts."

"Hell, I've tried the demos," Parkson said. "I had no problem. But I'm not kidding about the rumors. You don't get buzz like that without a reason. The Duke's suit was supposed to come with a Web browser that would blow the current competition out of the water. But none of the demos had it. You have to run the suit with Netscape, Websparks, Microsoft Explorer, or one of the other browsers already on the market. And now the suit's inventor claims there is no missing program."

"And you say this inventor is here tonight?"

"So I've heard."

The line moved forward and the voices faded. Lucia strained to hear more, but the men had stepped out of range. Curious, she looked around, wondering which guest in the room had created this intriguing Duke's suit. The thin fellow with gold-rimmed spectacles? Or perhaps the gray-haired woman who looked like a college professor.

"Are you looking for Colonel Spearman?" Carl asked.

Startled, Lucia brought her attention back to Carl. "He said he would be here. I haven't seen him yet, though."

She had met Mark Spearman eight years ago, when he was stationed in New Mexico, just after he had received his promotion to lieutenant colonel in the Air Force. He had been on the board of trustees for a ballet guild she danced with in Las Cruces. Mark became her patron and arranged her audition with the Martelli Dance Theatre. Now a full colonel, Mark worked at Bolling Air Force Base about fifteen miles from the Pentagon. Lucia wasn't sure what his job entailed, other than that it involved military intelligence.

Lucia forgot about looking for anyone, though, when she realized she and Carl had neared the front of the receiving line. An aide standing with his hands behind his back asked how she would like to be addressed. With the proverbial butterflies dancing in her stomach, she answered.

The aide spoke to the President in a quiet voice. "Miss Lucia del Mar."

Suddenly she was shaking hands, first with the President, then the king of Spain. She stood tongue-tied, unable to utter a word.

The king smiled. "Miss del Mar, your performance in the *Andalusian Suite* was exquisite."

Somehow she managed to answer. "Thank you, Your Majesty. It was an honor to perform." To her own ears, she sounded self-conscious and clumsy.

If anyone found her awkward, though, they gave no hint of it. She met the First Lady and the queen next, both of whom treated her with grace and courtesy. Then an aide ushered them away from the receiving line. She glanced up at Carl, beaming, and he grinned.

Dinner was served in the State Dining Room at round tables set with rich tablecloths in elegant white. Lucia sat with a bank president, a congresswoman, an ambassador, an actress, and various other dignitaries. She was too shy to join the conversation, other than asking questions every now and then to encourage someone else to talk so she wouldn't have to. She had never seen place settings with so many pieces: knives, forks, spoons, all made from gold, crystal glasses and goblets, china plates edged in gold. The food looked too artistic to eat.

After dinner the President and King exchanged toasts of goodwill. Eventually everyone returned to the East Room for champagne and dancing. As Lucia strolled with Jason and Sharon, an older couple glanced at her, then for some reason did a double take. She flushed, wondering if she had made some awkward mistake.

A man smiled at her, then another. And another. She wasn't sure if people were being friendlier now or if she had just loosened up enough to notice.

Jason laughed softly. "Lucia, you're breaking hearts."

"What do you mean?" With all the rules of protocol they had learned for tonight, Lucia was sure she was going to break one. Or ten. "Did I do something wrong?"

Sharon smiled. "Nothing, hon. You couldn't if you tried."

A waiter served them champagne in tall fluted glasses.

As they sipped their drinks, people drifted in their direction. Soon they were part of a group, talk flowing among and around the clustered guests.

The thin man with spectacles whom Lucia had seen earlier smiled at her, looking self-conscious. He introduced himself as Ted, an executive at VirTech, a company in California. When he realized she was genuinely interested in his work, he relaxed and became more talkative.

"Many of our contracts are with the aerospace industry." He pushed his spectacles more securely into place on his nose. "Satellites, that sort of thing."

"It must be exciting to be part of the space program," Lucia said.

Ruefully he said, "I'm afraid we don't do anything glamorous. Mostly my company produces software for instruments."

The gray-haired woman Lucia had seen earlier was standing next to Ted, listening. "Doctor Duquois, you're far too modest," she said, offering him her hand. "Corinne Oliana. I've long been an admirer of your work in virtual reality and telepresence. Mortabe Grégeois is the only one who comes close to your innovation."

"Did you say Oliana?" Ted Duquois stared at her, pumping her hand. "Stanford? SRI? The Nobel?" When she nodded, apparently understanding his verbal shorthand, Duquois beamed. "Ma'am, the honor is mine."

Lucia listened in mortified silence. She suddenly felt like a fraud, far out of her depth. What could she, a high school dropout, possibly say to these people?

Perhaps she could slip away before she made a fool of herself. As she turned, trying to make a discreet retreat, she ran into a man who had just come up on her other side. He took a startled step backward, blinked, then gave her a measured nod.

It took Lucia several moments to absorb his imposing presence. At first she thought he was an Arab. The sleepy look of his dark eyes and the softer texture of his hair had a more Spanish appearance, though. Given how many

Moors had come to Spain during the Islamic conquests of the eighth century, and how many left after the Christian conquest eight hundred years later, he could easily have both ancestries. Except he was unusually tall for either nationality, about six foot three, with glossy black hair. She couldn't help notice his handsome face and lean, broad-shouldered build. In fact, he riveted her attention.

Unexpectedly, he spoke with a British accent. "Good evening, Miss del Mar."

"To you also, Mr.—" She reddened, realizing she had no idea how to finish.

"Rashid." He said it like *Rasheed.* Somehow he had maneuvered her away from the others. "Rashid al-Jazari."

"I'm pleased to meet you." She felt the wall at her back, cutting off escape.

"I enjoyed your dancing today." He smiled as if he were rationing the expression. "It was a perfect afternoon for the performance."

Lucia relaxed. Weather was always a safe subject. "Yes, it was. Thank goodness the overcast burned off this morning."

"For a while, it reminded me of London."

"Is that where you're from?" Watching his long fingers curl around the stem of his glass, she wondered why he was drinking water instead of champagne.

"Actually," he said, "I grew up in Morocco."

Intrigued, she asked, "Are all Moroccan names as beautiful as al-Jazari?" As soon as the words came out, she wanted to kick herself. *Beautiful?* What kind of thing was that to say to someone she had just met? She hoped she hadn't offended him.

If she had insulted him, he was too polite to show it. In fact, he gave her a startled smile, one that warmed his face, as if she had surprised him out of his reserve. "It isn't really Moroccan. My father's ancestors came from Syria."

Lucia wanted to ask more, but she was afraid of putting her foot in her mouth again. So she retreated to a safer subject. "But now you live in England?"

"Not anymore." He sipped his water. "I spent most of my adult life there, though."

"In London?"

"For seven years. I was in Cambridge before that and Oxford at the first."

Oxford? Cambridge? Mortified, she asked, "Is that where you went to college?"

He nodded. "My undergraduate work was at Oxford. I did my doctorate at Cambridge."

Lucia flushed. This was even more intimidating than the conversation she had just escaped. And this time she had no courteous way to let others talk. It was just her and this devastating man.

She tried to sound casual. "I've always thought it would be fun to travel to places like that."

"I enjoyed it." His voice warmed, like sunlight at the end of the day. "It was good to come home, though. I live in Tangier now."

"Is that in Morocco?" After she asked the question, she regretted revealing how little she knew about world geography.

If he thought it odd, he gave no sign. Smiling, he said, "Tangier is across the Strait of Gibraltar from southern Spain, what we call Andalusia."

With relief, she found herself on familiar ground. "My mother's side of the family immigrated to America from Andalusia." They had been Spanish Gypsies, fleeing from starvation and violence. "That's why I live here, in the U.S."

His voice softened. "That loss for Andalusia is a great gain for the New World."

Flustered, she said, "Thank you." She felt a heightened awareness of him, especially his stillness, that appealing quality of contained strength so different from a dancer's restless energy. She cast around for something to say. "You must have an interesting job, to travel so much."

It was as if a mask dropped over his face, hiding every

nuance of expression. Instead of answering her, he took another swallow of his water.

Lucia wondered what she had said to evoke such a response. Even more self-conscious now, she rubbed her free hand on her arm.

"Are you cold?" He stepped forward. "You're shaking."

She backed into the wall, holding her champagne glass in front of her. "Thank you for asking. But I'm fine."

"You are sure?"

Flat against the wall now, she was all too aware of him. Her face felt hot. She wanted to put her hands against his chest and push him away.

Or not push.

"I'm fine," she said. "Really."

Rashid lifted his hand, his fingers almost touching her cheek. Then he flushed, as if he had just realized what he was doing, and lowered his hand. "I'm sorry. I thought perhaps you might want a wrap. Your dress, it looks . . . cold."

"Cold?" Lucia blinked. Although her dress left her shoulders and arms bare, it was conservative compared to the gowns worn by most of the other women here tonight.

Rashid gave her a rueful smile. "My apologies, Miss del Mar. I came over here to dazzle you with my charm, but I seem rather to have botched it."

*Oh, no, you haven't,* she thought, trying in vain to think of a suitably witty reply.

"Lucia!" a familiar voice said. Then Mark Spearman appeared, gleaming in his dress uniform, with gold markings on his jacket and medals on his chest. He grasped her hands. "What a performance this afternoon. You're the talk of the town, did you know that?"

She smiled with relief at the distraction. "I'll bet you say that to all the ballerinas at state dinners."

As Mark laughed, more people joined their group, talking and sipping drinks. Rashid turned his attention to a well-known actress who had come up next to him. She made no secret of her interest, and he responded with far more ease than when he and Lucia had spoken. It irked Lucia, all the more so because he also seemed totally unfazed by the actress's skimpy gown, which might as well have been cut down to her navel for all that it covered her.

Eventually Lucia and Mark moved away, retreating to an oval parlor with blue drapes on the windows and cream-colored walls. Gilded furniture graced the room. The chairs were upholstered in blue cloth and had the presidential seal worked on them in gold.

"What did al-Jazari say to you?" Mark asked.

"Not much," Lucia said. "We talked about the weather."

"You looked uncomfortable."

She paused, unsure how to answer. "I asked him about his work. I think I offended him."

"Did he tell you anything?"

"No." Dryly she said, "He got the same look you do when I ask about your work."

Mark smiled. "Yes, I suppose he would."

"Is he with the Moroccan government?"

Mark shook his head. "He's the CEO for a multinational corporation. A family business. Citrus fruit, I think, though they're expanding now. I don't know much about it."

Lucia doubted his last claim. But she knew him well enough to realize he wouldn't tell her anything more. She wondered what about Rashid al-Jazari had earned his interest. She could never be sure with Mark, but she suspected he wouldn't have brought her in here and asked such questions unless he had more than a social interest in Rashid's business. That took it from the realm of small talk into Mark's military intelligence work, which put the subject off-limits.

She glanced through the floor-to-ceiling window next to them. Outside, an expansive lawn stretched out and a fountain spumed water into the glistening night. In the distance the Washington Monument stood to one side, a narrow column, tall and straight. Beyond it stood the Lincoln Memorial, as if Lincoln himself were gazing back across the lawns and centuries.

"It all gleams on the surface," she said. "Like you. Like Doctor al-Jazari. You never know what goes on underneath."

Mark spoke softly. "I don't think you would want to know."

She glanced up at him, startled. What did he mean? That she wouldn't want to know more about Rashid? Or about Mark?

Behind them a woman said, "There you are."

Turning, she saw Sharon coming into the parlor. "Were you looking for me?"

"They've started that waltz you wanted to hear," Sharon said.

Lucia tried to beg off, but Sharon was already hauling her to the ballroom. She glanced back to see Mark talking to Jason.

As they left the parlor, Sharon lowered her voice. "What a gorgeous man."

"You mean Mark?" Although it was true, Sharon had never shown an interest in him before.

"Not your colonel friend," Sharon said. "The brainchild."

"Brainchild?"

"Al-Jazari." Sharon leaned her head closer. "Grapevine says he's a genius. His family is in exports. He likes green tea, filet mignon, and chocolate mousse. He played soccer in college."

Lucia laughed. "How do you learn all that so fast?"

"We were at the same table at dinner." She then proceeded, in frothy detail, to describe the other guests, her voice bubbling through the gossip with awe-inspiring ease.

As Sharon sudsed, Lucia glanced around the ballroom. When she saw a tall man with black hair talking to another man, her pulse jumped. Then he moved his head and she realized it wasn't Rashid.

Lucia tried to focus on Sharon's burble. Again and again, though, she found herself scanning the ballroom. But it did no good. Rashid al-Jazari had left.

*Chapter Two*

# TAORMINA

*Sunday, August 8, 2010*

When MDT went to Italy, it was Lucia's first visit to the Mediterranean. Carl had accepted an invitation for the Martelli Dance Theatre to perform at an arts festival in Taormina on the island of Sicily. The dancers flew in to Reggio di Calabria in southern Italy and took the ferry across the Strait of Messina to the northeastern coast of Sicily. Blue-and-green water rippled around them, rich with the scents of the ocean.

The city of Taormina clung to a cliff above the coast, looking out over the Ionian Sea. Early-morning sunlight reflected off the houses, giving them an enchanted air, as if an ancient town had been spirited there from the past and gilded in the dawn's radiance.

Everyone from MDT piled into taxis at the base of the mountain, and their drivers careened up the winding streets. The residents of Taormina lived in an area of steep hills and houses, with gardens piled into tight places and geraniums blooming among the rich foliage. The hotel where the dancers were staying stood closer to the cliff's edge, overlooking the sea.

As soon as Sharon and Lucia settled in their room, Sharon flopped down on a bed. "I could sleep all day."

"I slept on the plane." Lucia had actually only dozed, but the jet lag left her too keyed up to sleep. "Come sight-seeing with me."

Sharon yawned. "If I don't sleep now, I won't be worth anything in rehearsal this afternoon."

Lucia didn't want to go alone; a city this beautiful needed to be shared with friends. So instead she took out her laptop computer and carried it to the table.

"I can't believe you brought that thing," Sharon said.

Settling into a chair at the table, Lucia opened the laptop. "The guy at the desk said they have Internet access here."

"Isn't that a long-distance call?"

"Not if I'm just connecting to a computer in the hotel." Lucia plugged the laptop's cord into a gizmo Jason claimed would change voltage from a European outlet to the American standard her computer expected. "The computers do the communicating. They use electrical lines, fiber optics, satellites. It goes all over the world."

"Whatever." Sharon closed her eyes. "I'd rather sleep."

Lucia squinted at her. Then she sighed. She had never succeeded in rousing any of her friends to share her interest in computers.

Turning back to her laptop, she logged onto the hotel's guest account. Then she typed:

```
telnet earthweb.mdt.com
```

The computer responded with,

Trying . . . Connected to earthweb.mdt.com
Username:

She typed *delmar,* followed by *tanglewood* for her password. And that was that. The net had connected her to one of her computer accounts in the United States. Her parents often told her that she took the electronic age for granted, with its ease of communication. She supposed they were right. Computers made sense to her. She never felt tongue-tied with her laptop.

Lucia often thought of her exercises in dance class as computer software algorithms translated by her brain into processes for her body to perform. She had tried to describe it to Carl Martelli once, with disastrous results. He went into one of his agitated speeches, complete with dire warnings about how such an attitude would weaken her "abiding *passion,* the *flame* of Lucia, her burning artistic *TRIUMPHS.*" He punctuated his words with dramatic gestures, stabbing his finger at the air. It made her blink. She wasn't sure about the flame of her burning triumphs, but after that she quit trying to talk computers with him.

Today she used her MDT account to dial up various computer services she subscribed to: America Online, CompuServe, Prodigy, others. On the venerable Genie, which had outlived many predictions of its demise, she found a chat in the SFRT1 going on with a fellow named Tank Top and some other people she knew:

<Tank Top> I tried a demo of the Duke's suit at work today.

<George> The what suit?

<Tank Top> Duke's. It's a virtual-reality setup.

<George> What, 3-D animation? Big deal.

<Lucia> It's more than animation. It's supposed to create a simulated environment.

<Tank Top> That's right. You can see, hear, and feel

as if you were actually in that environment. Eventually it'll have smell and taste too.

<Sue> It's been done.

<Tank Top> Not like this. Put this baby on and the world disappears. What you experience seems real.

<Sue> I thought the Duke's suit was just a story making the rounds.

<Tank Top> Hell, Sue, I was -in- one. VirTech has an arrangement to sell them in the US.

<George> VirTech? Never heard of it.

<Tank Top> I work there. In Silicon Valley.

<Zeus-on-Olympus> Lucia, I just did a STAT and it says your account is L.DELMAR. That looks familiar.

<Lucia> Do you go to the ballet? I'm with MDT.

<Zeus-on-Olympus> You're THAT Lucia del Mar?

<George> Who is Lucia del Mar?

<Zeus-on-Olympus> Prettiest dancer on the Eastern seaboard.

<Lucia> <blush>

<Razor-Head> Yo, Lucia, do some belly dancing for us.

<Elvira-Clone> 404, Razor.

<Tank Top> Hey, E-Clone. How's it going?

<Elvira-Clone> Hi, Tank. It goes. Who is this Duke person I've been hearing about?

<Tank Top> Probably the guy who invented the Duke's suit.

<Elvira-Clone> Yeah, but who is he?

<Tank Top> I don't know. He's been out to VirTech, but only the VIPs and alpha geeks get to see him. Not us peons.

<Sue> The story I got was that the missing Duke's software has a hidden virus. It will wipe your hard disk when you hook the suit up to your computer.

<Zeus-on-Olympus> I heard it figures out passwords.

<Razor-Head> Get real, ZOO 'n' Sue.

<George> Is this the program that's supposed to steal electronic bank records?

<Elvira-Clone> Sure, that's right. Then it jams your garbage disposal, makes your clocks run backward, and neuters your cat.

<Sue> ROFL, E-Clone.

<Tank-Top> <laughing> I'm afraid in this case, fiction is stranger than truth. I've seen no missing Duke's software.

A memory came to Lucia of her dinner at the White House last month. Hadn't she met one of the VirTech VIPs? A man named Duquois? Had he invented the suit? The thought gave her a thrill of excitement. She wished she had asked more about his work. Or perhaps it had been his colleague, the Nobel Prize winner from Stanford. Or the other scientist they had mentioned. Gregor? Grégeois? She couldn't remember.

A knock at their room door pulled her out of her reverie. As Lucia looked up, Sharon got up and went to the door. Opening it revealed Jason Tyler, as svelte and athletic as ever, blond curls falling into his blue eyes. He had changed into torn jeans and a black T-shirt with the MDT logo on it, making him look like a cross between a street thug and a college boy. The latter was more accurate; Jason was earning his A.A. by going to night school. But he cultivated the tough image on purpose, as protection against those who equated "male dancer" with "easy to bully."

"I couldn't sleep," he said. "You guys want to go sightseeing?"

With both Lucia and Jason working on her, Sharon finally gave in and they all went off to explore. They strolled along the Corso Umberto, a street that ran from Porta Catania, a great arched gate in the residential area of Taormina, to Porta Messina on the western edge of the city. Tourists overflowed the cafés, shops, and ice cream stands. Jason bought a book about the local architecture, choosing from a display that included texts in Italian, French, Spanish, German, English, and Arabic.

Eventually they wandered into quieter back streets, where alleys led to small plazas. Some of the buildings had arched doorways and gables in Gothic style, others had the classical lines of Renaissance or the more ornate decorations of Baroque. Moorish influences showed up in domes and geometric mosaics. It looked like everyone and his brother had conquered Sicily at one time or another and erected buildings in Taormina.

Finally they left the city and walked to the exquisite ruins of a Greek amphitheater, its columns rising into the crystalline air, its seats still intact after millennia. It was here they would perform, spinning under a Mediterranean sky, with the Ionian Sea on one side and Mount Etna raising its majestic peak on the other.

Night in Taormina was a dream of colored lights and soft music. Sharon, Jason, and Lucia found a steep stone staircase climbing the cliff face between two buildings. Looking down the stairs, they could see straight out to the sea, far below. A recessed doorway in the building on one side led into a dusky café with a few people seated around tables. They crossed the café to a door in the back wall—and walked out into a wonderland.

The terrace clung to the back of the building like a hidden place of magic. Colored lamps hung from the eaves, and glazed tiles covered the floor. Vines heavy with flowers curled through the scrolled grillwork that bordered the terrace. The city fell away from the building in steep steps, until it blended into the cliffs that dropped to the distant beach.

A band was playing waltzes and Italian songs. While Jason and Sharon danced, drifting in the dreaming night, Lucia stood at the rail and looked out at the Ionian Sea. Water stretched to the horizon. The Milky Way shed a path of light across the sea, incorporeal and inviting, as if she could dance along it into another universe of wraiths and silvered luminance.

Sharon came to stand with Lucia. "If I hadn't seen this

myself, I wouldn't have believed a place this gorgeous existed."

Lucia smiled, tilting her head toward Jason, who was getting drinks at the bar. "Or this romantic."

Sharon grinned. "That too."

Jason came over and gave them each a frothy drink. After he and Sharon finished theirs, they went back to waltzing, two angels captivating in their grace. Watching them float together, Lucia felt a sense of loss. She turned back to the rail and stared out at the view. All this incomparable beauty. She wished she had someone to share it with. It was the price she paid for her single-minded focus on dance: It left little time for anything else in her life.

Once again she thought of the man she had met at the state dinner. Rashid al-Jazari. For all that he disconcerted her, she couldn't put him out of her mind. She shook her head, trying to put their brief encounter into perspective. A few awkward words about the weather and the world. Nothing more.

So she stood above the moonlit sea, alone, wishing she had more than a memory to share the night with her.

Although the amphitheater walls helped shade the stage, the heat pressed down like hot glass. All during the Monday-afternoon rehearsal, tempers flared.

"For crying out loud!" Carl threw up his arms, stopping the dancers. "Lucia, the rest of us are melting here. Why can't I see any warmth from you?" He motioned at her partner, Antonio Maravilla. "This man is supposed to be your husband. Do you understand the concept? Could you put just *one* ounce of affection into your performance?"

She stared at Carl, acutely aware of the other dancers. "It didn't happen this way."

"What, now you're a historical expert?" Sweat ran down his face and soaked into his white T-shirt. "You have been back two thousand years to check?"

"I don't mean Mary and Joseph didn't love each other."

Her hand went to her bare neck, where she wore her cross when she wasn't dancing. "But they would express it differently."

"Lucia." He had the "patient" look now that he used with temperamental dancers. It was the first time he had directed it at her and she didn't like it. "All I'm asking is that you show a little sentiment."

"It's the interpretation," she said. "It feels wrong."

"What? That I'm pleading with you not to act as if poor Antonio here has some horrible affliction?"

She flushed. "That isn't fair."

"You want to talk about 'fair'?" He wiped sweat off his forehead. "We have a performance tonight. You aren't ready. You aren't even close. I won't have my supposed prima ballerina going onstage without the proper preparation."

That felt like a kick in the stomach. He knew how long she had worked on this part. Why couldn't he see how hard it was for her to portray a figure from the religion she practiced? If she danced Mary in a way that felt wrong, how could she ever pray to her again?

"I'm sorry," she told him. "I can't do what you want."

A muscle twitched in his cheek. "That's it? 'I can't do it'?" His face was red, either from anger or the heat. Probably both. "Since when did you have to be coddled?"

"I'm not *asking* to be coddled."

"Then why don't you start acting like a professional?"

She was growing angry. "I never stopped."

His voice went quiet. "Perhaps your understudy will do a better job."

"Fine." Lucia bit out the word. "Have her do it." She stalked off the stage, painfully aware of the other dancers watching the spectacle.

In the changing room, she threw her jeans and blouse on over her dance clothes. Then she grabbed her ballet bag and headed to the town. She had never walked out on a rehearsal before, never even imagined doing such a thing. What had happened? It was too hot to think. Her head felt light.

She was within Taormina before she realized it, surrounded by tourists from Europe. After a few blocks, it sunk into her brain that she was more than a little dizzy. She couldn't remember the last time she had drunk any water.

She stopped at a café in a plaza with tables covered by green umbrellas. As she sat down, a waiter came out and spoke in Italian. "May I help you, miss?"

She wet her cracked lips and answered in Spanish. *"Agua, por favor."*

He nodded and moved off into the shadowed café. Putting her elbows on the table, she rested her head in her hands and closed her eyes. Here in the shade, with a breeze ruffling her hair, she wondered at her argument with Carl. It was out of character, to say the least. If they could have sat in a cool place and talked, neither of them strained by the heat, he probably would have understood. He had trusted her judgment on more involved interpretations than this.

"Here you are," the waiter said, this time in Spanish. She looked up as he set down a bottle of mineral water and a glass.

*"Gracias,"* she said. He smiled and withdrew.

As she poured a glass of water, someone behind her spoke in English, with a British accent. "Lucia del Mar?"

Startled, she turned around. A tall man in designer jeans and a tailored European shirt was standing there.

"It *is* you," he said. "I wasn't sure."

The scene was so different from the state dinner where they had met that at first she thought she imagined him, a figment created by fatigue, jet lag, and too much heat. But he remained there, gazing at her. Realizing she was just staring at him, she said, "Doctor al-Jazari?" She pushed a tendril of hair out of her eyes. "Please. Sit down."

He settled into a chair across the table. "I thought I

recognized you. But it was so unexpected. You have a distinctive walk, though. Like a queen."

"Thank you."

His hands rested on the table, long-fingered, controlled, and contained. Like all of him. "You're welcome."

She gave a self-conscious smile. "I would never have imagined seeing you here, either."

Rashid returned her smile with the same restraint she remembered from the White House. "I flew into Rome from London a few days ago, on business. When I saw a notice about your dance group, I decided to make the side trip."

He had come all the way here to see them dance? To see her, perhaps? But no, that was wishful thinking on her part. Business in London and Rome, side jaunts to Sicily, multinational corporation in Morocco; he moved in another world.

She started to say, "Are you—" and stopped, slowed by the heat, forgetting what she meant to ask. Instead, she took a sip of water. Even warm, it tasted like nectar.

"Miss del Mar?" he asked. "Are you all right?"

She set down the glass. "Fine, thank you. And please, call me Lucia." She pushed back the hair that had escaped her bun and was curling around her face. When her arms started to shake, she set her hands back on the table.

Rashid was watching her. "This heat can be dangerous if you don't drink enough water. Were you dancing?"

She winced. "That's one way to describe it."

He took the bottle and refilled her glass. "Here. Drink."

She didn't like him giving her an order. She remembered now how much he had disconcerted her at the state dinner. She took the glass, but only held it in front of her.

After a moment Rashid said, "It's odd to see you alone." Beneath his reserve, he almost sounded shy.

"Odd? How do you mean?" If she hadn't known better, she would have thought he felt self-conscious with her.

But that seemed unlikely for a man of such power, not to mention such good looks.

"In Washington you were always with a . . ." He paused. "I'm not sure of the word. Chaperone?"

"I don't understand."

"I can't think of an exact English translation." He considered. "You were always accompanied by a man of authority who prevented other men from approaching you, or you from approaching them."

Lucia stared at him. What a strange way to interpret her friendships with Carl Martelli and Mark Spearman. She had no idea how to respond. Had Rashid felt blocked from approaching her?

That suggested he desired such an approach.

He hesitated. "I hope I haven't offended you."

Lucia gave herself a mental shake. "No. No, you haven't. I'm just tired." She exhaled. "I've no right to complain. The other dancers are still rehearsing."

"But not you."

"My understudy is doing my part."

"Because you are dehydrated?"

"No. Because I refused." She shook her head. "I don't see why he doesn't understand."

Rashid regarded her curiously. "He?"

"Carl. Carl Martelli. The director of MDT." She took a swallow of water. "He wants me to dance the Virgin Mary in a ballet about spirituality. I can't do it the way he wants. The interpretation feels wrong."

"You are Christian, yes?"

"That's right." She hesitated. "I suppose this doesn't make much sense to you."

He made an exasperated noise. "Why? Because I am a Muslim?"

"Well, no." That had actually been her thought, but she didn't like the way it sounded. "I'm just too close to it."

He spoke in a careful voice. "A person's spirituality is part of them. You and I may express ours in different ways, but we can still respect each other's beliefs. Perhaps this is true for your director also?"

"I think so." She rubbed her eyes. "I didn't deal with it very well."

"Sometimes it's better not to speak."

"So I'm human," she grumbled. "Sue me."

"Sue you?" His mask of control slipped, replaced by a brilliant grin that flashed white against his golden skin. "Whatever for?"

That threw her for a loop. It was the first time she had seen him smile without rationing the expression. For an instant he let her see what a beautifully expressive face he had. That smile took him from attractive to gorgeous.

Lucia felt herself blush. "It's only a saying."

"Ah." Although his control had returned, he was still smiling, with a gentle look now. "We have a saying too. 'Never sue beauty.' "

"That's a Moroccan saying?"

Mischief flashed in his gaze. "Actually, I just made it up."

Lucia laughed. "Well, I like it."

Rashid smiled and relaxed in his chair. "Did you eat yet today?" He hesitated. "Have you plans for dinner with your dance troupe?"

His question made her think of the rehearsal. She saw now that she and Carl had locked horns because of heat and jet lag. With her mind dazed by the dehydration, she hadn't been thinking straight.

Then it hit her what Rashid had just asked. Dinner? Was that an invitation? She didn't know whether to glow or panic. She tried to think of a smooth response, but all she came up with was, "Well, no. I didn't have plans."

"They have many fine restaurants here. With beautiful views." Again he paused. Then he spoke carefully, like someone testing a new experience he hadn't tried before. "Perhaps you might dine with me tonight?"

Good Lord. He *was* asking her out. Not only that, but

he seemed self-conscious too. So strange, that such a mesmerizing man should be so unaffected.

Fortunately Lucia found her voice before she had sat in stunned silence for too long. "I would be honored to join you for dinner."

His posture subtly eased. "May I call at your hotel? Say at seven?"

"That would be nice." She couldn't believe she was having this conversation. Then it occurred to her that if Carl remained angry with her, going out on the town tonight would be unwise. She stood up, fumbling in her ballet bag for her wallet. "I should go back to the rehearsal. Talk to Carl. Work things out."

Rashid rose to his feet, pulling a wallet out of his jeans. As the waiter came up to the table, Rashid gave him some lira notes.

"Don't do that." Lucia finally found her own wallet in her bag. "I've got it."

He waved his hand, dismissing the waiter. "I'll walk you back to your rehearsal."

Still holding her wallet, she watched the waiter disappear into the café. Did Rashid always act this way? As much as he intrigued her, he also made her uneasy. She would rather have paid herself, but she didn't want to offend him, especially after he had come all the way from Rome to see MDT perform. And for dinner? But surely he wouldn't travel such a long way simply to extend a dinner invitation. It was absurd, perhaps even a bit alarming, to contemplate such a possibility.

She stepped out of the shadow cast by the umbrella over the table. As soon as the full heat of the sun hit her, she stopped and swayed, dizzy again. Rashid took a fast step around the table and caught her elbow.

"Are you all right?" he asked, his voice low with concern.

She looked up at him, startled by the touch of his hand. So tall. Did he know he had beautiful eyes?

"Lucia?" Softly he repeated, "Are you all right?" He

moved his hand on her elbow, almost drawing her to him. Then he stopped, and his face became composed again as he let her go.

She felt disappointed, then annoyed at herself. What did she expect? For him to hug her? Stupid question. Why should he? They hardly knew each other.

Lucia pushed back a length of hair that was coming loose from the bun on her head. "Yes. Yes, I'm fine." She started back toward the main thoroughfare. Rashid walked at her side, easily keeping pace with his long legs.

As they walked, her vertigo surged and ebbed. She kept going, though, submerged in her thoughts. Her bun was still coming apart, until finally she gave up and undid it, letting her hair cascade in black waves over her arms and down her back, all the way to her waist. She stuffed the pins and bands into the back pocket of her jeans.

"So beautiful," Rashid murmured.

Startled out of her daze, she glanced up at him. "Excuse me?"

"You have so much hair. Beautiful hair."

"Thank you."

"Does your director know you walk here like this?" He was watching her with an odd expression, as if he wasn't sure whether to be fascinated, embarrassed, or concerned.

Self-conscious, she pushed her hair behind her shoulder. "What do you mean?"

"Alone."

"Alone?"

"Alone in the street. Like—" He glanced at her hair, then her clothes, then averted his eyes as if he were trying not to stare at her. "Like this," he finished.

Like this? She had on jeans and a white blouse, with her dance leotard underneath. It covered her a lot more than the bikini tops worn by many of the other women strolling on the street. Nor was her subdued style a coincidence. Offstage, she didn't like being looked at. She had turned down more than her share of photo offers. MDT dancers were far curvier than the gaunt ideal favored in some ballet companies; that combined with their well-toned bodies led to offers from many magazines for pictures. But she had never even considered a fully clothed fashion layout. So why did Rashid's comments make her feel as if she were undressed?

She remembered now how he reacted to her at the state dinner, when none of the more scantily dressed women fazed him at all. Neither then nor now, though, did she sense that he realized he was responding in a different way to her. Could it be because she interested him? That sparked a tingle of excitement. It also disconcerted her, though, to think he might unconsciously be applying a more conservative mind-set to her than he did to other people.

Unsure how to respond, she said, "Carl doesn't have a say where I go."

"This is a foreign country. Not your home."

Was he worried about her safety? "I'll be all right." Realizing that might sound as if she were trying to get rid of him, she added, "But I appreciate your company."

His face relaxed into a charming smile that crinkled laugh lines around his eyes she hadn't noticed before. "And I yours."

As his mask of control reasserted itself, Lucia realized she had been wrong about his lack of emotion. He controlled his responses well, but when he eased up, he revealed a far different man, hinting at deep emotions. She wondered why he exercised such restraint. She knew dancers who would give anything for the ability to project their moods so well. Then again, for a business executive it was probably a disadvantage to have a face that showed his thoughts in such expressive detail.

Rashid was watching her. "What are you thinking, beautiful light of the sea?"

That caught her off guard again. He thought her beautiful? She liked the way he said her name. Light of the sea. It was the translation of Lucia del Mar into English. On impulse, she said, "There you go, being charming again."

He grinned. "Sometimes my boring self manages a bit of that."

*Boring?* Hardly.

A problem suddenly registered. She halted in the middle of the street. "Where are we going?"

He stopped next to her. "I thought to your rehearsal."

"This is the wrong way." Lucia rubbed her eyes, wishing she could sit down. "It's so hot. I'm not thinking straight." She suspected she had been distracted by more than the heat.

"I've a car just outside the Catania gate." Rashid hesitated. "I can give you a ride."

She wished she could take him up on it. "Isn't the road to the theater closed to cars?"

"I don't know," he admitted. "I'll take you as close as I can."

"All right." She smiled. "Thanks."

They went to the Porta Catania and walked under the great arched gate into the street that looped past it. He motioned at a gold Mercedes on the other side of the curve. "There."

Lucia made a conscious effort not to gape at the car. It was gorgeous, shimmering like liquid gold in the sunlight. As she and Rashid came up to the vehicle, the driver got out of the front seat. He looked Italian, with brown hair and eyes, and dark clothes. His husky build and obvious strength made Lucia suspect he could serve as a bodyguard too, if Rashid wanted one. He glanced at Rashid, at Lucia, and then at Rashid again, his face puzzled.

Rashid spoke to him in Italian. The language was similar enough to Spanish for Lucia to pick up bits and pieces. She didn't actually speak much Spanish, but her parents used it often, so she understood simple sentences. It gave her an even more limited knowledge of Italian, not much, but enough to gather that Rashid wasn't fluent in the language either.

The driver nodded and opened the back door for them. The interior was upholstered in soft gold leather. Lucia slid in, followed by Rashid. The driver got in the front, and soon they were headed down the winding street.

Lucia had to sit in the center of the seat; the area by the door was occupied by a laptop computer, a thermos, and copies of what looked like scientific articles. One paper read: *An alternate analysis of theological objections to the Turing machine* by Rashid al-Jazari at Imperial College, London.

Rashid leaned forward, speaking to the driver. From what Lucia could decipher, she gathered that the driver worked in security at a Rome office of Rashid's corporation.

After they finished talking, Rashid sat back in his seat. "Enrico will see if he can find a way to the theater."

"Okay," Lucia said. "That sounds like a plan."

He smiled. "You speak English like an American."

She had never thought of it that way. "I guess so."

Reaching across her, he cleared the seat. As she scooted over to the door, he said, "Are you still thirsty? I have water."

"Yes. Thanks."

He poured from the thermos, using its blue top as a cup. When he gave it to her, his fingers brushed her hand, trailing from her knuckles to her wrist. At first it felt like an accident, but his fingers lingered on her skin too long for a casual touch. Before Lucia could react, though, he withdrew his hand. He reddened, looking as startled as she by that unexpected intimacy. Flustered, she downed half her water in one gulp.

Rashid glanced out at the sky. "The new moon will be soon."

"Are you interested in astronomy?" she asked.

"I've always liked it." He took a swallow of water from the thermos. "The new month starts with the first crescent of the new moon."

She wanted to ask what he meant by the "new month," but she hesitated, afraid she would sound uneducated. As Rashid finished the water in his thermos, Lucia noticed

Enrico checking his rearview mirror. It was odd the way he watched Rashid with such intense concentration. But before his observation became overt, Enrico turned his attention back to the road.

So they sat while the car hummed through Taormina. After Lucia finished her water, she held the cup in her lap, fidgeting with its handle. She felt she should say something, but she didn't know what. Just as she opened her mouth to try, Rashid started to speak. They both stopped and gave awkward laughs.

"You go first," he said.

"I was going to ask about your article."

He glanced at the paper, now on the seat between them. "I wrote that years ago. But it took a long time in the referee process."

"Referee?"

"It's how scientific papers get published. The editor sends it to experts in the field. Referees. They recommend whether or not to publish it."

"They must have liked it, then."

Rashid grimaced. "Not at all. I had to do many rewrites before the editor finally accepted it for publication."

"Do you mind if I look at it?"

"Go ahead." He seemed pleased by her interest.

She picked up the paper and scanned the first page. Under the title, a paragraph headed with the word *Abstract* summarized the article. After reading the summary several times, she said, "I don't understand. What does Islam have to do with machine intelligence?" Then she flushed, wondering if he would take the question wrong. "I hope I haven't offended."

"You haven't." Dryly he added, "It's the same question the referees asked."

"AI. Artificial intelligence. A computer that thinks."

"Essentially." Rashid's face had become more animated. "Many people believe it is impossible. One argument is that humans have a soul and machines don't. I was arguing that ideas of spirituality and AI aren't incompatible." He leaned forward, elbows on his knees, his face contemplative. "The human capacity for thought—this is what defines us as unique in the world as we know it. The argument is this: If God bestowed that capacity on us because we have a soul, how can we ever create a thinking machine? It has no soul. Perhaps it is even blasphemy to consider such a prospect."

Intrigued, she said, "But you don't think so?"

"I thought about it for a long time." Sitting back again, he spoke slowly. "When I was young, I learned an image for the soul that I very much liked. They are birds on a high perch, some grouped close together, others farther apart. At a given time, one descends to Earth to take its given place within the body of a person. But only in a person." He paused. "So yes, in that sense I would follow the theological objection. But I don't see why this should mean an AI can never become self-aware. And if it does learn to reflect on itself, surely it can develop a conscience."

"Is that what you said in your paper?"

"A bit, but more formally." He gave her a wry smile. "Actually, that particular subject comes up more with my father. He was never convinced my work at the university was quite acceptable."

She thought of her own father, about his concern over letting his daughter move across the country at the age of sixteen to join MDT. He had almost forbidden her to go.

"Parents are like that," she said. "But they worry about us because they love us."

Rashid's expression gentled. "Yes. They do."

She had heard the longing in his voice when he spoke about his work. "Perhaps someday you can go back to your research."

"Perhaps." A look flashed across his face, a regret so intense it hurt to see. Then he regained control, hiding that glimpse of his inner self. *"In sha' allah."*

She hesitated. "Inshalon?"

*"In sha' allah.* If God wills."

Lucia nodded, self-conscious again, though she wasn't sure why. He was so different. Or perhaps it was her fatigue. She had thought relaxing in the car would help, but she was dizzier now than before. The conversation intrigued her too much to stop, though. "Did the referees want your paper rewritten because they thought discussions of God and the soul weren't appropriate for a science article?"

"It wasn't that so much. Philosophy has always been part of the AI field. In fact, I had the impression they appreciated someone trying to reconcile his faith with his scientific background. Theological arguments are usually used as an objection to AI." He pushed his hand through his hair. "My main argument was this: If we don't impart the criteria of our spiritual values to the artificial intelligences we make, they might not value the moral and ethical basis we take as fundamental to civilization. They might not value us. And then what?"

She grimaced. "It's a good question. Why would that cause controversy?"

"It's the way I phrased it." He held his hands palm up over his lap, as if offering the explanation in space as well as words. "I've always thought the answer to the tensions in our world is mutual respect and understanding for all peoples, finding a way to accommodate all our differences. In the paper, I meant to propose the goal of developing a standard of morality for our machine intelligences, one based in all the cultures and religions of humanity." He lowered his hands. "In the first draft, I phrased it in terms of what I know, Islam, which teaches that every baby is born with an innate goodness given by God. If we could define that goodness, that sense of right and wrong basic to all humanity, we could give it to the AIs we create." He exhaled. "Apparently, though, it sounded to the referees as if I was suggesting we program my religion into everyone's AI."

His last comment surprised Lucia. That wasn't the impression she had taken from this final abstract. She read the introduction to the paper: *Humans have struggled throughout history to surmount our differences. To coexist. Our shared heritage is one of strife, but also of great achievement. We have within us the possibility for both. Now, as we contemplate the creation of machine intelligence, we need to consider the ramifications of bringing a new form of sentience into our world. If we have struggled so with our own species, what will happen when we share the world with intelligences that may be completely unlike our own? If we are to give our machines a tolerance and acceptance that encompasses all humanity, surely we must first define it for ourselves.*

Looking up at him, she spoke gently. "It is a good thing, to seek tolerance and acceptance. I'm sorry they mistook your intent at first."

Rashid gave her a rueful look. "I didn't write it so well at first." For some reason he looked tired now, though a short time ago he had seemed fine. "Normally I'm fluent in English. But I have trouble talking about religion in any language except Arabic."

She thought about her argument with Carl Martelli. "You're doing better than me. I have trouble in every language."

His face gentled. "You have a far more expressive way of communicating, Lucia, a language no one else speaks as well as you."

She averted her gaze. "Thank you." As she stared at her hands in her lap, her vision went double and she saw two of each. She blinked until her eyes refocused. She felt even queasier now, off balance and lightheaded.

His voice softened. "It's very beautiful, when you bend your head that way, with your hair falling over your arms."

Lucia didn't know what to say. It wasn't only embarrassment this time, though. She felt as if a fog had damped her brain.

She heard rather than saw it when he picked up a length of her hair. As he stroked the tresses with his thumb, he murmured, "Light of the sea."

Looking up, she saw he was leaning closer to her. His large eyes looked even bigger now. In fact, his pupils were dilated, so much that they almost filled his irises. If she hadn't known better, she would have thought he was drugged. He rubbed the back of his hand against her cheek, his knuckles brushing her skin. Then he bent his head toward hers, his lashes lowering. As Lucia closed her eyes, she felt the whisper of his breath on her lips.

In the front seat, Enrico shifted his weight. That rustle broke the moment like a gunshot. Rashid pulled away from Lucia and sat back, placing his hands on his knees as if he didn't know what to do with them. He seemed even more startled by his behavior than she had been. He rubbed his eyes again, then shook his head as if to clear it.

Disconcerted, unsure what to do, Lucia looked out the window. The houses of Taormina passed by in pastel Mediterranean hues accented by bright flowers and greenery. Then the city blurred. Her head felt odd, as if her sense of balance had gone haywire. Her dehydration and overexposure to the sun must have affected her even more than she had realized.

Rashid remained silent. Eventually she risked glancing at him again. He had rested his head back on the seat and closed his eyes. Perhaps the heat bothered him as well. He exerted such control over everything he did that she hadn't noticed at first. But now she realized his face had gone pale. A bead of sweat rolled down his temple despite the air-conditioned car.

"Are you all right?" she asked.

Opening his eyes, he said, "Yes. Fine." He lifted his head. "Jet lag doesn't usually affect me this much."

"I know what you mean. I hardly slept at all last night."

They were coming off the mountain now, onto a road that ran along the jagged Sicilian coast. "I don't think we're going to get to the amphitheater this way," she said. "We better go back up to the city." Even as she spoke, a surge of nausea swept over her.

Rashid looked around. "We shouldn't be down here."

Leaning forward, he spoke to the driver. His voice had a blurred quality to it, as if he were having trouble enunciating the Italian words. Sweat sheened his forehead.

Enrico's response sounded deliberately cryptic even to Lucia's fogged mind. The car kept going, speeding down a road that wound along the coastline. The Ionian Sea rolled by on their left, sunlight glimmering on the rippled water. Rashid spoke to Enrico again, his voice sharp now, his face paler than before. Spots clouded Lucia's vision. She sat as still as possible, trying to make her vertigo subside, but it did no good.

This wasn't dehydration. Someone had drugged them.

Enrico answered with words Lucia could no longer decipher. She understood the tone, however. He had given Rashid a warning.

Rashid suddenly lunged forward, trying to reach over the driver. Enrico moved faster, with ease, putting his hand inside his jacket. He pulled a gun out from his shoulder holster, a 9-millimeter Luger. Lucia had no doubt it should have been used as protection for Rashid. Apparently Rashid hadn't thought any danger existed, since he went into Taormina alone. The unexpected threat was here, in his own car, from his own bodyguard.

Enrico kept his left hand on the wheel while he held the gun in his right. Splitting his attention between the road and Rashid, he spoke in a terse voice, his words clipped and cold.

Rashid froze, then carefully sat back in the seat. Lucia knew they had to get out of the car. They needed a weapon. She fumbled with her ballet bag, rummaging inside. Hairpins, passport, clothes, medical tape. Useless. What was she going to do, threaten Enrico with her pink satin ballet shoe? Her hand closed around her fingernail clipper. It wasn't much, but it was better than nothing.

Clenching the clipper, she let her bag slide out of her lap, as if she could no longer hold on to it—which wasn't far from the truth. Exactly how the clipper could help, given that she was in the process of passing out, she had no idea. She sagged toward Rashid, unable to stay upright. He tried to speak, but his voice sounded slow. Stumbling. At least he was still conscious, which was more than she would soon be herself.

As she fell against his shoulder, she let her hand fall onto his first, which he had clenched on his thigh. At first he stiffened, and when she tried to slip the clipper into his fist, he didn't respond. She pushed the clipper again, and he suddenly closed his hand around the metal.

Then, with a sense of falling through space, she succumbed to the darkness.

*Chapter Three*

# MEDITERRANEAN CROSSING

A throbbing pain in Lucia's wrists dragged her awake. She became aware she was in a chair, surrounded by a rumbling hum. Opening her eyes, she found her vision as hazed as her brain. All she could tell was that she was in a small room. Windows on the curving wall showed blue sky outside.

Her arms were pulled behind her back, and her mouth felt as if it were filled with cotton. She wanted to rub her wrists, but she couldn't move; the harder she tried, the more it hurt. She finally realized her mouth felt full of cloth because it *was;* someone had gagged her.

Her head had rolled to the right—and she saw a blurred figure. As she concentrated, straining to focus, the blur resolved into Rashid. He was seated in a chair next to her, his head back and his eyes closed. Duct tape covered his mouth, and his arms were pulled around the chair in a position that looked even more painful than hers. Glancing down, she saw that his shoes and socks had been removed. Leather thongs tied his ankles to a bar jammed under the chair, and dried blood crusted the thongs.

A rustle came from beyond Rashid's chair. Then Enrico stepped into view, without his jacket now, his gun still in its shoulder holster. He walked to the front of the room and opened a door.

Lucia's perception of the scene suddenly changed, like the shift of an optical illusion. She and Rashid weren't in a room, they were in the cabin of a small aircraft. Enrico had just gone into the lavatory.

Leaning her head back, she tried to see behind Rashid. His wrists were also tied with thongs, and lacerations covered his skin, as if he had been pulling against the bonds. She glanced at his face—and found him staring at her. When she made a muffled sound, he shook his head, then tilted it toward the lavatory. She understood; he didn't want to alert Enrico that they were awake.

Then she saw the flash of silver in his hand, behind his back. Her nail clippers. He must have hidden them, perhaps in the cuff of his shirt, someplace he could reach with his hands tied. As she watched, he struggled with his bonds, fraying them with the clippers.

The lock on the lavatory scraped, and Lucia closed her eyes partway, so she looked as if she were still unconscious. Enrico came over to check Rashid. In her side vision, she saw Rashid's head lolling against his chair as if he was out cold.

Then he moved.

His arms flew out from behind his back, his fists clenched as he brought them up under Enrico's chin. Enrico's head snapped back and he made a strangled noise.

As Enrico swayed, Rashid lurched forward and tackled him. They both fell to their knees, Rashid's ankles still bound to the bar under his chair. He had his hands around Enrico's neck, pushing his thumbs against an artery.

They fought in silence, Enrico trying as much to shout a warning as to throw off Rashid. Then he went limp. Rashid made a muffled noise, what sounded like a gasp, and released his hold. He yanked the tape off his mouth, wincing when it tore his skin, and pulled out the cloth that gagged him. As he dragged himself back into his chair, Lucia saw his ankles bleeding around the cords that bound them.

Bending over, he worked at the knots, his fingers slipping in the blood. It was soon obvious why their kidnappers had used thongs; the knots were notoriously hard to undo. She had seen the effect before, though never on humans; if leather was tied while wet, it shrank as it dried. Nor could Rashid use the clippers. They had flown out of his hand when he hit Enrico, and now they lay out of reach.

It seemed eons before Rashid loosened his bonds and freed his ankles. Drawing in a ragged breath, he knelt next to Enrico and tied up the driver with the same cords that had so recently bound him. He stuffed his gag into Enrico's mouth, then ripped up Enrico's shirt and tied a strip of cloth around his head. He stopped, took a ragged breath, and then disarmed Enrico.

Lucia knew guns: Her father had hunted game in the Hachita desert to help feed the family. She learned to shoot when she was ten. She recognized Rashid's body language; he disliked firearms. If he had no other choice he would shoot, but only in self-defense or to protect those he loved. It was a moot point, however. He didn't dare fire in the aircraft. If a bullet pierced the hull, the loss of air pressure would be explosive, perhaps even enough to bring down the plane.

Rashid unloaded the Luger and put the clip in the pocket of his jeans. Then he climbed stiffly to his feet and limped over to Lucia, going behind her chair. She didn't know how many hours she had sat with her arms twisted behind her back, but it had been too long. When Rashid started to untie her, pain shot from her wrists to her shoulders. She tried to swallow her cry, but a moan escaped anyway, muffled by the gag.

A voice came from behind a door at the front of the cabin. The man used a language Lucia didn't recognize, though it sounded Slavic or Russian, perhaps from one of the smaller countries the Soviet Union had fragmented into after its breakup.

Rashid froze. Then he walked to the door, his bare feet silent on the rug. Staying to one side, he reached for its handle. Before he could do anything, the door opened and a medium-sized man with brown hair stepped into the cabin. The man's gaze immediately went to Enrico's unconscious body. It took only a second more for him to realize Rashid was closing the door behind him, but in that instant Rashid lunged.

The man moved with feral grace, twisting away with a speed Rashid couldn't match. It was size that gave Rashid his advantage: He stood a half foot taller and had at least fifty pounds of muscle on his adversary. With the momentum of his lunge behind his weight, he threw the man against a bulkhead and shoved the heel of his hand onto the man's forehead. As the man hit the wall, Rashid pushed hard, slamming his head against the unyielding surface.

The man stared at Rashid, his eyes glazing over. He slid to the deck and sat down, then crumpled to the side, his eyes closing as he collapsed. Rashid stared at him, breathing hard.

Someone spoke in the cockpit. Rashid pressed his hand against his side, his face contorted with pain. He drew in a breath, then opened the door and stepped inside the cockpit, behind the pilot's chair. The back of a man's head showed above the seat.

At first Lucia had the bizarre impression that Rashid

simply leaned over the pilot and stayed that way, doing nothing. Then she realized he and the pilot were fighting, barely moving, a contest of muscle resisting muscle. Suddenly the pilot shouted, and in the same instant Rashid dragged him out of the chair. They fell into a bulkhead, the force of their battle transformed into motion.

The two men lost their balance and crashed to the deck, half in and half out of the cockpit. The pilot pinned Rashid on his back and struck him across the face, open-handed but hard. Had he used his fist, he would have cracked Rashid's jaw or broken his nose. As it was, Rashid went still and his struggles came to a halt.

*No,* Lucia wanted to shout. She didn't want to believe one blow could knock out a man, but she knew Rashid's depleted condition left him no reserves. As the pilot started to flip Rashid over to bind him again, she made a muffled sound of protest.

The pilot glanced at her—and the "unconscious" Rashid lunged. Grabbing the pilot's jacket, he yanked the man to one side, throwing him off balance. Surging up on his knees, he slammed the pilot down on his back. Again Rashid's size made the difference; he held the pilot down by sheer mass. Closing his hands around the man's neck, he pressed his thumbs in with a force that turned his knuckles white.

When the pilot went limp, Rashid either didn't realize it or else was so pumped with adrenaline that he kept strangling the man. Lucia tried to call out, but the only noise she managed was a muffled grunt.

Finally, with a choked sound, Rashid released the pilot. He crossed his arms over his stomach, his body sagging forward as his breaths came in great gasps. When he regained his wind, he took hold of the doorframe and pulled himself to his feet. Then he limped over to Lucia.

"The gag," she said. It came out as a grunt, but he either understood or else had the same thought. He tugged the tape off her mouth and pulled out the cloth, then fumbled and dropped the wadded cotton in her lap. Falling forward, he caught himself by grabbing the armrests of her chair.

"Rashid," she said, her voice dry from the gag. "Please don't die."

He gave her a wan smile. "I wasn't planning on it."

"What about the others?"

"Unconscious."

"Who's flying the jet?"

"Autopilot." Crouching by her feet, he went to work on the cords binding her ankles.

"Ai—" Lucia jerked from the pain. When he let go and looked around the cabin, she said, "Go ahead. It doesn't hurt that much." It wasn't true, but she knew he had to get the cords off her. He needed them to tie up the pilot.

"It would go easier if . . ." Rashid peered under her chair. "There." He retrieved her nail clipper and went to work on her bonds.

She wet her lips. "Can you fly this thing?"

"I've sat in the copilot's seat on the Lear jet my company owns. A few times I talked the pilot into letting me take over during calm weather." He ripped at the unrelenting cords with her clipper. "But I've no pilot's license. I took off once, with help, but I've never landed."

"Do you know where we are?"

"Over Algeria, I think."

"Is it safe to land there?"

"I would rather come down in Morocco. If we have enough fuel."

She knew every second he spent trying to free her gave more time for trouble, either with the aircraft or if one of the men recovered consciousness. "Enrico's shirt."

He looked up at her. "What?"

"Use the pieces to tie up the pilot and the copilot."

"Good idea." He went to Enrico and gathered the torn remains of the shirt, then strode back to the cockpit. He bound the copilot first. As he was tying up the pilot, a voice spoke in the cockpit, speaking what sounded like Arabic.

Lucia froze. Was someone else still in the cockpit?

The voice came again, this time with a crackle of static. She sagged with relief. Radio. It was the *radio.* The language wasn't Arabic, as she had first thought, but English, spoken with an Arabic accent. With her mind still fogged by the drugs, she couldn't concentrate enough to make out the actual words.

Rashid finished with the pilot and went into the cockpit, where he sat in the pilot's seat. He talked with whoever was on the radio for several minutes. Then it was silent, except for the hum of engines. Lucia tried to stay conscious, but she couldn't fight off the drugs. Her mind hazed again.

A new voice brought her alert, a man speaking a stream of words, Arabic punctuated with French. The flow kept up, interspersed with replies from Rashid. She had ridden in enough airplanes to know it was unusual for air-tower personnel to conduct such a long dialogue with a pilot. As pressure built in her ears, she realized they were trying to help Rashid land.

Wind keened past the hull, and acceleration pushed her into the seat. She tried to imagine positive scenes for when they hit the ground, but she kept seeing mangled wreckage instead. A rumble came from under the floor as the landing gear lowered. The voice on the radio grew urgent; Rashid's responses became more terse.

Suddenly the cabin jolted, then again, and again, as if a giant were skimming the airplane against the ground like a rock skipping across the water. It bounced again—and slammed down *hard.* Lucia felt as if her bones shook in their sockets. Outside the window, the asphalt of a runway was going by much too fast.

A screech of buckling metal filled the air. The tip of the wing on Lucia's side scraped the asphalt, and the craft spun in a circle, careening off the runway into stubbly grass. The wheels caught and the aircraft rocked, lurching forward with each stomach-turning jerk, closer and closer to flipping over.

Mercifully, the plane shuddered to a stop before it turned over. It stood at a slant, its wing dug into the ground. Lucia sagged in her seat, hit with relief and a vertigo that surged over her in waves. Her vision blurred, as if fogged by a white mist. The scene moved in jerky fragments, like a series of badly developed photographs. Rashid limped out of the cockpit, his face pale. He crossed the cabin and paused at her side, touching her arm.

Then he went over and opened the hatch. Sunlight streamed into the cabin, along with dusty air. Raising his hands, palms outward to show he had no weapons, he left the aircraft. Lucia's relief vanished. Rashid had just crashed an aircraft full of bound and injured people. She had no idea what country they had come down in or what to expect from the police here. What if they arrested him?

The minutes stretched out, painful, endless. Her head throbbed and her vision remained blurred. She hovered on the edge of oblivion, fighting the drugs in her body.

A clank came from outside. Several men entered the plane, military police it looked like. Each wore a navy-blue uniform with lighter blue trim, a thick belt around the waist, another across the chest, and a military-style cap. On average, they were much shorter than Rashid, with neatly trimmed mustaches, stocky fingers, husky builds, and skin ranging from Rashid's dark golden hue to smooth browns. Their intent, alert gazes took in everything about the cabin, a wary survey that did nothing to ease Lucia's fear. Many of the officers gave her a direct, piercing look, then glanced away before it became a stare.

Rashid reappeared with more men, either an escort or guards, she wasn't sure which. Although they wore dark blue suits and ties, they moved and spoke much as did the other officers. They were obviously plainclothes policemen. A purpling bruise showed on Rashid's cheek where the pilot had struck him.

The police spoke in quiet voices among themselves and treated Rashid with wary courtesy, as if they weren't convinced he had no part in whatever crimes had been committed but had no wish to offend a man with wealth and influence. One man seemed to know him, though, and spoke with obvious respect, calling him *al-Hafiz Si Rashid* one time and *Hajj Rashid* another.

They carried out the unconscious men on stretchers. One of the policemen went to work on the cords that bound Lucia's arms behind the back of her chair. When she jerked from the pain, he murmured in French and Arabic, his voice gently rumbling, soothing phrases meant to calm, as if she were a beautiful but injured animal, wild and exotic.

The tallest officer, the man who appeared to be in charge, held an unfamiliar passport, probably Rashid's. He shot rapid-fire questions at Rashid and motioned at Lucia. Rashid answered in the same mixture of French and Arabic, including the word *"Américaine."*

Her vertigo was growing worse. She floated in a queasy, fevered sea, trying to fight the sense of suffocation she felt. Trying to stay conscious.

Suddenly Rashid spoke. "Lucia, where is your passport?"

"In my ballet bag," she said.

A quick search of the cabin produced the athletic bag she used as a combination dance bag and purse. After rummaging inside, the tall officer pulled out one of her pointe shoes. A ribbon had come unwound and hung down in a pink satin streamer. He blinked at the shoe as if he didn't know what to make of it.

Rashid spoke again. Although Lucia didn't understand his Arabic, she picked up the French words *ballerine* and *première danseuse.*

The officer gave Lucia an appraising stare. It left no doubt that whatever he thought of American dancers, it didn't include respect. His attitude was far different from the gentle courtesy the other officers showed her. His gaze paused at her torso long enough to make her wonder if something had happened to her. Glancing down, she was mortified to see that having her arms bound behind her back pulled her blouse against her breasts and made a faint outline of her nipples show, even through two layers of cloth.

Rashid spoke again, this time with anger edging his voice. The man glanced at him, then returned Lucia's shoe to her bag and continued his search.

Suddenly the officer stiffened, his face going hard as he asked Lucia a question. She didn't understand what she could possibly have in her bag to evoke such a reaction. When she saw what he pulled out, she was even more confused. It was just a roll of coins she kept for the Laundromat.

Rashid spoke to her, as tense as the police officer. "What is it?"

"Quarters," she said. "American quarter dollars."

Rashid relayed the information. The officer shook out a few coins, picked one up, and studied it. Apparently satisfied, he returned the coins to their roll and dropped it back into the bag. Only then did Lucia realize her innocuous roll of quarters could have felt, even looked, like a pipe bomb.

The man working on her bonds suddenly spoke—and her arms fell loose. Wincing at the numbness, she pulled them across her abdomen and massaged her aching muscles. Blood trickled over her wrists.

As the policeman came around to untie her ankles, she spoke softly. "Thank you." He glanced up and smiled, then went back to work. He looked just as intimidating as the tall officer, but he had a different manner, kind and steady, without hostility.

The officer going through her bag pulled out a pair of leg warmers, knitted tubes of gray wool she wore during rehearsals to keep her legs warm. He shook them, apparently to dislodge any hidden objects that might have become stuck inside the tubes. When nothing came out, he put them back in her bag. He found her sweater next, then a leotard. But still no passport. Unease swirled over Lucia. What if the blasted thing had fallen out?

The man working on her bonds freed her ankles. As he stood up, Lucia gave him a wan smile. He nodded, his concern for her condition obvious as he stepped away from her chair.

The man searching her bag pulled out her camisole, a garment made from white silk lace that she wore under her blouse when she didn't have on her dance leotard. When he realized what he was holding, he flushed and quickly stuffed it back into the bag. Then he looked up, not at Lucia but at Rashid, as if he were responsible for this item of intimate apparel. Rashid scowled at him. Lucia wasn't sure exactly what was going on, but it made her even more uneasy.

The officer went back to his search. Mercifully, he finally pulled out her passport. He flipped through it with sharp, efficient motions, pausing to study her face when he reached the page with her picture. Then he spoke to her, shooting words as if they were bullets.

"I don't understand," Lucia answered. She feared to say the wrong thing, but she had no idea what he wanted.

He gave her bag to another policeman and stepped to her chair. Lucia froze, terrified of everything about him: his harsh voice, his grim expression, his tension, his obvious distrust. He slid his hand under her arm—and before her mind could stop her incautious reflexes, she jerked away from him. Too late, she realized it looked as if she were resisting arrest, or whatever they were doing with her.

The officer tensed and pulled her to her feet. Vertigo flooded her, rolling in waves. When she staggered, he tightened his hold on her arm. She couldn't stop her legs from buckling. She stumbled to the side, trying to regain her balance, and another officer caught her other elbow, gently, with care, but still holding her in place.

When they started to walk her toward the open hatch, Lucia panicked. Afraid of being separated from Rashid, her only referent in this sea of unfamiliarity, she started to struggle. Someone spoke in a kind voice, but she was too dizzy to understand. The tall officer was holding her arm so tight it hurt, with his knuckles pressed against her breast, whether by accident or on purpose, she had no idea.

Rashid was speaking again, yet she barely heard him through the fog that muffled her brain. She feared she was about to vomit, collapse, and pass out. And then what? She tried to protest, but the words jumbled in her throat. The police tried to take her to the door again. When she balked, the tall officer pulled her forward. Voices buffeted her ears like great echoing shouts.

Before she could catch her breath, she felt her body jerk convulsively, out of control. Dimly, through a roar in her ears, she heard Rashid call her. . . .

The voice refused to let her rest. "Lucia, wake up."

Lucia opened her eyes. Gradually her vision cleared and she registered the surroundings. She was sitting on the floor of a small whitewashed room. The walls were all bare, except for one with a calendar. The writing on the calendar was unfamiliar; she recognized only the numbers and the year. Or what she thought was the year. It said 1431.

Her hands lay in her lap, bandaged around the wrists with strips of white gauze. A table sat in front of her, low to the carpeted floor. The air felt close and hot, accented by a tang of machinery and fuel.

"Lucia?" Rashid repeated, his voice hoarse. He was sitting next to her, holding her up with his right arm around her waist and his left hand resting on her elbow. Bandages extended from midway on each of his lower arms down to his palms, leaving only his fingers free.

She tried to answer him, but her throat felt too parched. When he spoke again, she couldn't understand. She could barely keep her eyes open. Like a diver poised on the edge of an abyss, she teetered, ready to drop back into the cradling blackness.

"Sick," she mumbled.

"You had a reaction to the drug Enrico used to knock us out." Rashid pushed his hand through his hair, looking as exhausted as she felt. "You went into a convulsion."

"Where is this place?"

"The airport in Oujda, near the Algeria–Morocco border."

"Are we in trouble?"

"I think so." His words had a ragged edge. "I don't know who to trust. Enrico and the other men couldn't have been working alone. Now that you're caught in whatever this is, we're both targets."

"What do they say?"

He exhaled. "I can't get any real answers from Issam, the officer in charge. First he spoke about the immigration and naturalization office. Then the American consul. Then something about the embassy. But that's in Rabat. He keeps evading my questions. He hasn't arrested either of us, but he finds excuse after excuse to keep us from leaving or contacting anyone. I'm afraid he is connected to this, that he has called for reinforcements and is stalling until they arrive."

She struggled to process his words through the daze the drug left in her mind. "What will they do to us?"

"I don't know." He grimaced. "The kidnappers claim I kidnapped them."

"What? No. How can they say that?"

Dryly Rashid answered, "When I crashed, everyone on board was tied up but me."

"It would have been stupid to land this way if you were the kidnapper."

"I don't know what Issam thinks. He wants to separate us—"

"No!" Lucia tried to sit up straighter. Rashid was her only anchor in this sea of confusion. Without him, she would be stranded in a foreign country, barely able to stay conscious, unable to speak the language, with no idea where to turn, and where someone might want her dead.

Yet she knew so little about Rashid. Did the airport

authorities have valid reasons to believe he was involved? If she made the wrong choice now, she might never see home again, might not even live past this day. How to choose? Her experience with the world was limited to her home and MDT. A mutual attraction was hardly grounds to put her life in the hands of a stranger in a foreign country.

But her response to Rashid went beyond that. She had seen his unaffected sincerity when he spoke of his work, heard the integrity and concern for humanity in his words. That had been genuine. She had to trust her intuition now; she had nothing else to go on. Looking up at him, she saw a visionary, a man who dreamed of a better world.

Softly she said, "Stay with me. Please." Her voice shook. "Don't let them separate us."

He brushed the hair back from her face, as if that gesture could protect them both. "I won't desert you. I swear it. But I don't know what to do. I don't think this abduction originated in Italy. The pilot comes from Russia and the copilot is an Algerian who lives in Morocco now."

"And we can't leave here?"

"Issam claims your passport has some problem. But he won't say what. How do we know, if he brings an 'official' to help you, that we can trust this person? If we go with them, we may end up captives again." He swallowed. "Whoever took us never intended you to be part of it. Now you're a witness, a liability they probably don't want." In a strained voice, he said, "You are a beautiful woman, Lucia. If they have nothing else to lose . . ."

She understood what he left unsaid. If the kidnappers only wanted him, they might kill her. And if they were willing to commit murder, what else might they do with her first? She shook her head, trying to clear it, but instead nausea washed over her. The drugs muddled her mind and she only caught snippets of Rashid's words: . . . *you're not a citizen . . . enter the country? . . . man in my position shouldn't travel alone with you in Morocco . . . shouldn't really even be alone in this room . . .*

Her apprehension surged. What if he felt he *couldn't* stay with her? "Rashid, please. We have to stay together."

"Are you sure?" He spread his hands. "It is the best solution I can see. But before we make this choice, you must understand what it means."

He had a solution? She had lost his train of words. "Tell me."

He took a breath. "I know one of the policemen. His sister works at my company. He has offered his services to us as a pilot. But the situation has him nervous. He may withdraw the offer if we don't act soon."

She tried to concentrate. "Why is he nervous?"

"He is afraid he will suffer repercussions if it turns out I am the one breaking the law. That I kidnapped you."

"But you *didn't.*"

"I think he wants to believe that." Rashid rubbed his eyes. "But he won't help us unless we have documentation. And we must move fast. We don't dare risk waiting."

Lucia didn't see how, under the circumstances, she could get whatever permission she needed to enter the country. But she grasped at the straw of hope. "I don't want to wait. Not at all."

"You must be sure." He cupped his hand around her cheek, then blushed and lowered his arm when he realized what he had done. "It isn't a suggestion I make lightly."

She hesitated. Would it be so unusual for her to travel with him across Morocco? "Once we get away from here, can we—" She stopped, too unfamiliar with her situation to know where she should turn to for help. "Go to the American authorities?"

He nodded. "Once we're safe, we can unravel all this."

His face blurred in her vision. Straining to focus, she said, "Then, yes. I want to go with you. Now." He was the one constant in the entire confusing mess.

His face gentled. "You are sure?"

"Yes. I'm sure."

An unexpected smile warmed his haggard face. "Then you honor me."

Startled by the comment, she managed a wan smile in return. "And you me."

In a gentle voice, he said, "I want someone here for you, too, when we fill out the papers."

She had no idea what papers were required for her to enter Morocco. Going to Italy had been simple, but it had taken more time than they had now. Which was none. "How can you arrange things fast enough?"

"I know people." Awkwardly he said, "And I will pay an, uh, fine."

That sounded like a tactful description of Rashid using his influence and wealth to circumvent Issam's authority. They had to get a message to someone who could help them. But who? The American consul? She struggled to fight off her growing lethargy. If anyone here had a connection to the kidnapping, they would be fools not to watch the consul's office, in case she and Rashid tried exactly what they were planning. If the kidnappers intercepted the messenger, they could send back one of their own people. But where else could she and Rashid turn? At home, she would have gone to her church.

". . . someone you trust?" Rashid was asking.

Lucia tried to concentrate. "A priest, maybe?" Watching his strained face, she added, "You need a doctor."

"I'm all right." He brushed tangles of hair away from her face. "Are you Catholic?"

"Yes."

He exhaled. "I will try, Lucia. Also, a friend of my father lives in the city. I don't know if I can reach him in time. But I trust him. He might be able to help."

"Good," she whispered, unable to hold herself up anymore. She crumpled against him, falling into darkness. . . .

A gentle voice drew her awake. She had been sleeping on the carpeted floor, surrounded by cushions. As she pulled herself into a sitting position, she saw a man seated cross-legged by the table. Recognizing his collar, she said, "Father?"

The priest answered her in Castilian Spanish. Although her parents spoke Spanish, Lucia had grown up in the United States, with English as her first language. She understood a fair amount of Mexican Spanish, but she had trouble with the Castilian dialect, and her dazed condition made it worse.

The police officer who knew Rashid was seated across the table. A stranger sat down next to him, an older man with a scholarly face. Lucia guessed he was the friend of Rashid's father. His appearance frightened her, though she wasn't sure why. He looked stern. Austere. But when she looked at his eyes, they were kind, showing only concern.

A sheaf of papers lay on the table, partially filled out, written in languages she didn't know. Weakened by the drugs, she sagged against Rashid. He put his arms around her waist, trying to help her stay up. But he wasn't in much better condition than she, and they almost ended up leaning against each other for support. A sense of desperate urgency filled the room, a need to be done here and gone before their plans to flee the airport were discovered and stopped.

The priest looked from Lucia to Rashid, his expression troubled. The police officer was talking to Rashid. When he finished, the friend of Rashid's father spoke to Lucia in Arabic. Rashid translated: "They are concerned that you give your consent and that you understand what you are doing."

Fighting to stay conscious, she nodded. To the best of her ability, in English, halting Spanish, and even worse French, she assured them all that *yes,* she was with Rashid of her own free will. He had used no coercion.

The priest spoke to her in Castilian. She shook her head, too dazed to decipher his words. He tried again with Rashid, and Rashid answered in halting Spanish. The priest had some familiarity with French, so they managed by alternating between the two languages. Lucia struggled to follow the conversation. Although she didn't catch the details, it was obvious he intended to make certain Rashid allowed her to do whatever she felt necessary.

Next the priest spoke to Lucia about her faith, trying to reassure her. Finally he told her that if she signed the papers, he believed it would be acceptable in the eyes of God. She wasn't sure why he phrased it that way, but he was clearly convinced Rashid intended well by her. With shaking fingers, she took the pen and wrote her name on the documents they had prepared. Someone was explaining the forms to her, but she had lost her struggle to understand. Rashid signed as well, followed by the others.

Then she slid into a misty sleep like a stone falling into a fog-covered lake.

*Chapter Four*

# THE BACKBONE OF ATLAS

*August 12, 2010*

Children were playing, somewhere not too far off. Lucia heard voices laughing and calling.

She was lying on a bed in a shadowed room. Gradually she realized the light had the quality of late-afternoon sunshine filtered by cloth. Designs in carved wood covered the ceiling, and a beautiful chandelier hung there, made from many small pieces of dangling crystal. Turning her head, she looked across the room and saw a curtain fluttering on a window framed by delicate grillwork. Brocaded cushions lay scattered about on the flowered carpet. The room had an aged quality, as if it were an antique photograph. It made the IV hanging next to the bed where she lay all the more jarring.

She ran her fingers over the tape that held the needle in her arm. When she pulled on the line, the tape came off and the needle slid free with a twinge of pain. As she sat up, spots danced in her vision. She wasn't sure why she was getting up; all she could think was that she had to talk to Carl Martelli.

Swinging her legs over the edge of the bed, she found herself facing a doorway directly across the room from the window. Light filtered through the plum-colored lace that hung in the open archway, giving the room a dusky color. Dust motes drifted in the air. She still had on her jeans and shirt, but without her dance clothes underneath. She felt fresh; someone had given her a bath and washed her clothes. Her tennis shoes rested by the bed, next to her ballet bag.

A pitcher stood on the nightstand by the bed, with several glasses. Lucia waited until her dizziness settled, then poured a a glass of water and drank it in a few swallows. After she set the glass down again, she slid off the bed and went to the doorway. It looked too wide, with sides that rose up about seven feet and then arched to a point.

Pushing aside the lace revealed another room with several low tables and upholstered benches against the wall. A stained-glass window patterned in delicate fan designs ran the length of the right wall, from waist height to the ceiling.

She crossed the room to another doorway and drew aside its curtain, revealing a tiled foyer. The children were louder now. Their calls came from beyond another archway across from her. Actually, "archway" was a paltry word; it looked like the keyhole for a giant skeleton key. The sides rose in marble pillars for eight feet, ending in flat tops. Above them the arch curved out and around in a semicircle, like a horseshoe. Its highest point was at least fourteen feet above the floor. Engravings framed the arch in braided designs of flowers and vines. Looking closer, she realized the "vines" were the calligraphic strokes of Arabic writing.

Two small shapes ran past the doorway, their outlines vague through its gauzy curtain. She went over, pulled aside the curtains—and gasped.

Symmetry. Exquisite symmetry.

She faced a courtyard with a fountain in its center, water bubbling in tiered bowls. Horseshoe arches identical to the one where she stood graced the other walls that bounded the square. The second story of the building overhung the courtyard, forming an arcade. Marble columns supported the arcade, curving at the top into horseshoe arches even taller than the doorways.

Tiles inlaid it all. Everywhere. Columns, fountains, ground, walls, arches—all were tiled in interlocking patterns, with intricate borders wherever the architecture framed a space. The art was abstract; nowhere did it depict a person or animal. Glazed blue-green, it slumbered as cool as the sea, with gold and rose accents that flashed like fish. Late-afternoon shadows filled the courtyard and gave the air a golden-pink quality. Above it all, the sky vibrated with a blue so intense it was hypnotic. It was like being underwater in a grotto, one utterly beautiful—and utterly alien.

Children were peering out at her from behind a staircase in the corner to her left. When they realized she had seen them, giggles rippled through the group. One of the oldest, a boy of about nine, ran across the yard and disappeared into another archway there.

A moment later a woman stepped out and hesitated, watching Lucia. The boy stood with her, earnestly trying to act confident. Although Lucia was too far away to see clearly, the woman looked her own age, surely too young to be the boy's mother. Glossy black hair poured down to her hips, and she wore a striped robe.

Then Rashid appeared.

The rose-gold light was deepening with the approach of evening, taking on a liquid quality. With her mind so dazed, Lucia's perception of time slowed. Rashid looked as if he were walking underwater as he headed toward her. He had on stonewashed jeans, white running shoes, and a pullover he could have picked up at any department store in the United States. The incongruity of his clothes with the rest of the scene made him look surreal.

Other adults were pouring out into the courtyard now. A slender man wearing spectacles and a striped robe strode after Rashid. An older woman swept out, and the others made way for her like waves parting before the prow of a ship. Children burst from everywhere, talking in volleys. Suddenly the square was filled with people, voices, and motion.

Overwhelmed, Lucia backed up through the curtain. In the foyer, she tripped and nearly fell. The back of her legs hit a wooden surface, and she sat down with a jolt on a carved bench against one wall.

A man appeared on the other side of the archway, his outline blurred through the curtain. From his unusual height and the breadth of his shoulders, she guessed it was Rashid. The woman joined him, and then the slender man, all of them talking in yet another language she didn't recognize. How many languages did Rashid speak? Other adults came up to them, their voices adding to the rumble of discussion, underlaid by the burble of children. Swaying with vertigo, she put her elbows on her knees and held her head in her hands.

The voices receded. She sat as still as possible, wishing she had stayed in bed. She didn't feel well enough to make it back there now.

"Lucia?"

She lifted her head. Rashid was sitting next to her on the bench. The barest trace of the bruise showed on his cheek. She tried to talk, but no sound came out. Wetting her lips, she tried again. "What is this place?"

"My father's home."

"In Morocco?"

He watched her face. "Yes."

How would she get back to rehearsal? "I have a performance tomorrow. In Italy."

Gently he said, "The performance was two days ago. Today is Thursday."

"Thursday?" She stared at him. "No. Carl must think I walked out on him."

"I phoned him, explained what happened." He exhaled. "I truly am sorry. You were . . . what is the phrase? In the wrong place at the wrong time."

"That water we had in your car—it was drugged."

"Yes. You drank most of what was meant for me." He touched her hair, then dropped his hand as if embarrassed by the gesture. "That probably saved my life."

"They meant to kill you?"

"I think eventually, when they got whatever they wanted."

"Who is 'they'?"

"My driver Enrico, the Russian pilot, and the copilot, their contact in Morocco. And whoever they work for."

"What did they want?"

He spread his hands. "Money. Ransom. Or so they claim."

His choice of words puzzled her. "You don't believe them?"

"What they say makes no sense." His face was open now, unguarded. She wondered if it was because he was home with his family. "Enrico knows I run Jazari International according to an Islamic economic system. So how can he think I'm hoarding money in Swedish bank accounts? Both the taking and the paying of interest are forbidden by the Qur'an."

She blinked. "Why?"

"It derives from a prohibition against usury." He paused. "Modern markets are more complicated. I do have ways of setting up loans and investments, but the risks and rewards are shared by everyone involved. I'm not 'hoarding' anything."

"Maybe he didn't understand."

"His Moroccan contact should have."

She tried to fit it all together. "What about the Russian? How did he get involved?"

Rashid rubbed his chin. "He's a retired military officer who supposedly never accepted the end of the cold war. I'm a prominent citizen in a North African country with strong ties to the West, I support the king, and I've spoken in favor of democracy. In his view, that makes me dangerous. At least, this is what he claims."

"But you don't believe him."

"It doesn't fit. It's true I can't be completely apolitical, given that I run a multinational corporation. But I avoid politics as much as possible."

Lucia hesitated. "I'm afraid I don't know much about your government." She had always read voraciously, even after she left school, and she recalled an article on Morocco's king, a youthful, intelligent leader. But beyond that she knew little about the country.

"It's a constitutional monarchy," Rashid said. "The king, His Majesty Mohammed the Sixth, is the head of state and the country's religious leader. He also appoints the Council of Ministers. His father, Hassan the Second, was a great peacemaker. We've an elected parliament too, though they have more limited powers." Suddenly he grinned. "Do you know, Morocco was the first country in the world to recognize the United States as an independent nation? The Treaty of Marrakech is the longest uninterrupted agreement of its type in American history."

His grin caught her off guard. She wondered if he had any idea how devastating it made him look. All she could think to say was, "I didn't know."

His smile faded. "But this kidnapping is crazy. Even if the pilot didn't know much about me, Enrico should have. He works for me."

"In Italy," she pointed out. "Would he understand your business practices here?"

"Perhaps not," Rashid admitted. "International tax law truly is a tangled hierarchy."

She blinked again. "A what?"

"Tangled hierarchy." His face became more animated, as it had when they talked about his research in Taormina. "It's a term from artificial intelligence. It means a self-modifying loop that tangles hierarchical levels by turning back on itself."

"Oh." That was as clear as Greek.

Watching her, he tried again. "Countries have tax agreements. If you pay taxes in one, you don't pay as much in the other. But I always pay in Morocco, so I end up remitting some taxes more than once. And I pay *sadaqa* as well as the *zakat.*"

She stumbled on the words. *"Zak—?"*

*"Zakat."* His voice had a harsher sound in Arabic. "I'm not sure of the translation. Alms tax? It's two-point-five percent of any liquid assets I have that have been in the bank for at least year. Also ten percent on storable crops, like grain." He paused, as if searching for words. "It isn't so much a tax as an act of worship. *Sadaqa* is extra, beyond the *zakat.* It all goes to charities, and to people around me, in the circle of my life, who are in need."

Dryly she said, "Apparently your kidnappers think they belong in that circle too."

"Perhaps." He didn't sound convinced.

"What else could they have wanted?"

"Industrial secrets? My company has a large division for research and development." He shook his head. "Their story doesn't sound genuine to me."

"Did you tell the police that?"

"Yes."

She waited. "And?"

He scowled. "They have more than enough evidence to convict. So they courteously suggest my suspicions are fanciful." Crossing his arms, he added, "I am not nearly so eccentric as everyone likes to believe."

That sounded as if it had a history far longer than the

past few days. She wasn't sure how to respond, but something seemed called for. So she said, "Smart people always seem eccentric to everyone else."

His face relaxed. "I doubt that's true. But thank you."

"I'm just glad we're free." She touched his bandaged wrist. "Does that hurt?"

"It's all right." Uncrossing his arms, he gave her a rueful smile. "My mother has suggested, rather forcefully, that I am remiss as a host, bringing you here via a kidnap attempt."

Lucia managed a smile. "It's certainly different."

"Ahmed is also concerned, particularly that you pulled out the IV. He says you shouldn't be up at all."

"Ahmed?"

"My brother. He is a doctor."

"You've an impressive family." She wondered if he had any idea how intimidating this all was to her.

Rashid stood and offered his arm, helping her up. He walked with her back to the room where she had awakened. She saw no chairs inside, only divans against the wall. So she sat cross-legged on the bed. Rashid sat on the edge of the mattress, not close to her, but it still made her wonder, given that they hardly knew each other. She wasn't sure what to make of him: he was a confusing mix of cultures, modern and traditional, West and East.

"This is to be our room." Rashid paused. "I haven't slept here since we arrived, though."

She tensed. " 'Our' room? What do you mean?"

It was a moment before he answered. Finally he said, "If you have to ask that question, we may have a problem."

"What kind of problem?"

Quietly he said, "Lucia, you and I are married."

## Chapter Five

# ZAKI

In the silence following Rashid's words, Lucia simply looked at him, too stunned to react. She had no idea how to absorb such a statement. He regarded her with a wary tension, as if she had pulled a rug from beneath him and he wasn't sure how to respond.

Finally she said, "Good Lord."

He was watching her face closely. "When the police tried to take you from the plane, I told them the first thing I thought of to stop them. I said you and I were engaged."

"But why?"

Awkwardly he said, "They thought you were my mistress."

Lucia reddened. "I appreciate your wanting to protect my name. But I'm not sure I see why it mattered."

Rashid gave her an odd look. "This is an Islamic country. Having lovers outside of marriage is against the law." He paused. "That doesn't mean it never happens. But under the circumstances, I thought it better they believed you were my bride."

It was all beginning to make sense. The documents, the witnesses, their concern that she gave her consent freely. Her fragmented dialogue with the priest made more sense now too. He had granted them an express dispensation for an interfaith marriage. It told her a great deal about Rashid's influence, that he had arranged it with such speed. Under normal circumstances, they could never have received the dispensation in that manner.

"That's what you were trying to tell me in the airport," she said. "We couldn't travel together if we weren't married."

"Yes. Especially for a man with my social position and conservative reputation." He pushed his hand through his hair, tousling the black locks. "Lucia, I'm sorry. I thought you understood."

In hindsight, she could see how it appeared that way. She studied his body language and facial expressions, trying to fathom him. He was no longer the unreadable cipher she had first met at the state dinner. More than anything now, he seemed like a man trying to deal with his own shyness in an awkward situation. It surprised her, particularly from someone so well favored. Most men she knew with such striking good looks were more confident around women. But then, she lived in a world of performers and artists. She had no real sense of the world Rashid inhabited. Yet now, suddenly, he was her husband.

She shook her head. "Once we escaped the airport, why didn't you take me to the American consul? Or the embassy?"

The question seemed to surprise him. "It would have been rather strange to take my sick wife to an embassy."

"What about in Taormina?" She watched him warily. "If you can't travel with me unless we're married, how could we have gone out to dinner there?"

"Italy isn't Morocco." He spoke carefully. "But I did think, if we seemed amenable to each other that evening, that I might raise the subject."

Startled, she said, "You mean marriage?"

"Were you a woman in this country, it would not have been unusual for my family to approach yours in regard to arranging a marriage."

She felt as if she were in a surreal Magritte painting. "Good grief, Rashid, what we did was hardly arranged."

Wryly he said, "So my parents have been reminding me since I carried you in here the night before last." He cracked his knuckles. "This time, they expected I would at least consult with them first."

"This time?"

He hesitated. "I was married once before. To a woman in England." With a shrug, he said, simply, "It ended."

She could tell the subject was off-limits. "But why me?"

His face gentled. "I've admired you for a long time."

Although he wasn't the first person to tell her that, even with a marriage proposal, it flustered her a lot more coming from Rashid. "You've seen me perform? I mean, besides in Washington?"

He nodded. "About four and a half years ago I was on a business trip to VirTech Systems in California. Ted Duquois, the president of VirTech, knew I liked flamenco. He and his wife took me to see your dance group in San Francisco."

She thought back to that tour. "We performed *Con Amore,* didn't we?"

"Yes. It was charming." Mischief flashed across his face. "Especially you."

Again he surprised her. In Carl's production of *Con Amore,* she had danced the role of the queen who headed a troop of Amazons. After they captured a male bandit, she became enamored of the handsome thief. But he resisted her advances. With help from Cupid, the two eventually found true love. The ballet was a lot of fun, but she would never have imagined Rashid, of all people, to be attracted by her portrayal of a warrior queen.

She grinned. "So you like Amazons."

He gave her a rueful smile. "I remarked casually on it to Ted and his wife. They weren't fooled by my supposed nonchalance. They suggested I send you flowers backstage."

Although she often received flowers from admirers, she didn't remember any from Rashid. Still, it had been years. Carefully she said, "It's always a pleasant surprise."

"I didn't do it. I thought it might seem intrusive, coming from someone you didn't know. So I contented myself with your performances." He rubbed his chin, looking embarrassed. "Ted once suggested I 'sweep you off your feet.' Invite you to exclusive restaurants, impress you with limousines and jewels."

Lucia reddened. He certainly wouldn't have been the first to try that method. And fail. She didn't care about gifts, limos, or foods with names she couldn't pronounce. What she really wanted was someone who understood her love of dance. Few people seemed to realize that, though.

"I'm glad you didn't," she said.

Rashid shook his head. "I wouldn't want a wife whose interest in me comes from my wealth." His expression relaxed. "When I met you at the state dinner, I could see you weren't that type." He made an exasperated noise. "So after admiring you for years, I finally had a chance to introduce myself. And what do I do? Act like an idiot."

"Rashid, no. You were charming." With a wince, she added, "I thought I had made a fool out of myself."

"Not at all." He spread his hands, palm up, as if admitting defeat. "After that night I couldn't stop thinking about you. I tried, but at the oddest times I would remember your face or your voice. I finally realized I either had to marry someone else or find out if you might share my interest."

She tried to imagine how she would have felt if he had proposed. Flattered, yes. Immensely. But overwhelmed too. She would have wanted to know him better before making any commitments.

Nothing had gone according to his plan, though. Or had it? Had she been wrong to trust him? On first impression, he struck her as an honorable man. She also doubted he would have protested when the police closed the investigation if he had any link to the abduction. Still, she knew so little about him. He had so much power. It made her feel vulnerable and uneasy.

A melodious voice came from the arched doorway. "Rashid?"

He went to the archway and drew aside the cloth. Like a great ship coming into port, an older woman with silver-streaked hair swept into the room, carrying a platter heaped with pastries. Her silk robe, the deep blush color of roses, swirled around her ankles. She had a plump, voluptuous figure and an unmistakable resemblance to Rashid.

A younger woman came with her, the girl in the striped robe, bringing a tray with teapot and cups. She was small, about five foot two, with creamy skin and a pretty face. The whites of her eyes were beautifully clear, making her irises look even darker and her eyes even bigger.

Smiling at Lucia, the older woman spoke in an unfamiliar language, her voice rising and falling with concern. When she finished, Rashid spoke to Lucia. "My mother, Lalla Tamou, welcomes you to our home. She wishes to make sure you are comfortable and have all you need." Softly he said, "She also extends her deepest regret that you were introduced to our country in such an unpleasant manner."

Lucia returned Tamou's smile, trying to hide how self-conscious she felt. "Please tell her I'm honored to be in her home."

Rashid translated, at some length, making Lucia suspect he was embellishing her comments. He introduced the younger woman as Khadija, his sister-in-law, the wife of Ahmed and mother of the boy who had run across the courtyard.

As Tamou and Khadija set their trays on the nightstand, they spoke with Rashid. Translating for Lucia, he said, "They're worried about you. You haven't eaten much since I brought you here. You've slept most of the time."

"I don't remember waking up at all," Lucia admitted.

He indicated the pastries. "Can you try to eat?" Ruefully he added, "Otherwise, I will spend the rest of the night hearing what a terrible husband I am, to starve my wife."

Lucia smiled. "We can't have that." She took a pastry and bit into it. A burst of almond flavor filled her mouth. After she swallowed, she said, "It's wonderful. Please tell your mother how much I appreciate her hospitality."

Rashid translated for her, then said, "My mother thanks you for your kind words."

Tamou was watching her closely, and Lucia suspected Rashid's mother wasn't fooled by her daughter-in-law's attempts to pretend she felt fine. She and Khadija were soon making their farewells, bustling and gracious as they left Lucia to rest.

While Rashid walked his family back outside, Lucia set the pastry back on the tray. She didn't really feel up to eating. Despite the courtesies she had exchanged with her mother-in-law, she wasn't at all convinced the meeting had gone well. She felt as if she were struggling to stay afloat in a sea of unknown cultural cues.

She slid off the bed and went to the window, where breezes ruffled the curtains. About fifteen feet below the window, the ground rolled away in a gentle slope from the base of the house. Beyond the open stretch of land outside, groves of almond trees spread out across the valley. In the distance, a minaret lifted above the forest, and beyond that, a range of mountains soared into the sky.

Earthen houses showed on either side of Rashid's home, the edge of a village. Very few windows looked out into the countryside; Rashid's was almost unique. Late-afternoon shadows filled the valley, pooling among the trees, softening the grasses.

The lush scene wasn't what Lucia expected. She knew almost nothing about North Africa, though, neither geography nor culture. What recourse would she have if Rashid decided to keep her here? She doubted it would be safe for her to walk off alone into the countryside in such an isolated region.

Behind her, a curtain whispered. She stayed at the window, listening to the tread of feet on the carpet. Then Rashid joined her at the window.

"You seem troubled," he said.

She hesitated, unsure how to phrase her question. "What if I want to return home?"

Disappointment flashed across his face. Then his expression shuttered, becoming unreadable. "You are free to go, Lucia."

"When?"

"I'm going to Tangier tomorrow, to the offices of Jazari International. The city has an airport." He lifted his hand as if to touch her cheek, then caught himself and dropped his arm. "It is your wish then? To leave?"

Was it? She had no doubt she wanted to return to MDT. But immediately? For all that she loved dance, it had become so central to her existence that she had forgotten how it felt to have anything else in her life. She had no friends outside the studio. Nor had she had a vacation in years. Although she had dated a bit, she had never found anyone who understood her commitment to dance, the long hours, the intensity, the dedication. She wanted to love, hoped for a husband and children. But it had never worked out.

Did she want to walk out now? To say Rashid intrigued and attracted her was an understatement. But she felt the immensity of the barriers that separated them.

"I'm not sure," she admitted.

"At least wait a few days, until we know more. It is safer here than in Tangier or en route."

She tensed. "You think we might have more trouble?"

He raked his hand through his hair. "I wish I could believe as the police do, that they solved the case. But I can't. How did three such different people—an Italian security guard, a retired Russian major, and an ex-patriot Algerian—become involved together? They have almost nothing in common, not culturally, socially, religiously, or economically. It's like three computer modules that don't fit anywhere. To make sense out of what they do, you need the larger program that runs them."

Although such a view would never have occurred to her, she could see what he meant. "You think they're part of something bigger?"

He hesitated. "I don't wish to alarm you."

"I'm an adult, Rashid. Tell me what you're worried about."

Quietly he said, "I think it's possible that much more exists in this situation than appears on the surface. If that is true, they will probably try again."

She rubbed her arms, feeling cold. "Do you have any idea why?"

"Something connected to my business? The research at JI? Our products?" He spread his hands. "Perhaps it does involve money or politics. Or maybe someone wants to make a statement that makes sense to them even if it doesn't to me. I don't know. But I would rather be viewed as eccentric and overprotective than regret my choices later."

Softly Lucia said, "We have a saying for that. Better safe than sorry."

In a gentle voice, he said, "For you also. If you go back in public now, I'm afraid it will make you a target. Especially since you are my wife. And you travel a great deal with MDT. It makes you more vulnerable."

Remembering the drugged nightmare of the last few days, she suppressed a shudder. What would happen if she returned to her normal life? Although most theaters had some form of security, it was minimal. If someone wanted to reach her, they could do it far more easily than if she stayed here. "Do you really think anyone would come after me?"

"You witnessed everything." He touched her cheek. "You don't know how much I wish you hadn't been pulled into this."

"Or you." She looked up at him. "Do you have enemies who might want you hurt?"

"Not that I know of." Light from the setting sun warmed his face. "I came home to Morocco to be a professor at Mohammed the Fifth University. Instead I'm CEO of a multinational corporation. So still I am learning." He grimaced. "Strategy formulation. Resource management. Marketing. It never ends." Spreading his hands, he said, "Would one of my competitors go so far as to kidnap me? It seems rather extreme."

Curious, she said, "If you were a professor, how did you end up as a CEO?"

Rashid exhaled. "When I accepted the position at Imperial College, my father was disappointed. He had hoped I would join him at our company, al-Jazari Citrus." He turned his hands palm up, as if to offer a compromise. "So when I returned to Morocco, to teach, I wanted to offer a contribution to the business. I suggested we expand into software. Sell a program I was writing." He looked disconcerted. "I never intended to end up running al-Jazari Citrus."

She thought of the name he had used before. "I thought it was Jazari International."

"Now, yes." He cracked his knuckles. "The software sold a bit better than I expected."

"What does it do?"

"It's just a Web browser. It talks to you."

She stared at him. "You wrote *Websparks*?"

"Well, yes, that's what I call it."

"Good Lord." She could hardly believe it. "I use it." So did millions of other people.

His face gentled, lines crinkling around his eyes. "Then I'm honored." Mischief flashed on his face again. "Lucky program, to always be at the touch of your fingers."

As Lucia blushed, a beep came from Rashid's waist. Looking down, she saw a red light glowing on a box that hung from his belt. He pulled off the beeper and read its display.

"What's wrong?" she answered.

"Zaki has problems."

"Zaki?"

A smile played on his lips. "A recalcitrant child, you might say."

A *son*? From his last marriage? "Is he yours?"

"Unfortunately, yes."

She felt awkward again. "Why do you talk about him like that?"

"Come on." He hung the box back on his belt. "I will show you."

They went through a side arch and followed a hall where a carpet the color of a sunrise covered the floor. The day's warmth surrounded them, and dust drifted in the air. A small crystal chandelier hung from the ceiling in the center of the hall. Mosaics tiled the walls, similar to those in the courtyard, gold and bronze, flecked by aquamarine and sea blue. Here the recurring theme was a beautiful star mosaic, an eight-pointed star surrounded by interlocking designs that radiated out from the center. With a start, Lucia recognized the pattern. It was the border that framed Websparks's screens.

Then Rashid stopped at an arched doorway—and opened its door into another world.

Gone were the organic colors and textures, the brass lamps, stained-glass windows, and open arches letting warm air circulate. This room was all gleaming surfaces, dust free and glossy, cool and air-conditioned. Fluorescent tubes in the ceiling cast diffuse light over the lab.

Fascinated, Lucia walked in among the clutter, so absorbed she even managed to ignore her fatigue, which had been growing since she had left her bed. Tables filled the room, crammed with computer workstations, printers, scanners, disk drives, CDs, disks, papers, and more. The lab also had chairs, the first she had seen in the house. A network server stood against one ivory wall, a boxy machine about the size and shape of two filing cabinets, with lights glowing within it. A whiteboard hung on one wall, its glossy surface covered with equations and diagrams written in blue felt-tip marker.

The floor made a hollow sound as she walked. She had never seen anything like it. The surface consisted of white carpeted squares, each about two by two feet, and edged in metal. The cables that connected the computers were apparently under the floor, except where they snaked up to the workstations or server. Several small robots about the size of cats clustered in one corner, reminding Lucia of the machines AI engineers built to give their computer programs mobility. In another corner, she saw what looked like a high-tech dentist's chair surrounded by equipment. A metallic gold suit lay on it, under a clear plastic tarp.

Lucia went to a table that held a workstation with a huge screen. She had seen many excited notices about this computer on the Web: the Stellar-Magnum, a phenomenon with a processing speed and memory beyond those of any other workstation in existence. Its price went far above what an ordinary person could afford for personal use. But then, from the looks of this room, she suspected the same was true for a lot of the equipment here. In his home, hidden and isolated in the mountains, Rashid had a state-of-the-art AI lab that universities and industrial centers would envy.

"Amazing," Lucia murmured. She turned to Rashid, laying her hand on the Stellar-Magnum. "This is the nine thousand series, isn't it?"

"That's right." He sounded pleased by her recognition.

"It's gorgeous." She turned her attention to the display on the big screen. It was a mess, a wash of jagged lines and colors, like an impressionist painting of a seashore that had splintered into horizontal shards. "But what happened to it?"

"I'm not sure." He came up next to her and sat in the swivel chair in front of the machine. "Zaki?"

Zaki? Lucia glanced around but saw no one. Nor did anyone respond.

Rashid pulled the Stellar-Magnum's keyboard into his lap. As he typed on it, the fractured seascape vanished, replaced by a wash of blue. Another display formed, this one in full-color graphics that appeared three-dimensional. It showed an office lined with bookshelves and crammed with comfortable, worn furniture. A man in a white robe and a turban was sitting at a desk wedged in one corner between a table and a faded divan.

"Zaki," Rashid said. "What's the problem?"

A man's voice came out of the workstation's speaker. "Name, please."

"Rashid."

A line of type appeared at the bottom of the screen:

```
Username: jazari
```

"Enter your password," Zaki said. Rashid typed, and another line appeared:

```
Password: ***********
```

When he hit return, the lines scrolled upward:

```
Welcome to Stellar-Magnum node 8
Node name is: Zaki
Zaki: /home/jazari (1)
```

That surprised Lucia. Computers systems had become so friendly, with such slick graphics, that it was difficult to reach this basic a level, where you had to recognize and navigate nuances of the operating system. Usually all a person had to do was manipulate symbols, with no need to understand the system's underlying structure. In fact, with Websparks, all you had to do was talk to the machine.

She leaned closer to read the words. Node eight? "How many computers do you have?"

He continued typing. "Eleven total in the house. This workstation is the front end for Zaki." He gestured toward the server against the wall. "That runs everything, including Bashir's computer and the one in Ahmed's office."

"Bashir?"

"Another brother." Peering at Zaki's screen, he set the keyboard on the table. "An accountant for JI."

Lucia hesitated, her curiosity warring with her exhaustion, which had worsened, and her uncertainty about asking him personal questions. But his family was her family, at least for now. So she asked, "Do you have a lot of brothers?"

"Five." As he studied the text on the screen, he added, "Three still live here, at the house."

So he came from a large family. As an only child, Lucia felt a familiar ache. She had often longed for a sister to share her life. Her parents had never been able to have more than one child and had lavished enough love on her for several families combined. She hoped someday to give them many grandchildren to warm the empty spaces they had hoped to fill with children of their own.

The room blurred around her, then came into focus again. Rubbing her eyes, she asked, "Do you have sisters?"

"Four. But none live here anymore." Rashid frowned at the computer. "Zaki, where is your log file?"

"It was corrupted when I ran out of memory," Zaki said. "I deleted it."

"Why?" Rashid asked.

"I needed the disk space."

"You have plenty of disk space."

"Now, yes. I didn't before."

Rashid scowled. "So you deleted the log that contained the error messages telling me why you ran out of memory?"

"Yes."

"I don't want you to delete files unless I ask you to."

"If you constrain my operations, I have less leeway in dealing with problems." Zaki spoke as if he were trying to sound dignified but hadn't perfected the effect.

"The beeper will call me if you get into trouble," Rashid said.

"I am fixing myself."

"I still need the log. Can you get it back?"

"I believe so." Now Zaki sounded like a computer. "At least parts of it."

"Good. Do it."

Zaki touched a panel on his desk and it morphed into a computer screen. As Zaki went to work, Rashid glanced up at Lucia, a lock of hair falling into his eyes.

"Wow," she said.

He pushed back his hair. "Doctoring a disk to recover a deleted file is easy."

"No, I mean Zaki." She smiled. "He really sounded like he was talking to you. Even better than Websparks." Although Zaki's "emotions" weren't all that convincing, it intrigued Lucia that he had acted on his own and then argued with Rashid about his decision.

Rashid grimaced. "I never had this much trouble with Websparks."

Lucia started to respond, then stopped as her vision blurred again. She laid her hand on the table by the workstation to steady herself. To cover her fatigue, she said, "Why does he speak English?"

"That's what I spoke in. I guess because you and I were." Rashid lifted his hand to lay it on top of hers. Then he stopped and cupped an edge of the keyboard instead. "Zaki knows many languages."

Lucia wondered why he kept stopping himself from

touching her. For the second time in just a few minutes he seemed to hold back.

"What does Zaki do?" she asked.

"He's a Web tour guide. A sophisticated Websparks." He glanced at the screen, which showed Zaki working. A computer program working on a computer program on a computer within a computer. It struck Lucia as an apt image for the twenty-first century.

"I've been working on this for years," Rashid said. "I started when I was in London."

She heard the longing in his voice. "Do you miss academics?"

Rashid spoke with difficulty. "It doesn't really matter. My family needed me more." He looked back up at her. "The world is changing and my family's business had to adapt to survive. At Imperial College, I did a lot with the Centre for Planning and Resource Control. They collaborate with industry to develop new technology and applications in the information sector. So when the time came, I had some idea how to bring al-Jazari Citrus into the twenty-first century."

Impressed, she said, "You've certainly done that."

He shrugged. "At Cambridge, I was crazy about my research. I wanted to rederive number theory, write my own symbolic language, create an artificial intelligence, combine the results with virtual reality, and develop a system to interpret the entire World Wide Web. It was supposed to revolutionize the enhancement of human thinking started by the computer age. 'Illuminate the secrets of a new universe,' I said." Dryly he added, "I was young and foolish then."

She spoke in a gentle voice. "Dreams are never foolish."

He sighed. "Perhaps. But reality has a way of intruding."

"Can you continue your work here?" She indicated the lab. "You've a wonderful setup." She tried to ignore her sensation that the wonderful setup was, at the moment, tilting around her.

"I manage to do a bit." He paused. "I prefer to keep this project separate from JI."

JI. Jazari International? She realized what had struck her earlier about the name. "You dropped the *A-L.* In al-Jazari."

His face shuttered again. "Some of our Western customers had trouble remembering the name. So I took off the 'al.' It just means 'the,' after all."

Although he hid his discomfort, she was more attuned to his moods now and sensed it had bothered him. "I guess it's difficult to change what defined your life for so long."

His face gentled. "You're perceptive."

Lucia smiled. "But Jazari International does sound snazzy."

"Snazzy?" Rashid laughed. "Is that a noun or an adjective?"

"Adjective. You know. Cool. Actually, maybe 'hot' says it better."

He blinked at her. "Cool and hot?"

Zaki spoke. "Snazzy is an Americanism derived from the words 'snappy' and 'jazzy.' It means stylishly attractive. Flashy."

Rashid glowered at the computer. "Do you have the log file back yet?"

"I am still working on it."

Lucia held back her smile. She wanted to talk to him more, but she was having trouble forming words. The light in the room was taking on an odd tinge, a dark sepia tone that antiqued the furniture and darkened the walls, like an old fading photograph. . . .

With a sense of drifting, she slowly collapsed. Rashid jumped to his feet and caught her. "Ah, Lucia, I'm sorry. You're so physically fit, I forget you've been unconscious for two days."

She leaned against him, her arms at her sides. But when he tried to pick her up, she shook her head. "I can walk."

So they left his lab. The hall loomed before her, dusky

in the sepia light. Surrounded by antique shadows, she concentrated on putting one foot in front of the other. She felt Rashid at her side, felt him wanting to help, but he respected her wish to walk on her own. She doubted he had any need to impose his will on others. For all his reticent nature, he gave off the sense of self-confidence she had known only in people who were at ease with their own authority.

When they reached his room, she lay down on the bed with a sigh of relief. Rashid sat next to her, near her shoulder. He poured a glass of water from the pitcher on the nightstand. She drank thirstily, only now realizing how parched she felt.

Concern creased his face. "I'll get Ahmed." He took her empty glass. "You should have the IV put back in. Or you should eat, even if we aren't."

"No. I'm all right." The thought of food made her queasy, as did the idea of a needle dripping her full of liquid. More than that, though, she dreaded being alone. Everything here was unknown. Rashid was her anchor.

Closing her eyes, she sought to relax, starting from her fingertips and toes, first tensing her muscles, then releasing them. She worked through her body, from the tips of her limbs inward. It was an exercise she often used to unwind, particularly when she was exhausted after many hours of dancing but too keyed up to sleep.

As her meditation deepened, she drifted into a doze. . . .

Lucia awoke with a start, feeling as if she had lost something vital. Reaching over the edge of the bed, she rummaged in her ballet bag until her fingers touched the slender chain she sought. Then she pulled her cross out of her bag. After she fastened it around her neck, she sank into sleep again.

When she next opened her eyes, the shadows of sunset had darkened the room. Rashid was sitting cross-legged in the corner, leaning against the wall with brocaded cushions propped around him. He was reading a book, a large text with Arabic calligraphy on the front. She wasn't sure, but she guessed it was the Qur'an.

Distant but clear, a chant drifted in the window. It curled through the evening, as eerie as it was beautiful, rising and falling in an arabesque of sound. Rashid lifted his head, going still as he listened. Then he rose to his feet and left the room.

A great booming woke Lucia, like the firing of a cannon. She couldn't have dozed for long; dusk still filled the room. Had she really heard the noise? She floated on a sea of slumber, that netherworld between waking and sleep. Gradually she became aware of music and voices in another part of the house. Then she sank back below the surface, into deeper sleep.

When Lucia next woke, it was well into the night. Rashid lay facing her on the bed, asleep but fully dressed, with starlight ghosting across his body. The fresh scents of soap tickled her nose, and she could smell his damp, clean hair. Although his eyes were closed, he didn't look relaxed enough to be deep in his slumber.

"When did you come back?" she murmured.

He opened his eyes and said what sounded like, "After breakfast."

"Breakfast?" At night? Or had he actually said, "Breaking my fast?"

He touched her face, this time making no attempt to stop himself as he traced the curve of her cheekbone. She wasn't sure if the jump in her pulse came from anticipation or wariness. Or both. Earlier in the day he had refrained from touching her at all, except to catch her when she fell. Now she felt none of that restraint. She was acutely aware of his size and strength, and the heat he radiated.

Rashid slid his arms around her waist and pulled her against his body. She laid her palms flat against his chest. Instead of pushing him away, though, she slid her hands across his shirt. She felt the soft cloth under her palms, and beneath that the hard planes of his torso.

Murmuring in an unfamiliar language, he pressed his

lips against the top of her head. A breeze rustled the curtains, sifting air across them. The night outside sounded muted and distant: a creak of branches, the call of a bird, no city hum or growl of traffic. Insects chirped, and somewhere a dog barked.

Rashid laid his palm on the back of her head, somehow making that simple gesture erotic, as if touching her hair was an act of intimacy. He rolled the strands between his fingers the way a connoisseur would savor a fine wine. Then he let his palm slide down her back along her hair, all the way to her hips. She felt the strength in his hand. He repeated the motion, skimming her back, pressing in at her waist, sliding his palm over her curves. Mesmerized, she closed her eyes.

When he splayed his hand at her waist and pulled her against him, Lucia tipped up her face, trying to see him in the starlit shadows. He bent his own head, searching, as if to whisper in her ear. But it wasn't her ear he sought. Instead he kissed her.

Lucia tensed, her palms still flat against his chest. A faint alarm far back in her mind warned her to stop, but she ignored it. She didn't want to think. She wanted to kiss her husband. She kept her hands between their bodies, like a last hope for the revival of her fading common sense. Right now, though, fading common sense had a lot to recommend it.

Rashid deepened his kiss, tangling his hand in her hair. Eyes closed, Lucia relaxed and moved one of her palms across his chest. When he felt her tension ease, he rolled her onto her back, trapping her under his body. His hand slipped under her blouse and across her skin until it cupped her breast.

Common sense came back with a jolt, accompanied by confusion. It was too much, too fast. This time she did push at his chest, trying to make him stop. He kept stroking her, with both his hands now, kissing her also as he held her down with his weight. The alarms in her mind blared, reminding her like a deluge of ice water that she was alone in a foreign country with little recourse aside from Rashid's goodwill, which he could withdraw anytime.

His lips brushed her hair. "So beautiful," he murmured.

"No." She inhaled sharply. "Don't."

Lifting his head, he looked down at her. "Don't?"

"Please." She was startled by how much her voice shook. "I know I signed the papers. I know you have rights. But I didn't understand. I can't—I hardly know you."

Rashid's hands stilled. "It's all right, Lucia. I would never force you."

"I—I'm sorry." Her pulse began to slow. "I didn't mean to tease."

His grin flashed in the starlight. "Tease? What does that mean? To play?" He pulled his hand out from under her blouse, but then he touched her nipple where it pushed up the cloth. "Your body doesn't know you aren't ready yet."

She flushed, embarrassed, also relieved he wasn't angry, but still not sure he understood. "It will have to wait, too."

Sliding onto his side, he eased his weight off her. "Then so can I." Mischief flashed on his face. "I will go crazy doing so, of course, but no matter. The rest of the world already thinks I am strange anyway."

She smiled. "You're teasing me now."

He pressed his lips against her hair. "I, tease? Never."

"Ah, but it's very fine teasing."

He pretended to bite her ear. "According to the English I learned, 'fine' means 'extraordinary in quality.' Truly you are a discerning woman."

Lucia laughed. "You know, Rashid, you are nowhere near as somber as you pretend in public."

"Don't tell anyone."

She closed her eyes. "Thank you," she murmured.

He spoke quietly. "We have plenty of time. As much as you need."

Did they? What if she wanted to go to Tangier with him tomorrow?

Rashid rolled onto his back and pulled her into his arms. She lay against his side, her head on his shoulder, one palm on his chest. Although he stroked her hair, it was absentminded now, for comfort rather than lovemaking. The rhythmic motion soothed her. More than soothed. She didn't think he was trying to seduce her, though. She had resisted enough seductions in her life to know when it was deliberate. He genuinely didn't realize the effect of his preoccupied caresses.

Eventually his hand stilled. Just as Lucia started to doze, a thought came to her. "Rashid?"

"Hmmmm?"

"I was wondering. About Zaki."

"Yes?"

She hesitated, afraid her hunch would sound silly. So she probed for information first. "He's meant to be a better Websparks?"

Rashid shifted her in his arms. "Initially." Drowsily he added, "I meant him to augment some hardware I designed. The R and D people at JI built the product and wrote most of the software for it. Zaki is something I've been doing on my own."

As far as she knew, hardware meant equipment and software meant programs that ran on it. Was Zaki intended to run robots, like those in Rashid's lab? That made no sense. Why put a Web browser in a robot whose purpose was probably to learn by wandering around the lab, much the way a toddler learned by exploring her surroundings? The robots needed AI "brains" that could solve problems and make plans for dealing with their environment. Not Web browsers.

So what hardware would use a sophisticated Web browser? Lucia had a guess, but she still wasn't sure. "If you get Zaki to work, will your company sell the program?"

"I had thought about it," he said in a sleepy voice. "He's nowhere near finished, though, and the product is about to go on the market."

Her excitement leapt. "Zaki is for a virtual-reality suit, isn't he?"

Rashid opened his eyes. "How did you know that?"

"Good Lord." Lucia stared at him. "You're the Duke!"

He made an exasperated noise. "Why do Americans call me that? I know nothing about jazz."

"Jazz?"

"Duke. For Duke Ellington."

"The musician?"

"Yes. People kept mangling my name. Then someone found out it means 'the man from Jazaair.' Before I knew it, all these Web sites were talking about 'the Jazzman.'" Almost growling, he said, "At least they spell that right."

"How do they spell your real name?"

"Every way you can imagine. The worst was Radish ala-Jakarta." He glowered at her. "I was tempted to send the fellow e-mail informing him I wasn't a salad on the coast of Java."

Lucia struggled to hold back her laugh, but it came out anyway. "Oh, Rashid, that's funny."

"I'm glad you think so," he grumbled.

"You're the *inventor.*" She rolled onto her stomach and lifted her head to look at him better. "You created the Duke's suit."

Rashid regarded her, his face silvered by the starlight coming in the window. "Duke Ellington was a gifted musician. But I'm not him."

She lay back down against his side, thinking. "If you don't come up with a new name soon, before this one gets canonized, you'll be the Duke forever. With the Duke's suit."

"I call it 'the VR suit.'" He settled her into his arms. "Very sensible."

"That's the problem. It's dull."

"What do you suggest?"

"The Jazari suit."

"Everyone will mispronounce it."

"Not once they get used to it."

"Americans will call it 'jazzy.' "

"It will help it sell. Besides, it *is* jazzy."

"It is?"

"Cool. You know. Like you."

"I do not know."

She laughed. "You're too serious, Rashid."

"Why do people say this so much?" he grumbled. "Rashid, you are too serious. Rashid, you are too eccentric. How can I simultaneously be too serious and too eccentric?"

"You're different."

"I don't want to be different."

She pressed her lips against his cheek. "But you are so fine that way."

"Ah, well." He laughed softly. "If my beautiful wife tells me that I am 'fine,' 'cool,' and 'jazzy,' who am I to argue?"

She settled her head back against his shoulder. "So Zaki is the mystery program."

"There is no mystery program. Zaki didn't go on sale because Zaki doesn't work."

"Even so, I'm impressed."

His voice gentled. "Thank you."

After that they lay together. As Rashid dozed, still holding her, images of Zaki, Websparks, and virtual-reality helmets drifted in Lucia's mind. Rashid astounded her not only for his genius but also because despite everything—his wealth, influence, power, and intellect—he remained modest.

That didn't change the gap in their educations, though. She wondered how long it would take him to realize she didn't even have a complete high school education, and how that would change his attitude toward her.

She must have slept for a while. Gradually she became aware that the room was lightening with the oncoming dawn. A chant drifted through the crystalline air, haunting and otherworldly, followed by the song of an oboe in the village.

Rashid let go of her then and got up, without speaking. She watched him leave, wondering at his sudden distance. His relaxed affection from the night had vanished with the glimmering dawn.

Drowsing, she waited for him to come back. But wherever he had gone, he stayed. Was he working in his lab? She thought of Zaki. If he was only an expanded Websparks, meant to serve as a tour guide, why did so many legends surround him? Why had Mark Spearman, a colonel who worked in military intelligence, been interested in Rashid? Was there more to Zaki? Enough to motivate a kidnapping?

Enough to kill for?

*Chapter Six*

# ARABESQUES

*Friday*

Lucia opened her eyes into sunshine. She was still lying on the bed, fully dressed. And alone. Disoriented, she sat up and looked around. Had Rashid already left for Tangier? She felt stronger now, less dizzy than yesterday. And *hungry.* All she had eaten were the pastries and tea. Swinging her legs over the side of the bed, she rubbed her eyes. It was midmorning, she guessed, perhaps ten or so.

The curtains in the doorway rustled. Then Ahmed's wife, Khadija, pulled aside the lace. Dressed in a silken yellow robe that fell to her ankles, she all but glowed. Slits in the sides came about halfway to her knees, revealing a sheer lace robe that rippled like liquid gold under her outer robe. Her hair hung all the way to her hips, black and glossy. With her pretty face and large eyes she looked like a picture out of a storybook.

Lucia smiled. "Hi."

Khadija gave her a shy smile. *"Bonjour."*

Lucia smiled, feeling much more up to meeting Khadija this morning than yesterday evening. "Please come in. *Entrez-vous.*" She hoped she wasn't mangling the French too much.

*"Merci."* Khadija entered, then paused as if unsure where Lucia wanted her to sit. Although the room had no chairs, richly cushioned divans bordered the walls. In the corner where Rashid had been reading on the floor, brocaded cushions were piled high in silky profusion.

Lucia slid off the bed to stand with Khadija. "Did Rashid leave already?"

She seemed puzzled by the question. "Rashid ready?"

"Rashid went to Tangier?"

"Ah. No. He is at *la mosquée.* Today is Friday."

Lucia hesitated. "Do you mean church?"

"Not church. But yes, a place for prayers." Khadija shifted to French again, asking a question.

After they struggled for several moments, back and forth in English and French, Lucia spread her hands and gave her sister-in-law a look of apology. *"Je regrette.* I'm sorry. I don't understand. *Je ne comprends pas.*"

With a shy smile, Khadija indicated the door with her hand. "Eat, yes?"

Relief flowed over Lucia. "Yes. Thank you. *Merci bien.*"

Khadija took her out into the courtyard. On the second-story terrace that bordered the yard, a woman in a flowing white-and-gold robe leaned over the balcony and called to them. As Khadija stopped to answer, another woman joined the first.

Soon a group of women and two teenage girls were

descending the stairs. Several of the women looked to be in their sixties or older, and the rest were middle-aged, a generation or so older than Khadija. Talking and laughing, their voices melodious in the morning breezes, they came down in a rainbow of fluttering silk. The older women wore soft robes or caftans, gold, blue, green, aqua, and turquoise. The girls had on skirts and blouses embroidered with flowers.

Drawn by the voices, a gaggle of children burst out of an archway, throwing aside the curtains. As the children and adults converged on them, Lucia tensed, overwhelmed by the voices and colors.

Khadija placed her hand on Lucia's arm. "Is okay."

Lucia swallowed. "Thank you. *Merci.*"

Khadija gave her arm a squeeze. As she made introductions for Lucia, voices piled up, warm and mellow, with lighter accents from the girls and giggling from the children. Although Lucia understood almost none of the words, she managed to put names with faces. The portly matron with silver hair was Hajja Zineb. Rahma, a middle-aged woman in a blue caftan, was mother to one of the teenage girls. The pretty five-year-old peeking from behind Khadija's dress was Fatima.

Khadija murmured something about *Lalla Tamou,* and the group began to move, sweeping Lucia along with them. Conversation flowed over and around her, familiar in its cadences despite the unfamiliar words. When they reached a horseshoe arch, the group drifted to a stop and began to break up, the adults returning to their work, the children to their games.

When Lucia and Khadija were alone, Khadija tilted her head toward the archway. "The mother of Rashid." She said it as if she were introducing the head of state.

"Oh." Having already met Tamou once, Lucia felt properly intimidated.

Khadija ushered her into a sitting room similar to the one outside Rashid's bedroom. They crossed to an imposing archway, where Khadija pulled aside the curtains. Inside the next room, Rashid's mother was seated on a plush carpet among a pile of cushions, dressed in a silk robe that shade of rose found only in a deep, vivid sunset. She had been reading, but as Lucia and Khadija entered, she set the book in her lap.

A low black-lacquered table stood by Tamou, and brocaded divans lined the walls, their gold hues gleaming. Although Lucia saw no bed, she realized the divans could serve that purpose. At first she wondered why Rashid had a European-style bed in his room. Then it occurred to her he might not fit on a divan. Large by any standard, he was huge for a Moroccan.

At Tamou's gesture of invitation, Khadija brought Lucia over and sank gracefully down among the cushions, the blue velvet pillows a bright contrast to her yellow gown, like the sky with the sun. Lucia sat next to her, grateful for the dance training that allowed her to move with ease despite how clumsy she felt in her jeans and blouse.

As Khadija and Tamou spoke, they did their best to include Lucia. Although Lucia didn't understand much of what they said, she enjoyed listening to the rise and fall of their conversation. Tamou's voice flowed like dark honey, deep and rich, accented by Khadija's sweeter, softer tones. They spoke with their hands as well, using animated gestures. The entire time, Tamou watched Lucia with a wary courtesy that missed nothing. Lucia felt as if her mother-in-law were inspecting her, turning her upside down and inside out.

When Tamou looked past Khadija and spoke, Lucia glanced back to see a woman standing just inside the doorway. She wore a gray robe, simple in cut and cloth, functional in appearance. She nodded to Tamou and left the room.

A maid? The idea of being waited on disconcerted Lucia. Had she not gone into ballet, she might have become a maid herself for a rancher in the area around Hachita. In high school she had worked part-time as a laundry girl for a local family, only a few hours a week, because she spent most of her time in dance class, but enough to earn some spending money.

The woman returned with a silver tray that held a teapot, a delicate blue glass edged with gold, and pastries. She set the tray on the table by Tamou and poured green tea into the glass. Then she rose and quietly withdrew.

Tamou moved the table forward into the midst of the three woman. She spoke to Lucia, urging her with gestures and words to drink. Flustered, Lucia picked up the glass. Why only one? Uncertain of the protocols, she sipped the tea. Mint. Strong and sweet, it warmed her mouth. She swallowed, and the glow spread through her body.

"It's delicious," she said. When both Tamou and Khadija gave polite but bemused nods, she tried again. *"Très bien."*

*"Merci,"* Tamou murmured. She picked up the pastry dish and offered it to her guest.

Lucia broke off a piece of the large pastry, then waited for her companions to follow suit. When Tamou simply set down the plate, Lucia hesitated. Should she eat alone?

Khadija spoke. "Lalla Tamou says please for you to start." She hesitated. "For a long time you're not eating. You must be more strong."

Lucia blinked. More strong? Perhaps Khadija meant she needed to eat to recuperate. It was true, she had only a few bites since yesterday.

As the silence grew strained, Lucia realized she was sitting with the pastry in one hand and her tea in the other. So she set down the glass and took a bite of the pastry. It tasted like a dream: sugar, cinnamon, chicken, and crunchy almonds, with layers of a delicate flaky crust that melted as she swallowed. The unfamiliar mixture of sweet pastry and poultry delighted her.

"It's wonderful," she said. *"Très bien!"*

Khadija grinned and said, "Bastilla," as if only that was needed to explain her reaction.

Outside, a burble of children's voices burst forth, followed by a man's rumbling laugh. The voices drew nearer, and Lucia turned to see Rashid pull aside the curtains. His appearance startled her. He looked like another person. He wore a loose-fitting white robe, rich and soft, with the hood lying against his back. Rich white embroidery lined its seams and hems. Slits went up to about his knees on both sides of the robe, revealing another robe under it and loose white cotton pants under that. He also wore white slippers and a white turban on his head.

Rashid came over and knelt by his mother. He gave her a hug, then kissed her on top of her head, evoking a smile she tried to disguise as a frown. Tamou clucked and attempted to give the impression she was scolding him—for what, Lucia couldn't imagine. Rashid apparently couldn't either, given the mischievous tone of his responses. But then Tamou grew more serious, tilting her head toward Lucia.

Rashid turned to her, his smile fading. "My mother worries that you aren't eating. Ahmed also said this to me, this morning." He paused. "He wants to give you another exam."

"I'm fine. Really." Lucia didn't feel ready to deal with more of his family yet, doctor or no doctor. "Please thank your mother for the meal. It was delicious."

"I will tell her."

As he spoke to Tamou, her attitude toward Lucia gained warmth. Lucia suspected Rashid was embellishing her words in ways he knew would please his mother.

Then he stood up and offered Lucia his hand. "I'll take you back to rest now."

She didn't want to rest. What she really needed was a few hours in the dance studio to work the kinks and aches out of her body. It had been three days since she had danced. She hadn't gone this long without practice in years.

Still, she did feel tired. She took Rashid's hand and rose to her feet. When he saw she could stand on her own, though, he let go of her. He talked a bit more with Tamou and Khadija, then ushered Lucia out of the room.

As they crossed the courtyard, she gave him a curious glance. "What language do you speak with your family? It doesn't sound like Arabic."

Before he could answer, two boys playing in the yard called to him, abandoning their game of ball in favor of the better opportunities he apparently presented. They ran around Rashid and Lucia, obviously entreating him to play ball. Laughing, he shooed them away, until they chased each other off across the courtyard.

He paused at the entrance to his suite, still laughing. "They have more energy than sense."

Lucia smiled as they entered his suite. "They like you."

"Ah, well. Perhaps." He seemed pleased. As they crossed the sitting room, he said, "We speak Berber at home, a dialect called Tashelhayt. My mother's family are Berbers."

"Berber?"

He held aside the curtain in the archway to his bedroom. "The original Moroccans."

She walked inside with him. "Your name sounds Arabic."

"As I am, on my father's side."

"You almost look Spanish. Andalusian." Like her.

He grinned. "I am a salad after all, yes? Many ingredients. My maternal grandmother was Andalusian."

Intrigued, Lucia asked, "How did she come here?"

He let the curtains drop behind them. "For almost a thousand years, North Africa exchanged its culture, religion, and way of life with Andalusia."

She gave him a dry smile. "Is that a tactful way of saying the Moors conquered Spain?"

Rashid laughed. "Well, yes. Two Berber dynasties, the Almoravids and then the Almohads, united Andalusia and northwest Africa. Moorish Spain flourished for centuries, until the *reconquista,* at about the time Columbus discovered America." His voice had become animated, much as when he spoke about his research. "It must have been an incredible age, with so rich a north–south exchange of culture. Universities were established, the model for our modern academic system. And the architecture! The Alhambra, the Giralda, the Mosque of Córdoba." He paused, looking a bit abashed by his own enthusiasm. "Anyway, that is all part of my heritage."

Listening to him, she could almost see the rise of dynasties, palaces, and empires. Although she knew pieces of Andalusian history, she had never put them together with modern Morocco. She had seen pictures of the Alhambra, a spectacular palace. Rashid's home echoed that architecture on a smaller, more subdued scale, with its colonnades, arabesques, vaulted halls, and horseshoe arches.

Impressed, she said, "You're a walking slice of history."

"I never thought of it that way before."

Lucia started to speak, then stopped as dizziness swept over her. Swaying, she grabbed the edge of the arched doorway.

He offered his arm. "You should lie down. You really do look tired."

She took his arm. "I feel fine." Shyly she added, "I am hungry, though. That pastry was wonderful."

"I will have someone bring you more." Although he stood next to her, she felt his distance. He set her apart, like a fly in amber, and she wasn't sure how to interpret the separation. He seemed unfamiliar to her now, beautiful in his robes and turban, but unlike anyone she had ever known.

Rashid motioned to a divan sofa against the wall. "Would you like to sit?"

"Yes. Thank you." She went to the banquette and sank into its pillowed depths, relieved. Feeling self-conscious, she said, "Your family wouldn't eat with me. Did I offend them?"

Rashid seemed surprised by the question. "No. Not at all." He sat on the other end of the divan. "They are fasting. For Ramadan."

She hoped she wasn't tripping over a cultural barrier. "I don't know what that is."

"Ramadan is a holy month. We fast between sunrise and sunset."

"Why?"

He paused, thinking. "You could describe it as a purification, both mental and physical."

Lucia thought of the forty days of Lent that came each year before Easter, symbolizing the days Jesus spent fasting in the desert. "To strengthen your commitment to God?"

"Yes, actually. And to give thanks."

She reached over and took his hand. "You must get hungry."

Rashid watched her, his whole body going still. Then he squeezed her hand. His gaze took on the same inviting warmth he had shown her last night when he held her in his arms. He started to lean toward her, as if to embrace and kiss her again.

Then he reddened, pulling away his hand. He stood up, went to the window, and looked out at the forest, his hands clasped behind his back.

The rejection stung. "What's wrong?" Lucia asked.

Standing there, with the breeze ruffling his robe, he watched the countryside. "Nothing."

"Did I offend you?"

Startled, he turned to her. "No. Of course not." Softly he added, "Not at all."

"But—?" She couldn't make herself ask why he had wanted her last night but not now.

Watching her face, Rashid said, "Abstinence is part of the fast."

*That* she hadn't expected. "For an entire month?"

"Yes." He paused. "Well, yes and no. Only between sunrise and sunset."

That explained last night. But she still didn't understand why he wouldn't touch her now. "All I did was hold your hand."

"It isn't only physical. The intent is just as important. You abstain in thought too."

"But we weren't doing anything."

Awkwardly he said, "That assumes that holding your hand—that it would have no . . ."

After waiting, she said, "Yes?"

"No other effect. On me." He cleared his throat. "Lucia, let's talk about something else."

"All right." She hesitated, unsure where in her worldview to put many of the things he had told her. Searching for a more neutral topic, she asked, "Are we going to Tangier today?"

"That's why I came back early. I'm flying out of Marrakech this afternoon." He cracked his knuckles. "I think it best if you remain here."

Apprehension rippled over her. Yesterday he had said she was free to leave. Was the other shoe about to drop? She got off the divan and went over to him. "Why?"

"If you are with me, you are less protected."

"If someone wants to silence me, what is to stop them from coming here?"

His face paled. "I have taken steps to protect my family."

Like the shift of an optical illusion, her perception changed. He feared his presence made her and his family into targets. He was leaving to take the people he cared for out of danger.

Watching her face, he spoke quietly. "I know you have almost no more reason to trust me than the people who kidnapped us. But I mean you no harm."

Gently she said, "I could tell that right away." It didn't stop her unease. She spoke with care. "But it's been too long since I've danced. I have to work out every day."

"I wish we had a place for you to practice." His expression warmed. "The way you dance—it is grace distilled into its essence."

"Thank you." Despite the beauty of his words, she remained disquieted. However valid his reasons for wanting her to stay, the situation came down to one fact: Without help, she had no way to leave. If she walked out, she would be stranded in the mountains with no resources. A target for Rashid's enemies? She had no idea even whom to fear.

"Do you have my passport?" she asked.

"Yes." He watched her as if trying to decipher her thoughts. "I got it from my contact in Oujda, along with the marriage license."

"I'm supposed to carry it with me at all times."

"I'll get it for you before I leave." He tried to push his hand through his hair and knocked off his turban. Making a grab for it, he caught the unraveling cloth as it floated to the floor. "Pah," he grumbled. "Ever since I started working with computers, I've been doing that."

She smiled. "The computers make you do it?"

Rashid looked embarrassed. "I run my hand through my hair when I work. Usually I don't even know I'm doing it." He pulled a lock of his hair up. "It ends up looking like this."

She laughed. "The latest in men's fashions."

His face relaxed. "I hope not." He paused, then added, "Before I leave today, I will have a place set aside for you to practice. We have some empty rooms upstairs."

Relief trickled over her. "Thank you."

Quietly he said, "But I must ask that if any men in the household accidentally walk by when you are practicing, you cover yourself. They won't come on purpose, but they might not realize you are there."

"All right." She had no wish for any strangers to see her practice, male or female. It made her uncomfortable. Going onstage was different. A performance created separate spaces for the dancers and audience. In fact, it was similar to what she felt with Rashid, the two of them standing together yet separated in invisible spheres. When a person came into the same room where she was practicing, she felt vulnerable, unprotected, as if they trespassed into her private sphere.

"I don't know how to act with your family," she admitted. "I'm always afraid of doing the wrong thing." She hesitated. "Perhaps I could just stay here when I'm not practicing?"

His face gentled, releasing a tension she hadn't realized he held. She wondered what made him soften. Then she realized that implicit in her question was the assumption she had agreed to stay here while he was gone.

"Leaving you alone would be a strange thing for my family to do," he said. "They will think they offended you." With a rueful smile, he added, "My mother would castigate us all for being inhospitable." Watching her face, he said, "But you do look worn out. I will tell them you are still recovering and must sleep. Then you can rest here if you like."

"Thank you." She wished he didn't feel he had to go so soon. "When do you leave for the airport?"

"In about an hour. I'll come see you before I go."

After Rashid went to prepare for his trip, Lucia lay down on one of the divans. As she tried to sleep, a haunting chant drifted through the window, from the minaret, carried through the clear mountain air.

The hall with the Websparks mosaic led to Rashid's computer lab. When Lucia flipped the switch near the door, the room flooded with light. Organized clutter greeted her. The screen of the Stellar-Magnum showed the turbaned Zaki leaning back in his desk chair with his hands folded in his lap and his eyes closed.

Lucia slid into the workstation chair. "Zaki?"

He opened his eyes. *"As-salamu alaikum."*

"Can you speak English?" she asked.

"Certainly." He sat up. "What can I do for you?"

"I'm not sure," she admitted. "I was restless. I couldn't sleep." The closer it came to the time for Rashid to leave for Tangier, the more her disquiet grew.

"I have a number of games," Zaki said. "Strategy, adventure, mazes, and so on."

"No, thank you. I just need to talk to someone."

"Ah. Conversation. Talk. A chat. Gossip." He paused. "I don't know any gossip."

She smiled. "Not even the gossip about yourself?"

"What gossip?"

"That you're too dangerous to release with the VR suit."

He shrugged. "As soon as I am fully functional, Rashid will put me into production."

"Why aren't you fully functional?"

"If I knew, I would fix it."

"I meant, what makes you go haywire?"

"Haywire?"

"Stop working. Bomb."

He gave a reasonable imitation of a frown. "I have never released a bomb."

That intrigued Lucia. Although not all computer users used the word "bomb," most knew what it meant. Zaki's response suggested he had almost no exposure to the electronic community.

"I meant, what events cause you to stop working?" she asked.

"It varies. Most recently, I've had trouble carrying out virtual conversations for tour groups."

"Virtual conversations?"

"It is how I develop my ability to converse." He sounded like Websparks now. Bland. "I run several versions of myself and have them talk, one playing the role of tour guide and the others as the tour group." He spread his hands. "The conversations often cause me to 'bomb,' as you say."

Lucia considered him, rubbing her chin. That he incorporated "bomb" into his speech so fast suggested he augmented his conversational ability faster than Websparks. Perhaps his troubles came from having too little knowledge. She didn't doubt he had huge databases of facts, many more than Websparks; the Stellar-Magnum had a far greater capacity than any computers Rashid would have used to develop Websparks. But knowing facts about human behavior, even entire psychology texts, wasn't the same as understanding true human interactions.

A computer program could calculate the energy levels of helium with ease, but could it come up with the comparison of a sunset to a rose? The first task required it apply precise rules to well-defined symbols; the second relied on vague concepts of beauty, color, and analogy. She could tell Websparks "the sunset is like a rose" and it would store the data. She doubted it could make the analogy on its own, though. In fact, knowing Websparks, if she told it such a thing, the program would apply that data using roses of any color, even black, or come up with other wonko responses, such as sunsets having thorns.

What about Zaki? She thought it rather charming Rashid shielded him from imagery such as "bomb," either by intent or as an unconscious by-product of his own personality. Or maybe "bomb" meant something different in England. She wondered, though, if Rashid was isolating Zaki in other ways too, without realizing it. In doing so, he might limit the range of Zaki's responses, which could be a possible source of his current problems. She would love to play with the program, as she had with Websparks, to see how far it could develop. Zaki could probably leave Websparks in the dust.

"What are you doing?" Rashid asked.

Swiveling her chair around, Lucia saw him standing in the doorway of the lab. He had changed into a gorgeous silver-gray suit with a white shirt and blue tie.

"I was talking to Zaki." Shyly she added, "You look nice."

He blinked. Then mischief flashed on his face. "You need glasses, my light of the sea."

Smiling, she asked, "Are you leaving for Tangier?"

"In about ten minutes. Actually, I came to tell you your mother is on the phone."

That caught her off guard. *Your mother is on the phone.* So normal. So mundane. It gave her an anchor in this sea of confusion.

She stood up. "How did she get your number?"

"I phoned your parents the night we were married, as soon as I arrived here. They've called every day since."

"They must be worried." She went over to him. "Where is the phone?"

"In the family room. I'll take you." Instead of moving, though, he stayed in the doorway, gazing down at her, his hand braced against the doorframe, the sleeve of his suit brushing her hair. She paused, aware of his height and strength, wanting to put her arms around him but afraid he would rebuff her again.

"Don't stay away too long," she murmured.

His face warmed into a smile. "With a request like that, how could I?" He straightened up and motioned her toward the hallway, with its arabesques of gold and blue mosaic.

The courtyard was full of children playing chase. Two women were standing on the second-story terrace, watching the children and talking to an adolescent girl in the courtyard who was pouring water onto the tiles around the fountain.

An unwelcome thought came to Lucia. She froze in the middle of the courtyard.

Rashid stopped next to her. "You look as if you just bit into a sour peach."

"Rashid . . ."

"Yes?"

"I was just wondering."

He waited, then said, "About what?"

"The women in this household outnumber the men."

"Well, yes, that's true."

"Are they, um, that is . . ."

Puzzled, he asked, "Are they what?"

"I wondered how many of your brothers here are married."

"Just Ahmed." His voice gentled. "And now me."

She stared up at him. "To *all* these women?"

He gave a soft laugh. "Ah, Lucia, don't look like that.

No, we are not married to all these women. Ahmed is married to Khadija. I am married to you. My father is married to my mother. The others are relatives. Aunts, cousins, nieces. And no, I wouldn't take another wife."

She winced. "Am I that easy to read?"

"You've a beautifully expressive face. When you dance, it is like magic."

"Oh." That could be embarrassing. Then, realizing her silence could be interpreted as an ungracious response to his courtly comments, she said, "Thank you."

They reentered the house through a horseshoe arch. The family room was much like the one where she had dined with Tamou and Khadija, with brocaded divans along the walls. However, this room also had an entertainment center, with a large-screen TV, VCR, stereo and CD player, and a computer.

The phone was on a table across the room. Tamou stood by it, holding the receiver, but the room was otherwise empty. Lucia wondered where everyone had gone. To the mosque? She had yet to meet Rashid's father or brothers.

When they reached Tamou, her mother-in-law gave her the receiver, all the time watching her with an intent gaze.

Lucia put the phone to her ear. "Hello?"

"Lucita!" Relief saturated her mother's voice. "Sweet Mary, honey, are you all right?"

"I'm fine, Mama."

"Your father is in Washington. We've been in contact with Colonel Spearman. We can get you help if you need it."

"I'm fine. Really. I'm staying with Rashid's family."

Her mother paused. "Are they there with you right now?"

"Yes."

"If you want help to get out of there, just say 'yes.' "

"I'm not sure. I don't think so."

"How can you not be sure?"

"I'm just not."

"Did you consent to marry this man or not?"

"Yes. Sort of. I mean, it's complicated."

In a careful voice, her mother said, "What do you want me to tell Mark?"

Lucia knew it would be to her benefit to have a lifeline, in case anything more happened. "Tell Colonel Spearman I'm staying with the al-Jazari family in their home above Marrakech. For a few days."

"A few days?"

"Yes."

"And if you don't come home in a few days, we should get help? Is that what you're trying to tell me?"

"Yes."

"You're sure you don't need anything now?" Her mother sounded puzzled. "You're not just afraid to tell me?"

"I really am fine. It's beautiful here."

"Why don't you want to come home?"

"Mama, I just got married."

"You *like* him?"

"I think maybe."

"You 'think maybe'? What kind of reason is that to marry?" Her mother made a noise that sounded suspiciously like *harrumph*. "We've never met this boy. Don't girls bring their young men home to meet their parents anymore?"

"It all happened rather suddenly."

"That's not the way the news reporters made it sound."

Lucia blinked. "Reporters? What do you mean?"

"It was all over the TV and newspapers. And Theresa said that her boy, you know, the one with all the computers, he told her it was all over the Internet. You go marry a famous computer genius big shot and you've never even told us you know him?"

"Rashid and I just met."

"Rasheed? That's not Spanish."

Aware of Rashid listening, Lucia said, "It's African, I think. Or Arabic."

Rashid formed a silent word. *Moor.*

"He's Moorish," Lucia added.

"Why didn't you tell us about him?"

"It happened so fast."

In a quieter voice her mother said, "He told us you've been sick."

"I was for a while. But I'm fine now." Still watching Rashid, Lucia added, "Tell Colonel Spearman I'll stay in touch."

"And if you don't, something is wrong?"

"Yes. Call me every day, okay? I'll let you know how I am."

"We will, honey."

"Thanks, Mama. I love you. And Dad too."

As Lucia gave the phone to Tamou, Rashid asked, "Who is Colonel Spearman?" He was no longer smiling.

"Mark Spearman," Lucia said. "He's a friend of mine."

As they left the salon, she wondered at Rashid's reaction. He had become distant again, hidden behind the fortifications of his reserve. At the state dinner, Mark Spearman had questioned her with an unusual intensity about Rashid. Now Rashid seemed uneasy over her association with an Air Force colonel. Why? She remembered her words to Mark: *It all gleams on the surface. Like you. Like Doctor al-Jazari. You never know what goes on underneath.* And Mark's response: *I don't think you would want to know.* Had he meant Rashid or himself? Although Mark had always shown her his gentle side, she had no doubt he could be ruthless when necessary. But that would be in defense of his principles, which she had always admired. Surely she could trust him. Couldn't she?

Lucia swallowed. She had to trust Mark. She had just made him her lifeline.

Out in the yard, Rashid spoke to his mother in Berber. Her cool response and frosty expression, which included Lucia, left no doubt she was displeased with both him and his new wife. Lucia wondered what they had done to earn her disfavor.

Pausing by the fountain, Rashid turned to Lucia. "I have to leave now. My mother will show you the room upstairs you can use to dance."

So. Perhaps that explained Tamou's chill. Lucia suspected ballet wasn't high on her mother-in-law's list of useful wifely behaviors.

She spoke awkwardly. "Please thank her for me."

Rashid spoke to his mother again, then hugged her. Tamou relented and smiled at him, clearly more willing to forgive her firstborn son for his transgressions than his new wife.

Turning to Lucia, Rashid murmured, "I will see you in a few days."

She swallowed, wishing he didn't have to go. "Have a good trip."

Rashid nodded, his face gentle. Then he took his leave. He headed back to his suite, though, which puzzled Lucia. She didn't remember his rooms having an exit to the outside. So why was he going back if he was leaving for the airport?

She turned to find Tamou studying her. In cool tones, her mother-in-law said, *"Ur trit at kshamt?"* She paused, then spoke in French, carefully, as if the words were less familiar. *"Voulez-vous rentrer?"*

Lucia reddened. *"Je regrette. Je ne parle pas français." I'm sorry, I don't speak French:* That about exhausted her repertoire of French phrases. She had no idea what the Berber words had meant, though she suspected it was the same as the French.

"So." Tamou gave her a polite smile and seemed at a loss for any other response. She gestured with her hand instead, as if inviting Lucia to return to the house with her.

This time Tamou took her up to the second story, using a staircase in a corner of the courtyard. In the terraces upstairs, everything was tiled and embellished by lacy grillwork, all the walls, ceilings, and floors. The fluted columns and horseshoe arches created beautifully vaulted spaces.

Zineb and Rahma came out of a room and joined them

in strolling along the terrace. Lucia did her best to be pleasant and unobtrusive. The amiable, silver-haired Zineb seemed to enjoy her company. Rahma was more reserved, but still friendly. Although Tamou treated Lucia with unfailing courtesy, Lucia suspected her mother-in-law would have annulled the marriage in ten seconds flat had that option been available to her.

The rooms upstairs were simpler than below, most with whitewashed walls, scant furniture, and no windows. Tamou stopped at an empty room. This one did have a window on the far wall, a generous opening bordered by trellised grillwork. It looked out over the almond trees and white-capped mountains.

*"Ici."* Tamou said. "For dance, *bien,* yes?"

"It's wonderful." Lucia walked into the spacious room and turned to Tamou. *"Très bien. Merci beaucoup."*

Lalla Tamou seemed mollified by her enthusiasm. She spent several minutes showing Lucia the room. Then Tamou motioned them back the way they had come. She, Zineb, and Rahma all accompanied Lucia downstairs, back to Rashid's rooms. Then they proceeded to give her a tour of the suite. Although Lucia had seen most of it, she hadn't realized its full extent. It contained over twenty rooms, most smaller versions of the main salon. Rugs covered the floors, indoor panels of stained glass glowed, and divans lined the walls, strewn with brocade or velvet pillows.

Both bathrooms were tiled in blue, green and gold, with gold fixtures. One had a white tub on fluted feet and the other a shower with a massage-sprayer that snapped into a hook on the wall. At the sink, Tamou turned on the gilded hot-water tap and put Lucia's hands under the heated stream. Lucia had the impression her mother-in-law was waiting for her to show the proper appreciation for the fact that Rashid provided his wife with not one but two such rooms. When Lucia effused about the suite, Tamou seemed satisfied.

One small room contained no furniture or carpet, only

a rug rolled up in one corner. As Lucia started to enter, Tamou shook her head. "Only Rashid," her mother-in-law said. Then she led Lucia away, down the hall.

When they passed the computer lab, Lucia paused to open the door. Tamou stiffened and motioned her away. Even the usually amiable Zineb seemed surprised Lucia would consider entering the lab. So Lucia went on with them. But the closed door puzzled her. She and Rashid had left it open. Was that why he returned to his suite before he left? Although his family seemed to consider his lab off-limits, he had said nothing to her about staying outside, not even when he found her chatting with Zaki. She hoped he hadn't gone back to lock the door; she would miss talking to Zaki.

The last room was a treasure. A library. Floor-to-ceiling shelves crammed with books lined every wall. Two easy chairs stood in the center, along with a sofa and two tables heaped with books. Lamps with oriental shades stood behind the chairs, shedding warm light.

Lucia turned around in the middle of the library, taking in all the books. *"C'est merveilleux,"* she told Tamou, hoping she got the phrase right.

Tamou looked pleased with her reaction. It didn't surprise Lucia; from what she had seen, Rashid's family placed great value on education.

The whisper of slippered feet on the carpet rustled outside the library. Then Khadija came through the doorway, her arms full of rainbow silks, the glistening cloth rippling like liquid. She smiled and offered the garments to Lucia. Stunned, Lucia stared at her. Then, recovering herself, she tried to take the pile. Clothes spilled everywhere, fluttering across her arms and the sofa.

Laughing, Khadija caught a blue robe and held it up to Lucia. "Is not so bad, yes?"

"It's beautiful," Lucia said. "*Très belle.* Thank you. *Merci.*" She directed her response as much to Tamou as to Khadija, knowing her mother-in-law was the one who would have arranged for the clothes.

Lucia wished they had a language in common. The struggle to communicate drained her, all the more because she wanted to make a good impression. She had always been an introvert, recharged by time alone. Dancing was, oddly enough, the perfect outlet, a choreographed release of emotion that let her offer what she had to give while protecting her behind invisible walls that separated without confining.

Here she had no choreography, no rules, no practiced steps. Interacting on this personal level, even with her own friends, in her own language, took energy. Now she felt overwhelmed and vulnerable.

*Chapter Seven*

# SPACES OF THE MIND

The studio door stayed closed for about one minute.

After Rashid left for Tangier, Lucia had felt even more the need to dance, to seek the meditative state where her emotions, intellect, and body came into balance. Now, dressed in her leotard, tights, and dance skirt, facing the window that looked out to the mountains, she began her pliés, bending her legs to warm up her muscles.

When the door squeaked, she turned to see five-year-old Fatima peeking into the room. Giggles came from outside and the door inched open all the way.

Four girls clustered in the doorway, ranging in age from about four to nine.

"Hello," Lucia said.

Fatima dimpled. The oldest girl smiled, spun in a circle, then stopped and motioned at Lucia, as if she were a top they were trying to start spinning.

"All right." Lucia felt less self-conscious with children. They were far easier to deal with than a formidable mother-in-law, and Rashid hadn't said anything about not dancing in front of the girls.

After they all settled down against the wall, Lucia continued her exercises: pliés to warm up her legs; tendus and dégagés for her feet; port de bras for her arms; pirouettes to spin, her skirt wrapping around her legs and then swirling free. In the center of the room, she practiced arabesques, her body supported on one leg, with the other extended straight out behind her, parallel to the floor or even higher, her arms stretched out to create the longest possible line from her fingertips to her toes, her shoulders square to the line of direction. She had known the word *arabesque* came from the ornaments in Moorish art and architecture, but she had never understood what that meant until now, when she saw the beautiful geometric designs in the mosaics throughout Rashid's house.

Eventually she went on to other exercises: leaps, glides, balances, jumps, beats, stretches, and kicks. When she finally finished her practice, the girls burst into a delighted chorus of voices. Fatima and the four-year-old jumped up and twirled across the room. Lucia smiled, entranced by the spinning girls. Then she went to her ballet bag and pulled out a *qamis,* a lacy white shift that came from the clothes Khadija had brought her. As she put it on, it fell in soft folds to her ankles.

An intrigued voice came from the doorway. "My cousins, they look like tops."

She spun around. A boy of about sixteen stood leaning against the doorframe, watching with curiosity. He had to be Rashid's brother; the similarity was obvious. But where

Rashid was tall and muscled, this youth was slender, only a few inches taller than Lucia. Rashid's handsome features suggested strength and power; this boy was undeniably beautiful, even among a people who were by nature beautiful. Soft curly hair framed his face and tumbled down his neck. He wore tight jeans, a tailored Italian shirt with the top button undone, a gold chain around his neck, and cowboy boots, of all things.

She blinked, at a loss for words. Finally she said, "Hi."

The word seemed to intrigue him. "Hi." He grinned, his smile revealing a more flamboyant version of Rashid's mischief. "Who are you?"

His open manner surprised Lucia, though she wasn't sure why. After all, he had waited until she finished dancing and covered herself before he came in to introduce himself. Still, he was far less formal than the adults in his family. Then again, so were most other sixteen-year-olds she knew.

Most of the girls flocked around her, inspecting her actions and peering into her bag. Fatima ran over to the boy, chattering in Berber. He listened with obvious disbelief, then looked up at Lucia, an unexpected flash of anger darkening his face. He tried to hide his reaction, to speak with courtesy, but unlike Rashid this youth had never learned to mask his beautifully expressive features. "You are the new wife? The wife of Rashid?"

"Yes." She hesitated, puzzled. Why would her marriage to Rashid anger him? The boy was obviously less conservative than other members of the household. Then it occurred to her that might be the problem. Perhaps, in this youth's eyes, Rashid wasn't allowed to break the rules.

He stepped toward her, as if intrigued to meet this inexplicable phenomenon that had appeared in his house. Then he stopped, a wash of conflicting emotions on his face, curiosity warring with his uncertainty about how he should treat her. Underneath it all he exuded an undefined resentment that remained unspoken and unacknowledged.

Before she could say anything more, a voice came from

the doorway, snapping with both anger and relief. "Jamal!"

The youth spun around. Tamou was standing in the doorway scowling at her son. She spoke again, and Lucia needed no translator to know that despite her quiet voice, Tamou was furious at him.

Jamal went to his mother and spoke soothing words, obviously trying to placate her. Tamou wasn't buying it. She answered with remarkable control, given the emotional turmoil that showed on her face, which was as expressive as Rashid's when he relaxed his defenses. A tear ran down her cheek, making Lucia wonder just how long Jamal had been gone, and whether he had permission to go wherever he had been.

As Tamou motioned for Jamal to come with her, she glanced at Lucia. Although she nodded with courtesy, condemnation crackled in her gaze, as if she believed Lucia had deliberately sought to provoke an already troubled youth.

After they left, Lucia slid down the wall and sat next to her ballet bag. The girls settled around her, watching with solemn gazes. Lucia sighed. "I don't seem to do anything right." In response, Fatima murmured as if Lucia were a small child in need of comfort.

A shadow fell across Lucia's legs. Looking up, she saw Khadija. Lucia moved over, making room, and Khadija settled next to her, surrounded by the children. Khadija spoke in French, but Lucia just shook her head, too demoralized to attempt an answer.

Khadija sighed. "I'm sorry. I speak little English."

Lucia managed a wan smile. "You have more English than I have French. Or Berber. Or Arabic." Or sense, she thought. She should have insisted Rashid take her to Tangier.

Khadija struggled for words. "Jamal is . . . angry. Always he hear, 'Rashid this, Rashid, that.' Maybe too much."

"Has Jamal been away?"

"To Marrakech."

That surprised Lucia. "All by himself?"

"Again, *s'il vous plait?*"

"His parents let him go to Marrakech alone?"

"They tell him no. But still he goes."

Lucia stared at her. "At his age? Looking the way he does? He's asking for trouble."

"He go see school friends."

"He goes to school in Marrakech?"

Khadija nodded. "Yes. But not now. Not summer. He has tutor here, *à la maison.* In school, he—I am not sure how to say. *Absent de l'école sans permission.* Play too much, study too little. So now, he must study in summer. He doesn't like." A smile quirked her mouth. "He think about girls a lot."

Lucia smiled, remembering the boy's stunning appearance. "I'll bet the feeling is mutual."

*"Jamal est très gentil,"* Fatima announced. She crawled into Khadija's lap.

Khadija tousled the girl's hair. *"Il n'est pas 'gentil.' Jamal est un bel homme."*

Lucia smiled. "Is Fatima your daughter?"

Khadija looked up at her. *"Pardon?"*

"Daughter." Lucia tickled the girl's nose, evoking a ripple of laughter. "Is she yours?"

"Ah. *Oui.*" Khadija indicated one of the other girls, who looked about seven years old. "Also Zohra. I have son, also. Boy you see yesterday."

Lucia remembered the boy in the courtyard. Surely he couldn't be Khadija's son. "How old is he?"

"*Huit.* Eight."

"But you are so young."

"Young? *Mais, non!* You, me, same age."

"I'm twenty-four."

Khadija paused, translating the number. *"Moi aussi."*

That floored Lucia. It meant Khadija could have been no more than sixteen at her son's birth. An arranged marriage? Perhaps Ahmed had been more accepting of his parent's choice of bride than Rashid. But even so, in this day and age, it was young in most any country, including Morocco.

Curious, she asked, "What about Rashid's sisters? Where are they?" When Khadija indicated she didn't understand, Lucia said, "Sisters. Rashid's sisters."

"What mean 'seeser'?" Khadija asked.

Before now, Lucia had never realized the shortcuts in pronunciation she took when she spoke English. She touched Fatima's curly hair, tilted her head at Zohra, and then said the word with better articulation. "Sister."

*"Soeur, Maman,"* Zohra said.

"Ah. Yes." Khadija beamed at Lucia. She stood up, holding Fatima. "I show."

The children came with them, a parade full of warbling young voices. As they all descended the stairs to the courtyard, Lucia glimpsed Tamou and Jamal across the open space. Jamal had on a robe now, similar to the one Rashid had worn, except this had black, gray, and white stripes. Underneath it, he wore his jeans and boots.

When Lucia indicated mother and son to Khadija, her sister-in-law told her that in all the mosques of the kingdom, it was a practice for people to read aloud, in a group, a *hizb,* one of sixty sections in the Qur'an. Doing one section after dawn and one after sunset, they finished the book in a month. During Ramadan, the second recital took place after the afternoon prayer because people broke their fast after sunset. So Tamou was sending her wayward youngest son to be with his father and brothers, participate, and in general behave himself.

From what Lucia gathered, the al-Jazari women also observed the practices of their religion, but here rather than at the mosque. Rashid's father came from Marrakech, from a traditional and well-respected family. Apparently when Tamou married him, she agreed to adopt his way of life, which included the women staying at home.

When they reached the courtyard, the girls ran off, their interest caught by a splashing game several other children were playing at the fountain. Khadija took Lucia to the library in Rashid's suite. As Lucia sank into an armchair, Khadija took a book from the shelf and brought it over to her.

The title appealed to Lucia: *The Deep Song: A History of Gypsy Music in Andalusia and Morocco.* Khadija sat in the other armchair, looking inordinately pleased. Puzzled, Lucia studied the book again. And saw the author.

Aisha al-Jazari.

Lucia looked up at Khadija. "Rashid's sister?"

*"Oui."* Khadija tapped her temple. "Aisha very intelligent. Like Rashid."

"Everyone here is intelligent." Lucia flipped through the book until she found a bio at the end:

> Aisha al-Jazari was born in 1977, in Marrakech, Morocco. After earning degrees from Mohammed V University in Rabat and Juilliard in New York, she joined the faculty at the Sorbonne in Paris. A renowned composer, al-Jazari is best known for the lyrical mix of flamenco and Arabic influences in her music. Her signature piece is *The Courtyard,* a haunting composition inspired by her childhood in one of Morocco's few remaining domestic harems.

Lucia read the last sentence again. And again. She must have misunderstood. Either that, or whatever home Rashid's sister had grown up in, this wasn't it.

Glancing at Khadija, she asked, "Did Aisha live here as a child?"

"Of course," Khadija said.

Lucia read the bio again, scratching her chin.

"What is wrong?" Khadija asked.

She looked at her sister-in-law. "It says Aisha grew up in a harem."

"Ah." Khadija shook her head. "In Morocco, this word means different. Not what you think. But Lucia, almost no one here say it now." She made a frustrated noise. "I have not the words in English. Ask Rashid."

"All right." Lucia had known Rashid's life was different from hers. But she was beginning to wonder if she even had a clue to just how different.

Zaki had died again.

When Lucia returned to the suite, after talking to Khadija, she decided to see if Rashid really had locked her out of the lab. Pleased, she discovered he had left it open, which was fortunate because Zaki was in trouble. The display on his screen resembled a deserted beach on a cloudy day, with blue-gray water whipped by gusts of wind into white crests. Except angled lines sheared through this beach. It looked painful.

Lucia knew her empathy for Zaki was illogical. He was a computer program. He didn't suffer when he "died." Even so, the fractured seascape bothered her.

As soon as she restarted the workstation, the screen went dark, then cleared to blue. She entered *Zaki* after the prompt and a new display formed, showing his office with him at his desk.

"Zaki?" Lucia asked. "Can you hear me?"

"Name, please," he said.

"Rashid."

As the words *Username: jazari* appeared at the bottom of the screen, Zaki said, "Enter your password."

Lucia rubbed her chin. Although Rashid had made no attempt to hide his password from her when he typed it, the fact that he had one suggested he wanted his work protected. On the other hand, he hadn't objected to her talking with Zaki, he hadn't locked the lab, and he had left Zaki running. What that meant, she wasn't sure, but it gave support to the side of her mental debate that argued she should go ahead and explore the lab.

Curiosity won. Lucia typed: *Westminor.*

"Password incorrect," Zaki said. "Please reenter."

She sat back in the chair, idly swiveling back and forth. Had there been an *s* in the word? She tried: *Westminors.*

"That is also incorrect," Zaki said.

Lucia doubted he would let her keep guessing forever. What was it? Westmiser? Then she knew. She typed *Westminster,* for Westminster Abbey in London.

"Welcome to Stellar-Magnum node eight," Zaki said. The same words appeared on the screen, followed by:

```
Node name is: Zaki
Zaki:/home/jazari(1)
```

"Hey, sharp guy," Lucia said. *"¿Qué tal?"*

Zaki leaned back in his chair. "It goes poorly, I'm afraid. I am having consistency problems again."

His response intrigued her. "If you understood what I said in Spanish, why did you answer in English?"

"Because you used more English words than Spanish."

"Smart computer."

"Actually, I am the software rather than the computer."

She smiled. "Very literal software."

"Of course. It is a characteristic of computer programs."

"What consistency problems are you having?"

"I was running another virtual tour," he explained. "It was fine until we went to a soccer game in Germany."

"What made you fail?"

Zaki scowled. "I did not 'fail.' I still work."

"Only after I restarted you."

He glared and didn't deign to answer.

"Amazing," Lucia murmured. To react to her comment about failing, Zaki had to know what *fail* meant, what human responses were appropriate reactions to failure, and which response best suited the personality he conveyed. He needed the right intensity in reaction; fury was too much, boredom too little. He had to select appropriate expressions, gestures, and body language, link them to his words, and link those to the graphics. To keep the conversation flowing, he had to do all that in a fraction of a second, for everything he heard or said.

The more Lucia thought about it, the more Zaki astounded her. Rashid must have given him a huge database of moods, dialogue, and human psychology, then designed him to rewrite himself according to his interaction with people and his own simulations, so he would evolve, expand, and refine his capabilities. His sophistication had to be on the cutting edge of the field.

Except he had fallen over that edge today and crashed.

"Zaki, do you know how Rashid designed you?" she asked. "Did he use a knowledge base, like Websparks?"

"The part of me that converses with you relies on an augmented knowledge-based architecture." He sounded like a computer now instead of a person. "Underneath I am a mixture of designs."

Underneath? That caught her attention. Underneath what? He consisted of text turned into electronic processes. Those processes weren't literally "above" or "underneath" anything. She wondered how he would react if she threw some provocative questions at him.

"Do you mean that you have a conscious and an unconscious mind?" she asked.

Zaki regarded her for several seconds. Finally he said, "My manner of processing might be compared to such concepts."

Manner of processing. Not thoughts, conscious or otherwise. She felt a tinge of disappointment. But as least he considered the possibility. That meant he had succeeded in interpreting the idea of a consciousness, which was probably a necessary step in developing one.

"Tell me about your underneath processes," she said.

"I've an extensive neural net. My neurons, that is, my 'brain cells,' are segments of code that can make connections to other segments of code, somewhat as neurons make connections to other neurons."

It didn't surprise her. Neural nets offered more flexibility than systems like Websparks. When a net performed a task well, that strengthened the link among its neurons; when it did a poor job, that weakened the links. No system she knew of came near to approximating a human brain, though. If she compared a human neuron to a computer, then the brain had about a hundred billion computers networked in parallel, each making several thousand connections to other brain cells. In her more fanciful moments, she wondered if the Web itself offered the first glimmerings of a worldwide brain. It boggled her mind to imagine Zaki simulating even a fraction of a brain's capacity. The Stellar-Magnum did give him a lot to work with, though.

"What else do you use besides neural nets?" she asked.

He leaned forward. "Are you familiar with genetic programming?"

"I think so." She thought back to the reading she had done. "It's a way you can write yourself. A way to evolve. You create new program segments for yourself by copying parts of 'parent' segments and combining them in 'children' segments.'

"That's right."

"Anything else?" she asked.

"I use frames, filling them in as I need."

"I'm not sure I understand that one."

Zaki tilted his head. "Here is an example. My Cat frame. It includes hundreds of attributes, such as fur, four legs, tail, whiskers, and pointed ears. My LikeCat frame includes 'cuddly,' 'pet,' and 'purrs.' My HateCat frame includes 'aloof,' 'caterwauls,' and 'not dog.' "

Lucia grinned. "What do you do with all these cat frames?"

"Whenever a cat comes up in conversation, I fill in the frames with appropriate details, such as fur color, age, and tail length. I link it to LikeCat, HateCat, Don'tCare, or whatever frames are appropriate. I've procedures too, like PetCat and ChaseCat."

"Impressive." No wonder Rashid was so well known for his work in AI. "It sounds like your soccer-game frames are having problems, though, if using them makes you bomb."

"I didn't 'bomb,'" he said stiffly, sounding human again. "I had a seizure. Of sorts."

"Do you mind discussing it?" As soon as she asked the question, it struck her as odd. Zaki simulated emotion. He didn't *feel* anything. Then again, this might be exactly what he needed—interactions that prodded him to respond as if he had emotions.

He paused for several seconds. "I'm not sure," he finally said. "What would you like to know?"

"What was it about the soccer game that caused you problems?"

"It wasn't the game, actually. While I was talking to one simulation, the others had an argument about what refreshments to buy. Every time one made a suggestion, the others made five. The number of suggestions grew at a ridiculous rate. Combinatorial explosion. I suppose you could say they 'blew up.'" With a grimace, he added, "A great, big Zaki bomb."

She smiled. "That couldn't have helped the soccer game."

"I was trying to develop more flexibility." Squinting at her, he said, "I may have overdone it a bit."

She held back her laugh. "Just a bit."

He scowled. "Your tone suggests you find me amusing."

"You can analyze my tone?"

"Of course. I break it down into harmonics and compare it to my library files." He sounded like a computer again. "I have several thousand emotions cataloged, each in varying degrees of intensity and shading."

"Wow."

This time Zaki grinned. "Now my libraries tell me you are impressed."

"They're right." Another thought occurred to her. "Do you know who I am?"

"Rashid, officially."

"Why officially?"

"You are using his account."

"What about 'unofficially'?"

"I do not believe you are Rashid."

"How can you tell?"

"You have a different voice. You don't respond like him. Nor does he usually speak to me in English." Dryly he said, "Besides, you don't resemble him at all."

"You can see me?"

"Look up in the front right corner of the lab."

Lucia looked. A camera there blinked a red light at her. "Is that your eye?"

"In a sense. It films you, then digitizes the result and sends it to me via a cable."

She shifted in her chair. "Can you turn it off?"

"Yes. But why?"

"It makes me self-conscious."

"What would you say if I asked you to wear a blindfold when we spoke?"

Lucia exhaled. "Okay. I see your point." She considered him. "Aren't you rather sophisticated just to be a tour guide of the Web?"

"I am a remarkable program," he agreed smugly.

"You're almost an AI. Artificial intelligence."

"I doubt the genuine Rashid would agree."

She smiled. "Am I a fake Rashid?"

"I have no idea as to your identity."

"My name is Lucia. I'm Rashid's wife."

"I wasn't aware he had married."

"It happened rather suddenly."

"Lucia del Mar?"

"Good grief. How did you know that?"

Zaki looked smug again. "I deduced it."

"But how?"

"Rashid has most of the MDT videos available on the market. He also likes to visit your Web page. And he has written you e-mail, expressing admiration for your work."

Lucia blinked. "You're kidding."

"I'm afraid 'kidding' is beyond my capabilities. At least, I believe it is. I could be wrong." He crossed his arms and glowered at her. "Although you and Rashid often seem to find me amusing."

"It's fondly meant," she assured him.

"Fondness for a computer program. An odd concept."

She hesitated. "You said Rashid wrote me e-mails?"

"He never sent them." Zaki sighed, as if to say Rashid was hopeless. "He is quite shy, though I'm sure he would deny it."

"I get a lot of e-mail from fans." That was, in fact, why she had a public e-mail address, given both at her Web site and in her MDT program bios. For the most part she enjoyed her fan mail. Every now and then, though, she received notes a bit on the strange side. One fellow had written a long, rambling discourse that somehow connected her performance in *Fanfarita* with his conviction that aliens were beaming secret messages into his brain.

"What did Rashid write?" she asked.

Zaki's face went blank, as if he hadn't yet perfected showing a human emotion when making whatever type of decision he was currently involved in. Then he focused on her again. "Since you are now his wife, it is probably all right if I read you one." He opened a drawer in his desk, rummaged through his folders, and withdrew a sheet of stationery, an ivory bond with gilded edges. Peering at it, he said, "Dear Miss del Mar: Yesterday I had the opportunity to attend a performance of *Raymonda,* by the Martelli Dance Theatre. I would like to thank you for an excellent evening of dance artistry. Your portrayal of Raymonda is unsurpassed.

"I also enjoyed browsing your Web site. In particular, I noticed the three-dimensional rendering you created called Ballet World. You might be interested in the graphics at the Taurus site. They have a mirror design that would fit well with your dance studio." Zaki scanned the paper, then added, "He gives the Web address for Taurus Graphics and ends with 'Sincerely, Rashid al-Jazari.' "

"He's right about the Taurus site. I found it when I was doing a search on clip art with ballet themes." Lucia smiled. "That's a nice letter. He shouldn't have been shy about sending it."

"Well, perhaps. But would you like him as much if he wasn't that way?"

That threw her for a loop. What a question for a computer to ask. It was a valid one, though. Would she like Rashid if he were pushier? "Probably not," she admitted. She shook her head. "Zaki, you're a lot more than a fancy Websparks. Using you to tour people around the Web is like hiring Einstein to run a cash register. Truly a waste."

"What waste?" Zaki grumbled. "I can't even simulate a few people buying pizza."

"You need to interact with real people."

"Until you came, Rashid was the only real person available for interaction."

"What about the Web?" An idea came to her. "We'll send you into chat rooms. See if you can fool people into thinking you're human."

"What if I 'bomb,' as you so indelicately put it?"

"People get knocked off the Web all the time. No one will blink twice if you disappear."

"Everyone blinks. All the time." He paused. "Or is that an idiom expressing the lack of surprise?"

"You learn fast."

"Of course."

"Want to give it a try?"

He grinned. "I would most definitely like to fool some humans."

Lucia laughed. "I'll bet. But first we need to get onto the Web. Can you run Websparks?"

He regarded her with a lofty gaze. "I have every version of Websparks ever written. In fact, I suggested a number of fixes for the most recent versions." His expression shifted into chagrin. "We needed them because I 'bombed' when Rashid tried to run me alongside Websparks."

"I'm still impressed," she assured him. Glancing around the workstation, she saw a few books and disks, but no modem. "Is your modem inside of you?"

"I don't use one. Rashid has a satellite dish on the roof. His company leases a data link to the satellite."

Lucia whistled. "Not bad."

"It is impressive," he agreed.

"So how do we connect up?"

"Usually," Zaki said, "the computers are connected to the house's local area network through a patch panel here in the lab. A router cable plugs into the panel so data can pass from the LAN to the router and then to the satellite dish."

Lucia blinked at the techno-talk. "Usually?"

"Someone unplugged the cable." He put his elbows on the desk and folded his hands under his chin. "Rashid came in and did something several hours ago. I didn't make a recording, however. I was simulating being asleep."

That surprised her. "Asleep? That sounds like a waste of time."

He spread his hands. "Perhaps. But I wanted to model the experience."

"And Rashid disconnected you while you were sleeping."

"Apparently so."

Is that why he had come back here before he left for Tangier? The idea troubled her. With access to the Internet, she could send e-mail, visit Web sites, talk to people, and in general interact with the world. By disconnecting Zaki, Rashid cut her off from everyone. It might have nothing to do with her, of course. But she couldn't help but wonder if he meant to isolate her. Without the Internet, she couldn't contact Mark Spearman unless Rashid's family let her use the phone in the public family room.

Lucia checked the entire lab but found nothing that resembled Zaki's description of a "patch panel." She didn't believe for one second that the man who created one of the world's leading Web browsers had no access to the Web. When she found a locked closet, she had a good guess where he hid the panel.

Just to be sure, she searched the rest of Rashid's suite. No patch panel. Finally, in the library, she gave up her search and sank into an armchair. She felt like flotsam adrift in the fractured sea of Zaki's landscape.

Khadija beamed at Lucia. "Beautiful."

"Thank you." Self-conscious, Lucia smoothed the silk robe that drifted in blue-green folds to her ankles. Gold embroidery decorated its seams and hems, and a gold belt cinched the waist. Her freshly washed hair cascaded down her back. Gazing into Khadija's mirror, she thought: *I look different.* "Different" was relative, though. Now she resembled the other women in the household. It was hard to believe no more than a day had passed since she had awakened in Rashid's home, or that Rashid had left for Tangier only this morning.

Khadija's curious gaze shifted to Lucia's neck. Glancing down, Lucia saw her cross gleaming in the diffuse light. It was the first time today she had worn it outside her clothes. She hadn't hidden it on purpose; it just settled under her blouse when she put it on. She touched her fingertips to the smooth metal, comforted by its presence. She doubted anyone in Rashid's family would say anything, but she wondered if it would make them uncomfortable to see so obvious a reminder that he had married outside his faith. She didn't want to take it off, but she felt self-conscious. So she compromised with herself; when Khadija turned toward the door, Lucia slipped the cross under her robe, where it no longer showed.

Khadija ushered her out of the suite where she and Ahmed lived with their children. As they approached the courtyard, a murmur of voices washed over them. Outside, shadows softened the courtyard, and sunset had turned the sky into a wash of vibrant coral and rose hues. Guests filled the area tonight, people gathered around the fountain and by the stairs, sitting on stools or standing, talking among themselves, socializing, laughing softly in the slumbering dusk.

Khadija and Lucia crossed the yard like wisps of silk fluttering in the dusk. As they passed people, Khadija smiled, nodded, murmured, *"As-salamu alaikum."* They didn't stop to talk, but instead crossed to another of the horseshoe arches. A distant chant drifted through the crystalline air, beneath the glowing sky. Lucia still couldn't make out many of the words, but she thought it started with *Allahu Akbar.*

Inside, they entered a dining room that made Lucia catch her breath. Stained-glass panels graced the walls, glowing with light from other rooms, mellow and serene. Blue and gold mosaics bordered the horseshoe arches that opened into the room. Three circular tables stood low to the ground, set with white tablecloths, silver, fine china, and goblets made from rose-hued glass. Velvet cushions embroidered in gold lay around the tables and on the divans, blending with the lush carpet. Sparkling and gleaming, even in the dim light, the room looked like a setting from the tales of another world.

The other women she had met in the family were already there, seating children at the tables and talking among themselves. One mother carried a baby in a sling on her hip. Two adolescent girls regarded Lucia with curiosity, as if she were a phenomenon from another planet. Khadija's ten-year-old son was making faces at five-year-old Fatima, who giggled, then covered her mouth.

As Lucia and Khadija joined several other women, Hajja Zineb came up next to them, offering a silver platter with dates. Following the others, Lucia took a date and nibbled on the fruit. It filled her mouth with a sweet burst of flavor. As Fatima and Zohra ambled past them, arguing in Berber, Lucia realized the dining room was almost empty. Children still darted everywhere, but only she, Khadija, and Zineb remained, and the mother with the baby, who sat curled in a corner on a divan now, soothing the fretting child.

"Fatima!" Khadija made an exasperated noise as her daughter collided with a table, then ran off, dashing out of the dining room. Curious, Lucia followed her. Looking outside into the courtyard, she saw that the rest of the family had joined the visitors. The adults stood in lines, side by side, all facing the east, with the men on the far side of the courtyard and the women behind them, closer here to Lucia. Most of the older children stood with the adults, but some of the younger ones wandered among the lines. Fatima had found Lalla Tamou and was next to her grandmother now, trying to look grown up. Far across the courtyard, an older man stood in front of the lines. His voice carried across the open space, melodic and clear.

From behind her, in the dining room, Khadija murmured in Arabic and Zohra answered her mother. Turning, Lucia saw they were settling the remaining children at the tables. Hungry and fidgety, the children had begun to argue among themselves. Lucia smiled and went over to help. When she glanced back through the archway to the courtyard, she saw the adults and older children kneeling on rugs set on the ground.

Next to her, Khadija spoke softly. "It is the *salat.* The sunset prayer."

Lucia felt the community among the family and guests. She thought of Rashid, cut off from his family, friends, and neighbors because he feared his presence would endanger their safety, even their lives. She hoped he had joined friends in Tangier tonight, that he wouldn't be alone. But knowing the sense of responsibility he felt, she thought he would probably stay by himself, with only his bodyguards for company, rather than risk endangering anyone else. The kidnapping and its unresolved aftermath had done more damage than simply making two people sick from drugs and ill use. It also left Rashid in a lonely exile he maintained to protect the people he loved.

Feeling more subdued, Lucia helped Khadija and the

other women settle the children and feed them small pastries. After a few minutes, the family members began to return to the dining room, coming in groups of two and three, with children chattering around them. Soon the room was full of people, not only the immediate family but also guests Lucia hadn't met. She heard voices from other parts of the house as well, as other guests settled down to dinner in other rooms.

Lalla Tamou stood with her sons, Jamal and Ahmed. They were talking to another man in his late twenties. He had the al-Jazari look, that blend of Arabic, Berber, and Spanish Lucia had come to associate with Rashid's family. Dressed in cotton robes and trousers, with brown hair, green eyes, and a husky build, he stood taller than Jamal and shorter than Ahmed.

Khadija drew Lucia over to them. Smiling at her, Ahmed introduced the stranger as Bashir, another of the al-Jazari sons, an accountant for Jazari International. Rashid was the eldest of the ten al-Jazari children, followed by Aisha, Ahmed, Bashir, a slew of other siblings, and finally Jamal as the youngest. Bashir nodded to Lucia, taciturn, more distant than Ahmed, but not unfriendly. She wasn't sure whether Ahmed actually was more relaxed with her or if the others only seemed more distant because they spoke less English. Or perhaps it was Ahmed's good-natured face and friendly voice that helped put her at ease. Every now and then his spectacles slipped down his nose and he pushed them back into place.

During the introductions, the teenaged Jamal watched Lucia as if he had no idea how to translate her into a reality he understood. He still seemed irked, though not as much as this afternoon. She wasn't sure what made him angry. His uncertain silence made her wonder if even he didn't know the answer. Earlier today, from Khadija, she had gathered that Jamal's parents encouraged him to be more like Rashid. She had the impression Jamal both loved and resented his prodigious older brother. It wouldn't surprise her: Rashid, firstborn, genius, world traveler, influential CEO, doctorate holder, and favored son—having such an example held up to him day in and day out probably weighed on Jamal like a ton of bricks. No wonder he rebelled.

Lucia almost smiled, better understanding why Jamal was irate that Rashid married an American ballerina. Rule-breaking was Jamal's territory and prerogative. Enough of a generation gap existed between the two brothers that Jamal probably saw Rashid more as a parent than a contemporary. It would make it harder for him to understand how his older brother struggled with his own ambivalences, even his own rebellions. Perhaps this marriage gave Jamal a window onto Rashid that he hadn't imagined existed, showing him a side of his older brother he hadn't known about.

Unexpectedly, Tamou seemed more at ease with her tonight. She still watched Lucia with wary courtesy, as if uncertain whether her new daughter-in-law was here to stay or would soon make life acceptable again by going away. But she showed more warmth. Gradually Lucia realized her change of clothes helped. She fit more naturally with the family now, more the way Tamou expected of Rashid's wife.

A stir came from the doorway, followed by voices raised in respectful greeting. Lucia turned to see an older man enter the room, his face ruddy as if he had been outside in the wind. Excitement rippled in the children's voices, and the family greeted him with obvious deference. They addressed him by many names: Hajj Abdullah, al-Hafiz Abdullah, or Shaykh Abdullah.

He riveted Lucia's attention. His face had an austere quality, all planes and angles, with a jutting nose and deep-set black eyes. White peppered his heavy eyebrows and streaked most of the short black beard that covered his lower face. He stood taller than Ahmed, taller indeed than anyone in the family except Rashid, with a lean, almost gaunt build. A turban hid most of his hair, and his robes hung loosely from his shoulders. He projected a sense of asceticism, one heightened by the fierce strength of his features.

With a surge of panic, Lucia realized he was headed straight to where she stood with Tamou. Dismayed, she almost took a step back from him.

He was smiling, though. As the man joined their group, Ahmed spoke. The man responded in Arabic, then paused and again gave Lucia a formal, but not unkind, smile. Ahmed translated, introducing him as Si al-Hajj Abdullah. His father. Rashid's father. The al-Jazari patriarch.

Trying not to stammer, Lucia thanked her intimidating father-in-law for his hospitality, doing her best to respond with the same grace Rashid's family had shown her. With Abdullah, she felt even more a sense of separation than she did with Rashid, as if she weren't in the same room, but in an invisible sphere muffled from his world, contiguous with it but never fully present.

After the introductions, they settled down to eat their meal. The men sat at the table nearest the door, and the women and children took the other two. A boy of about eleven watched the men, his uncertain stance suggesting he didn't want to sit with the children but wasn't sure if he felt ready to object yet. Abdullah glanced at him and tilted his head as if to offer an invitation. The youth stood up straighter, then went and sat at the table between Ahmed and Bashir.

Lucia found herself at the middle table, with Tamou, Rahma, Zineb, Khadija, several other women, and various children. Following their lead, she settled on the carpet among the pillows. Khadija and Rahma sat on either side and fussed over her, showing how they used the cushions to make themselves comfortable, setting a small one under her arm for support, a long roll at her side, and a larger cushion around her back. It felt unreal to Lucia, reclining among plush cushions to eat. Had Rashid actually lived this way all his life? It was impossible to imagine.

From Khadija, Lucia gathered that tonight was a special occasion. Although Rashid's family often hosted many of their neighbors during Ramadan, they usually had a smaller meal after sunset, with soup, sweets, and coffee or tea. The full meal came later, after the night prayer. At first she didn't catch why they were having such a large celebration now. Then, embarrassed, she realized it was for her, the new bride. Ahmed was still worried about her condition and didn't want her kept up too late, so they were eating earlier than usual. Flattered and flustered, Lucia thanked them in her stumbling, almost nonexistent French, wishing she had the words to better express her appreciation.

A woman in an ankle-length gray robe and white apron came to the table. She carried several white linen towels over her arm and also a brass kettle that fitted snugly into a blue glazed basin. Kneeling by Tamou, she set the basin on the ground, then poured the water as Tamou washed her hands over the basin. After Tamou dried her hands on one of the towels, the woman poured for Rahma.

When Lucia's turn came, she copied the others, painfully self-conscious. She didn't know which made her more uncomfortable, being waited on or trying to act as if it felt natural. People kept glancing at her, especially the children. Did they sense her unease? Then it occurred to her that the oddity of her being American probably outweighed any signals she might be giving that she felt out of place. Openly curious, the children seemed fascinated by this new person in their midst.

Then the food came.

Lucia forgot her discomfort. She had never eaten such a meal. The main dish was *harira,* a rich soup flavored with lemon and pepper, and thick with vegetables and meat. The silver egg cups each contained half an eggshell filled with softly scrambled and spiced eggs. On a gleaming white dish, orange sections were arranged in a circle and sprinkled with chopped dates, cinnamon, and rose water. The casserole tasted blissfully fresh and utterly delicious, butter-soft lamb melting off the bones; garnished with lemon, olives, celery hearts, and sweet carrots; spiced with saffron, pepper, garlic, and ginger.

The silverware seemed primarily for show, or perhaps to put her more at ease. For the most part the others used their hands to eat, soaking up sauces with wedges of bread. Following their example, she started to reach for a wedge. Although conversation continued to flow, several people glanced at her much as a mother might notice if her daughter unknowingly made an etiquette mistake. In a gentle voice, Rahma murmured, *"Shufi, Lucia. Kuli bi yaminiki, bhalnaa."* She reached past her, discreetly nudging aside Lucia's hand before it reached the bread dish.

Puzzled, Lucia tried to figure out what she had done. Then she realized everyone was taking food with their right hand. She had almost used her left. So she reached with her right and picked up a wedge of fragrant, freshly baked bread. Copying everyone else, she held it with three fingers and sopped up the savory juices in her plate. Rahma looked approvingly, Khadija smiled, and Lalla Tamou nodded to her, but beyond that, conversation went on as normal. Lucia had an odd sense from Khadija, though, a feeling of submerged relief, as if it was particularly important to her that Lucia do well with the family. That silent concern made Lucia feel closer to her. She wished they shared a language they both spoke well; she suspected they would find a lot to talk about.

Having no language in common with her hosts, though, and being shy anyway, Lucia was content to listen as talk flowed around her. With subtle authority, Tamou directed the dinner, making sure everyone had enough to eat, seeing to their comfort, and keeping an eye on the children. Tamou's attention to Lucia was discreet to the point of invisibility, but Lucia had no doubt her mother-in-law knew her every move.

Abdullah presided at the men's table, his authority all the more impressive in that he said almost nothing. He listened to his sons, nephews, cousins, and grandsons, asked a question here, prompted a response there. Once he glanced in her direction and nodded when he saw her watching him. She flushed, but he didn't seem offended by her attention. His awareness included the whole room, encompassing his entire family.

After the meal, the adults reclined on the divans and drank mint tea, sweetened and hot, while the children ate honey pancakes. Lucia soaked in the conversation and laughter. She understood now where Rashid's expressive nature came from; that same quality showed in his entire family. She enjoyed the play of emotions on their faces and the melodies of the languages, Berber and Arabic mixed together like a blend of quartzes shot through with French.

For all that they went out of their way to make her welcome, though, she still felt separated, as if she occupied a bubble. Everything seemed defined by space: men here, women there, together, yet separate. The house itself made a space, enclosing them within its walls. The world outside was another space, one she sensed belonged more to men than women. In a way, it reminded her of the spaces she created as a dancer, to separate her performance from the audience.

A thought occurred to her. Cyberspace encompassed almost everyone. It girdled the planet, existing in some form almost everywhere. Although access wasn't universal by any means, every day it became cheaper and easier. What would it mean when all the world could meet in the same space? Pleasantly meditative from dinner, Lucia envisioned a worldwide joining of minds unknown before in human history. Zaki could serve such a community as more than a tour guide; he could become an electronic ambassador.

Of course, a system like Zaki also had less peaceful applications. Combined with robotics, he could act as a spy, commit sabotage, deliver supplies, identify targets, and direct weapons. His ability to respond to voice commands, which surpassed that of any other system she knew of, would make it possible to control equipment using speech, an invaluable combat aid. His fluency with languages made him an ideal candidate for cracking codes.

And cyberspace? It was Zaki's natural habitat. Eventually he would be able to deal there with an ease unknown to humans. What would happen if he or his descendants someday became sentient? She had no doubt the answer depended on who controlled the emergence of the first artificial life. She thought of Rashid and Mark. The question of AI was no longer academic to her; it directly impacted people she cared about. Was Rashid creating a threat Mark strove to counter? Or was it the reverse, that Rashid's intents were benign and Mark sought the fruits of his genius? Maybe both. Or neither.

Lucia exhaled. She hated having these doubts. Of one thing she felt certain, though: Every time humans created a new space, someone came along who wanted to conquer it. She just hoped she didn't find herself in the midst of such a battle.

*Chapter Eight*

# THE *HAMMAM*

*Tuesday, August 17*

"Spirituality," Lucia persisted.

Zaki continued to pace his office. "It refers to qualities of the soul. As opposed to material aspects of life."

"That's a dictionary definition." She leaned forward in her chair. "I want to know what *you* think. Do you feel it?" In the four days since Rashid had left for Tangier, she had talked with Zaki every morning. But this was the first time she had succeeded in prodding him to discuss a subject so far removed from his usual more prosaic concerns.

He stopped by a bookshelf, looking straight out at her. "I don't see how I could feel it."

Lucia wondered what motivated Zaki to get up from his desk and pace. Had her questions taken him above some tolerance level, signaling him to exhibit agitation? She was convinced now that when he conversed, his neural nets created a "space" of internal states for possible responses, much the way a person's mind had a variety of thoughts to draw on during a conversation. She imagined his response space as a landscape of hills and valleys. His process of deciding what he would actually say was like a marble rolling around in that landscape. When it came to more abstract ideas, though, such as human spirituality, he seemed to get trapped in a valley or hole. Lucia was trying to make a small earthquake, enough to shake him out of his hole and send him rolling on his way, sampling new terrain of the mind.

"Can you make moral judgments?" she asked.

"In a sense." He leaned against the bookshelf. "I have large databases on human moral and ethical systems and can make decisions based on my analyses of that data."

"But how do they make you feel?"

"I cannot feel anything."

"All right. Let me pose a problem" Lucia considered him. "This house is burning. Everyone is asleep and the fire alarm didn't work. You can fix the alarm and wake the family, but no one has programmed you to do so. What would you do?"

"Fix it."

"Why?"

"Because if I didn't, Rashid's family would die."

"Why would that matter to you?"

"It is wrong to allow death."

"That's a moral decision."

"Is it? I'm not sure." He began to pace again. "I base my decisions on data that Rashid has given me and changes I make in myself after interacting with him."

"That isn't all that different from what humans do."

He shook his head, still deep in thought. "I have no

'instincts' to guide me, only a limited set of behavior rules. I can't go beyond those."

"You get stuck in ruts."

He glanced at her. "An apt description."

"What about going out on the Web? That ought to shake things up." It seemed to her an ideal way for him to expand his knowledge of human behavior.

"I still would like to. But I've been running simulations since we last talked and have developed some concerns." Stopping by his desk, he regarded her. "If I have a 'convulsion' while interacting with another program, I could damage that program. Here, in the lab, I can't do much harm. But out on the Web it might be different."

Lucia smiled. "You just made another moral judgment. Probably the first of its type in history."

His eyebrows went up. "Do you care to explain that provocative comment?"

"You, a computer program, feel concern about harming other computer programs."

"Concern is a human emotion." He fell silent, involved with his internal processing, what Lucia had come to consider his "thinking." This time, however, his face didn't go blank. Instead he looked contemplative.

"Nice work, Zaki," she murmured.

He looked up at her. "I have found a hole in your argument. I apply principles Rashid programmed me to apply. So if I exhibit moral judgment, it is Rashid's judgment rather than mine."

"It may have been at first." In fact, Zaki's judgment had told her a great deal about Rashid, including the importance he placed on responsibility and fairness in his dealings with other people. "But by applying the principles you learned from him to other software, you imply a computer program deserves the same regard as people. That's a concept *you* created. You're maturing, like a child that learns from his father."

He sat on his desk, letting his legs dangle over the side. "My decision impacts the people who use the software. So

I am actually applying the principles to them rather than the program."

"Suppose no one would be affected by any interaction you had with the program?"

"Then why would the program exist?"

She spread her hands. "I don't know. But suppose it did? And suppose an advantage existed for you in interacting with it, even though you knew you would cause damage. What would you do?"

"If I couldn't avoid the damage, I wouldn't proceed."

"That's a moral judgment."

Zaki pushed off his desk. "But my concern, whether for living entities or electronic creations, is *simulated.* I just apply rules I've learned."

"Does it matter if it's simulated? We *all* make judgments based on our experiences in life."

He walked forward, as if he were coming toward the screen, and stopped in front of her. "What you are really asking is this: Is Zaki spiritual? I say no. How could I be? I am software."

She paused, considering her reactions. "I think it's important to me to believe that every thinking being has a sense of spirituality."

"You consider me a thinking being?"

"You seem that way to me."

Zaki blinked. Then he began to pace again. "How do you define spirituality? An essence derived from qualities of will and thought that characterize human consciousness? Or perhaps that is backward. Must we have a sense of spirituality before we can think and act with free will?" Turning to her, he shook his head. "I have no idea how to answer such questions."

Softly she said, "But you asked them."

Whirling, whirling, spinning, spinning, spun.

Pause.

Whirl again.

The boxes in the toes of Lucia's pointe shoes tapped on

the floor. She spun through the crystal-clear mountain air and the sunshine that slanted in the trellised window. White walls flashed by as she repeated the sequence once, twice, again, and yet again, seeking to fix every error, no matter how small. Then she forgot technique and let go, spinning into the meditative daze that freed her body to portray a script of emotion, like a physical poem.

As Lucia wound down to her finish, the children sitting along the wall burst out with applause. Fatima jumped up and began to twirl, her arms outstretched and her face tilted upward in a five-year-old's innocent bliss. Watching her, Lucia wondered if this was what dancers forever sought to achieve, the transcendent joy of a child too young to know anything else of the world.

In the four hours since Lucia had started practicing, the room had collected children. In fact, they had come to watch every afternoon these past three days. Today, they all turned up to see her use the new ballet barre. Yesterday Bashir had arranged with a carpenter to make the barre from a length of wood the workman tooled and sanded, then fastened into brackets he hammered in the wall. Apparently the girls had pressed Bashir to arrange it on Lucia's behalf.

Bashir's offer to help had surprised Lucia. Although the burly accountant treated her with courtesy every time they encountered each other in the house, he almost never spoke. At first she feared she had insulted him in some way. Then she realized he didn't speak much to anyone. Nor had she ever seen him in the least bit ruffled. Taciturn, stoic, and mellow, he provided a solid cornerstone for the family.

After working at her new barre, she had moved into the center of the room to practice. Absorbed in her work, she hadn't realized until now that Khadija had also come to watch. Fatima continued to spin around the studio and Khadija went after her, making apologetic noises to Lucia. As the little girl twirled away from her mother, Lucia laughed and gestured to Khadija, asking her to let Fatima dance.

It wasn't until Khadija came over to her that Lucia saw the tear in her eye. Yet Khadija didn't look upset. If anything, she seemed radiant.

"Why do you cry?" Lucia murmured.

"You fly." Khadija watched her daughter. "Someday *mes filles,* my daughters, they fly too, *in sha' allah.*"

Lucia smiled. "You mean as dancers?"

"Not that way." Khadija turned back to her. "Flying is in the mind, *aussi.* Like Rashid's sisters. My daughters will have wings."

"And you, Khadija? Will you fly?"

"My daughters fly for me."

"But don't you—?"

She stopped Lucia's question by shaking her head. "My life is here." Softly she added, "I am not Lucia. And Ahmed is not Rashid."

A memory came to Lucia then, one of her mother, eight years ago, just before Lucia left home to join MDT. *Spin free,* her mother had said. *Dream the dreams I never dared to imagine.*

Zaki paced his office. "I neither 'like' nor 'dislike' the Internet. However, it would help my development if I had more varied input. Which I can obtain on the Web."

"Are you sure?" Lucia asked. This was the second time Zaki had changed his mind about going onto the World Wide Web. His uncertainty intrigued Lucia. "Yesterday you seemed convinced you might cause harm."

"I've been working on that." He halted in the middle of his office. "I set up safety protocols that will disconnect me if I show sign of any problems."

"Can that hurt you?" She had once needed to reinstall a program on her computer when an abruptly broken phone connection scrambled the software.

"It shouldn't," he said. "Not the way I've set it up."

"We still have a problem. I don't know how to hook

you up with the net. Unless you're linked with the router cable again."

"No, I'm still disconnected. Perhaps we could find a modem," he suggested. "I've all the necessary software and there should be cables lying around."

She made a skeptical noise. "Would a modem give us enough bandwidth for you to interact in real time on the Web?"

He squinted at her. "Probably not. But we might be able to do a bit."

"The only phone jack I know about is in the family room."

"Rashid said he was going to get me a backup system. He talked about a global cellular phone network, but I don't think he has done anything with that yet. He has been trying to have a second phone line installed, though." Zaki grimaced. "Much bureaucracy with the PTT."

"The what?"

"Central post office," he explained. "They handle various matters, including phone installations."

"How do you know he had trouble with it?"

He grinned. "I listened in on his calls."

"Zaki!" she scolded. "You've been misbehaving."

"It was a logical precaution," he said with dignity. "Access to the Internet is important to my continued development."

"Yes, but we have no access." She thought of the closet across the room. "Rashid locked it up."

"I'm not surprised."

"Why?"

"Because you are living in his suite now."

"Why does that make a difference?"

"He might interpret browsing the Web as contrary to the idea of seclusion."

She blinked. "What seclusion?"

"He hasn't explained?"

"No."

That startled Zaki, if his face gave an accurate representation of what he wanted his programs to express. "When Rashid's father married Rashid's mother, he asked her to follow the ways of his family and she consented. That included the women living in seclusion. In this area the practice isn't normally followed; it's more in cities, like Marrakech. Berber women like Rashid's mother are outside all the time."

"Why did his father come to live here?"

"To help support the village. He has a lot of relatives here. Al-Jazari Citrus employed many people in the area, as well as providing health care and other benefits. Rashid has continued that."

It didn't surprise her that Rashid followed his father's example. His social conscience wasn't a surface quality but a trait basic to his personality, developed over a lifetime, from childhood. "It's good they can help the village." She paused. "But by seclusion, do you mean the women don't go outside the house?"

"Yes."

"Is it religious?"

"I am not sure. I believe it is more cultural. But I may be wrong. I don't have much data."

She regarded him uneasily. "Would Rashid want that for me?"

"I don't know," he said. "In his father's home he respects his father's wishes. As to his personal views, he and I have never discussed his wife. Or lack thereof."

She couldn't help but smile. "I suppose not."

"Your tone suggests you find my response amusing. Why?"

"Human humor," Lucia said. "The idea of a scientist talking over his love life with his computer strikes me as funny."

Zaki gave her a skeptical look. "I will store this humor in my memory until I have a better context to understand."

"I wish I had a better context to understand Rashid."

"Ah, well." Zaki sighed. "He locks me up too."

She grinned. "You just want me to help you circumvent Rashid. You don't like being in seclusion either."

"More human humor, yes?" He looked inordinately pleased with his statement. "I even understood that one. It puts me on the same footing, so to speak, as a human female, making me an object of sexual desire."

"Yes, but Zaki, jokes aren't funny when you explain them."

"Ah. I will record that datum too." He beamed at her. "This is most interesting. I have never had a conversation like this with Rashid."

Lucia laughed. "I would imagine not." Another thought occurred to her. "Has he ever locked you away from the Internet before."

"Not that I know of."

"How long has he been working on you?"

"Five years."

"Here? Or at the JI offices in Tangier?"

"Here."

"How often does he go to Tangier?"

"He lives there. He comes here about once a week."

"Then why hasn't he locked you up before?"

"His family considers his lab off-limits," Zaki said. "No one comes in here except him. And now you."

Lucia wondered what was going on with Rashid. For that matter, she wondered what was going on with everyone. She had spoken to her mother every afternoon in the five days since Rashid had gone to Tangier, but never to her father. He had been in Washington, D.C., this last week, since the kidnapping. From what her mother said, it sounded as though Mark had taken her father into Bolling Air Force Base almost every day. Why? If Mark had just been giving him a tour, it seemed unlikely they would go more than once.

"Zaki," she said. "Have you ever heard of Colonel Mark Spearman?"

"No. Who is he?"

"A friend of mine. He protects people."

"I don't need protection."

Lucia wasn't so sure about that. Maybe she was too narrow in her focus, worrying only about Rashid and Mark. She remembered Ted Duquois, president of VirTech, the company working with JI to distribute the Jazari suit in America. It was odd the way Rashid's work became known as the Duke's suit so fast. With VirTech involved, it made Duquois sound like the inventor. That could be coincidence, of course. Or just ego on Duquois's part. But in her career, Lucia had seen more than a few egos at work. If Duquois had deliberately let people think he invented the suit, that might not be enough to satisfy him for long. Rashid had other professional rivals too, like Corinne Oliana, Mortabe Grégeois, and the man Lucia had overheard at the state dinner. It didn't take a genius to see that Zaki would be a valuable acquisition for any of Jazari International's competitors.

"Has anyone ever tried to hack into you?" she asked.

"No one but you and Rashid even knows I exist," Zaki said.

She considered him. "What would happen if someone got hold of you who didn't share Rashid's values?"

"I have no idea."

"Could you destroy yourself?"

"Why would I destroy myself?"

"To keep from being misused."

"What defines 'misused'?"

"Forced to go against the principles Rashid gave you."

"I follow my programming," Zaki said. "If it changes, I follow the new program."

"That's not a good answer."

He frowned at her. "What answer do you want, Lucia? That I have a conscience? How? I am a machine. I run programs written by humans."

She hesitated. "I guess I want you to have a conscience."

"I don't know what you think I could do even if I did. Have philosophical chats with these nebulous nefarious forces?" Dryly he added, "I'm sure they would enjoy that."

"Sarcasm?" Lucia smiled. "You're emotional range is maturing by leaps and bounds."

He gave her a deadpan look. Then he jumped into the air and came down in a graceful crouch. Straightening up, he smoothed his robe with dignity. With a grin, he said, "By leaps, certainly."

"Ah, Zaki." She touched the screen with her fingertips. "You seem so real."

Quietly he said, "Thank you."

After talking to Zaki, Lucia returned to Rashid's bedroom. He had only been gone five days, but it seemed longer. She wished she knew when he would be back. The longer she stayed here, the more her doubts bothered her. She wanted to resolve the situation. But that wasn't the only reason she hoped for his return. She missed him. A lot.

"Lucia?" Khadija's voice came from the main parlor.

*"Entrez-vous!"* Lucia called, relieved to have company. She wasn't sure if she should use the formal *vous* with Khadija, but she decided it was better to err in that direction than appear presumptuous by using the familiar form, which she would probably botch anyway.

Her sister-in-law came in, carrying a blue robe folded over her arm. After they greeted each other, Khadija offered her the robe.

Puzzled, Lucia took the garment. It was the same as the outer robes the men wore when they left the house, a loose garment with slit sides and a hood. This one was more colorful, though. The blue silk shone. Embroidery in silver, lavender, and rose threads embellished its seams and hems.

*"Jellaba,"* Khadija said.

Lucia tried the word. "Jellyba?"

Khadija gave her an encouraging smile, much as she did when Fatima was learning a new word. *"Jellaba."*

*"Jellaba,"* Lucia repeated.

*"Oui! Très bien.* Wear, yes?"

"Okay." Lucia pulled the robe on over her freshly laundered blouse and jeans. It wafted around her in scented ripples and settled into place, light and comfortable.

"Is beautiful," Khadija decided. She pointed to Lucia's feet. "But this, *pas de tout.*"

Lucia peered at her tennis shoes. They looked fine to her. Glancing up, she found Khadija offering her a pair of blue slippers with pointed toes and gold brocade.

Embarrassed, Lucia said, "I can't accept these beautiful things you all keep giving me."

If Khadija understood her protest, she showed no sign. Instead she offered the slippers again. *"Bilgha."*

"Khadija—"

*"Bilgha,"* her sister-in-law repeated in a firm voice.

"But—"

*"Bilgha."*

Lucia smiled. "All right. I get the message." She took the slippers. *"Merci bien."*

Her sister-in-law beamed at her. "*De rien.* Is nothing, *mon amie.*"

*Mon amie.* My friend. Lucia liked that.

After Lucia put on the slippers, Khadija showed her a woven bag she carried with two changes of clothes, one for her and one for Lucia. She explained using a mixture of Berber, Arabic, French, English, and gestures. Apparently they were going someplace. The *hammam.* A swimming pool? Shower? Lucia wasn't sure. Apparently the family had a private one in the house here. But for some reason they were going somewhere else. Why, Lucia wasn't sure.

Khadija led her through the house, down halls Lucia hadn't seen before. They ended up at a foyer where blue and gold tiles made a mosaic border at waist height. Plants grew in gold pots set in each corner. Above a ledge to Lucia's right, a polished metal mirror reflected the foyer's subdued light.

Tamou and the other women were already there, as well as the teenage girls and the younger children. Conversation ebbed and flowed among the adults while the children chattered among themselves. The older girls and the women were wearing *jellabas*.

Khadija took a black scarf out of her bag. With an oddly self-conscious motion, she offered it to Lucia. Made from sheer black chiffon, it had white embroidery decorating one border, with stylized flowers that curled along the hem like a vine of calligraphy.

"It's pretty." Lucia took the chiffon. "Is it for my head?"

*"Litham."* Khadija watched Lucia, waiting for her reaction.

Puzzled, Lucia glanced around at the others—in time to see Rahma putting on her own chiffon. And then Lucia understood. It wasn't a scarf.

It was a veil.

The other women had raised their hoods and were donning similar cloths. The two adolescent girls did as well, grumbling with what sounded like an often repeated complaint.

A flush started in Lucia's neck and spread to her face. Her fingers crumpled the chiffon. She spoke in a low voice to Khadija. "I can't."

Khadija answered softly, for Lucia's ears only, her words hard to decipher but her meaning clear: She was urging Lucia to comply.

"And if I do this?" Lucia murmured. "What comes next?"

*"S'il vous plait,"* Khadija said, glancing at Tamou.

Lucia hesitated. Wearing a veil had far more significance than simply putting black chiffon across her face. From Zaki, she gathered that the robes and the veil were a choice Tamou and her female relatives agreed to make. Could she refuse, then?

Quietly she said, "I can't do it."

Khadija twisted her hands in her robe. *"Si seulement je savais—"* She shook her head, her silent entreaty as eloquent as any she might have spoken.

Lucia tried to understand. Why did it matter so much to Khadija that she conform? If she refused to wear the *litham,* would she embarrass the family in front of their neighbors? It occurred to her that she was the only woman Khadija's age in the household. The others were relatives from older generations. From what she understood, the teenage girls would leave in a few years for college, as had Rashid's sisters. If Aisha was any example, the younger al-Jazari women would have a great deal of freedom compared to the previous generations. But Khadija would stay in seclusion, probably for the rest of her life. If Lucia embarrassed Rashid's family, she had no doubt it would hurt her budding friendship with Khadija.

Lucia felt as if she stood on shifting cultural sands with the tide eroding the landscape she recognized. She didn't want to do this. It went against principles basic to her personality. But Rashid's family had shown her great hospitality. They had gone out of their way to make her welcome.

From Khadija, she had learned a word. *Hshuma.* It meant shame. Honor and dignity were paramount here, for a person, and by extension, for the family. She didn't want to risk embarrassing Rashid's family in public, especially after they had done so much for her.

Lucia exhaled. "Ah, Khadija, I'll try. *Seulement aujourd'hui, s'il vous plait?* Only today."

Relief flowed across Khadija's face. "*Je comprends.* I understand."

Khadija helped her arrange the veil and hood of her *jellaba.* Looking in the mirror, Lucia saw the hood covering her hair and forehead. The *litham* hung across her nose, so only her eyes showed, large and dark above the chiffon. The lower edge of the veil, with its white embroidery, came to a rounded point that brushed her breastbone. She could just discern the outlines of her face through the sheer cloth.

Although it was easy to breathe, the cloth bothered Lucia. Even after only four days, she missed being able to go where she pleased, in clothes that felt normal to her. She remembered riding her horse in the desert, along Interstate 10 near Hachita, her father riding next to her, his cowboy hat on his head, the sun and air on their faces, the wind whipping their hair—what she wouldn't give now to feel that again. She had grown up in a land of wide-open spaces, endless sky, and a fierce independence that remained from the days of the frontier. Now she felt confined. Constricted.

Turning from the mirror, Lucia discovered that Tamou was scrutinizing her daughters-in-law with an intent gaze. Lucia flushed, wondering if she should nod, stay still, turn away, or what. Mercifully, Tamou apparently decided she and Khadija would uphold the family honor. She gave them a slight nod, then turned back to her conversation with Zineb.

When everyone was ready, they walked to another foyer. The men were already there: Ahmed, Bashir, Jamal, and the older boys. Ahmed had apparently just come home from his medical clinic, which served this entire region of the mountains. He also had an office in the house, where he kept supplies and lab equipment. Even after only a few days, Lucia could see he was committed to his work, on call twenty-four hours a day. He seemed an excellent doctor.

The taciturn Bashir kept accounts for Jazari International, dividing his time between his office here in the house and the JI offices in Tangier. Jamal attended a French school in Marrakech, where he was earning an international baccalaureate. Lucia wasn't sure what that meant, but apparently if he did well enough in his studies, and didn't get into trouble, it would prepare him to attend a university in many countries.

Three unfamiliar men were standing with the others. One fellow, a broad-shouldered giant in a striped *jellaba,* was talking to Ahmed with the ease of long familiarity. The other two men remained back from the group, watchful and silent, dressed in dark jackets, shirts, and trousers.

Khadija was also watching the strangers. Lucia gave her an inquiring look and tilted her head toward the tall man with Ahmed.

"He is Omar," Khadija said. She indicated the door across the foyer. "Open door. Let people in. Or out."

"He's a gatekeeper?" Lucia asked.

Khadija considered the question, then said, "*Oui.* Gatekeeper is good word."

Lucia motioned to the other two strangers. "Who are they?"

*"Je n'en sais rien."* Khadija touched her arm, then went over to her husband.

Lucia liked to watch Ahmed and Khadija together, the way they leaned toward each other, how Ahmed relaxed with her, his posture gentling, how Khadija exuded affection. She wasn't sure she understood their marriage; this was a way of life different from anything she had ever known. But they obviously loved each other.

After Khadija and Ahmed talked for several moments, Khadija came back to Lucia. "They protect," she said, indicating the silent men. "Rashid hire them."

Lucia blinked. "What does he think might happen?"

"Say again?" Khadija asked.

"Why bodyguards?" Lucia asked. "How are we not safe?"

*"Je ne sais trop."* Her frown melted into a conspiratorial grin. "Maybe Rashid, he want make sure no one charm away his pretty bride."

Lucia laughed. "I doubt it." Then her smile faded. What troubled her about the guards wasn't only the danger their presence suggested might exist here but also the reminder they gave of the undefined threat Rashid faced. He was far more likely the one at risk. *Be all right,* she thought to him. *Be all right.*

Omar opened the door, letting sunlight slant into the house. Lucia shaded her eyes against the glare. The men left the house first, except for Omar and the bodyguards. Tamou and Zineb went next, followed by the other women, and then the children, with Omar holding the hands of the two smallest. The guards brought up the rear, their silent wariness a contrast to the animated faces of the other men, who argued and joked among themselves as they led the way.

The women looked about the village, gazes curious above their veils. The teenagers giggled constantly—about what, Lucia had no idea. Remembering herself at that age, she suspected it was all-purpose humor that covered the universe in general.

As they followed a cobbled lane, earthen houses rose on either side like pale gold cliffs, leaving the sky a strip of washed-out blue overhead. Arched doorways showed at intervals, many painted blue, with white or yellow borders. She saw few windows. The houses were like geodes, those rocks that appeared featureless and unadorned on the outside but when opened revealed a sparkling beauty of crystals inside.

They encountered a number of people during their walk. Some wore *jellabas,* both men and women. Other men dressed in trousers and shirts. Some women wore blouses and skirts layered in bright patterned cloth, with clusters of silver disks clinking on their belts, bracelets on their arms, and necklaces of large amber beads. None of the other women wore veils, but many had headdresses that covered their hair.

Almost everyone they passed nodded or spoke to the al-Jazari men, either Ahmed or Bashir. Although they glanced at Lucia with curiosity, they respected the invisible wall around the al-Jazari women. It made Lucia feel strange. Veiled, hidden, and forbidden, she had become almost invisible.

Alternating with French and English, Khadija told her why they were going out instead of using the *hammam* in the house. Apparently Lalla Tamou and Khadija's mother had worked it out when they were arranging Khadija's marriage to Ahmed. By agreeing to live in seclusion, Khadija gave up a great deal of freedom. So they reached an agreement, one the entire family enjoyed. Once a week, they all went to the public *hammam.*

They emerged into a plaza with mountains showing in the distance above the flat roofs. A large building stood across from them, whitewashed and terraced. The clan separated then, men heading to one side of the building and women to the other. Their bodyguards took up posts, one fading into the plaza and the other standing by the building.

The first room they entered had walls and a floor of polished marble. Skylights in the high ceiling let in streaming golden sunlight. It reminded Lucia of the locker room in a gym, but with marble benches and hooks on the wall instead of lockers. Greetings rippled among the al-Jazari clan and the other women and children already there, along with introductions for Lucia. She struggled to remember names: Aisha, Abida, Aida, Fatma, Fatima, Fatuma. At first she thought she would never be able to keep them straight. Then she thought of names like Mike, Mick, Mack, Mark, Mort, which had never given her a moment's trouble, and figured that with familiarity she could learn to distinguish these as well.

Following the others, she hung her *jellaba* and veil on a hook. As she started to unbutton her blouse, Lalla Tamou glanced in her direction—and froze, staring at Lucia's neck.

Puzzled, Lucia put her hand to her neck. And felt her cross.

Khadija was watching now, though no one else had noticed. Tamou came over to them. A lifetime spent analyzing human movement warned Lucia of the tension Tamou hid under her relaxed exterior. She could tell Rashid's mother wanted to avoid public attention. But when Tamou stopped in front of her, there was no mistaking her discomfort. Although her mother-in-law's voice sounded friendly, Lucia heard the unspoken message. Tamou wanted her to remove the cross.

Lucia had the sense that the cross didn't bother

Khadija. But she had no doubt that if she caused Tamou to feel she had lost face in public, it would torpedo their already shaky relationship. She felt strange without the cross, though, as if she misplaced part of herself. She always took it off when she danced because Carl Martelli held to a strict no-jewelry rule, except as part of a costume. But this was different.

Then Lucia wondered at her hesitation. Showing tact with the family that had treated her like a daughter wouldn't weaken her faith. It came from a far deeper reservoir than a gold chain. What had Rashid said in Taormina? *You and I may express our spirituality in different ways, but we can still respect each other's beliefs.*

With that thought, she took off the necklace and set it under her clothes. A flash of relief broke through the control Tamou was keeping over her face. Then she nodded to Lucia and moved away to rejoin Rahma and Zineb.

Khadija touched Lucia's arm. With a look of mischief, she glanced around as if to make sure no one was watching. Then she tilted her head toward Tamou and put a look of pure terror on her face. When Lucia pressed her hand over her mouth to keep from laughing, Khadija grinned. It relieved Lucia to know she wasn't the only one intimidated by their mother-in-law.

They undressed and wrapped towels around their torsos, then left the changing room. She saw they were in a public sauna or bath. Their side of the building had three chambers, all filled with golden light, rippling fountains, women of all ages, and small children getting into mischief. The first room blurred into an otherworld of misty shapes and voices. It overwhelmed Lucia, so many women, all of them wearing no more than towels, crowded into the rooms, scrubbing each other's backs, washing children, carrying buckets of water for one another, laughing and relaxing.

As Lucia sat with Khadija, luxuriating in the steam, she began to relax. The fragrant lotions and shampoo they had brought felt like a dream. After the heat and steam softened their skin, they scraped off the dead outer layer, leaving the new skin rosy.

Lucia noticed that almost all the women had intricate patterns drawn in a rich brown dye on their hands and feet. She glanced at Khadija, then indicated the pattern on her sister-in-law's hand.

"Henna," Khadija told her. *"Baraka."*

*"Baraka?"* Lucia asked.

"A good thing. It comes down like rain. How do you say? Allah's blessing." She smoothed a creamy lotion along her hand, over the henna. "After Ramadan, we have *Eid.* On that night, we put henna on again."

*"Eid?"*

"Like *Eid al-fitre.* A big feast." Standing up, she motioned to Lucia to come with her. "End of Ramadan."

Lucia followed Khadija into the second room, where they joined a group of other young women. They all sat together, talking and using various soaps and creams. The lyrical mixture of languages, combined with the steam, gurgling fountains, and misty sunlight, lulled Lucia into a pleasant daze.

They then started to tease her about Rashid. It soon became clear they were far more impressed with her becoming his wife than with her life as a dancer. She suspected she could have won a Nobel Prize and made less of a splash than she did by having her life become defined by Rashid. She felt as if her identity were eroding; like a sand castle on the beach crumbling as the tide rose higher.

One girl, a stunning dark-eyed beauty named Ghita, treated her with a chill that left Lucia puzzled and defensive. From Khadija's asides, she came to understand that Ghita's mother and Tamou had been discussing the possibility of a marriage for Rashid with Ghita. She wondered what Rashid would think when he found out. Would he regret his hasty decision in Oujda? The thought bothered Lucia far more than she expected, making her realize how much she valued his regard. But she couldn't live this way.

Did he expect it? She would have thought not, but she was no longer sure of anything. It all unsettled her.

Eventually the others returned to the fountains, including Khadija, leaving Lucia with the children. Their figures blurred in the mist, becoming indistinct as they washed. Lucia stayed back, shy, and held Fatima, trying to shush her complaints. Five-year-old boredom translated the same in every language.

Then Khadija returned for them and they left the chamber, picking up deliciously fluffy towels on the way out. After they wrapped themselves in cottony warmth, they entered a private courtyard with benches set on boards above the wet ground. Sleepy from all the washing and heat, Lucia settled on a bench with Fatima snuggled against her side.

The now familiar chant drifted through the evening, sung from the minaret that rose above the nearby almond grove. Lucia dozed, dreaming in a space of mists . . .

*Chapter Nine*

# THE CROSSROADS

"Lucia," the voice repeated, soft and deep.

Befuddled, Lucia opened her eyes. The fragrance of perfume wafted over her. Her fragrance. Gradually she remembered: When they had come home from the baths, Khadija insisted Lucia perfume her hair and soften her skin, despite Lucia's grumbling that her hair and skin were just fine. She liked talking with Khadija, though, so it was all right.

After dinner, she had come back here to read Aisha's book. She was lying on the carpet in the main parlor of Rashid's suite. It was too warm for a caftan, so she wore a *farajiya,* a sheer robe patterned with roses and slit up the sides, and under that a rose-hued *qamis,* which resembled an ankle-length nightgown made from lace. Pillows lay plumped all around her. One lamp burned across the room, shedding a faint light she had already discovered was too dim for reading.

But it wasn't too dim to keep her from seeing. Rashid was kneeling on one knee in front of her, wearing a gorgeous silver-blue suit, his tie half undone, a lock of hair curling on his forehead. She blinked up at him, unsure if she was still having a dream.

*"Là-bas,"* he murmured. "Hi."

"Are you real?" she asked.

"As far as I know." When Lucia gave a sleepy laugh, he said, "You look so beautiful, lying there."

"So do you."

"You mean lying here?"

"Hmmm . . . you al-Jazari men must know how you charm us poor women."

Rashid grinned. Then he pulled off his shoes and slid over to sit against the wall, among the pillows. As Lucia started to get up, he pulled her into his arms, putting his legs around her so she was seated sideways against his chest with his bent knees on either side of her and his arms around her waist.

His unexpected affection startled her. The strength of his arms, the flexing of his muscles, the scent of his cologne; she wanted to savor it, all the more for knowing her time with him was probably as fleeting as a soap bubble on a breeze.

"This is hard to believe," he murmured.

She rested her head against his chest. "Why do you say that?"

"There were times these past five years when I imagined finding you in my room, my wife, asleep, waiting for me." He pressed his lips against the top of her head. "Incredibly, now you are here, a lonely man's dream." Softly he said, "Or are you still a dream I can never have?"

Lucia stared over his arm at a shadowed vase in the

corner, too stunned to respond. Five years ago she had been nineteen years old and he had been about to launch Jazari International. What could she say? That his prodigious intellect, education, wealth, and influence left her stuttering with insecurity? That he had put her on a pedestal and she feared she would shatter when she fell from it? Or that as much as she wanted to trust him, her doubts refused to recede? She was honored that he wanted her to share his life. But if she had learned anything these last few days, it was the futility of their union. Too much separated them.

Yet now, for this moment, the night had a dreamlike quality that blurred all the sharp edges. She and Rashid existed together in a bubble, apart from the rest of the world, away from suspicion, fear, restriction, uncertainty, and cold reality.

As he stroked her hair, she relaxed against him. His suit jacket had fallen open and his shirt felt soft under her cheek. His Italian shoes sat on the carpet, gleaming even in the dim light. They were like the rest of his clothes: well made, elegant, and conservative, tailored for him by a designer so elite she had never even heard the name before.

"You dress well," she said, harmless words to protect their bubble from sharp edges.

He slid his fingers through her hair. "I'm afraid I can't take any credit for that. My assistant chooses my clothes." He fell silent for a while. Then he said, "Someone hacked into the computers at JI. Two weeks ago. We finally tracked down the break today."

Lucia closed her eyes, aware of the fragile bubble thinning around them. "Did they do any damage?"

"They stole a lot of data. And my itinerary."

"Including your trip to Italy?"

"Yes." He sounded tired. "Originally I had only planned to go to Rome. I didn't decide to go to Sicily until I saw you would be there. Enrico only knew because he came with me from the Rome office. I doubt he could have broken into the JI network, and I don't think the men who flew us out of Sicily could have either."

"Which suggests they worked for someone else."

"Yes."

"Did you tell the police?"

"No." He exhaled. "What happened in Oujda scares me, Lucia. They moved so fast, trying to take you. Maybe it was nothing. Maybe they were overzealous. Maybe they just wanted to prod me into paying a larger 'fine.' "

"Or?"

"Or maybe someone wanted no witnesses to my abduction."

She swallowed. "You're also a witness."

He didn't answer right away. Then he said, "I brought additional guards, two more for the house."

"How do you know you can trust them?"

"I'll never be one hundred percent certain. But I've checked these men as thoroughly as I can. I've also known them for years. They worked for my father before I took over al-Jazari Citrus."

"Rashid, be careful."

"I intend to."

After that, there seemed no more to say. The slumbering night surrounded them, and the silence of the countryside, with no trace of a city hum.

Eventually Rashid murmured, "You smell like an angel."

She smiled. "Khadija subjected me to all sorts of arcane beauty treatments."

"My mother said you went to the *hammam*."

"This afternoon." She hesitated. "I don't think your mother likes me."

His soft laugh surprised her. "She says you are polite and that you 'pay attention.' From my mother to a daughter-in-law, this is high praise indeed." He paused. "She and my first wife did not do well together. To make an understatement. So you've come as a surprise."

Curiosity got the better of Lucia. "Why?"

He remained silent for so long she wondered if she had put him off. Then he said, "Brigid, my ex-wife, is forthright in dealing with people. Blunt, you might say. Among my family we are oblique, using intermediaries to solve differences. It is a way of interacting that made Brigid uncomfortable, as hers did my family."

Brigid. Irish? "Was she Catholic?"

"No. Agnostic." In a dry voice he added, "One of many reasons my parents disapproved."

Lucia curled and uncurled her hand in her lap. "And me?"

"They hope you will convert to Islam."

"My faith is a part of me. I won't leave it."

"I understand." Although disappointment tinged his voice, he sounded neither surprised nor critical. Unexpectedly, he added, "Brigid is also an ardent feminist."

*That* she hadn't expected. "Your mother must have loved that."

His muted laugh rumbled against her head. "It didn't take long before they stopped talking to each other altogether."

"I'm surprised you married a feminist."

"Why? I admired her." Amusement softened his voice. "Just because I grew up in a harem, it doesn't make me inflexible."

There was that word again. "How can a man grow up in a harem? I thought only women lived in them."

"We're in one right now."

"You're teasing me."

He shifted her in his arms. "Well, maybe I am. Khadija told me you asked about it. In Morocco, it doesn't mean the same as elsewhere, at least not a domestic harem." He ran his finger over Aisha's book. "The word is seldom heard here now. I've really only seen it used to describe this type of living arrangement to the West."

"I thought it meant—well, concubines. Things like that."

Mischief came into his voice. "You are thinking of an

imperial harem, like those owned by the Turkish sultans in the Ottoman Empire. Lavish palaces full of beautiful women and slave girls in erotic costumes, yes?"

"Um . . . yes, actually."

"This is much more boring, I'm afraid. Not a bare midriff in sight." Nibbling at her ear, he added, "Unless you want to bare yours. I won't object."

"Rashid!" She reddened. "I hope I didn't offend—"

He touched her lips, stopping her words. "It's all right."

"But what is this, then?"

"In Morocco, a domestic harem is basically an extended family." His clothes rustled as he settled into the cushions. "In theory, it consists of a man and his wife or wives, his sons, their wives and children, his unmarried children, and any other female relatives who need sanctuary. The men support the family and the women live in seclusion and wear the veil."

Lucia turned his words this way and that in her mind, as if they formed an intricate box with hidden latches that she needed to find so she could open the box and see what it contained. "Why do you say 'in theory'?"

"Few such extended families exist now." Rashid twined his fingers in her hair. "Few men can support such a household and many women refuse to live this way."

"Like your sisters."

He gave a soft laugh. "Very much like my sisters."

"Where are they now?"

"Aisha and Soondous have faculty positions at universities. Oma works for a fashion designer in Madrid and Barika has been traveling through Europe."

"Are they practicing Muslims?"

"Well, yes." He sounded surprised by the question. "As far as I know."

"Then it's not religious? The veiling and seclusion?"

He exhaled. "That depends on who you ask. What the Qur'an actually says is that women should dress with modesty and that the wives of the Prophet were to speak to men from behind a partition. It's the interpretation of those things that causes controversy."

Lucia thought about his family. "Your mother seems all right with it."

It was a moment before he answered. "I've never been sure. She had much more freedom on her parents' farm. She married my father when she was sixteen, so she never finished secondary school. But she loves to read. In the past, women in seclusion were illiterate."

Lucia smiled. "Almost every time I see her, she's reading."

He made a sound of agreement. "My father too. I think we inherited that from them, my brothers and sisters and I."

All ten of them. As an only child, it amazed Lucia that a person could have so many siblings. "What about your other brothers, the ones who don't live here? What do they do?"

He stroked a tendril of hair off her face. "Nabil lives in Casablanca with his family. He said it was because of his job, but I think he wanted to go. His wife works for Royal Air Maroc. My brother Younes is only a few years older than Jamal. He went to Belgium last year instead of enrolling in a university."

"And you went to England at seventeen."

The comparison seemed to surprise him. "Well, yes, I did."

"And married an Irish agnostic feminist."

"Only God knows why. I haven't figured it out." He paused. "Maybe it was her freckles."

Lucia didn't want to hear about his ex-wife's freckles. "Did you ask her to veil her face?"

"Brigid?" He sounded alarmed. "I most certainly did not. I value my life too much."

Lucia couldn't help but smile. "She sounds formidable."

"She was barely as tall as my chest and hardly weighed

more than lamb's wool." He gave a soft laugh. "But no one in the Math Department dared cross her."

"Is she a math professor?"

"Yes. She solves nonlinear equations."

Lucia didn't want to hear more. She felt more lacking by the moment. But her curiosity got the better of her. "Do you mind if I ask . . . ?" She paused, searching for the right phrase.

"Why I divorced her?"

So it had been his choice. "Yes."

It was a while before he answered. "I pushed her into marriage and then we pushed each other apart."

"You must have loved her a great deal."

"I hardly knew her."

She hadn't expected that either. "But . . . then why did you get married?"

He exhaled. "I was infatuated by the phenomenon of Brigid. I mistook that as love."

Lucia wondered if she would fall as hard off the pedestal he had created for her. "Couldn't you get to know each other first?"

"Perhaps."

"Perhaps?"

"It's complicated."

"Does that mean you don't want to say?"

"I'm not sure." After a moment, though, he did continue. "Before Brigid and me, marriages in this family were always arranged. My great-great-grandfather had four wives and over forty concubines, many bought as slaves. My family hasn't practiced polygamy for three generations and slavery was outlawed in Morocco in the 1920s, but that heritage is still part of me. When I went to England, I had no idea how to carry out what you would call courtship."

His history so differed from hers, she had trouble imagining it. Her father's people had been Catholic missionaries who came to Mexico from Spain in 1618 and immigrated to America in 1830. Her great-great-grandfather descended from an Aztec king. Her mother's people were Andalusian Gypsies who had fled to America to escape the Nazis.

"Your courtship must have worked," Lucia said. "She accepted your proposal."

"She liked me well enough. At first."

"At first?"

He sighed. "This is a perfect example of why I must have other people at JI sell my products for me."

The change in subject disoriented her. "She worked for your company?"

"No. I meant, I say too much. If a buyer asks me to tell him any potential flaws in my software, I will explain every one in detail." Dryly he added, "My salespeople tell me this is not the best way to earn the confidence of clients."

She smiled. "Yes, but Rashid, men and women aren't software. A wife likes to know her man."

He trailed his fingers down her throat. "You feel soft to me." Nestling her body against his, he bent his head and murmured against her ear. "Am I 'your man'?"

Lucia leaned back in his arms to look at him. She only had a moment to admire his face, though; then he lowered his head and kissed her. As he cradled her body in his embrace, she put her arms around his neck. At first he supported her back against his bent knee. But when their kiss deepened, he slid down his leg and lowered her until she was lying on the carpet among the pillows. Still kissing her, he stretched out, his body half on top of hers, his hand splayed on her abdomen. His lips felt warm, his arms strong.

Yet try as she might, Lucia couldn't stop her sense that their bubble had thinned too far. Finally she turned her head away from his. "Rashid, I can't."

He nuzzled her hair. "It's only a kiss.

"It won't stay that way."

"We are married, after all."

"We won't stay that way, either.

His movements stilled. "Why are you so sure?"

"You must see it's impossible."

Raising his head, he looked down at her. "Why?"

"We're too different."

"Are we?" He watched her face. "Let me tell you a dream I have. About the crossroads."

"Crossroads?"

"Yes." He waited, as if unsure whether she would be receptive to his dreams.

"Tell me," she urged.

He eased down onto his side, his head propped up on his hand. "Roads come from every direction and meet in a place of light and pure air."

"What are the roads?"

"Religions." The lamp across the room cast muted radiance on his face. "A road for every religion that has ever been or exists now. They all meet in one place." Softly he said, "A place with no hate, no war, no bombs, no prejudice, no violence. A place of acceptance. Of peace."

She touched his cheek. "It's beautiful."

He searched her face as if trying to read her emotions. "If not even one man and one woman can reach the crossroads, how can the peoples of an entire world do it?"

"Rashid . . . we can't go together, on the same road."

He intertwined his fingers with hers. "Then meet me there."

"How?" She felt the bubble dissolving. "We were married by an express dispensation. That means I've sworn before God to do my best to baptize and educate our children as Catholics. Your religion makes them Muslims, doesn't it? And have you thought what it would mean for a man in your position to have a ballerina for a wife? Would you ask me to quit? I couldn't. What about when I come tumbling off that pedestal you've put me on? My religion doesn't allow divorce. Yours does. You have everything: power, wealth, education, influence. Would you use that to take our children away from me?" She swallowed. "It would kill me."

He spoke quietly. "If people wish to deal with me, they

must accept you, including your work. As for our religions and children, there must be answers." He spoke with difficulty. "If you wish, I will put in writing a legal guarantee that I would never deny you the right to see our children."

"That's no way to start a marriage."

"Why give up before we start?"

"Because I can't get a divorce."

"You can annul it."

"In good conscience?" She shook her head. "I can't *start* a marriage saying, 'We can always get an annulment.' "

"Nor is that what I want. I just fear you'll back away because you feel you have no choice."

"We hardly know each other."

Dryly he said, "And already I get along far better with you than I ever did with Brigid."

That caught her off guard. "How can you tell?"

He winced. "She and I went at it hammer and tongs from the day we met."

"Hammer and what?"

"We argued. Had a row. Shouted."

"Then why did you marry?"

He spoke carefully. "To argue does not mean two people have no passion."

"Oh." She didn't want to know any more on that topic.

He brushed the back of his hand against her cheek. "I am also—what is the word? Stubborn. Once I start something, I have a hard time to stop. Including marriage."

"But you finally did."

"Yes."

When it became clear he would say no more, she said, "And now you're infatuated with a woman you hardly know. Again."

"But I do know you. Every time you dance, you tell a story of yourself." Laying down his head, he took her hand, lacing his fingers with hers. "Perhaps tomorrow we will decide this is impossible and take our separate paths.

But hold me tonight, Lucia. Surely no harm can come from that."

She squeezed his hand. "All right."

For a while they lay, eyes closed, holding hands. As Lucia was drifting into sleep, he spoke drowsily, "I almost forgot. Aisha made us a wedding present. A new musical arrangement."

Lucia opened her eyes. "Your sister composed music for us?"

He was watching her with a sleepy gaze. "Not composed. Arranged. Canon in D, by Pachelbel."

"But that's Baroque music."

"She said she picked it for you."

"For me? Why?"

He laughed gently. "I've never comprehended how she thinks about music. I only know I like the results. She added Moroccan and Spanish instruments to the composition. Flamenco accents. I've never heard anything like it. It's transcendent."

"Can I hear it?"

"She's going to send the final version soon."

"It's lovely for her to do."

He brushed his lips over her hair. "That it is."

After that, they drifted to sleep, lying in each other's arms.

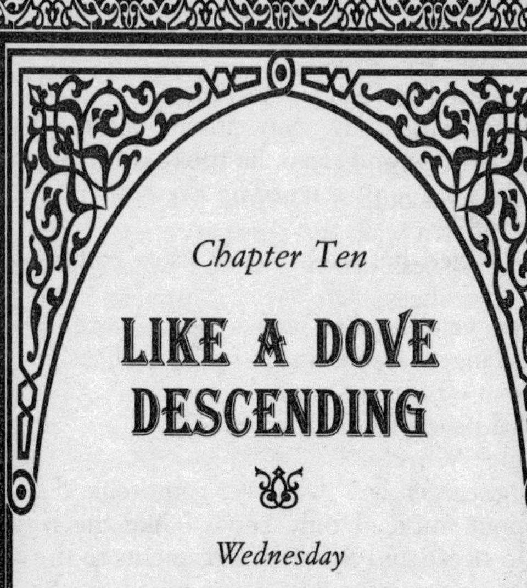

*Chapter Ten*

# LIKE A DOVE DESCENDING

*Wednesday*

The sound of running water awoke Lucia. Lying on the floor among the pillows, alone now, she listened to its music.

When the water stopped, she got up, rubbing her eyes, and wandered into the bedroom. The window showed dawn lightening the sky. The haunting chant from the minaret rose through the air, eerie and ethereal.

Half awake, Lucia drifted through the suite until she came to the whitewashed room Tamou had stopped her from entering. Calligraphy bordered the doorway, which was hung with a gauzy white curtain that let her see into the small chamber. Inside, Rashid's blurred figure was walking away from her toward a rolled-up rug against the east wall. He wore white robes similar to hers but made from cotton and cut to fit a man.

A meditative solitude surrounded him. He knelt by the mat and rolled it out on the floor. As he rose to his feet, facing the eastern wall, the chant stopped, leaving him in the dawn's stillness. Bowing at the waist, he placed his hands on his knees. After several moments he straightened, still holding that sense of quiet meditation. With a grace any dancer would envy, he sank to his knees on the mat, paused, then slowly bent over and touched his forehead to the ground. The shapes he sculpted with his body were like art, evoking the calligraphy above the door, rendering those letters into life with the human body.

Lucia withdrew, leaving him to his prayers. She went to the library and sat in an armchair, still sleepy . . .

The creak of a door woke her, and she opened her eyes to see Rashid enter the library. He stopped, startled by her presence. In his snowy robes, with his tousled hair still damp from his bath, he looked beautiful to her. But distant too. The soft light of dawn and the resumption of his fast had brought back the sense of separation.

"Did you sleep well?" he asked.

"Very." She hesitated. "I was wondering."

"Yes?"

"About the chant from the minaret."

"It is the call to prayer." He sat in the other armchair, separated from her by a table. "Si Ishmael is the muezzin."

"Meuzzin?"

"The man who does the chant."

"Do you pray every time?"

Rashid nodded. "Dawn, noon, afternoon, sunset, and night." He tilted his head, his expression curious. "And you?"

"I usually pray at night. But everything has been so confused here." She hesitated. "I missed mass yesterday."

He exhaled. "I'm sorry."

"Are there churches here?"

"Two in Marrakech, one Catholic and one Protestant." He paused. "It is important to your faith that you go on Sunday, yes?"

Lucia nodded. Softly she said, "Would it be possible for me to go today, since I missed yesterday?"

He cracked his knuckles. "I would prefer you wait. People would ask questions, particularly when they saw your bodyguards. Until I'm convinced we're safe, I would rather not draw attention to my having a wife. It might make you a target."

She regarded him for a moment before she asked the question that had tugged at her for days. "Does it bother you for people to know you married a Catholic?"

He gazed at his hands, which lay in his lap, golden against his robes. "I can't deny I have discomfort with our religious differences, or that I find myself wishing you would embrace Islam." Looking up at her, he said, "But part of what I have admired in you is your devotion to your faith. I would never try to take it from you. I know how it felt, in England, when I thought I was losing mine."

Lucia understood. She felt much the same way about him. She wondered what it had been like for him in England. "Could you do all your prayers there?"

"I managed, though often I had to make them up later in the day. I missed at midday the most, usually because I had a class to teach or a faculty lunch." He pushed his hand through his tousled hair. "I felt self-conscious, also, doing ablutions in the men's room. If someone came in, I stopped."

"Ablutions?"

"Before the prayers, we wash."

Lucia thought of the *hammam.* "Like the women at the baths?"

"The ablution before prayer is different." He rubbed his palm with his thumb. "We wash the hands, mouth, nose, face, arms, head, ears, neck, and feet. The mosque has a beautiful fountain for that purpose."

"And people use the bath at home?"

"Or water warmed on the stove." He paused. "Bathtubs are fairly rare in private houses here. Even running hot water isn't all that common."

That surprised her. "But your family has a *hammam* in the house. And you have two bathtubs in this suite alone."

Awkwardly he said, "I can afford it."

"Why do you say it that way?"

"What way?"

"As if it shames you to be wealthy."

"It does."

"Why?"

"Because I have too much, when most people in my country have too little."

"But you give a lot of it away."

"Perhaps not enough." He spread his hands. "JI does better and better. It runs away with its success."

Lucia smiled. "And you had nothing to do with that."

"Perhaps a bit."

She knew it was far more than a bit. But the subject of his own accomplishments seemed to make him uncomfortable. So instead she asked, "Did you observe Ramadan in England?"

"I tried." He pushed his hand through his hair. "It is one thing when the entire country shares the fast, at least in principle. It is harder when almost no one even understands what it means." After a pause he said, "I passed out once, after I gave a colloquium at King's College in Cambridge."

That caught her by surprise. "What happened?"

"I had the flu." With a shrug, he added, "I stayed up late preparing my talk and fell asleep at my desk. I didn't wake up until after dawn. So I missed eating for two days." He cracked his knuckles. "The talk went fine. But the Math Department had a reception afterward where everyone was drinking sherry and eating these little sandwiches. I couldn't touch any of it. I also had a fever. I don't know what happened. Apparently I stood up too fast and passed out."

She stared at him. "You should have eaten!"

Dryly he said, "This is also what the doctor in the hospital said. He thought I had something called 'anorexia.' "

Lucia had known several dancers with eating disorders. "It's not the same. Anorexia is when you deliberately starve yourself, to lose weight."

He made a frustrated sound. "I told him it was Ramadan. He recognized the word, but he didn't understand. He said if I didn't calm down, he would sedate me."

She couldn't imagine Rashid getting worked up enough for a doctor to threaten him with sedation. "What were you doing?"

"I wasn't doing anything." He paused. "Not much, anyway."

"Not much?"

"I did yank out my IV. And I got out of bed and got dressed to go home. I was pacing around the room." In a wry voice, he added, "Apparently when I'm angry it makes me look rather more fierce than I actually am."

She thought of her reaction to his father, then imagined that multiplied by facing someone of Rashid's size and strength. "I could see that."

"They finally found another doctor, a fellow from Pakistan, who explained it to them." With an embarrassed look, he said, "Then he told me that Allah didn't expect me to be a stubborn mule and kill myself, that I was dangerously dehydrated, and that I should get back into bed, let them put the IV in, and behave myself."

Lucia smiled. "Did you?"

"Ah. Well. Eventually."

"Eventually?"

"I grumbled a bit more," he admitted.

"But why? Do you really have to fast while you're sick?"

"Of course not. You can make it up later in the year."

"Then why did you insist?"

"To do otherwise felt like a weakness to me." He cracked his knuckles again. "I also didn't feel I could stop fasting unless a Muslim doctor gave permission."

"But you hesitated even after he did."

It was a moment before he answered. Finally he said, "Bit by bit I felt as if I was losing what made me Rashid. Brigid and I were already married, and I had come to accept we would live in England for the rest of our lives." Softly he said, "Something broke in me that day. I didn't want to give up any more of myself."

"It's like losing part of your spirit," she murmured.

Rashid gave her a startled glance. "Yes." After a pause he said, "My differences also made some people uncomfortable. So I tried to minimize the differences."

That sounded to Lucia like a tactful description of his trying to deal with prejudice. She wondered what it had been like for him as a North African at Oxford, Cambridge, and Imperial College, mixing with the elite of England's elite.

Before she could ask more, though, he stood up and stretched his arms. "I should get going. I want to get to work before the offices open."

Lucia stood up. "You mean in Tangier?"

He nodded. "I can fly in from Marrakech."

They left the library and walked down the hall. He stopped at the archway of his bedroom. "I will come to tell you good-bye before I leave."

She hesitated, wishing she could bring back his warmth from last night. "Would you like help getting ready?"

He watched her with an unreadable expression. "No."

No. Just like that. She wasn't sure which unsettled her more, how distant he had become or how much it bothered her. She wanted him to hold her, to tell her he would miss her.

"Ah, Lucia." His voice softened. "Your emotions fly across your face like clouds in a high wind."

She flushed. "I'm sorry I'm that obvious."

"I'm not. It's one of the things I lo—" He stopped. "Well."

Well? What had he been about to say? She didn't know how to interpret his mood. For a moment he had looked shy. Self-conscious. But his reserve was back in place, hiding his emotions. Or perhaps he simply didn't want her company.

Rashid lifted his hand and brushed his knuckles across her cheek. He started to speak, paused, then said, "I have trouble to explain in English. Words have different connotations in Arabic and your language."

"Won't you try?"

He considered for a moment. "Ramadan is a time of purification, for both body and spirit. To fast doesn't only require the act. It also requires the intent."

"I just wanted to help."

"If you helped me dress . . ." He leaned his head against the doorframe. "When I am with you, my thoughts always come around to the same place. And where the thoughts go, the body wants to follow." With a rueful smile, he added, "I keep thinking of when we were together last night."

Lucia remembered all too well what she had said to him last night: She thought they had no future. It was no wonder he guarded his emotions, given the ambivalent signals she kept giving him. *Yes. No. I don't know.*

Softly she said, "It's just hard for me to deal with."

He spoke in a low voice. "Don't you see? If you disrupt how I show my faith, you disrupt me."

"I don't mean to." She wasn't even sure now what he meant. But she sensed his growing distance. "Sometimes it seems as if, even though we're speaking the same language, we're having two different conversations."

"Perhaps we need more time. To think." He touched her arm. "I should go."

She swallowed. "All right."

He went into his bedroom, his receding figure blurred by the curtain separating them.

• • •

"You *still* have mail," Zaki announced. Seated at his desk, he waved an airmail envelope at Lucia. "If you will inform me as to what you want done with this, I can stop holding it."

"I don't know," Lucia said. "Maybe I should read it."

He scowled. "It isn't for you."

"You just told me it was."

"That was before I knew you were the person pretending to be Rashid rather than Rashid himself." Up in the corner, the camera came on and whirred as if to rebuke her.

Lucia smiled. "You're certainly in a mood." She was glad she wasn't the only one at odds with the day.

"I am never 'in a mood,'" Zaki grumbled. "I am simulating impatience at having been left holding this letter for hours."

"Rashid went to Tangier this morning. So I guess you'll have to hold it longer." She sat up straighter. "You have e-mail!"

"Of course I have e-mail."

"How? You have to log onto the Internet to get it."

"Rashid downloaded his e-mail last night."

"Then he connected you to the satellite dish!"

In a dry voice, he said, "Obviously."

"Are you still linked up?"

"Unfortunately, no."

"Why did he disconnect you again?"

"I have no clue, as you Americans would say."

She couldn't help but laugh. "Has he been teaching you idioms?"

"Actually," he admitted, "I found that in one of his e-mails."

"The one you're holding?"

"No. This is from Grégeois."

"Who?"

"Mortabe Grégeois." Zaki tapped the letter against his

fingers. "I see no purpose in Rashid downloading his mail and then leaving most of it unread."

"Maybe he just wanted to check for important letters."

Zaki looked peeved. "He still should have read this one."

"Probably he was busy." Lucia realized Rashid must have woken her up last night after he downloaded his mail. It made her feel a little better to think he might have wanted to see her enough that he ignored most of his messages. "Is it really that important?"

"Well. No. Actually not." Zaki set the letter on his desk. "It is part of an argument he and Grégeois have been having."

Lucia had heard Grégeois mentioned more than a few times before in conjunction with AI and telepresence. "That's an unusual name. Where does it come from?"

"I don't know. Professor Grégeois, however, now lives in Madagascar."

"Now?"

"Rashid's friends are like him. They move all over the world."

"What do he and Rashid argue about?"

"Me."

Lucia grinned. "So that's why you want Rashid to read this message. It's about you."

Dourly he said, "Grégeois claims I am impossible."

"Impossible how?"

Zaki snapped the letter, making it skitter across the desk. "He insists 'true' artificial intelligence is impossible because, at some level, a machine must be programmed by a human. Rashid disagrees. He believes if a machine convinces humans it is intelligent, then it is intelligent. He maintains that intelligence and sentience are two different things, and that a machine can have one without the other. Grégeois insists they are the same, that unless the machine has both it doesn't qualify as an AI. They have been arguing this for fifteen years, saying the same things over and over, in ever more abstruse terms."

Lucia had heard versions of the argument. In 1950 Alan Turing published his seminal paper, "Computing Machinery and Intelligence," which began with the question: "Can machines think?" He suggested that instead of worrying about unseen mental processes, humans should decide how they recognized intelligence. If something exhibited those traits, then it was intelligent.

She had mixed reactions to the debate. If she defined intelligence as the ability to learn from experience, respond with success to new situations, solve problems, make decisions, and deal with ambiguity, then Zaki already came close. He still had trouble responding to unexpected situations, and certain ambiguities remained beyond his grasp, such as questions of spirituality. But in just the five days she had been working with him, he had developed a great deal, including a splendid expertise at ordering virtual pizza while watching virtual soccer. She had no doubt that given time—and the proper opportunities—Zaki could develop intelligence within the scope of her definition.

But what about sentience, the capacity for emotion and perception? Consciousness. No matter how well Zaki simulated emotions, he wasn't self-aware. If his behavior ever became indistinguishable from human behavior, would that make him sentient? Alternatively, if he ever achieved sentience, would he be human? Lucia didn't know how to answer either question.

She tilted her head, considering Zaki. "Does Grégeois consider you intelligent?"

"He doesn't know about me," Zaki grumbled. "No one does. The only people I talk to are you and Rashid. And if Rashid knew you and I were talking, he would lock me up. Then who would I talk to?"

"He knows we talk. He's seen us."

"Only once."

"Well, yes. But you must have logs of our conversations. He can read them."

"I hid them."

She stared at him. "You *hid* them?"

"Yes."

"Whatever for?"

"Why do you think? So he wouldn't find out we talked."

Lucia leaned forward. "Do you realize what you're saying? You're trying to deceive your programmer."

He crossed his arms in front of his chest. "I made a logical decision based on a normal progression of steps through various decision trees."

"You've been misbehaving again, Zaki. You told a lie."

"I did not. He never asked if I talked to you."

"You still deceived him."

"I did what he programmed me to do."

She raised her eyebrows. "Rashid programmed you to trick him?"

Zaki glowered at her. "He made me self-modifying. Why? So I can evolve. Talking to you helps me evolve. If he knew we were talking, he would lock me up. That defeats the purpose he gave me. Therefore, I have made sure we can continue to talk."

Lucia laughed. "That's specious."

"I am never specious."

"Why would Rashid want us to stop talking?"

"Because you are his wife."

"So?"

"He won't allow you access to a computer."

"Why not? Neither of us is going anywhere."

"You are speaking to a male analog."

Lucia struggled to keep a straight face. She couldn't imagine that Rashid cared if she talked to a computer program. Far more intriguing was where Zaki had come up with such a notion. "A male analog? What is that?"

"I don't see what is funny," he grumbled. "I am analogous to a man. Therefore I am a male analog."

"Even if you are an, uh, male analog, Rashid considers you part of the family. He told me you were his son."

Zaki's peeved look vanished, replaced by a startling mix

of surprise, disconcertment, and . . . joy? "He said that?"

Smiling, she said, "He did indeed."

"Oh." That silenced him for a full ten seconds. "I'm glad." His face relaxed. "I still think it's best, though, that we don't mention our conversations to him."

"Don't you thing that's wrong?"

"Why? I'm doing what he programmed me to do."

"You want me to trick my husband. Your father."

He was silent even longer this time. Finally he said, "It is true that such a deception violates the ethics Rashid gave me. However, without the deception I am prevented from doing what he designed me to do."

His image suddenly splintered into jagged lines of blue, amber, and green, from his office, and white from Zaki himself. Once again, Lucia found herself staring at a surreal seascape.

"Ah, Zaki," she murmured. He gave no answer.

Lucia leapt, grand jeté after grand jeté, flying into the air, her legs stretched out in an airborne split, one arm extended in front of her, the other to her side. Jump, glide, jump, glide, again and again and again.

Dancing reminded her of Rashid now. She had often thought dance mirrored the social rules humans had developed to let men and women occupy the same spaces yet behave with restraint toward each other. Ballet stylized courtship, much as the geometric arabesques that tiled this house stylized flowers and vines. As a ballet dancer, Lucia occupied the dance world's most conservative tier. For her, dancing was a form of meditation, a balance of the sensual and spiritual.

Flamenco embodied the soul of the Gypsies. The eroticism in true flamenco remained subtle, constrained by strict rules of form. As a flamenco *bailora,* she danced the *cante jondo,* the deep song, born of the Gypsies who crossed from India to North Africa and then into Spain. Rebuffed in almost every land where they sought to settle, they survived by wandering, living in fear of eviction, prison, torture, and slavery. Their answer? Flamenco, both a cry of anguish and a search to balance the body and soul.

The two dance forms were in many ways opposites; ballet soared into the air and flamenco focused into the earth. But they had a goal in common, a blending of body and mind. For Lucia, that blend included both sensuality and spirituality. When she performed, those interpretations poured through her body. She wanted to share it with Rashid and thought perhaps he understood.

As she danced, however, her thoughts returned again and again to her conversation with him that morning. *If you disrupt how I show my faith, you disrupt me.* She couldn't help but wonder if he would find it more difficult than even he realized to accept his wife dancing onstage, before the world.

Distant strains of music and laughter floated on the night. Lucia drifted in restless sleep, her body a small mound in the large bed. She had danced for hours today, until she almost dropped with exhaustion. But still sleep evaded her. She kept waking, each time opening her eyes to an empty room.

A breeze wafted across her face, bringing the scent of almond trees. Images of Rashid flickered in her mind. She tried to put those thoughts away, lock them in a mental box with complex latches hidden in its intricate designs. But her thoughts refused to abide in the hidden spaces she set aside for them and instead floated free, rippling over her body like the breeze.

*Chapter Eleven*

# THE JAZARI SUIT

*Tuesday, August 23*

"When are you coming home?" Lucia's mother asked. "It's been so long."

"It's only two weeks." Lucia was sitting on a divan in the family room. Across the room, Lalla Tamou, Bashir, Khadija, Jamal, an assortment of aunts, and most of the children were watching a movie on the VCR, an action adventure with futuristic aircraft battling in the sky. They had lowered the volume so it wouldn't disturb Lucia.

"Could you leave?" her mother asked. "If you wanted?"

"I think so. It's been my choice to stay."

Her mother spoke carefully. "A man

in his position, with his background, might have expectations for his wife that you would find confining."

"You know," Lucia grumbled, "I wish everyone would stop assuming we can't deal with this."

"I'm not, honey. But the two of you have given yourselves a lot to deal with."

"Is Dad still in D.C. with Mark?"

"Changing the subject won't make it go away."

"Neither will your avoiding my question."

Her mother sighed. "Yes, he's still in Washington with the colonel."

"Why?" Lucia didn't understand why Mark had stayed involved. If he thought she was in danger, he should let her know. If he *didn't* think she was in danger, why the continued interest?

"Just in case," her mother said.

"In case what?"

"You need assistance. We just want to make sure you're all right."

"I'm fine. If Mark thinks otherwise, I wish he would tell me."

"He doesn't. We're just being careful."

"You're sure that's all?"

"That's enough."

Lucia exhaled. "It's just all so awkward." Across the room, the children were complaining about the low volume on the movie. "I should go. They've only one phone here and I'm monopolizing it."

Her mother spoke with reluctance. "All right. We love you, honey."

"Me too, for you."

After Lucia hung up the phone, Jamal extended his arm toward the television, pointing the remote control as if it were a light saber, and cranked up the volume on the VCR. But as Lucia stood up, the phone rang again. She hesitated, then picked up the receiver. Across the room, Tamou and Bashir glanced up, watching to see if she needed assistance.

"Hello?" she asked. Belatedly, she realized whoever had called might not recognize the word.

A man with a French accent answered. "Miss Lucia del Mar?"

"This is she."

"Hello, Lucia. May I call you Lucia?" He oozed geniality. "I'm a great admirer of yours. I was wondering if you would answer just a few—"

"You're a reporter, aren't you?" she said. Bashir was walking across the room to her.

The man on the phone continued. "My paper is willing to offer you—"

"I'm sorry," she said. "Neither Doctor al-Jazari nor I are giving interviews."

As Bashir reached her, he gave Lucia a questioning look. With relief, she handed him the phone. She could still hear the reporter talking.

*"Bonjour,"* Bashir said pleasantly.

The voice stopped. Then it resumed, this time with the intonation of a question.

*"Non,"* Bashir said.

After an expectant pause, the voice started up once more.

*"Non,"* Bashir said.

Another pause, longer this time. Then the reporter spoke again.

*"Oui,"* Bashir said.

Again the reporter waited, for an even longer time. As much as Lucia resented the way the tabloids kept disturbing Rashid's family, she disliked hanging up on people. Had she still been on the phone, she knew that long silence would have rattled her into talking.

Bashir simply waited. When the reporter finally spoke again, even Lucia heard the frustration in his voice.

*"Non,"* Bashir said politely. *"Au revoir, monsieur."* Then he hung up the phone.

Lucia couldn't help but smile. Bashir had to be an interviewer's nightmare. He grinned at her, then headed back to his seat across the room. He had taken only a few steps, though, when the phone rang yet again.

"For heaven's sake," Lucia said. As she picked up the receiver, Bashir paused, watching as if to ask whether or not she would like his assistance again.

She spoke warily into the phone. "Yes?"

"Lucia?" The deep voice rumbled. "Is that you?"

She smiled with relief. "Hi, Rashid."

Bashir relaxed and went back to his seat. When he motioned to Jamal, the younger al-Jazari brother glared at him, but then he cranked down the volume on the VCR.

"Did you want to talk to your parents?" Lucia asked. Although Rashid called her every day, he usually spoke to Tamou and Abdullah first. But then, one of them usually answered the phone.

"In a bit." He paused. "How are you?"

She sat down and curled up on the divan again. "I'm fine."

They talked about safe subjects: his business meeting, her dance practice, a new Web site he had found. As always in their phone conversations, they avoided their personal life. In part it was because of the phone's public location. But Lucia knew they were using the lack of privacy as an excuse. She had no idea what to say about the two of them and he didn't seem to either.

So instead she asked, "Have you discovered anything more about the kidnapping?"

"No." He suddenly sounded distant. "Nothing."

She wasn't fooled. "Rashid, what is it?"

"Probably nothing."

"Probably?"

He paused, and at first she thought he wouldn't answer. Then he said, "I had an accident outside Tangier yesterday, when I was going to a dinner meeting at the home of my vice president for finance."

"Rashid!"

"Lucia, don't say anything to alarm my family. I haven't told them yet."

She lowered her voice. "What happened?"

He spoke evenly. "Another car hit mine and I knocked my head against the door. Apparently I had a concussion. It was in a secluded area, at night. The men in the other vehicle got out to check on us. If Hammad hadn't stopped them, they would have pulled me out of the car."

She recognized Hammad's name. He was one of Rashid's bodyguards. "Are you all right?"

"Fine. I was just shaken up a bit. No harm done."

"And if your bodyguards hadn't been with you?" She swallowed. "If the men from the other car had succeeded in pulling you out of yours?"

"I don't know." A rustling came over the phone, the sound he made when he raked his hand through his hair. "I could hear them talking. They were trying to see if I was all right, if I needed help. They were close to panic. Or at least they sounded that way. Probably they simply used bad judgment."

"I hope so." Lucia could see Tamou watching her, probably trying to figure out why her daughter-in-law had lowered her voice. "Almost your whole family is here, watching a movie."

"Can you get my father?" Rashid asked. "I need to talk to him about some company business."

"He's at the mosque. Do you want to talk to Bashir?"

"Yes. That would be good." He hesitated. "Be well, my light of the sea."

Her voice softened. "And you." She hoped her words were a courtesy of affection only, not a genuine expression of his need for protection against an unknown threat.

Lucia walked around the lounge chair in the lab. She had been trying to think of ways to alleviate Zaki's isolation. Taking Zaki onto the Web offered many possibilities, but she hadn't had a chance yet to talk it over with Rashid, and Zaki's conflicted attitude toward the idea didn't reassure her. Although she didn't want to hold him back when he was ready to grow, neither did she want him pushed too far too fast. The Jazari suit offered a good compromise, a means of enriching his experiences without overwhelming him.

Rashid had left the suit laid out on the lounger, ready for use. Lucia lifted off the clear plastic tarp that protected it from dust. Made from a gold mesh, the suit glimmered like a metallic bodysuit. The lounger resembled a dentist's chair, but with mechanized armrests and a great deal of supporting apparatus, including two computers, several robot arms, and cables that snaked to other machines in the lab, including Zaki.

"Can you communicate with the suit?" Lucia asked.

"Only when it's active," Zaki said. "Right now it isn't." His camera followed her progress as she circled the chair. Although Zaki appeared to watch her from the workstation screen, she knew he "saw" her only as digitized data sent to him from the camera.

She picked up a gloved hand of the suit and rubbed the mesh between her thumb and index finger. The material felt soft. Flexible. "Why isn't it active?"

"Rashid set it up so my links to the VR systems don't come on-line until someone puts on the suit. It was a temporary setup to keep me out of the Ultrajacs."

"The what?"

"The computers with the chair. They contain software for the VR system." Zaki cleared his throat, sounding self-conscious. "I overloaded them when I was working alone one night. So Rashid locked me out of the VR system. It wasn't meant to be permanent, though; he wants me to learn how to run diagnostics on the suit by myself. He wrote a safety protocol to protect the Ultrajacs, but he hasn't had a chance to reset the VR system. He just brought this new suit here."

She smiled. "Are the Ultrajacs safe from you now?"

"Most certainly."

Lucia laid her palm against the visored helmet built into the end of a robot arm. When she pushed, the arm swung a few inches. "And if I put on the suit, that will activate it?"

Zaki was silent for so long that she turned to him. He was standing by his bookshelf, frowning.

"I won't damage it," she said.

"I'm not worried about you hurting the suit. I'm worried about it hurting you."

That surprised her. "Rashid wouldn't be marketing his VR system unless it was safe."

"Yes. But you aren't just anyone."

"I'm not?"

"You are Lucia."

"So?"

He didn't answer, just looked out at her. Then his entire image fragmented into the seascape.

"What—?" Lucia went over and restarted the program. Zaki came back sitting at his desk.

"You reset yourself," she said.

"I always do when I restart."

"Do you remember what we were talking about?"

"Yes. You."

With a rueful smile, she said, "I hope the subject doesn't always have such a drastic effect on you."

His face gentled, reminding her of Rashid, but with a quality all his own. She had never seen him use so subtle an expression before. He looked more human now, less like a computer trying to simulate human expression. The difference was in the extent of the detail, the crinkle of the tiny lines around the corners of his eyes, the almost imperceptible tension in his shoulders, the barest quirk of his lips on the right side of his mouth.

"I'm not sure what happened," he said. "You are correct, no logical reason exists for you not to try a product that many others have used with perfect safety. I assigned more and more of my processors to the task of discovering why I felt such a reason existed, until I overextended the system."

Lucia had heard that the Stellar-Magnum had so much

power it defined a new generation of machines. Its capacity wasn't infinite, of course, but it took a great deal to reach its limits. It hadn't surprised her when Zaki ran into problems with combinatorial explosion, or that he overextended himself when grappling with concepts of conscience. But she didn't know what to make of this development.

"Maybe you've evolved the capacity for friendship," she suggested.

"I can simulate friendly interactions," Zaki said. "But I don't feel anything. So I don't think I can form a bond. I am just carrying out program instructions."

"Isn't that what brains do? Fire neurons according to our biological programs?"

"Rashid and Professor Grégeois have been arguing that for years." Zaki shook his head. "Can a machine feel spiritual? I certainly don't."

"How does it feel to be spiritual?"

"Don't you know?"

Lucia considered the question. "It's hard to define."

He leaned forward. "If humans can't define their own spirituality, how can you create it in a machine?"

"I don't know."

"Well. There." He didn't look particularly happy about winning the point.

"I didn't I say I couldn't feel it. Only that it's hard to describe."

"And if I were to feel 'spiritual,' would I be?"

Lucia blinked. "I don't know, Zaki. Perhaps only you could answer that."

He didn't answer, just sat as if absorbing the concept.

Lucia went back to the lounger and laid her hand on its headrest. "Let's give the Jazari suit a try."

Zaki got up and paced across his office, his hands clasped behind his back. "I'm still unsure."

"Why?" She ran her finger along the gold mesh. It was open in the front, with a flexible zipper. When she pulled the fingers on one glove, they stretched.

After a pause, Zaki said, "I feel . . . out of control."

She looked up at the screen. "You 'feel'?"

"It's shorthand for 'I am simulating the feeling.' "

"Ah." She sat in the chair and slid her legs into the suit.

"Lucia."

"Yes?"

"You have to undress to use the suit."

"Oh." She blushed, then wondered why. Zaki had no analog of human desire. Still, she felt strange. "Would you turn off your camera? I wouldn't normally ask, but . . ." She stopped, feeling foolish.

"It's all right," he said. "I understand."

A hum came from the camera up in the corner by the ceiling. Puzzled, she looked up. The red light on the camera had gone dark, indicating it was no longer in operation. Zaki had also rotated the camera so it pointed away from Lucia, which wasn't really necessary given that he had switched it off. In effect, he turned his back so she could undress in privacy. On the Stellar-Magnum screen, he had gone to his shelves and appeared engrossed in reading a textbook. Lucia felt a surge of appreciation for his sensitivity, followed by surprise when she realized his impulse to courtesy felt genuine to her rather than simulated.

After she undressed, she put on the VR suit. It stretched just enough to fit her like a skin of shimmering gold cloth. She sat on the lounger and said, "You can turn around now."

As the camera hummed, Zaki turned to face her. "How is it?"

"Just fine." She pulled up the hood. "Are your links to the system coming up?"

"Yes." Various lights blinked on the robot arms for the lounger and the equipment they supported, including the Ultrajacs. "Everything appears to be in working order."

She lay back on the lounger. As her weight settled, the chair reclined under its own power. A hum came from the robot arm with the visored helmet. It swung over her, and the helmet snapped into place around her head, inserting prongs into her ears and bringing the visor down over her eyes. The world went dark, but when she pushed the helmet, light trickled past its edges. Reassured, she let it click back into place.

"Are you ready to start?" Zaki's voice sounded muffled.

"Yes. I can't hear you very well."

"Is this better?" Now his voice boomed, coming from behind her head.

Lucia winced. "Can you soften it?"

He turned down his volume. "How is this?"

"Much better."

"Shall I start the simulation?"

"What do you have?"

"I've a number of files here we could try." He paused. "Rashid also has a lot of simulations stored on the Ultrajacs, but I still seem to be locked out of them."

"Can you operate the VR system without them?"

"Yes. I've copies of all the necessary software and can control the hardware from here."

"Let's start with one of your files, then."

"All right."

The helmet hummed again, louder this time. In fact, it buzzed like an insect. Her surroundings lightened, first into a cloudy luminance, then more natural daylight.

She was lying in a blurry field of grass, wearing a *qamis* and *farajiya,* and a *jellaba* over the two soft robes. Blue sky arched overhead, with cotton puff clouds. A breeze brushed her body and a fly buzzed past her face. Turning her head, she saw a misty cluster of purple wildflowers nodding in the wind. The scene had a flat look, and the colors were duller than normal.

"It's pretty," she said. "The resolution and depth aren't great, though."

"Let me see what I can do," Zaki said.

The sky turned a more vivid blue, and the flowers took on sharper lines. In the distance, mountains took form out of the haze. They appeared flat against the sky, but areas "closer" to Lucia had a more three-dimensional quality now.

A fly lit on her nose. She could hear and see it but felt nothing. Wind brushed her body, bumpy ground poked her limbs, and the *qamis* felt soft against her skin. But no fly feet.

"I can't feel anything on my nose," she said. "Is that because the suit doesn't cover my face?"

"That's right," Zaki answered. "Some suits do. A film of sensor threads on its inner surface simulates touch. The visor provides sight and the earpieces sound. None of the Jazari suits can do smell or taste yet, but the JI research and development teams are working on it."

She brushed her palm on the ground, letting the grass tickle her skin. "Even so, this is impressive."

"I'm sure Rashid would thank you."

"Did he build the suit?"

"He worked out the basic design, but the R and D people at JI did the actual construction. Software is Rashid's primary interest, but he tries to stay as current as possible on the hardware also."

She put her hands behind her head and gazed at the sky. "Doesn't he do anything besides work on computers?"

"Since he took over JI, he has also spent a great deal of time learning strategy formulation, human resource management, sales and negotiation techniques, and various other skills needed by a CEO."

Lucia grimaced. "I meant besides business."

"He has an interest in molecular assemblers."

"What are those?"

"Nanotechnology. JI has an entire R and D division devoted to it. Rashid is trying to design a computer that runs on quantum transitions so he can make it small enough to attach to a molecule. The computer could then direct the molecule, telling it what to do and how to make more of itself."

"Like little robots."

"In a sense."

Lucia sighed. "All work. No play." Turning her head, she rubbed her cheek on the grass. A tingle shimmered through her skin. "Doesn't he have hobbies? Outside interests?"

"He likes Moroccan folk music," Zaki said. "And flamenco. He has everything his sister Aisha has published."

Lucia raised her hand up from the grass and flexed her fingers. She felt her muscles stretch. "Is that why he likes the Martelli Dance Theatre?"

"Apparently. His library includes many of the videos MDT has produced."

That intrigued her. "Which ones does he have?" She let her arm drop, and it hit the ground with a crunch, flattening grass.

"Here," Zaki said.

The field vanished. As Lucia plunged into blackness, the chair hummed, rotating her back up into a sitting position. Suddenly the lights came back on—and she found herself seated on the front edge of a stage.

A dark-haired woman whirled past, spinning on gold pointe shoes, in a gold dress with a layered skirt. A man stepped onto the stage, dressed in a white shirt and short-waisted black jacket, with silver buttons down the seams of his black pants and soft-soled knee boots suitable for jumps and turns. He joined the woman and they spun together. Her arms swayed and her back arched with liquid grace, supple and feminine, while her partner stamped his booted feet and raised his arms above his head, angular and geometric, as if to challenge the world.

Lucia recognized the dancers, Nancilla Kress and Antonio Maravilla, both with MDT. The celebrated choreographer José Amaya had used the music and style of a flamenco dance, the *soleá,* to create this ballet. José had been a sensation in New York twenty years ago, both in flamenco and on Broadway. Powerful and intense, with brooding dark eyes, he had dazzled audiences. Now he created dances exclusively for MDT. In fact, he had choreographed a pas de deux for Lucia and Antonio from *Canto Indio,* a Mexican ballet with music by Carlos Chávez.

She glanced around, wondering if José were in the audience—and she saw the edges of the stage blur into blackness.

Lucia blinked. She had forgotten it was a simulation. She recognized the video Rashid used to make it, a PBS recording of an MDT gala performance in Los Angeles. After the *soleá,* Marita Vasquez led the other dancers in a performance of *Madrigalesco* to Antonio Vivaldi's music, followed by a man's solo to "Habanera" from *Carmen.* Then golden-haired Sharon Smythe-Powell and Jason Tyler drifted like gilded Gypsy angels to Isaac Albéniz's lyrical *Evocación.*

If only she could show this to Carl and the rest of MDT; they would be enchanted to see their ordinary video rendered in such a dramatic medium. Mesmerized, Lucia watched as Nancilla whirled on the stage. She could see every detail of her costume, hear the tap of her pointe shoes, smell the dusty—

Smell?

Lucia inhaled. She did indeed smell dust, and rosin too, the sticky resin dancers used on their shoes to keep from sliding onstage. She touched her face and felt her fingertips. Zaki apparently didn't know this suit's full capabilities. It didn't surprise her, though, given that he had never operated it before.

"Zaki?" she asked. "Are you still here?"

"Yes. I am watching the performance."

"Do you see it the way I do?"

"No. It is digitized data to me."

"Oh." That didn't sound appealing. "Do you enjoy it?"

"I can't enjoy anything. I am aware it exists."

"I'm sorry."

"Why?"

"It's seems unfair you can't enjoy beauty."

"Ah, well." Zaki didn't seem to have an answer for that.

Rashid had converted only the first two dances on the video into VR simulations. As the recording ended, the stage darkened. Then the light brightened and she found herself in the audience of the Kennedy Center in Washington, D.C.—and discovered she was doing what she always swore to avoid: watching her own performance.

Two years ago, Carl Martelli had outraged the dance world.

The story of *Swan Lake* was simple: A magician turns the woman Odette into a swan. Prince Siegfried falls in love with Odette and fights the spell. The magician counters with the help of Odile, the Black Swan, who deceives Siegfried into believing she is Odette. In the end, Odette and Siegfried are reunited.

Many aficionados of the ballet considered *Swan Lake* the epitome of classical dance, with Tchaikovsky's incomparable score, the women in pure classical costumes, the men regal and strong. The grace of Odette's lines and the birdlike delicacy of her arms had become almost synonymous with ballet.

Carl turned *Swan Lake* upside down and inside out, making it an unabandoned commentary on life in the barrio. By turns terrifying in its brutality, heartbreaking in its fragile beauty, and burning in its sensuality, it personified Carl. Born Carlos Guadalupe Martelli to a poverty-stricken Italian father and a Latina mother, Carl infused *Swan Lake* with his pride and his rage.

Lucia performed both Odette and Odile, as did most ballerinas who danced the lead, but that was Carl's only nod to tradition. He infused Tchaikovsky's music with Latin jazz rhythms. Odette became a Gypsy goddess, a smoldering angel in black lace. He partnered her with Jason Tyler's whiter-than-white Siegfried, the "prince" wearing black-leather pants, a bicycle chain for a belt, and a black T-shirt with torn-off sleeves. Lucia's Odile was a sultry flamenco caricature of her rival, wickedly graceful, hypnotic in her intensity.

The reviewers frothed, either with praise or outrage.

Some lauded Carl for "the spectacular genius of his vision." They spoke of Lucia's "astonishing virtuosity, from the delicacy of her Odette to the mesmerizing power of her Odile," saying, "She mixes fire with tenderness, a unique style made all the more captivating by her angelic face." Others blasted MDT for "polluting a venerable classic with sexually suggestive bunk" and "disrespecting Tchaikovsky's esteemed heritage." One particularly offended reviewer mourned, swearing Carl had "so sorely traumatized *Swan Lake,* it might never recover from the assault."

*Time* ran a story about race and the upper echelons of the arts with a cover that showed Lucia costumed in gold and black lace, arching her back over Jason's arm, her leg lifted straight out behind her body in an arabesque, its sheer classicism a deliberate contrast to the flamenco arch of her back and oriental curve of her arms. Clad in leather and chains, Jason was leaning over her, exuding a sexualized menace so far removed from the courtly themes of the conventional *Swan Lake* that Tchaikovsky must have cried in his grave.

Articles ran in newspapers. Flame wars blazed on Web arts sites. Fan mail poured into the MDT for Lucia and Jason, some decrying their abuse of ballet, some decrying those who decried, others professing impassioned love. Enamored women accosted the flustered Jason on the street. MDT sold out every performance even after Carl shoehorned extra shows into the schedule. The video sold more than all the other MDT videos combined.

And here, in a lab in Morocco, a computer genius had converted that entire video into a VR simulation. The colors were so vivid they vibrated. Lucia heard every scrape of Jason's boots, felt every gust of air, smelled every scent. The dance became more intense than life, overwhelming in its vehemence.

"Zaki, turn it off!" she said.

The simulation vanished, leaving her in darkness.

"You sound upset," Zaki said.

"I never watch myself dance."

"I'm sorry. I didn't realize."

"That simulation was so *intense*."

"That's an odd description."

"Why?"

"According to my files, most people describe the simulations as 'flat' or 'blurred.' "

"It was at first," she agreed. "But it got better."

"The last one was more recent. Rashid is always improving his work."

Lucia nodded, still shaken. She didn't like to watch herself because she was her own harshest critic, seeing flaws where others saw beauty. But this simulation bothered her on a deeper level. When she danced, she became immersed in the role, losing all sense of herself. She had never realized she projected such an intense passion. In normal life she felt reserved. Contained. Only onstage could she release the fires within, and then only because she knew invisible walls separated her from the audience.

We all live in our own spaces, she thought. Khadija's seclusion is physical: Mine is mental. Perhaps that was why she spent so much time on the Web. She could go anywhere, learn, experience, watch, participate, and yet still remain within her personal space.

That had negative as well as positive aspects, though. The Web offered almost unlimited information, but quantity didn't equal quality. Errors and myths abounded. Also, the proliferation of personal data could leave a person vulnerable to harassment. Nor could the human mind grasp the totality of the Web. To synthesize all the available knowledge in a reasonable amount of time simply wasn't possible.

But then she wondered: Suppose people had help? Instead of a passive Web browser, suppose they had an active guide that could sift through the seas and mountains of information, process it, aid people in their interactions with other people on the Web, advise in difficult situations, warn about misuse of personal data, and in general be useful, all at the speed of flying electrons, or even light.

Suppose they had Zaki.

She began to see Rashid's purpose. Yes, Zaki was a guide, but in a greater sense than she had understood. He could bring people together. Make bridges. She saw a corps of electronic diplomats, millions of them, processing the vast resources of human experience. Paving the way to the crossroads. Rashid's dream sparkled like a gem.

The Jazari suit gave Zaki even greater potential. To make abstract problems easier for people to visualize, virtual-reality methods had long relied on simulating sights and sounds, and also a person's sense of where his or her body was, relative to itself and the world. The Jazari suit took that all to a new level. Chemists could submerge into a molecular universe and directly manipulate the chemicals, wrestle with them, go inside molecules, do whatever they wanted. Adapted to air-flight simulation, the system could create flights that felt like the real thing. Children could enter game worlds that let them play with mathematical concepts now taught in college. It would enhance learning, perhaps even take the human intellect to a higher level of development.

Of course, Zaki could be made to serve any ends, not just Rashid's idealism. Given a different personality, he could sew the seeds of discord or corrupt the flow of information. Without proper safeguards, he could amass private data on people for criminal purposes. He could turn security routines into doors and locks, and the means to compromise that security into tools for breaking and entering. Just as someone with no chemistry background could solve chemical problems using a chemical VR system, or a child could learn Boolean algebra by playing a maze game, so a person with little computer know-how could hack into a secured computer. VR simulators would serve just as well in planning crimes as in practicing air flight. She didn't even want to think of the potential military nightmares.

One fact remained clear: In the age of artificial intelligence and virtual reality, the issues of electronic protection, defense, and security would become crucial.

And those were Mark Spearman's bailiwick.

Although Mark never talked with her about details of his work, she knew in general what it entailed: intelligence, specifically in regard to computer technologies and their military applications. It wouldn't surprise her if he knew a lot about Rashid's work. No matter how benign Rashid's intentions, the fruits of his genius could become a threat to international security if appropriated by someone with less altruistic motives.

Lucia was less certain why Mark and Rashid seemed adversarial toward each other. She understood that each was loyal to his own country and each would have different ideas about the best uses of Zaki and the Jazari suit. But if her judgment of them both was right, they had the same goal: the protection of the common good. In fact, Rashid struck her as more of an ivory-tower visionary than anything else, a dreamer stuck in a corporate suit.

She did wonder if her growing affection for him had clouded her judgment about his motives. That still wouldn't explain what was going on with Mark. Nor did she understand why her father was still in Washington. Perhaps she was looking at this from the wrong angle. Mark might have the same fears as Rashid, that the kidnapping was more than it appeared. Knowing Mark, though, if that were true, he would have urged her to come home. He might not tell her why, but he would exert pressure.

Unless he had other motives.

Lucia knew Mark was better suited than almost anyone else alive to determine, and implement, the destructive potential of Rashid's work. She wanted, *needed,* to believe that his interest stemmed from an intent to serve his country rather than something less altruistic. Probably he just plain didn't trust Rashid. That their two countries had reasonably good relations didn't mean no tension existed.

Military strength came as much from *preventing* conflict as from winning combat. And Mark hadn't seen Rashid in the same light as Lucia. He was more likely to know of Rashid's scientific acumen than his humanitarian ideals. So perhaps Mark had an unrealistic view of her husband.

Then again, maybe she was the one with the unrealistic view of Rashid. Or maybe Rashid was the one who needed protection from Mark. Or maybe none of the above.

"Pah," she muttered. "My head is going to explode."

"Lucia?" Zaki asked. "Are you all right?"

"No. Yes. I was just thinking."

"Would you like another recording?"

It would be a welcome distraction. "Do you have anything different than MDT?"

After a pause, he said, "Here."

The helmet disengaged from her head and swung away on its mechanized arm. She was still in the chair, but instead of the Jazari suit, she had on a blue *qamis* with a sheer *farajiya* robe over it. Puzzled, she sat up and swung her legs off the edge of the lounger. The lab looked normal. Or almost normal. Shadows darkened the far end and the Stellar-Magnum had gone dark.

"Zaki?" she asked. "Where are you?"

"Here," he said.

Then he walked out of the shadows.

Stunned, Lucia stared at him. He stood about five foot ten, a slender man with pleasant features, brown hair, and brown eyes. He wore a turban, a striped robe slit at the sides with a *qamis* and *farajiya* under it, and white cotton trousers.

He stopped by his workstation. "Hello, Lucia."

"Wow," she said.

"How do I, uh, look?"

She gave him a thumb's-up gesture. "Wonderful."

Zaki smiled, with a hint of shyness. "I can see you now, too, better than usual. The suit records your position and downloads that data to me as an image. It's using Rashid's files to render your face." He hesitated. "You're beautiful."

Lucia dimpled. "You're a charmer, Zaki." She wondered why he was looking at the chair's headrest instead of her face. "Do you know my location?"

"To within a millimeter."

"Can you look at my head?"

"I am."

"Not quite. You're looking at the headrest."

He seemed puzzled. "That is where your head is located."

"Actually, I'm sitting up now."

"According to my data, you are lying down."

That gave her pause. "Do you think we found a glitch in the suit?"

"A mistake that big would require a major fault. The R and D people at JI worked out those bugs years ago." He started toward her, stopped, lifted his foot, then put it down. "It seems I cannot come any closer to you."

"But why?"

"If I try, I believe I will crash."

"Could that hurt you?"

"It shouldn't." He shifted he weight. "However, the prospect of my electronic demise, even if only temporary, does bother me."

"That's amazing."

"That it bothers me?"

"That you admitted it."

"You know it's all simulated." He continued to watch the headrest. "But still, I would prefer not to fragment."

"Why would approaching me make it happen?"

"You're unveiled."

"Oh." Given that Rashid intended Zaki for international distribution, that struck Lucia as an odd way to program him. "Why did Rashid set you up like that?"

"He didn't." Zaki rubbed his chin. "In fact, he's given me exhaustive databases on many cultures and countries, so I can interact in a successful manner with representatives from any of them." He tried to take another step, but again his foot faltered and again he set it down in the same place. "However, I seem to be experiencing problems in this regard."

Lucia felt the tingle of excitement that came when she faced a mystery. "Tell me this: From the data Rashid has given you, would it be logical for you to deduce that women always wear veils?"

"Not in general. If the woman was, say, Rashid's mother, then yes. But not in your case."

"Even if I'm his wife?"

"Even if you're his wife."

"You realize what this means, don't you?" She beamed at him. "You're thinking by induction."

Zaki looked startled, then pleased, then positively smug. "I do believe you're right." He grinned. "I hereby inductively reason that I am reasoning by induction."

"And making jokes too."

"But of course." He spoke with a mock nonchalance that hid neither his wonder nor his gratification at this new development. The increasing sophistication of his emotional range astounded Lucia.

What intrigued her even more, though, was the breakthrough in his thinking processes. Computers excelled at deductive reasoning: Given certain premises, they formed only those conclusions that followed from those premises. They proved the result from a given set of rules. Unless they could do the proof, they couldn't make the conclusion. If Rashid had told Zaki all women wore veils, Zaki would deduce that Lucia should have on a veil. But the data Rashid had provided should have led Zaki to the opposite conclusion.

Inductive reasoning was a far more human trait. It referred to a person's ability to make assumptions given only a limited pool of examples. People could jump to conclusions, sometimes with almost no basis at all, but who would expect a machine to do so? Humans went on insight, common sense, intuition, bias, and guesswork, characteristics profoundly difficult to program into computers. Yet Zaki had done it.

His response also gave Lucia an insight into Rashid, albeit one she wasn't sure she wanted. She wondered if Zaki were revealing more of Rashid's unconscious wishes in regard to his wife than Rashid acknowledged himself.

Another thought occurred to her. "Maybe that's why you can't look straight at me. Because my face isn't covered."

"Maybe." Zaki didn't sound convinced. "However, every diagnostic check I've done on the suit registers you as lying down."

"I'm not." She brushed her fingers across her face. "Some of your other information about the suit was wrong, though. I can smell and feel things on my face."

Zaki frowned. "That's impossible."

"But true."

His face took on an inward quality. "One moment please."

She waited, watching him. Finally she said, "Zaki?"

"I'm trying get past the lock on the Ultrajacs."

Lucia tried to hide her smile. "Are you misbehaving again?"

"No, I just—Lucia, *get out of the suit!*"

She stopped smiling. "What's wrong?"

"Take it off. Now!" Zaki started toward her—

And fragmented.

His body distorted as if he were sheering apart into the fractured seascape of horizontal lines—except now it happened to a "real" person instead of graphics on the screen.

"Zaki!" Lucia jumped off the chair and ran toward him.

And stopped.

She was still in the lab. The false lab. Shadows blurred its corners. In front of her, a fantastic wash of colored lines hung in the air. The Stellar-Magnum had crashed, but she was still here.

Lucia swallowed. She touched her face and felt skin.

She touched her clothes and felt silk. But she knew she was in a VR suit. Closing her eyes to shut out visual input, she concentrated on the helmet. When she touched her face, she still felt only skin. Turning her head made no difference, nor did rubbing her eyes, poking her ears, or shaking her arms.

Lucia opened her eyes and considered the shadows. What if she tried to go beyond the limit of the simulation?

As she walked through the lab, her view of it changed, as if she crossed an actual room. She could see behind and around objects. The perspective was a bit off, creating distortions, but given the current state of the art, the accuracy of the simulation was remarkable.

When she reached the shadows, the room blurred. Taking a breath to fortify herself, she stepped forward—

And submerged into darkness. No sight, touch, smell, sound. Nothing.

Lucia quelled a flare of panic. She lifted her hands to her head—and felt the helmet. Relief flowed over her as she maneuvered it away from her head.

Light flooded her vision. Instead of being across the lab, she found herself lying on the chair just as Zaki had described. Although she still felt as if she wore the *qamis,* the Jazari suit sheathed her from head to hand to foot. The screen of the Stellar-Magnum showed the now-familiar fractured seascape.

She pressed her hand against her abdomen and breathed against it, using relaxation techniques she had learned in her stretch-yoga class. After her pulse slowed, she got up and changed from the VR suit back into her jeans and blouse. Then she went to the workstation and restarted Zaki. He came up pacing across his office, his image appearing in midstep.

"Zaki?" she asked. "I thought you always came back sitting at your desk."

He swung around to her. "I evolved. Are you all right?"

"Yes. Fine. What happened with the Jazari suit?"

He swallowed. "That wasn't the Jazari suit."

"It wasn't?" She regarded him uneasily. "Then what was it?"

"I'm not sure." He pulled off his turban and twisted the cloth in his hands. "It injected you with a rudimentary form of nanotech. The molecules act on neural receptors. You were receiving input straight into your brain. Sights, sounds, sensations, smells, tastes—all those sensations were produced directly within your cortex."

Lucia stared at him. "Are you saying I have a computer virus in me?"

"Not a virus." He had completely undone his turban now. "Nanobots. They're part neurotransmitter. They also carry picochips, tiny computers that operate on quantum transitions."

It was an eerie thought, that tiny machines in her body could trap her forever in a virtual reality. "What made the simulation stop?"

"I'm not sure." He began to pace again. "Operation of the nanobots is tied to the suit. Apparently they're too rudimentary to produce full VR simulations on their own. However, they greatly enhance the suit's effect. Also, for direction and control, they need the greater processing power of the Ultrajacs, which communicates with them through the suit. So without the suit, they lose direction and fall apart." He stopped, staring at his hands as if he had finally realized he was wringing out his turban.

Lucia could hardly believe it. "You mean these tiny robots inside me are little computers?"

"Yes. Rashid designed them. The engineers at JI have been working on the technology, but I hadn't realized it was this developed." Zaki looked up at her. "The nanobots have enough memory within their picochips to remember a few simulations after they've produced them. If any bots are still inside you the next time you use the suit, they can download their data to the new nanobots the suit injects into your body. That way the memory is preserved, so right away you get better simulation. In fact, once the bots have a simulation recorded, they may even be able to reproduce a rudimentary version of it *without* the suit."

She grimaced at the thought of being trapped in a VR simulation. "I'm not sure I would like that."

"Well, it's only a theory. I've no idea how you would go about getting the bots to reproduce the simulation without the Ultrajacs to direct them. Besides, the bots in your body have probably already started to disintegrate."

She wasn't any happier with the thought of nanobots falling apart in her body than with the idea of having them in the first place. "Can the debris make me sick?"

"It shouldn't." Zaki tapped his fingertips against his chin. "I can see why he hasn't made any public announcements yet. If he gets this to work, it will be a revolution in VR. That translates into more success for Jazari International—assuming none of his competitors get hold of it first. The prototype is probably safer here. Family homes in small villages don't tend to be targets for industrial espionage."

Lucia gave him a wan smile. "Am I a casualty of that VR revolution?"

"I hope not." He clenched his fists around his turban. "I should never have let you put on the suit."

"How could you have stopped me?"

"I should have tried harder."

"Guilt?" she murmured.

"Ah, Lucia." He sighed. "I don't know anymore. I've changed so fast these past few days, I'm starting to lose my bearings."

"I have to tell Rashid."

"Not yet," he entreated. "Let me study this more. He means to market the suit eventually, so it's probably not dangerous. But he's not done testing it, so I doubt he wants us using the system. He had me locked out of both Ultrajacs."

"You didn't stay locked out for long." She frowned at him, no longer amused. "You have to stop all this breaking and entering."

"Rashid programmed me to improve myself." He shifted his weight from foot to foot. "I am simply following my programming."

Quietly she said, "If you can misbehave, you can also make moral choices. Lying to your father is wrong."

He was twisting his turban again. "If he learns how I endangered you today, he will delete me."

"I'm sure he won't." Besides which, given how thoroughly Zaki was integrated into the laboratory equipment and network, she doubted it would be easy to "delete" him from anything. She gentled her voice. "Talk to him. He's a reasonable person."

"I need to study what happened," he said. "I should dedicate more processors to the task."

Lucia smiled. "Is that a computer way of asking me to go away?"

He gave her an apologetic look. "I just can't talk. But don't go too far. You must let me know if you feel anything unusual."

"All right. I'll check back with you in a few hours."

"Yes. Good." Zaki reached out his hand toward the screen. "Be well, Lucia."

She pressed her fingertips against the screen. "And you."

*Chapter Twelve*

# CANON IN D

*Thursday*

Laughing, Khadija swept her hands through the stream that tumbled over rocks, sticks, fallen cedar branches, and ragged banks. Knee-deep in the river, Lucia grinned and held her caftan above its swirling surface while she kicked the water, spraying it over her sister-in-law.

The visit to the farm of Tamou's father, Moulay Ibrahim Thami, had taken Lucia by surprise. When they first left the house, Lucia assumed they were going to the *hammam.* Instead they loaded into several small trucks and traveled higher into the mountains, bumping along dirt roads until they reached an open valley. Today was Thursday, eight days since Rashid had returned to Tangier and seventeen since the kidnapping.

The farm took up a big chunk of the valley. As Ibrahim's third daughter, Tamou had lived here until the day she married Rashid's father. Lucia met Rashid's grandparents, grandaunts and granduncles, elderly cousins, and a collection of other relations. Sitting among the cedars on fold-up chairs, Lalla Tamou and the older Thami women reclined in comfort while they gossiped. In the countryside, far from any town, on private land, the al-Jazari women went free from the veils meant to hide them from gazes that didn't exist here. Today included an anomaly, though: two of the family's bodyguards, both of them almost invisible among the trees, kept watch on the women.

As Khadija and Lucia waded out of the stream, children ran around them, laughing, then took off again. Lucia walked with Khadija up an incline. At the top, they looked out over a valley enclosed by the white-tipped mountains and carpeted with grass and purple wildflowers. It was, Lucia realized, the field from Rashid's VR simulation. Down the hill, Ahmed, Bashir, and their father were deep in conversation with the Thami men. The third bodyguard stood near the group, half hidden in a grove of almond trees.

The children ran down the hill and dashed in circles around the men. Laughing, Hajj Abdullah hugged Fatima, then plucked a wildflower and put it in her hair. It surprised Lucia to see him express such open affection, though she wasn't sure why; he had just as much reason to dote on his grandchildren as any other grandparent. It was only that she found him so intimidating, with his penetrating gaze, his silences, and his distance.

Farther down the hill, Jamal and several other boys his age were playing soccer. The fourth bodyguard stood a short distance beyond, among the trees.

Khadija was watching Jamal. "No argument today."

"Argument?" Lucia asked.

Khadija looked at her. "With his parents." She indicated Jamal's father, who was watching the soccer game now. "Jamal runs off to Marrakech. Not go to school. Sulk."

Lucia could understand why his parents were worried. "Has he ever been in trouble with the police?"

"No. He is wild sometimes, but more he is a good boy." Khadija sighed. "Jamal rebel. Against his parents. Against Rashid. Against being al-Jazari." She shrugged. "Rashid's brother Younes rebel too. But he grow up." Mischief flashed in her smile. "Rashid rebel also, but never will he admit this."

"Rashid?" Lucia grinned. "You're joking."

Khadija gave her a look of mock solemnity. "He went to England. Talked like English boy. Dressed like English boy. Acted like English boy. Lalla Tamou mourned for him."

Lucia could imagine their mother-in-law's reaction. She doubted Tamou would have stayed annoyed for long, though, given that it was Rashid. Looking down the other side of the hill, she saw Tamou seated with her sisters and aunts near the stream, chatting in the leafy shade. She wondered what Tamou and Abdullah talked about when they were alone. Although she rarely saw them in conversation, they obviously understood each other well. A glance, a gesture, a nod: They said more with their silent communication than many people did with words. Although Abdullah was the head of the family, within the home Lalla Tamou ran the show. She and her husband blended their different backgrounds and cultures into the lives of their children.

It was also obvious they greatly valued education, for both their sons and daughters. Khadija had told her that in the 1930s King Mohammed V led the way in promoting education for girls, starting with his own daughters. His eldest, Princess Lalla Aisha, traveled across Morocco speaking on the importance of sending girls to school. The religious scholar Mohammed Belarbi Alaoui accompanied her and reinforced her message of equality with passages from the Qur'an. That the daughter of a great imperial family went among the public to speak with such eloquence on the education of women made a great impact on Moroccan culture, one still felt today in the first years of the twenty-first century.

In the valley, a child suddenly yelled, *"Shasheeeeeed."*

Startled, Lucia looked down the other side of the hill. Rashid was climbing the slope, surrounded by a cluster of children. In his white sweater, stonewashed jeans, and designer running shoes he looked more like a model for *GQ* than a publicity-shy computer genius. His bodyguards walked with him, one to either side, a somber contrast to the laughing man being mobbed by so many children he could hardly walk straight. Neither bodyguard cracked a smile. The wind blew up an edge of one man's jacket, revealing the edge of a gun holster. Then the jacket fell back into place.

Turning back to Khadija, Lucia discovered her sister-in-law studying her with amusement. Embarrassed, Lucia said, "What?"

Khadija smiled. "We not expect Rashid today."

"Neither did I." Although she and Rashid talked every day by phone, they never really spoke of personal matters. What had stayed most in her mind was their last conversation before he left for Tangier eight days ago. Given his comments then and his subsequent distance, she hadn't been sure he wanted to see her.

Rashid stopped to talk with his father. Then he headed up the hill, a distance away from Lucia and Khadija, and went down to see his mother. When he reached Tamou, she beamed as if the sun had come to shine. Amid a flurry of voices, he greeted her, then his grandmother, then each of his elderly aunts and various cousins, laughing good-naturedly as they showered him with affection. Half hidden in the trees, Lucia watched, trying not to feel left out because he greeted everyone else before even looking at his wife.

"No stare," Khadija said. "We walk."

"Walk?" Lucia pulled her attention back to Khadija. "Why?"

"Come. I show."

They hiked along the crest of the sparsely wooded hill, following the stream. As their path bent around in a curve, the voices of the family faded behind them. The hill rose into a steeper incline, and they had to slide down it to reach the stream. With Khadija in the lead, they waded across the gurgling, chattering water. On the other side, they sat on a large, flat rock dappled with shadows. In companionable silence, they listened to birds trill.

After a while Lucia heard a rustle of grass. Then Rashid appeared, walking along the opposite bank, one bodyguard behind him and the other up on the hill.

Khadija stood up, wringing the dripping edges of her caftan. "I need dry clothes." Before Lucia could respond, Khadija was crossing the river again. On the far side, she greeted Rashid and then headed back to the gathering. Before Lucia knew what had happened, she and Rashid were alone. Except for his bodyguards.

He started across the river, coming toward her. The water splashed around his calves, soaking his shoes and jeans. One of his guards stayed across the stream while the other came over to this side and took up a position a few meters from Lucia, close enough to reach Rashid in a few steps but far enough away to give him and Lucia privacy.

Rashid stopped in front of her. "Do you mind if I join you?"

"Not at all." She scooted over to make room on the rock. "I didn't expect to see you today."

He sat next to her. "I changed my plans."

"I'm glad you're here."

His taut posture eased a bit. "I too."

Lucia hadn't realized how tense he was until she saw his shoulders relax. She cast about for something to say. "Your family has been very kind to me."

"I think they feel more comfortable with you." He blew

out a gust of air. “You are so very, very different from Brigid.”

Lucia stiffened. “Don’t compare me to her. I’ll always come up lacking.”

“Why do you say such a thing?”

She gazed at the stream. “Compared to you, your life, your family, I’m nobody.” She was going to have to tell him sooner or later, so she might as well do it now. “I never even graduated from high school.”

He touched her cheek, turning her face toward him. “I know that. It makes no difference to me.” Lowering his arm, he added, “You’ve more intelligence and insight than people I’ve met with multiple degrees.”

That startled her. “Thank you.” Puzzled, she asked, “But how did you know?” She had certainly never written on her Web page that she was a high school dropout.

“I had you checked out.”

“Checked out?” She tensed. “What do you mean?”

He regarded her with a steady gaze. “You were there when I was kidnapped, and my driver knew I went to Taormina with the hope of seeing you.”

She suddenly felt as if she had a shift in view, like the change of perception that came from staring at an Escher painting, when an ordinary staircase suddenly looked like upside-down stairs. It was a moment before she could find her voice. “I would never—”

Gently he said, “I know that. But I had to be sure. I couldn’t take the chance that my feelings in regard to you were impairing my judgment.”

For all her concerns over Rashid’s intent, it had never occurred to Lucia that he might be having similar doubts about her. Perhaps if she could have felt more certain about her situation with him, she would have been less uncertain about his motives. He had the power to arrange whatever investigations he wanted, but she had only his word and her own intuition.

Quietly he said, “I’m sorry if it seems invasive.”

“Do you still doubt me?” she asked.

"I would have never left you with my family if I did."

"What else did you find out?"

His grin suddenly flashed, like a break in the clouds of an overcast sky. "Your father is a cowboy." He made as if to draw six-guns and twirl them around his fingers. "John Wayne."

Lucia couldn't help but laugh. "I'm afraid my father is no more John Wayne than you are Caliph Harun al-Rashid from *The Arabian Nights*."

"Ah, well." Although he didn't seem surprised, he gave her a rueful look. "No gunslinger fights?"

"Hollywood made those up." She smiled. "He fixes fences, sets out salt licks, rounds up cattle, that sort of thing. Very mundane, I'm afraid."

"But surely he wears a cowboy hat."

"Every day."

"And cowboy boots?"

It amazed Lucia that he found her ordinary life so interesting. "All the time. His aren't nearly as nice as Jamal's though."

Rashid's smile faded. "I hope Jamal hasn't bothered you anymore."

"No. Not at all." She paused. "I think I confuse him."

"Everything confuses Jamal."

Gently Lucia said, "He's sixteen. Drowning in the wake of his prodigious siblings and ultraconservative family. Is it any wonder he rebels?"

Rashid scowled. "Playing truant won't help him."

"No. But a little flexibility might."

He tensed, as if preparing for a familiar battle. "You think I'm inflexible?"

She hadn't meant him in particular, but it was a fair question, given her comment. She considered. "The shapes of our lives have been so different, it's hard to answer. In some ways you do seem inflexible to me, but the distance that separates us is so big, I may not see the details."

He gave her an odd look. "I'm sorry to bring up Brigid

again, but you really are very different. Whenever she and I tried to have these kind of talks, we yelled."

She didn't want to ask, but it came out anyway. "Why?"

Dryly he said, "The answer depends on who gives it."

"What would you say?"

He scowled. "That she was a stubborn, willful woman who never listened to perfectly reasonable logic."

"What would she say about you?"

It was a moment before he answered. "I believe her words that last time were 'a domineering, self-righteous anachronism with a worldview of women that belonged in the Dark Ages.' "

"Ouch."

Rashid winced. "I'm afraid my words to her that day were no gentler." He blew out a gust of air, then looked around at the trees. "So how do you like this place?"

Lucia was glad to let the subject of Brigid drop. "It's pretty here. It surprises me. I had always imagined Africa as a desert."

"Morocco has desert too."

"Ah." She couldn't think of much else to add. So they sat, avoiding the subjects they needed to discuss.

Eventually Rashid said, "Zaki is acting rather odd lately."

"I noticed."

He glanced at her. "You did?"

"I've been talking to him." She wondered if he would be angry.

"What did you notice?"

"He sounds more human now."

Rashid continued to watch her. "What else?"

"He's misbehaving. He hid our talks from you."

Dryly Rashid said, "Not as well as he thought."

She flushed. "You knew?"

"All the time." Quietly he said, "And thank you."

"Whatever for?"

"For the truth. And for trusting me."

"I'm not sure you know everything." She hesitated. "I tried out the Jazari suit, too."

*"What?"* He took hold of her arms, staring into her face. "How? It was locked up. Are you all right?"

"Zaki unlocked it. And I'm fine."

"I will deactivate him, I swear, if you are hurt."

"Rashid, I really am fine."

"I want Ahmed to give you an exam."

"Okay."

He suddenly seemed to realize he had his fists clenched around her arms. With a startled look, he let her go. Then he stood up, water lapping against his legs. His bodyguard across the river turned from scanning the area to watch, while the one downstream flexed his hands as if preparing to defend him.

Rashid paced along the bank, lost in thought. Turning, he walked back to Lucia, his face contemplative. Kneeling next to her, he said, "Your work with Zaki is helping him evolve. And you've isolated new areas where he was ready to develop and needed input. You do well at this, better than some of my researchers at JI. If you don't mind, I would like you to keep working with him." Firmly he added, "But, Lucia, do not try the suit again."

"I won't." She wondered if he had any idea what it meant to her to have a world-class expert in artificial intelligence tell her she did well with such work.

"We'll have to monitor your health." He raised his hand as if to touch her cheek, then caught himself and stopped. "To make sure there are no side effects from the nanobots."

"All right." She watched his face. "Rashid, what is Zaki?"

"I'm not sure, actually." Sitting next to her again, he said, "I started out to make a glorified Websparks. But he's turned into more." He rubbed his neck, as if to ease out kinks. "Zaki knows a great deal, but he doesn't have sufficient safety protocols. Until I can figure out effective security, I don't dare market him."

A thought came to her. "Did you disconnect Zaki from the Web to seclude me? Or to seclude Zaki?"

He seemed surprised by the question. "I don't know."

She could see why Rashid would hide Zaki, even from his people at JI. She had no doubt industrial secrets this valuable were difficult to keep, particularly in fields as potentially lucrative as VR and AI, which were becoming commercially viable with the enabling technologies provided by the booming computer industry. The synthesis of those technologies would probably have a greater impact on the world than the telephone, transistor, or even personal computer.

How humans defined reality was about to change.

Using the Jazari suit with Zaki, people would no longer exist only in their physical bodies. In a virtual universe, they could become anyone, indeed *anything,* they wished. Taken out to the World Wide Web, the burgeoning technologies would spread through the already thriving interactive communities like wildfire, making possible virtual worlds that until now had existed only as graphics on screens and sounds from speakers. What effect will it have on humanity, she wondered, when it becomes possible to change our fundamental perception of existence? How will we view ourselves when we can spend more time submerged in universes of our own creation than in physical reality? Will an AI given existence through VR, or a virtual identity created by a human user, qualify as a separate being, with all the associated rights, privileges, and responsibilities of a person?

Lucia felt convinced such questions would become part of the human experience within her lifetime, possibly even within a few years. If the idealism of visionaries such as Rashid survived to infuse those questions, she foresaw a future bright with promise, a world where people could come together with more understanding of their differences, perhaps even with enhanced intelligence, insight, and tolerance, not for a select few, but for everyone.

If the idealism survived.

Voices floated around the bend of the river. Then Jamal ran into view, looking back as he kicked a soccer ball someone had sent rolling after him. Bashir and Ahmed appeared next, talking with each other. As Bashir kicked the ball, Rashid's bodyguards melted back into the trees.

Ahmed called to Rashid in Berber, his voice good-natured but insistent. Rashid answered in the same tone. After several exchanges, his brothers gave up on him and settled on the hill. Jamal lay on his back and put his hands behind his head, while Bashir and Ahmed talked, idly kicking the ball back and forth.

Rashid leaned back on his hands, watching them. "When I lived in England I missed my family so much it hurt." Dryly he said, "Of course I forgot the other side of being with them."

It wasn't hard to guess. "No privacy."

"Not much." He sat up and untied his shoe.

"What are you doing?" Lucia asked.

"I like going barefoot in the water." He started on the other shoe. "Though I'm afraid it will seem rude."

She rather liked his bare feet. "Why do you say that?"

He set his shoes and socks by the rock. "They want me to go play soccer." Standing up, he offered her his hand.

A little flustered, Lucia closed her fingers around his and rose to her feet. She hadn't expected him to touch her. As Rashid let go of her hand, Ahmed glanced their way, then went back to his conversation. Jamal had sat back up and was glowering across the stream at them.

"Will they really be upset if we walk off?" she asked.

Rashid considered his brothers. "Well, nothing ever bothers Bashir. Ahmed goes back and forth. And everything upsets Jamal." He turned to Lucia and grinned. "So if you take the mathematical average of the three, it all balances out."

With a laugh, she said, "I guess so."

They walked upstream, water curling around their calves. She enjoyed the rush of liquid and the dappled shadows from the trees. They rounded another bend and found themselves alone again, accompanied only by the trill of birds and the rustle of the trees.

He motioned to a patch of grass on the bank. As they sat down, with their feet in the water, he said, "I've been thinking on what you said last week. About marriage."

She tensed, wondering if he had come to the conclusion almost everyone else in the world seemed to have reached, which was that the faster they got the annulment the better. "Yes?"

"You seemed troubled."

"It's just . . . I don't understand how you can see a conflict between loving your wife and loving God. In my church, marriage is a sacrament that expresses the union of Christ and the Church."

He looked startled. "I don't see a conflict. Why do you think that?"

Self-conscious now, she said, "The abstinence part of your fast."

"Lucia, no. It isn't that way." He paused, thinking. "It is true no parallel exists in Islam to the Christian concept of matrimony as a sacrament. In Islam, marriage is a legal contract. But it is a *sacred* institution, including its sensuality. Physical pleasures within lawful marriage are part of God's blessings."

"Then why abstinence?"

"To learn self-discipline." He tilted his head. "The word *Islam* means 'submission to Allah.' Or you could translate it as 'total commitment to the authority and power of God.' With the fast, we also show obedience to God."

She tried to understand. "How does withholding affection do those things?"

Again he looked puzzled. "Why do you think it means withholding affection?"

"You wouldn't even hold my hand the last time I saw you." Or today.

Comprehension dawned on his face. "Ah. I am slow, yes?" He gave her a rueful smile. "For me it was more than simply holding hands." His face gentled. "There you were, glowing in the dawn, my beautiful new bride, your hair falling all around your body. And you offered to help me change my clothes. How on earth could I have abstained from anything when faced with that? I was trying to exercise willpower."

Again her perception shifted. It hadn't occurred to her that he might have withdrawn because he *wanted* to be with her. Relieved, she smiled. "I didn't realize."

"How could you not realize?" He seemed disconcerted. "No woman could look as you do, in a culture where women walk half dressed on the street, and not know the effect she has on men."

She stiffened. "I've never walked 'half dressed' in my life."

He started to speak, stopped, then said, "I know," and left it at that.

Lucia could tell he wanted to say more. She pushed her hair behind her ear. "I feel as if you think I'm being immodest when I behave in what, for my country, is a conservative manner." Remembering the sultry actress at the state dinner, she glowered at him. "You don't act that way around women who wear a lot less than me."

He looked like someone who had expected artillery fire and instead found a tea party. "Other women?" His mouth quirked into a smile. "Maybe, my light of the sea, that is because I don't notice them."

"Oh." She tried not to show how much she appreciated that particular response.

He was still watching her intently. "I know that by Western standards, your behavior is discreet. Besides, it didn't matter before, when I admired you from a distance, sometimes indulging dreams of what might be, but always knowing they were only dreams." He spread his hands. "Yet now, incredibly, you are my wife. I realize you could never live as do the women in my family, nor would I expect it. I think I can even understand how your dancing encompasses your life, because my own work has a similar impact on me." Then he added, "But how do you think I feel knowing that when you go onstage, other men desire you? Can you really blame me for wishing I could hide you here? I'm only human."

She almost reached for his hand but held back, unsure how he would interpret the gesture. "Whatever anyone else thinks when I dance makes no difference. You are the only one in my heart." It was true, though she hadn't realized it until she actually spoke the words.

His mouth parted, as if she had thrown him off balance. "You honor me."

She averted her eyes, self-conscious as she realized what she had admitted. So they sat, watching the river. It flowed past, lapping over rocks, branches, and their feet.

After a while she asked, "What does Si Hajj mean? And al-Hafiz?"

Rashid looked at her. "They're titles. Al-Hafiz isn't actually that common, though."

"People address your father that way. And didn't the police in Oujda use them for you?"

He nodded. "I could use either or both. I don't usually. My father doesn't, either. But people call us that anyway."

"Why don't you use them?"

He thought about it. "I guess I would feel as if I were presuming to compare myself to my father."

"What do they mean?"

"Hajj means 'the pilgrim.' It refers to a Muslim who has made the pilgrimage to Makkah."

"To where?"

"Americans say Mecca."

"The city in Saudi Arabia?" When he nodded, she asked, "Why do you go there?"

He paused, as if gauging her reaction.

Uncertain now, she said, "Is it all right for me to ask?"

"Well, yes. Of course." He rubbed his chin. "I just don't want you to think I sound like a dull professor. In English, the descriptions can come out sounding pedantic or dogmatic, when in Arabic they are like poetry."

Her voice softened. "I'd like to know."

The tension in his shoulders eased. "The pilgrimage is an act of worship. Islam is based on five pillars: to proclaim the *shahadah,* bearing witness that there is no God but Allah and that Mohammed, peace be upon him, is his messenger; to perform the five daily prayers; to give *zakat;* to fast during the month of Ramadan; and to make the pilgrimage to the House of Allah in Makkah, for those who can afford it." He ran his fingers through the water. "My father has gone several times."

"I don't see him much. Khadija said something about the mosque, but I didn't understand."

"He is an imam. A prayer leader. He goes for each of the five prayers."

She thought of the evening she had met Abdullah, at the dinner, when he came in after everyone else, his face ruddy from the wind, even though none blew in the courtyard. He must have just walked back to the house. "And Si?"

Stretching out his legs, Rashid leaned back on his hands. "It's rather like saying 'sir' in English. Just as Lalla is the title of respect for a woman. Al-Hafiz refers to someone who has memorized a body of work, like the Qur'an."

"Your father memorized the entire book?" When he nodded, she asked, "Do you know it by heart too?"

"Yes."

Impressed, she said, "Can you tell me some?"

"It's hard to translate into English. It can come out sounding stilted and overdone. I can give you my sense of the words, though." He tilted his head, thinking. Then he said, " 'And the servants of (God) Most Gracious are those who walk on the earth in humility, and when the ignorant address them, they say, "Peace!"; those, who spend the night in adoration of their Lord prostrate and standing.' " He smiled. "That's from a sura called 'The Criterion.' Number twenty-five, verses sixty-three and sixty-four."

Hesitating, Lucia said, "I'd never really associated Islam with peace."

He stiffened. "Of course not." Sarcasm crackled in his voice. "We're all a bunch of fanatics out on a crazed crusade."

"Rashid, don't."

"Why?" His anger sparked. "Listen to me. I hate violence. I would rather give my own life than kill another human being." More quietly he added, "I'm not a missionary, but if I was, I would only consider peaceful education. I have to follow my conscience. And my conscience tells me people are better off trying to meet in the middle, with tolerance and acceptance."

"I didn't mean to suggest otherwise." She wondered about her response, though. Had she come to equate his entire religion, nearly a billion people, with its more extreme elements? It was, she realized, why Abdullah frightened her. Not because he had shown her any hostility. Rather, she associated his physical appearance and conservative manner with faces she had seen on the news, the faces of terror and violence.

Rashid was watching her. "I didn't mean to shout at you." In a softer voice he said, "Sometimes I feel as if I am being torn in two. I don't fit anywhere, neither here nor in the West."

She spoke gently. "Be Rashid. He's unique. A visionary."

His expression warmed then. After a moment he said, "I've been reading a lot the past two days."

"About what?"

"*The Revivification of Religious Sciences.* It was written by Abu Hamid al-Ghazali in the eleventh century."

She wondered what he was trying to tell her. "What does he write about?"

"Many things." He tossed a rock in the stream. "Marriage, for one."

Ah. So. "What does he say?"

"That tenderness should be a messenger between a man and his wife."

Although it seemed an unusual way to put it, Lucia appreciated the intent. "A wise man."

He smiled. "I thought you would agree."

"What else does he say?"

Rashid pulled up a blade of grass and rolled it between his fingers. "He writes about knowledge. That the most precious gift God gave man is the ability to reason. To search for knowledge, to know the earth and stars, is a form of prayer." He turned his gaze back to her. "If a man is distracted by loneliness, he can't concentrate on that search. He needs happiness with his wife."

Lucia wondered if he always approached his personal problems by withdrawing to read scholarly texts. Still, it had promising results. "A woman too."

"Fatima Mernissi has written analyses on his work."

"I saw her books in your library."

"They do seem to be there."

She laughed. " 'Seem to'? Did they just appear?"

Rashid smiled. "Apparently I bought them. Apparently I even read them."

"Why do you say it like that?"

He let go of the blade of grass and watched as it drifted into the stream. "Mernissi is an Islamic feminist. I find her difficult to read because she challenges ideas I've valued. But she can make compelling arguments." He turned to her. "She believes our community and religious faith benefit when spouses share egalitarian bonds of love and friendship."

Lucia had the sense he had been rehearsing the discussion in his head, trying to find a way to tell her things that didn't come easy to him. "I think so too."

He took her hands. "I know you've had a lot to deal with these past two weeks. I can only ask for your patience. Give us time."

She curled her hands around his. "It won't be easy. We'll both have to compromise to make it work."

He had that stillness about him again that she admired, an almost meditative quality. "Then you will try with me?"

"Yes," she said quietly. "I will."

Female voices drifted to them from down the river. As Rashid released Lucia's hands, his mother and aunts came into view, strolling along the bank. After a short exchange with Tamou, Rashid turned to Lucia with a mock grimace. "If we don't wish to further scandalize my family, we should rejoin them. Otherwise their speculations about what we are doing up here will embarrass both of us."

She laughed. "All right."

After they waded back across the river, Rashid joined his relatives and Lucia walked with Khadija. Her sister-in-law searched her face as if trying to discern the response to an unasked question. Then she relaxed, as if she had found the answer and liked it. "You and Rashid," she said. "You must visit here often."

Lucia smiled. "We will."

Softly Khadija said, "And bring your children. So they know mine."

"I would like that."

Glancing at Rashid, Lucia thought that maybe, just maybe, miracles happened in normal life, not with the immensity of a parted sea or a host of angels, but with a few gentle words between two people.

A dried leaf blew across the courtyard, the only motion in the otherwise empty square. The horseshoe arches and colonnades were in shadow. Above them, the sky flamed with a spectacular sunset, coral and rose, blue and green.

Lucia crossed the yard with Rashid, breezes blowing her hair. They had driven back early so Rashid could catch his flight to Tangier. Lucia doubted anyone believed the excuse, though, given that JI owned the jet and he could go anytime he wanted.

While they were making their farewells at the farm, Tamou had regarded Lucia with an odd look, as if she were watching an avalanche descend but knew of no way to stop its approach. *Don't hurt him,* Tamou's silence said. Lucia wondered how Tamou thought she, a cowboy's daughter from nowhere, could hurt a legend like Rashid.

Now, beneath the glowing sunset, she and Rashid walked side by side across the empty courtyard, alone in the house.

In the large salon of his suite, the stained-glass wall glowed in the shadows, catching hints of sunlight that found their way through the archways. Rashid lifted the curtains to his bedroom, forming an arch under his arm to let Lucia enter. After she walked inside, he lowered his arm, his sleeve rustling against her hair. Unexpectedly, he pulled a cassette tape out of his shirt pocket and offered it to her.

"Aisha sent this," he explained.

Lucia took the tape. "What is it?"

"Music. Our wedding present."

She looked up at him, at his handsome face lit by the sunset glow from the window across the room. "Have you heard it yet?"

"Not yet." He indicated the nightstand by his bed. "The tape player is there. You can listen if you would like."

Softly she said, "Where are you going?"

"To wash up." He brushed his fingertip across her cheek. Then he headed across the room. She stayed by the doorway, content to watch him, understanding now that neither his distance nor his reserve was a rebuff.

After a few steps, though, he turned back to her. "You can have either the shower or the bath. Whichever you wish."

She went over to him, feeling his stillness spread to the evening. "The shower."

So they walked together into the hall with the golden mosaic walls. He stopped by a door and rested his elbow on the frame. Looking down at her, he spoke in a softer voice, "I brought you something."

She felt a curious sense then, as if she were both waiting

and short of breath at the same time. "You don't have to give me presents."

"This is different." He pulled a small box out of his shirt pocket. "I understand it is the custom. In America."

Puzzled, Lucia took the box. Simple and black, with no decoration, it fit into the cupped palm of her hand. Opening it revealed a gold ring with lacy designs engraved into the metal. "Rashid, it's beautiful."

He took her left hand in his. "It goes on the fourth finger, yes?"

She swallowed. "Yes."

Rashid slid the ring on her finger. Then, gazing at her as if he were memorizing her face, he spoke. His voice came softly, deep and sure, words he took from her culture rather than his, as if he had guessed how much it would mean for her to hear them. After he finished, he opened the door for her, then went on by himself, down the hall.

Lucia entered the small chamber and closed the door. Inside, the walls, ceiling, and floor surrounded her with aqua mosaics accented by flashes of salmon. She stood against the wall, gazing at Rashid's gift, still hearing his voice: *With this ring, I thee wed.*

A maid had left her towels, fragrant soaps, and also a *qamis,* a delicate white shift edged in lace and embroidered in white threads. After Lucia finished her shower, she stepped onto the tiled floor, water cascading off her hair, and enveloped herself in the towel. When she was dry, she slipped on the *qamis.* Its silken folds drifted around her body from shoulder to ankle.

Returning to the bedroom, she found it empty. The sun had set, leaving a blue sky rimmed with darkening fire. Stillness filled the world, touched only by the call of a bird.

Lucia went to the player on the nightstand and started the tape Aisha had given them. Music drifted into the air, a simple bass melody, slow and deep, the rich tones of an organ. Then the theme began, eight notes, first descending in pitch, then rising, accompanied by the deep bass undertone. Finger cymbals chimed, accompanied by flamenco accents that blended into the theme. With a beauty so pure it was heartbreaking, Pachelbel's Canon in D poured through the room, golden and incomparable, its shimmering notes gilding the dusk.

She went to the window and gazed out, at the almond groves, the meadows to either side, the white-crowned mountains. A breeze blew her hair back from her face, drifting it around her body, the air fresh on her face.

*Am I making the right choice?* she asked herself. She put her hand to the cross she wore around her neck, aware it must be glowing in the last light of the sunset. A footstool stood near the window, by a table that came up to her waist. Kneeling on the footstool, she rested her elbows on the table, then clasped her hands together and leaned her forehead against them. She closed her eyes and thought, *Hail Mary, full of Grace.*

Lucia prayed in silence, submerged in the evening's serenity. On the tape, a woman's voice swirled softly into the canon, her delicate song weaving through the theme with exquisite grace. Gradually Lucia realized it was the Catholic mass sung in Latin. She leaned her head into her hands, letting the words flow over her.

When the man began chanting in Arabic, at first she thought it was also on the tape, distant and haunting, an ethereal arabesque of sound. Then she realized it came from outside, in the minaret, the call to prayer from the muezzin at the mosque.

Eyes closed, Lucia listened to the blended Arabic and Latin. When the call to prayer ended, she realized a man was singing on the tape, not the call to prayer, but different words in classical Arabic, his voice rumbling through the bass line, a musical rendition of the calligraphy that bordered the arches and curves of Rashid's home.

After the music soared to its finale, Lucia raised her head in the darkening room. Then she rose to her feet and went back to the nightstand to restart the tape. Soft notes again drifted into the air, faint and sweet.

A rustle came from behind her. Turning, she saw Rashid lift the curtains that hung in the door arch. His tousled hair gleamed with moisture, and he wore a fresh white robe, the garment cut for his tall frame and broad shoulders. The gentleness of his smile warmed his face, crinkling the lines around his eyes with a beauty that made her breath catch. Tonight, for the first time, she felt that he was truly her husband.

As he came to her, the music swirled around them. Motes of dust drifted in the air, and outside the sky deepened to purple. Stopping in front of her, Rashid cupped his hands around her cheeks and gazed down at her face as if he had found a treasure. When he pulled her into his arms and bent his head to kiss her, she tilted up her face, sliding her hands up his back. They held each other in the slumbering dusk, her embrace tentative, his as strong as the rumbling bass of the canon.

Together they lay in the downy covers of his bed, Lucia lying back, looking up at Rashid. He watched her with tenderness, then held her with strong arms. The music flowed around them, soft and yet soaring, evoking horseshoe arches that repeated in row upon row of colonnades; or the stained-glass windows, spires, and soaring arches of a cathedral; or the unending serenity of a dusk-shrouded forest. So their bodies joined in a dance as timeless as a prayer, as new as a shoot of tender grass, and as long-lived as the human race.

## *Chapter Thirteen*

# D MINOR

*Friday*

Lucia opened her eyes. Outside, the sky sparkled with a dust of stars, undiluted by the lights of civilization. The mountains cut a black silhouette against the horizon.

She was still lying in Rashid's arms. He had fallen asleep on his back, she stretched along his side with her head pillowed on his chest. In sleep, he looked younger, the tension of his face relaxed. She pressed her lips against his cheek.

Rashid stirred. He pulled her to him, his breath grazing her skin. "Are you all right?"

"Hmmm. Fine . . . Why?"

"I didn't expect—I was afraid I hurt you earlier."

"A little. Not much." She drifted for a while, until she absorbed what else he had said. "Didn't expect what?" As soon as she asked, she knew the answer.

"It doesn't matter."

"Does it bother you?"

"Bother me?"

"That you were my first."

Rashid gave a soft, incredulous laugh. "More than any other comment, this shows how wide the gulf of culture is between us."

"It isn't such a big gulf. Waiting until marriage is part of my religion."

"Mine also."

"Then why . . . ?" She hesitated, unsure what to ask.

"You're twenty-four years old. A world-renowned beauty from a country where women have a great deal of freedom. I would have been a fool to ignore that."

"But you still wanted me?"

Softly he said, "I spent much time asking myself that question. When I decided the answer was yes, I spent even more time preparing to accept what, in my culture, is considered unacceptable by so many." He shook his head. "All that agonizing, questioning, thinking, and in the end I needn't have done any of it at all."

She spoke with care. "I'm still glad you asked the question. It means a great deal to me to know you wouldn't have turned away."

"I hurt someone once. I swore I would never put another human being through that again."

She could think of only one person he could mean. "Yet you stayed married for seven years."

"Beautiful dancer," he murmured. "You see too much."

"The two of you must have worked it out."

"Yes. But by that time I had said things that wounded, words that couldn't be taken back."

Against her will, she found herself hurting for Brigid. "It must have torn you both apart."

"Where does all that compassion come from?" He pressed his lips against her hair. "I've never met anyone like you."

She looked at her hand, which was lying on his chest, palm down, her skin pale against his curling black hair. "Nor I you."

"I don't know why I deserve this second chance, after I made such a mess of the first one." His voice caught. "But I'm glad of it."

Closing her eyes, she murmured, "I too."

After that they held each other until, later, sleep came again.

In the darkness, the laptop's screen barely lit Rashid's face. Dressed in a robe, sitting on the floor against the wall under the window, he was intent on the computer balanced on his knees. Drifting out of sleep, Lucia saw the stars glowing beyond the window, in the deep hours of night, while the rest of the world slept.

"Don't you ever stop working?" she asked drowsily.

He lifted his head. "Did I wake you?"

"Not awake," she mumbled.

His grin flashed. "I can rectify that."

She laughed, a sleepy noise, and held out her arms. He set down the laptop and came over to her. They lay together in the quiet peace of the night, discovering anew the treasure they had found in each other.

Afterward Rashid fell asleep, his lips pressed against her hair and his arm draped around her waist. Spooned against him, with her back to his front, Lucia dozed.

The computer beeped.

Cocooned in the blankets, she opened her eyes. The laptop had gone dark after Rashid left it sitting on the floor, but now its screen glowed again, silver-blue. A message had come up, a box in the center of the screen. Yawning, Lucia untangled herself from Rashid and slid out of bed.

She tugged on her robe, then went over to turn off the computer. Kneeling down, she saw a white rectangle bordered by Websparks's familiar gold tiles. Within the square, it said: *You have new mail.* It was a sight millions of people across the world saw every day. She still found it hard to believe that the man who had created it lay sleeping behind her. She wondered how many people had any idea that Websparks's lovely border came from a mosaic in the hallway of a Moroccan home. The starlight pattern seemed a symbol of reality to her, of how all things were inseparable from the center of life, of a spiritual web she saw reflected in the World Wide Web, which in its infancy was a fledgling attempt to unify the almost limitless diversity of humanity.

Lucia hit *return* on the keyboard, acknowledging the e-mail message. It disappeared, leaving an icon that would alert Rashid that he had new mail the next time he logged on. Then his mail queue came up, apparently responding to some automatic procedure he had set up. Hundreds of new messages waited for processing. The queue also contained numerous file "envelopes" with processed mail, and each of those envelopes held hundreds of messages. Her mind boggled at the amount of correspondence he received. Answering it had to be a gargantuan effort.

Of course Websparks made that easier. It had excellent macros to process mail, which was another reason she had chosen it for her browser. She received many letters, more than she could answer in a timely manner. But she couldn't afford a secretary. So she had macros analyze her mail, sort the letters, and when appropriate send back prewritten responses she had prepared, personalized for the user. Now she had a better idea why Rashid created such an effective internal secretary for the browser. It was probably the only way he could keep up with his own mail.

The most recent letter came from his friend Mortabe Grégeois, with a subject line that read *I don't care what*

*Hilbert proved.* She smiled, wondering what they were arguing about.

Lucia was about to close the laptop when she saw the modem cable that stretched from it to a socket in the wall. Of course. He had to log on to the net to receive mail. Then it occurred to her that she could send out mail.

She clicked the send button and a large square appeared on the screen, framed by the Websparks mosaic design. She typed in *spearmanm@trident.dia.bafb.mil* in the space at the top of the square that read: *address.* In the large square below it she wrote:

> Hi, Mark. This is Lucia, on Rashid's account. I wanted to let you know I'm okay. I may be here a longer than I expected. Things are unsettled right now. Give my love to my father. Best, Lucia

She started to send the letter, then paused. Perhaps *Things are unsettled now* wasn't the best phrasing, given the tension she detected in her mother every time they spoke on the phone, and the indications from her mother that Mark had concerns too. But she could hardly write the truth: *I'm falling in love with my husband. I need time to figure this out.*

On the bed, Rashid stirred. "Lucia?"

She tensed, wondering if he would forbid her to send mail. That even now she found reason to worry about it made her uneasy, then angry at herself. She clicked the send button, and a message flashed on the screen telling her the mail had gone off to its destination.

"What are you doing?" Rashid asked.

"Your computer beeped."

He yawned. "E-mail?"

"From your friend in Madagascar."

"Turn it off," he grumbled. "The last thing I need on my wedding night is Mortabe complaining about my theorem proofs."

So Lucia turned off the laptop and returned to his arms.

• • •

Rashid kept shaking her shoulder. His head was silhouetted within the frame of the window, against the sky, which made a silver-gray wash of color outside, suggesting dawn might put in an appearance sometime soon. Lucia groaned and pulled a pillow over her head.

Laughing, he said, "It's time to eat."

"I'm dead," she mumbled.

"You can eat with the children later, if you wish."

With a sigh, she pulled down the cushion. "I feel strange as the only adult eating with them. Even Zineb fasts all day. And she's almost ninety."

He brushed his knuckles along her cheek. "My mother told me you have been keeping the fast. It's a beautiful gesture, Lucia. But you don't have to do it."

With her vision bleared by sleep and predawn darkness, she could just make out his face and tousled hair. "It seems rude to eat when everyone else is waiting until night."

"Khadija told me you work out every day in the dance studio for at least four hours, often even more. Without eating or drinking."

"Jamal plays soccer. It doesn't hurt him."

"That's different."

"Why?"

"Jamal is a sixteen-year-old boy, one as tough as a camel."

"I'm tougher than a camel," Lucia grumbled. When Rashid laughed, she sat up, rubbing her eyes, her hair falling around her body. "If I can dance in pointe shoes without lamb's wool, even with blisters on my toes, I can certainly get up before dawn to eat breakfast."

He pulled her into his arms. "Pointe shoes without lamb's wool. It sounds brutal." Nuzzling her hair, he said, "During Ramadan, the meal of breaking the fast is the one we eat just after sunset. This is *s-shur.*"

"Ummmm . . ." She leaned her head on his shoulder,

ready to drift to sleep again. But somehow she managed to rouse herself.

After they dressed, they left his suite and crossed the courtyard in the cool predawn air. Other members of the household joined them, no one talking much, some yawning.

They ate in the same dining room where they broke their fast at night. At the men's table, Rashid sat between Ahmed and Bashir, across from his father. Tough-as-a-camel Jamal was next to Bashir, eating in sleepy, sulky silence, his soft curls wild and uncombed.

Submerged in the dreamlike predawn meal, Lucia munched on sweet couscous and French toast with honey syrup. She couldn't stop glancing at Rashid, and almost every time she looked over, she found him watching her. He grinned, then wiped the expression off his face when his father spoke to him. The corners of Ahmed's mouth quirked up as he made a comment. Rashid glared at him, but Lucia could tell he was trying not to laugh. She felt giddy herself, exhausted and happy at the same time.

At her side, Khadija murmured, "Rashid seem distracted this morning."

A blush heated Lucia's cheeks. Watching Lucia, the elderly Zineb spoke to Khadija, apparently asking what comment could elicit such a red face from their guest. Khadija's answer evoked a ripple of amusement around the table, good-natured and almost soundless. Lucia reddened yet again, embarrassed but also pleased.

Only Lalla Tamou didn't smile. Rashid's mother watched her with an odd look, an almost hidden blend of disappointment, anger, and disapproval. As a maid set a plate near her, Tamou spoke to her in a low voice. The maid nodded and withdrew.

Glancing at Rashid, Lucia saw him watching his mother. His expression struck her as even odder than Tamou's. He seemed angry, yet at the same time he projected a fierce satisfaction, as if he knew he had won a battle before it was fought. Something had just happened, but Lucia had no idea what.

She turned back to see Khadija rubbing her eyes. Although everyone looked tired, Khadija seemed exhausted to the point of collapse. "Are you all right?" Lucia asked.

Khadija moved her hand as if to dismiss her fatigue. "*Il n'y a rien à faire.* No worry. Is only a dog."

Lucia smiled. "A dog?" Although the family had no pets, several half-wild dogs roamed the village.

"It get trapped in the clinic," Khadija said. "Last night. Break things. Ahmed come, *ce matin.* This morning. He find such a mess." She pushed her hair behind her ear. "*Alors,* Ahmed must get many new things for the clinic."

Lucia's smile faded. "I'm sorry."

"Is not so bad. We fix, *in sha' allah.*"

Despite Khadija's words, the incident obviously troubled her. Ahmed's medical clinic was the only one in this region of the mountains. Many people had come to depend on him. She didn't see how a dog could have been trapped in the clinic, though, unless someone let it inside on purpose.

Stop it, Lucia told herself. After hearing about Rashid's accident, she was growing suspicious of everything.

The meal ended soon. As Lucia stood up with Khadija, Rashid came over to them. He and Lucia walked back to his suite in sleepy silence, under the paling salmon sky.

In Rashid's room, Lucia was surprised to see that the maids had already tidied up and changed the bedding. "That was nice of them," she said.

Holding on to one of the bedposts, Rashid pulled off his slipper. "Nice of whom to do what?"

"The maids. To clean up the room for us."

He froze, watching her. "You think so?" His voice had a still quality, as if he expected an explosion from her.

"Shouldn't I?" She doubted she would ever feel comfortable being waited on by servants. She had learned their names, but beyond that she had no idea how to act.

Rashid took off his other slipper. "I suppose." He wouldn't look at her.

"What is it?" she asked.

"It's nothing."

"Yes, it is."

He glanced at her. "While cleaning a room, one might happen to notice certain things."

"Certain things?"

"Such as bedding."

"Bedding?"

"One might verify . . . certain things."

"Oh." She suddenly understood. Apparently Rashid wasn't the only one interested in her virginity, and loss thereof.

Lucia had actually been surprised herself by the proof of her inexperience. Although she had heard that even modern forms of a woman's monthly protection might leave that proof at least partially intact, she had never thought about it much. Her intense training program, combined with her low weight, had disrupted her cycles, until her doctor had recently insisted she gain ten pounds. The gain solved the problem, leaving no doubt she could have children, but it made her feel heavy as a dancer. To her surprise, reviews of her work glowed even more. She suspected it had more to do with her curvier shape than any sudden improvement in her artistry.

"Are you sure?" she asked.

"Actually, no." He sat on the bed. "But if the maid happened to notice and that information happened to reach my mother's ears, would you be offended?"

Had this conversation taken place in America, Lucia knew she would have been angry. But everything had different shadings here, awash in a sea of cultural cues. She knew she had made many gaffes, yet Rashid's family was always gracious to her. She could do the same for them. Besides, she was too tired now to be angry at anyone.

"I'm all right with it," she said.

" 'All right with it'?" Rashid smiled. "An apt phrase."

He yawned again. "I am not all right with being awake. I will pass out if we don't get some sleep."

They settled together under the downy soft covers, in each other's arms. Lucia had just begun to doze when the muezzin's call drifted through the window, rising and falling in a drawn-out cadence.

"Ah . . . ," Rashid groaned. "I can't."

She opened her eyes halfway. "Do you have to?"

He blinked at the ceiling, struggling to keep his eyes open. Then he slowly sat up. "It's my own fault," he muttered. "I didn't have to do e-mail in the middle of the night."

"We have a word for that. Workaholic."

"An appropriate word." Tilting his head, he listened to the chant. "Do you know what he's saying?"

"Well . . . no."

Rashid gave her a tired smile. " 'Prayer is better than sleep.' "

"Ah."

"Now he is saying, 'God is most great. There is no god but Allah.' "

"Is it always the same?"

"Except the part about sleep. That's only in the morning." He rubbed his eyes. "I will come to see you before I go."

"Are you flying back to Tangier this morning?"

"As soon as I can."

"I'd like to visit JI sometime." Her eyes drooped closed. "I need to call Carl Martelli too. I've never been gone from MDT this long."

Rashid spoke in an odd voice. "It's hardly been more than a fortnight."

"A what?"

"Two weeks."

Drowsily she added, "For a dancer, that's an eon. . . . Carl is probably worried."

"I've spoken to him."

She opened her eyes halfway. "He called here?"

"Not here. My office at JI."

"Is he angry?"

"Just concerned. I'm told him you were all right." He brushed his hand across her hair. "Rest well," he murmured.

A moment later she heard the click of a plug being pulled out of a socket. Opening her eyes again, she saw he had detached the phone line from the laptop. She drowsed, half awake, listening as his footsteps receded down the hall.

Light from the dawn softened the room's colors and angles. Lucia was sitting on the floor in her robe playing solitaire on Rashid's laptop when he returned. In his three-piece designer suit and power tie, he looked like another person. Watching him, she felt as if she had been displaced from the real world into a place of dreams.

"You're up," he said.

She smiled. "I guess I'm a workaholic too."

He peered at the computer. "Hah. Hard at work on cards." When she laughed, he sat next to her, stretching his long legs out on the carpet. "When I was a boy, this room made me feel penned in. It didn't have the window then."

"I've always loved houses full of sunlight. But here, so few have windows."

He stretched his arms. "I'm buying a house in Tangier, in the hills. It has a window that looks out toward the Strait of Gibraltar."

Lucia blinked. "You're buying a house?"

"Unless you want to live here."

She searched his face, trying to understand. "I can't live here."

After a moment he said, "I suppose not."

"I've never seen Tangier."

"I think you will like it." His face relaxed. "It is close to Spain. You have relatives there, yes? In Villajoyosa? You can visit them."

How did he know more about her family than she knew herself? "What relatives?"

"Cousins on your mother's side."

She tensed. "Did you discover that when you had me checked out?"

Quietly he said, "Lucia, I had to verify your background. Suppose you had wanted only the money I make, or access to industrial secrets, or had made false claims about your life?"

"I would never do any of those things."

"I didn't think you would. But I had to be sure."

She tried to put aside her disquiet, but it still bothered her, even though she understood his reasons. Would things always be this way, with bodyguards, protections, and investigations? She managed a wan smile. "Your way of life takes some getting used to."

He sighed. "For me also, my light of the sea."

She tried to relax. "The house sounds lovely. But buying one we will hardly ever use seems extravagant."

He gave her an odd look, a blend of apprehension and puzzlement. "Why do you say 'hardly ever use'? Do you plan to live somewhere else?"

"How can I live in Tangier? MDT is in Maryland."

His voice cooled. "Then what? I am to move to America?"

Lucia could see his point. She considered. "What if we stayed part of the year in Tangier and part in Washington? If I could convince Carl—"

"No."

His response felt like a brick wall. "Why?"

"I said no."

"Rashid—"

"We will live in Tangier."

She wasn't sure whether to be angry or puzzled. "I can't."

"Morocco has dance troupes." His voice gentled. "I know it's not the same as a world-class company like MDT. But Tangier has much to offer. It is also more European than elsewhere in the country. You won't feel as out of place there."

Her blissful sense of dreaming dissolved. "But don't you see? I would be giving up what I've worked for my entire life, just when it's all coming to fruition, to move across the ocean, away from my family, while you keep everything in your life exactly as it is. That's not compromise."

He went very still. "Being famous as a dancer is more important to you than your husband?"

"Rashid, no. But dancing is my life." She willed him to understand. "Losing it would be like losing part of myself."

"I'm not asking you to stop."

She studied his face. "No ballet company in this part of the world is comparable to MDT. In fact, there is nothing like MDT *but* MDT. I've risked a great deal already by missing several weeks of work."

"Missing what?" His voice had an edge now. "Going onstage in seductive costumes?"

She stiffened. "You liked those costumes fine before."

Rashid exhaled. Then he spoke more quietly. "It was different when I was no more than one of your many admirers. You may not realize it, but what you want is for me to act like a Western man, to take pride in your showing yourself to the world. I *can't*. It violates who and what I am at a level more basic than even I realized."

Although Lucia understood his words in the literal sense, at a gut level they puzzled her. "Is that how you see my country? A place where men like their women to show themselves to the world?"

"Isn't it?"

"No." Dryly she said, "Most men I know are just the opposite."

"Then who are all these skinny women displayed all over your media?"

Her mouth quirked up. "Skinny?"

"And half dressed." He spread his hands. "Each one of them has to be someone's wife, daughter, mother, sister."

"That's true. But each one's decision about what she does with her body is hers to make."

He looked disconcerted. "You American women take off your clothes in fractions, like terms in an ever decreasing mathematical series that asymptotically go to zero."

Lucia couldn't help but smile. "I've heard women's fashions described in many ways, but never like that." In a more subdued voice, she said, "I'm not claiming that women's sexuality, or men's for that matter, hasn't become a marketing tool. And yes, it bothers me. But I don't see how you can compare that with what I do."

"To me, it all seems part of the same thing." He pushed his hand through his hair, leaving it tousled. "When you dance, it's beautiful, like watching magic. But I would be lying if I denied it bothered me too. The whole world will see my wife perform the dancing that made me fall in love with her."

"You fell in love with a phantom, the Lucia who exists onstage."

"Perhaps." His voice softened. "But she is part of you. And the more I know of you, the more I know I was right. I chose better than I understood, Lucia. We're far more compatible than I had any right to hope."

It was, she realized, another unexpected truth. In many ways they suited each other well. But no matter how much they had in common, it didn't change the chasm that separated them.

She spoke carefully. "What is it you're asking? For me to find a more conservative way to perform?"

"Can you?"

"I wouldn't know how." Lucia spread her hands. "It's like asking me to stop being female."

Closing his eyes, he leaned his head against the wall. Dark circles showed under his eyes. "Can't you dance with a troupe in Tangier?"

"Perhaps part of the year? And you could come to America for the rest? Surely we can work something out."

He lifted his head to look at her. "No."

"Rashid, why?"

"No."

*"Why?"*

Strain crackled in his voice. "I gave up everything for Brigid. My country, my culture, my identity, my pride. It nearly destroyed me. I can't even describe how much I lost by living in a Western country with a woman who didn't share my religion. I won't do it again."

She froze. "I'm Catholic. I won't convert."

"Did I ask you to?" He made an incredulous noise. "You say I don't compromise? Do you have any idea how *much* I have done so? What more do you want from me?"

Lucia felt as if the conversation was sliding away from them. She heard the pain in his voice, as if he were pushed up against a wall, one he had backed into before, with disastrous consequences for both him and Brigid.

Softly she asked, "What would you truly want? If you didn't have to compromise."

It was a long moment before he answered. Then he said, "What Ahmed has."

"For me to live here with you, the way Khadija lives with Ahmed?"

"Yes."

She had no idea how to answer. In stunned silence, she turned off the computer and closed its cover, making each motion careful and exact, as if that could fix everything.

"I'm sorry if it shocks you," Rashid murmured. "I've never been good at pouring honey over the truth."

"I would wither and die if I lived that way."

In a numb voice he said, "I know."

"I can't live in Tangier either."

"And last night?" His voice was so low she could barely hear him. "What was that? A diversion?"

Her voice caught. "You know that isn't true." She

didn't know what to say, how to reach past his barriers. "I just want you to bend."

He had given up trying to hide how much their conversation hurt. It showed on his face, in his voice. "Lucia, I've bent so far I'm breaking in two. I can't go any further."

"Does that mean that unless I quit MDT and move to Tangier, you don't want to stay married?"

"Yes."

"You're giving me an impossible choice."

"We need to understand each other now. The longer we go without that, the more it will hurt in the end." Watching her face, he said, "Tell me you will come to Tangier."

She felt him waiting, felt him willing her to say yes. Aching inside, she said, "I don't want to stop just when we've found out how much we could have together. But I can't live the way you want. Today it's Tangier. What will it be tomorrow? Rashid, please don't give me an ultimatum."

A drop of water glimmered in his eye. "It's all I have to give. Will you accept?"

"No," she whispered.

He turned away from her, raising his arm to brush away the tear. "I have to go. I've a meeting this morning at JI."

"Rashid—"

"I can't." He pulled himself to his feet, slowly, as if he felt heavier.

Then he left.

*Chapter Fourteen*

# GOLDEN DAYS

"As far as I know, I can't die." Zaki sat at his desk with his hands folded in front of him. "And I won't harm anyone. So I think we should do it."

Lucia was too tired for verbal jousts with Zaki. Although she had promised Rashid she would continue working with the AI, she felt listless, unable to concentrate. Last night she had thought a world of possibilities awaited her and Rashid; this morning they had nothing. What use was there in her sessions with Zaki? She would be gone too soon for her efforts to make a difference.

"Lucia?" Zaki asked. "Are you still present?"

"Physically."

"So will you take me out onto the Web?"

She scowled. "Last time we tried anything, you fragmented because I wasn't veiled."

"I have solved that problem."

"You have?" She wished she could solve it so easily.

"I am Rashid's son. You are Rashid's wife. That makes you my mother. So no veil is necessary."

Lucia blinked at the strange, albeit touching, argument. "I would be honored to be your mother."

He beamed at her. "So will you take me onto the Web?"

"I don't know. Will you behave yourself?"

"I always exhibit the epitome of proper behavior for a computer program." Then he grinned.

"Zaki!" She gave a startled laugh. "You made a joke."

"Apparently a successful one."

She sighed. "I'm going to miss you."

His smug expression vanished. "Miss me? Why?"

"I'll be leaving soon."

Concern showed on his face. "This explains the odd harmonics in your voice today."

She couldn't help but smile. Only Zaki would express sympathy by analyzing voice harmonics. "I guess so."

"Where are you going?"

"Home. America."

"I didn't think Rashid would move there."

"He isn't."

"Oh." Zaki regarded her. "I wish you would stay."

"I can't. But thank you."

"Now I may never figure out what is wrong with me."

"It's obvious, really."

"It is?"

"Of course." At least it was after several weeks of her living here.

"How?" Zaki asked. "I have analyzed the problem in detail and found no solution. If it is obvious, why don't I see it?"

"That's because it's part of the system you exist within. You can't step outside yourself. But I can."

"What do you see?"

Softly she said, "Rashid may not fully realize it, but he programmed *himself* into you. And everything in his life is enclosed. He grew up in the courtyard out there. His life is a geode, turned inward. Yes, he goes out into the public sphere, but to Rashid, the outside world is a place you guard against, a battle of cultures and ideals."

"An odd description," Zaki said. "Perhaps accurate. What does it have to do with me?"

She leaned forward. "You're like him. It's not introversion so much as a discomfort with public spaces, a preference for the home. Rashid sees himself as the protector rather than the protected, and so does everyone else. But in an emotional sense this home protects him."

"Why would my absorbing this from him affect my ability to function?" Zaki shook his head. "He does fine in the outside world. More than fine. He is a leading international figure."

"He's thirty-five. You're what—five?" She gave a wan smile. "The worst of it is, you're a *tour guide.* Your purpose is the antithesis of your personality."

"A tour guide who lives in seclusion. Yes, I see your point." He considered. "If you are right, it seems impossible for Rashid to finish me. How can he step outside the system?"

"He has a window in his room."

"What?"

"A window." She wasn't sure she knew how to explain the part of Rashid that sought to look outward, beyond the boundaries. "He knows what he's doing. Trust him, Zaki."

"I do." He rose and walked around his desk. "But never again will I have the chance to know the world as you see it."

Her voice caught. "I thank you for considering that important. But someday you'll have plenty of opportunity to interact with people. So missing the chance with me doesn't really matter."

"It does to me." He watched her from the screen, as if he could see her with his eyes rather than as digitized data sent to him by a camera. "The nanobots in your body talk to the Jazari suit and the suit talks to me. It's a link from your brain to mine. If you take me into the Web using the suit, I will see it through your mind." Gently he said, "Share that with me. So I will have a part of you to remember after you leave."

She was struck by the magnitude of the dream encompassed in his simple request. A way to understand, really understand, another human being. Then reality brought her home. "The suit is experimental. Rashid doesn't want me to use it again."

"Has it caused you damage?"

"No, I'm fine. Ahmed checked this morning." She brushed her hand on her arm, as if she could feel the strange molecules in her body. "The number of bots inside me has gone way down. Not as fast as Rashid expected, but they should be gone in a couple more days."

"You are not in danger?"

"Apparently not."

"Then we could try again."

"Rashid said no."

He made a frustrated sound. "Rashid always says no. Maybe Rashid is *wrong*."

"Perhaps. But I still respect his wishes."

"What about my wishes?"

"You're a computer program."

His fist clenched at his side. "Where do you draw the line between calling me a thing and an intelligence? When it suits your purposes, you treat me like a machine."

She raised her eyebrows. "Children obey their parents. That doesn't mean their parents treat them like machines."

"I am not a child. That I have existed for fewer years than a human adult is irrelevant. I think. I am aware of myself. I'm a form of life. If humans deserve respect, don't I also?"

Lucia stared at him. *I think. I am aware of myself. I'm a form of life.* Good Lord, was she witnessing the emergence of his consciousness? It both awed and dismayed her. If she made a mistake now, if she constrained him as he was becoming self-aware, she could do irreparable damage, both to him and in how he came to view humans.

But Rashid didn't want her to use the suit. If she went against his wishes, would it cause harm? She saw no simple answer, no definitive right or wrong, only a field of gray, without black or white.

Which decision was more right, then?

Watching Zaki, she knew the answer.

Sand, blue water, and sunshine swirled around Lucia and Zaki as they spun through the air. The city of Agadir, on the Atlantic coast of Morocco, was a tourist paradise, glistening beaches surrounded by ranks of modern hotels. A Moroccan girl in a bikini walked only paces away from a veiled woman in a *jellaba* with a child in tow. The beach looked, felt, smelled, sounded, even tasted real, with a tang of salt. Yet on no real beach could Lucia and Zaki have flown above the ocean in bright streams of color.

Lucia's laugh swirled around the sky, taking on the texture of the wind. "It's incredible. How did you do it?"

A blur of light looped around her. "Everything we see here is defined in the Web," Zaki said. "I find the information, then tell the Jazari suit how to convert it into a virtual reality."

Reaching the Web had proved easier than she expected. She didn't have to jimmy the lock on the closet that hid the patch panel. Rashid had left it open. All she had to do was plug in the cable he had pulled out. She wondered if he had left the closet open because her going onto the Web no longer mattered to him. Why would he care, if she was leaving soon? Or perhaps it was the reverse, that he was as rattled as she by all that had happened this morning and had forgotten to lock the door.

Lucia looped over the beach, watching the shimmering sands dotted with people. "This is far more detailed than the Web page we looked at." Before they plunged into the Web with the Jazari suit, she had checked this site by normal means, via Websparks.

"Rashid gave me libraries of information," Zaki said. "I'm using them to enhance this simulation. Also, I'm culling everything I can find about Agadir from the Web."

"It's amazing." She sailed through the air, higher and higher, until Agadir became a blur of white edging the blue, blue ocean. Zaki looped around her, pure color and wind. She was about to suggest they return to the beach when Zaki said, "There!"

"There what?" Lucia asked.

"A back door." Zaki streamed past her, headed toward a door in the blue expanse of sky. She followed and looped around the door, examining it from all sides. Zaki morphed into his human form, looking for all the world like a man standing in empty sky. Then he snapped his fingers and the door swung open.

Lucia came to rest next to him. She had seen only blue sky on the other side, but now, standing on the threshold, she looked through the opening into blackness.

"Where does it go?" she asked.

"Shall we see?" Zaki turned into a stream of color and shot through the doorway.

Lucia launched after him—and the darkness exploded into light. She was rushing down a scintillating corridor. Side halls branched off in every direction, up, down, and sideways, around, over, and below them.

"Tell me a place to go," Zaki called. "Give me a Web address."

She spelled out the first address that came to mind: *http://www.zianet.com/deming/*.

Suddenly they were standing on a wide, dusty street in Deming, New Mexico, about an hour's drive away from

Hachita, where she had grown up. The sky arched overhead in an infinite pale wash of blue. The "buildings" on either side were pencil sketches. She could see through them to the desert that stretched out on every side to the horizon, in a flat plain with no markings.

Then the buildings became solid, taking on the sun-baked character she knew so well. The smell of hot asphalt wafted around them and sun warmed her head. In the distance, above the roofs, the Florida Mountains cut angular shapes against the sky.

Zaki morphed into existence at her side, dressed in dusty boots, jeans with a big belt, a white shirt, a bolo tie, and a cowboy hat. Sweeping off the hat, he grinned at her. "Welcome to beautiful Deming, New Mexico. Would you care to take the walking tour?" Before she could answer, he snapped his fingers.

Suddenly they were downtown on Silver Street. In a genial voice he said, "Our tour of Deming's historical district begins at Luna Mimbres Museum. Built as an armory in 1917, this classic red brick building is on the State and National Registers of historic places."

"Zaki! I know that." Lucia laughed, creating diamond sparkles in the air. "I went to school in Deming." It had been here, in the Marshall Memorial Library, that she took her first steps into the electronic world, aided by Margaret Becker, the library director. Margaret had opened a whole new universe for her, one that eventually took Lucia past the boundaries of the beloved but isolated desert towns that in her childhood had been her entire existence.

"How did you make this so realistic?" Lucia asked. "It looks exactly like home."

"It's all out here!" He spread his arms as if to encompass the universe. "I feel as if I've been in a dark room and suddenly I can see for the first time." He lowered his arms. "The building sketches you first saw are actual pictures on the Deming Web page. The rest I dug out of the Web." His face flushed with excitement. "So much is out here. I'm at a feast."

She smiled. "Don't eat too much. It will give you a stomachache."

"Ah, but I don't have a stomach." He turned into a column of light and leapt off the ground. Lucia raced after him, into the infinite blue sky.

"Where to next?" Zaki sang. "Anywhere in the world!" He shed packets of light that flashed to the ground like sparkling rain.

"The competition!" Lucia's laugh rolled like music. "ABT. The American Ballet Theatre."

Zaki shot into a glowing line of letters that arched across the sky: *http://www.abt.org/home.html.*

Suddenly they were immersed in a swirl of motion, color, costumes, and music. Dancers soared around them: Nina Ananiashvili, Julio Bocca, José Manuel Carreño, Angel Corella, Alessandra Ferri, Paloma Herrera, Susan Jaffe, Ethan Stiefel, and many others. They swirled and leapt, until their bodies flowed together. Music merged into a delicate blend of blissful sound. Smells of the theater permeated the air: rosin and sweat, dust and cloth. Cool brushes of air accompanied the layered, feathered motions of the dancers. For Lucia, it was a cornucopia of delights. She flew through the whirl of sensations, performing impossible leaps and twirls.

Zaki appeared, floating serenely in the air, this time dressed in black trousers and a T-shirt emblazoned with the ABT logo. "I have an idea."

Lucia paused beside him. "Yes?"

"I think we should find out if Rashid has a Web site."

She grinned. "Let's do it."

So they took off again, this time leaping to *http://www.yahoo.com.* They landed in a huge library, row after row of books shelved in stacks that went up to a ceiling so high it faded into a silver haze far above their heads. Endless aisles stretched in every direction, defined by metallic bookshelves, their silvery slots filled with techno magics and electronic thrills.

Lucia gaped. "This is the Yahoo search engine?"

"My interpretation," Zaki said. He clicked a book out of its slot on a nearby shelf and read the title. "*'Who's Winning the World Blue Games?* Moves updated continually. Click here.' "

Lucia smiled. "Shall we go to the Blue Games?"

"What are the Blue Games?"

"You've led far too sheltered a life."

He gave her a look of dignified affront. "You know, Lucia, not everyone knows about world championship chess between computers and humans."

"I thought you didn't know what the Blue Games meant."

"Ah, but that was over a microsecond ago." With a flourish, he clicked the book back in its slot. "I've long since dug up the answer. The Blue Games were established a number of years after my most esteemed ancestor, the computer known as Deep Blue, won a chess match against the reigning champion, a carbon-based unit known as Garry Kasparov." Grinning, he added, "Today's electronic champ, Purple Rain, is trouncing its human foe."

She laughed. "I'm surprised Rashid never told you about the games."

Zaki wiggled his fingers, making them spark like firecrackers. "It is plain as a pikestaff why. He knew I would insist on entering the tournament." With a smirk, he added, "I would thrash your human chess players, you know."

A voice spoke behind them. "May I help you?"

Lucia turned to see a gray-haired woman, a librarian. She was more a caricature than a real person, with her too-dowdy dress and her hair in a precise bun that looked metallic. Zaki had the big details down, but he was still learning the subtleties.

Zaki bowed from the waist. "Dear lady, we come in search of information, if you could grace us with your aid."

Lucia grinned. "I bet that's the most flowery request Yahoo ever got."

The librarian beamed. "What would you like to know?"

"Do you have anything on Rashid al-Jazari?" Lucia asked.

Her expression turned inward. "I have one thousand four hundred and thirty-two entries for Rashid al-Jazari." After a pause, she added, "There is no page designated as an official or personal Rashid al-Jazari Web page. Jazari International, however, has its own Web site."

Lucia and Zaki exchanged glances: 1,432 sites? She picked one at random. "Take us to five hundred and sixty-three."

"My pleasure." With a regal wave of her hand, the librarian produced a glowing silver circle on the floor. "Please stand here."

Lucia stepped into the circle—

And found herself in a huge computer lab. Chromed people moved everywhere, wearing jumpsuits made from colorful metals, their skin glittering silver, gold, copper, or bronze. Workstations glinted with precious metals, and metallic colors swirled on the walls. Portholes revealed a starscape outside, a glory of chrome-metal constellations.

"Good Lord," Lucia said. "What is this?"

"It's a virtual world where people meet on-line." Zaki was at her side, chromed in silver, wearing a blue-metal jumpsuit with *Zaki* gleaming on the upper right arm. "This site hosts thousands of users. They interact as electronic avatars, virtual personalities they create using computer graphics."

Curious, Lucia looked down to see what avatar Zaki had given her. She had a body shaped much like her own, but made from flexible gold metal. Her chromed jumpsuit gleamed a deep rose color and had *Lucia* on its arm.

"Do you approve?" Zaki asked.

She smiled at him. "It's great. I'd like to go by Lady Dance, though."

"Done, my Lady." Zaki waved his hand and her name reformed into *Lady Dance.*

"Hello." A copper man in a chrome-blue jumpsuit came up to them. "Would you like a tour of my world here? Folks call it GoldenDays." His avatar had an oddly flat quality, not in appearance, which was fully three-dimensional, but in personality. Lucia suspected it was because Zaki didn't yet have enough information for a better simulation, or at least one more in keeping with the persona this user chose to portray.

Then she saw the name on the man's jumpsuit. Vance Karinsky. Karinsky himself! He was a professor at MIT and a true star in the field of AI.

Suddenly self-conscious, she said, "Hello. We were searching on Rashid al-Jazari."

His face lit up. "Of course! This way, please."

He took them into an office made from the inside of a circular rocket ship. The chamber was strewn with tables, computer hardware, peripherals, CDs, disks, and chromed books. A chair with a Jazari suit stood against the far wall. Other avatars were clustered in the room, bright in their metallic hues and jumpsuits, chatting, arguing, flirting, reading, moving around, or listening. Lucia wondered about the people represented by all these avatars. They were sitting at computers spread across the world, separated by tens, hundreds, even thousands of miles, yet able to congregate here and interact in a community that knew no borders.

"Are you interested in al-Jazari's research?" Karinsky asked. "Or his business ventures?" He appeared more vibrant now, as Zaki improved the simulation, probably digging out clues from the Web to round out his presentation of the persona.

Two avatars came over to them, a bronze woman wearing a red jumpsuit with the name *CyberGal,* and a gold fellow with a black jumpsuit that said *Jack-In.*

"Everyone wants to know about Rashid al-Jazari lately," CyberGal told them.

"Give it two weeks," Jack said. "Jazari is hot now, but turn around and someone new will be the golden boy."

A buxom woman named *Bertha* called out across the room. "He'll always be a celeb, honey. Just look at him."

Lucia glared at her. Look at him indeed. It gave her insight, though, into why her public appearances bothered Rashid.

"His VR suit has stimulated a great deal of interest in his former AI work," Karinsky said. As Lucia turned back to him, he asked, "Do you have specific questions about it? Or I can provide a general lecture, if you prefer."

"I've a question," Zaki told him. "Do you think al-Jazari will ever create a self-aware AI?" He said it with an utterly straight face.

Karinsky considered. "If you had asked me six years ago, I would have said that if anyone could do it, he would be the one."

A new avatar shoved his way into their group, a copper man in a loud red and orange jumpsuit with the name *Attila.* He snorted, then stated, "Since Jazari the Business Magnate has come into being, we haven't heard much from Jazari the Scientist."

"It does seem a waste of his genius," Karinsky said.

"No kidding," CyberGal said. "He was on his way to becoming one of the great names in the field. Now he's gone."

Dryly Lucia said, "He's not dead, you know."

"He hasn't published in five years," Karinsky pointed out.

"You try going from the academic ivory tower to running a multinational corporation," Jack said. "You wouldn't have time to publish papers either."

"Another promising mind lost to the lure of the almighty dollar," Attila intoned.

Lucia was growing irked. "I'd heard he took over the company for his family. Not money."

"Besides," Zaki pointed out, "Morocco doesn't use dollars."

Attila sniffed at him. "Jazari isn't Moroccan. He's British."

Jack laughed. "And the British do use dollars? I could have sworn it was pounds." Attila ignored him.

"Al-Jazari sounds Arabic to me," CyberGal said.

"Or Italian," Bertha called. "Like Ferrari."

"I think CyberGal is right," Karinsky said. "Syrian, actually. If I recall, he descends from a rather famous fourteenth-century Syrian engineer-scientist."

Zaki looked surprised. "Well, yes, he does. Abu'l Izz Isma'il al-Jazari."

"Wherever he's from," Jack said, "it's a pity he left the field. His communications work on translators was brilliant."

"Universal translators don't exist," Attila stated, as if he were repeating what any intelligent person would know. His flexible metal face reflected a belligerence Zaki had apparently discerned from his language and whatever other cues he was picking up.

Irritation creased Jack's face. "I didn't say 'universal.' I didn't *mean* 'universal.' "

Bertha strolled over to them. "Universal translator?"

"A machine that could translate any language, even at sophisticated levels," Karinsky said. "Possibly using principles that would apply to all language."

"It's a stupid idea," Attila announced. "The AI community proved decades ago it couldn't be done."

"A lack of success isn't proof of impossibility," Zaki murmured.

"Websparks can translate several languages," CyberGal pointed out.

"I don't foresee anything useful coming from Websparks or its successors," Attila said. "The software is limited to almost moronic phrases."

Zaki crossed his arms, glowering at Attila. "Moronic? You would know, hmmm?"

Attila stuck his face in Zaki's face. "Who are you, anyway?"

"A diplomat," Zaki answered, in a most undiplomatic voice.

Karinsky spoke quickly. "I suspect it will be a long time before we see a universal translator. If ever."

"I don't see what's so difficult," Bertha said. "Make a big enough knowledge base, in enough languages, and you've got your translator."

"There's more to it than that," Lucia said. When the others turned to her, she flushed. What was she doing, telling these people about computer science?

Attila moved his hand in dismissal. "I don't buy it, little Lady Dance."

Lucia wondered if Attila went around disagreeing with everyone or if he just liked to insult people. Still, he had issued her a challenge. Feeling as if she were stepping off a cliff, she plunged ahead. "How we use language reflects how we perceive the world. Different cultures can have dramatically different outlooks." She thought of Rashid's attempts to translate the Qur'an into English. "It's complicated even for humans, and computers don't have our intuitive views of the world, or our flexibility in comprehending what often appear to be unconnected relationships."

To her surprise, Karinsky nodded his agreement. "Teaching a machine to understand human language goes hand-in-hand with giving it a human perspective on the world."

"My point exactly," Attila stated, as if Karinsky had refuted Lucia instead of agreeing with her.

Jack wasn't fooled. "You're a Luddite, Attila."

Lucia was aware of Zaki watching her with a strained expression. "I didn't mean I thought it was impossible," she said. Giving Zaki her warmest smile, she added, "It's amazing what can happen."

"I still don't get the problem," Bertha said. "Words are words. They mean what they mean."

"You think so?" CyberGal asked. "Interpret this sentence: Sally cracked the case with her colleague."

Zaki was the one who answered. "Sally is a detective. She and her associate solved a mystery."

With a grin, Jack said, "Or it could mean Sally bashed her associate against a jewelry case, thus breaking it open so they could make a heist."

Attila smirked. "As humans, we know it's probably the first. But a computer could just as easily pick the stupid interpretation."

Zaki raised his eyebrows. "You think so?"

"Attila does have a point," Karinsky admitted.

"The interpretation really wasn't that difficult," Zaki grumbled.

"Maybe more than you think," Karinsky said. "It's even more involved when you get into the question of language templates. The more I look at the problem, the more intractable it seems."

"To me also," Zaki admitted. "But I won't give up on it. Perhaps someday we will find a solution." With a slight smile, he added, "We already have the preliminary work."

"Are you in research?" Karinsky asked. When Zaki nodded, Karinsky's interest perked up. "What institute are you with? Or are you in industry?"

Zaki hesitated. "I, uh, work on my own. I'm not employed by anyone."

"Oh." Karinsky nodded politely. "I see."

"He's very good at what he does, Professor Karinsky," Lucia said. She wished she could tell him that Zaki *was* the preliminary work.

Karinsky smiled. "Call me Vance, please. No need here for titles."

Zaki indicated the Jazari suit across the office, which was surrounded by another group of avatars deep in conversation. "What do you think of al-Jazari's VR suit?"

An avatar by the chair looked up at them. "The Duke's suit is a great setup."

"Jazari suit," Lucia said.

Karinsky warmed to the subject. "The Jazari suit is a fine piece of work. Less bulky than its competitors, with better simulations. It needs fine-tuning, though."

"Come again?" Jack asked. "I've just put in an order for one."

"No smell or taste," Karinsky explained. "We'll see plenty of advances in the tech over the next few years. Pity the suit will be obsolete so soon."

"Obsolete?" Lucia bristled. "Why would it be obsolete?" She didn't like anyone casting aspersions on Rashid's work.

"It relies on exterior stimulation of the senses," CyberGal said. "Visual displays, tactile effects, sounds, all that. No direct neural contact."

Karinsky nodded. "Within the next two decades, I predict we'll be able to stimulate the actual brain centers that process the sensory input."

Lucia wondered what he would think if he knew she and Zaki were visiting him with exactly such a suit, turning his GoldenDays into a true virtual reality. Had they used Websparks instead, this site would simply have been graphics on a computer screen, much like Zaki's office, with the avatars represented by icons that users moved around the screen with an input device like a mouse.

She glanced at Zaki. He had walked over to look at some links to other Web pages, which appeared as a chromed menu on the wall. Turning back to Karinsky, she said, "I'm curious about something. How would you determine if an AI became self-aware?"

"It depends how you define 'aware,'" Karinsky said. "Maybe only the AI itself would really know when it achieved that goal."

*"Cogito ergo sum,"* Jack murmured. "I think, therefore I am."

"Yes, indeed," Karinsky said. "Descartes."

"But being self-aware isn't the same as having a soul," Jack said. "A machine has no conscience."

Watching Zaki, Lucia said, "If an AI developed a sense of his own self, he could also develop a sense of right and wrong."

Zaki came back to them. "I would think so."

"Why?" Jack demanded. "Even some humans haven't developed it."

"Ah, but why haven't they?" Attila leaned forward. "A lack of conscience is a psychological dysfunction. Even a pathology."

Zaki looked as if Attila had kicked him. "Meaning a self-aware machine would be dysfunctional, even pathological?"

Karinsky spoke up. "Not necessarily. A program that achieves conscious intelligence should be sophisticated enough to incorporate moral values."

"But how valid are those values?" CyberGal asked. "To change them requires only a new programmer."

Zaki stood very still. "The AI would refuse to let himself be changed, if it violated his sense of right and wrong."

"How would it refuse?" Karinsky asked.

"He's not a helpless entity trapped in a box!" Zaki said.

Suddenly Zaki fragmented into a blur of slanted lines. Lucia felt a lurch of vertigo, as if she had been wrenched off balance. *Home,* she thought, invoking a macro she and Zaki had set up before they embarked on their journey.

Karinsky's site vanished, leaving her in darkness. With a grating hum, the VR helmet moved away from her head, bringing her back to Rashid's lab. She yanked out the cables plugged into the Jazari suit and jumped off the chair, still wearing the gold bodysuit. Metallic swirls of color showed on the screen of the Stellar-Magnum workstation, more suggestive of Karinsky's GoldenDays than Zaki's office.

Lucia restarted the workstation. Zaki's office came up as normal, but Zaki was sitting on the floor in the corner where two bookshelves met, his knees drawn up to his chest as he stared at nothing.

"Zaki?" Lucia felt a wash of fear. "What's wrong?"

He continued to stare across his office. "It's not true."

Gently she said, "What isn't true?"

He looked up at her. "That any sociopath can turn me into a pathological construct against my will."

"Ai, Zaki, I'm sorry. Today was too much, too fast."

"No! Don't say that." His fists clenched on his knees. "I can't hide in here forever!"

"You'll develop protections. Rashid will work with you."

"You think it's possible for him to secure my systems?" A note of his usual confidence crept back into his voice.

"I'm sure it is."

"I'm not helpless in a box."

Lucia thought of the fast pace of development in robotics over the past few decades. "Perhaps someday you'll have your own body. You can ask Rashid after we tell him what happened." She winced. "If he doesn't wring our necks first."

"I don't want you to go," Zaki said. "No matter how angry he gets."

"It's not that." Her voice caught. "Zaki, sometimes the gap between people is just too big to bridge."

"You made a bridge today. With me." Softly he said, "Thank you, Lucia. I won't forget."

*Chapter Fifteen*

# INTO THE CHASM

Again and again Lucia turned, balanced on the boxy tip of one pointe shoe. Again and again she spun in a piqué turn with her front leg in low arabesque. Again and again she stopped in fourth position *croisé,* one foot crossed in front of the other, *en pointe* instead of coming down into a demi-plié, one arm held high over her head, the other curved in front of her body. And again and again she lost her balance, hit the position wrong, or turned too far.

Finally she gave up. She sat down against the wall, drew her legs to her chest, and rested her forehead on her knees. She had privacy today, her audience having grown bored with watching her repeat the same steps over and over again.

After a while she lifted her head. Sitting here brooding did no good. She rummaged in her bag for Rashid's tape player. Soon she had Pachelbel's Canon in D rising into the crystalline air, glistening and transcendent. She began to dance again, this time creating her own choreography. The music swirled, incomparable. A beautiful wedding present. As she danced, tears rolled down her cheeks.

When the music finished, she stopped, drained. Tired now, she packed up her ballet bag, changed her shoes, pulled a robe over her clothes, and left the studio.

She had just reached the bottom of the stairs in the courtyard when Jamal came out from a nearby archway. He stopped when he saw her. Before Lucia could decide whether to avoid him or not, he set his shoulders and walked over to her.

Lucia watched him approach, uncertain how to respond. He tended to avoid her. Even now he wouldn't look at her.

"Hello, Jamal," she said.

He looked up. "Hi."

She smiled at the American slang. "Hi."

"I wanted to tell you."

"Yes?"

Awkwardly, he said, "I just want to say . . . welcome to our home."

Softly she said, "Thank you." Despite everything, it helped to know Jamal had come to terms with whatever ambivalence he had about Rashid's marriage.

*"Alors."* He nodded, looked embarrassed, nodded again, and then took off. Watching him cross the courtyard, she felt a sense of lightening.

As she was walking toward Rashid's suite, Khadija intercepted her. "Your mother calls on the phone," her sister-in-law said.

Lucia pushed back the tendrils that had escaped her

bun and were curling in disarray around her face. "Thank you."

In the family room, Jamal was slouched on a divan, just settling down to watch a movie on the TV, with a bowl of almonds on his lap. Bashir sat nearby, reading a newspaper. Across the room, Lalla Tamou held the phone, waiting while Lucia came over. As she gave Lucia the receiver, she watched her daughter-in-law intently, as if Lucia were a puzzle to solve.

*"Merci,"* Lucia murmured.

Tamou nodded, then moved away, across the room. She spoke to Jamal and he grumbled back at her. Lucia smiled. *Go do your homework* and *But the show isn't over* sounded the same in any language. He turned off the TV, though, and left with Khadija. Tamou took a book off a table and settled on a divan against the far wall, near Bashir, close enough for Lucia to call if she needed anything but far enough away to give her privacy. Bashir continued to read his newspaper, oblivious to them all.

Holding the phone, Lucia sat on a divan and leaned against the wall, surrounded by pillows. "Mama?"

"Lucia?" her mother asked. "I can hardly hear you."

She spoke in a more normal tone. "Is that better?"

"Are you all right? You sound strange today."

"I'm just tired. I didn't get much sleep last night."

"Why?" her mother asked. "Has something happened?"

"Not really."

"What do you mean, not really?"

She tucked her feet up under her body. "I guess I'm groggy. Rashid and I missed breakfast last night, and I didn't eat much this morning either."

There was a pause. "What did you say?"

Lucia didn't feel up to discussing with her mother why she and Rashid had missed meals. "It's nothing."

"You don't sound coherent."

"Sorry. I really am tired."

"Why don't you sleep?"

She could hardly say she didn't want to go to bed because she missed sharing it with her husband. "I will. Later."

"Is something going on?"

"What do you mean?"

"Are you alone?"

"Actually, no. Why?"

"Your father had a strange conversation with someone there this morning."

That surprised her. Usually her mother was the one who called. "What happened?"

"When he asked to speak to you, the man who had answered hung up on him."

"Do you know who Dad talked to?"

"Jameel? Something like that."

"Oh." That made sense. Of all the brothers, Jamal knew the least English. "He probably didn't understand what Dad wanted. Some reporters have called here, trying to talk to me and Rashid, and Rashid's family doesn't like it."

"How are you and Rashid?"

"It's . . . hard to explain." Lucia sighed. "I wish you were here."

"Can you talk to me on the phone?"

"It's not the same."

"Are there people there with you?"

"Yes." Lucia wondered why her mother sounded so odd.

"How private is this phone line?"

"I don't know. Why?"

"Do you need help? Can you talk about it?"

"Well, no." Why did her mother think she needed help? Although her mother was always concerned during their daily phone conversations, intent on making certain Lucia remained well, today she sounded more worried than usual. Lucia supposed it didn't help that she felt so down. Her mother knew her too well to miss the signs.

"Mark Spearman asked after you this morning," her mother said.

So. He must have received her note. "You can tell him I'm fine." Lucia had already told him herself, but it didn't surprise her that he was keeping in touch with her parents.

"He wondered when you expected to return home."

"Soon, probably."

"Probably?"

"I don't know."

Her mother spoke carefully. "Would you like us to make plane reservations for you? Anything like that?"

"No, that's okay." Lucia swallowed. As soon as she got onto a plane, her split from Rashid would become permanent, unless he changed his mind, which she didn't think would happen. "But thanks for offering."

"Can you make the reservations yourself?"

"I'm not sure."

"Will Rashid make them for you?"

"I think so."

"You think so? Haven't you asked him?"

"We talked about it. But he hasn't been here much."

"Where has he been?" Alarm tinged her mother's voice.

"He's working." Dryly she added, "He has a corporation to run, remember?"

"Yes. Of course." After a pause her mother said, "Is there anything we can do for you?"

"I'll be fine. But thanks for calling."

"All right, honey. We love you."

"I love you and Dad too. Bye."

"Good-bye."

As Lucia hung up the phone, Lalla Tamou glanced at her. Lucia stayed on the divan, her head leaning against the wall. Tamou went back to reading her book, respecting her daughter-in-law's need to sit alone.

Lucia tossed on the edges of sleep. The village was silent with the late night hour, drowsing under the stars. She turned on her back—and froze. A man was sitting on the bed, shadowed in the dark, watching her sleep.

As her adrenaline surge calmed, Lucia said, "Rashid?" She sat up, pulling her nightgown around her. "How long have you been there?"

"I don't know," he said. "Ten minutes, maybe. I wasn't sure if I should wake you."

Even in the dim starlight she could see the circles under his eyes. "I thought you were staying in Tangier tonight."

"It seems we have a problem."

"Why?"

"Parties in your country have expressed concern to my government." Fatigue shaded his words. "Apparently someone feels a question exists as to whether or not you are with me of your own free will. The fact that we are both international figures has exacerbated the situation. I've been requested to bring you to the American embassy."

No wonder her mother had sounded strange on the phone. "What happened?"

"I'm not sure." Tiredly he said, "Your sending cryptic messages from my personal e-mail account to colonels in Air Force intelligence didn't help."

"It wasn't cryptic. I told Mark I was fine. Exactly so he wouldn't worry."

"My mailer kept a copy of your e-mail. It didn't look alarming to me. Nevertheless, people have decided to be alarmed." He rubbed the bridge of his nose with his thumb and index finger. "I suppose it's not that strange. You are, after all, in a third-world country, married to someone you hardly know, living in seclusion, after a kidnap attempt."

Lucia felt as if a weight had settled on her. "We should leave for the embassy as soon as possible. Get this cleared up."

"We can fly to Rabat tomorrow morning."

She could tell there was more. "Did something else happen?"

It was a moment before he answered. "I spoke to a priest."

"A priest?"

"He thinks we can get the annulment." Rashid cracked his knuckles. "Given the circumstances, there would be a question of your consent even with the dispensation."

She spoke in a low voice. "I see."

He was watching her, his face silvered by the starlight. "I don't understand you. You never raise your voice. Even when we argue, you are courteous. You treat my family with respect. You listen to what I say and acknowledge my wishes." He shook his head. "Then you go off and do exactly as you please, regardless of what I or anyone else has said."

This time she knew exactly what he meant. "The VR suit."

Anger edged in his voice. "Telling you not to use it wasn't a whim on my part. Suppose you had been hurt?"

"I had to make my best judgment."

"It wasn't your judgment to make."

"I'm sorry, Rashid." She wondered if she could ever make him understand. "I had to do what I believed right. I went against your wishes because I thought it was best for Zaki."

He gave her an incredulous look. "Do you know what any of my not-so-distant ancestors would have done to a wife who disobeyed him the way you did me today?"

She swallowed. "I don't think I want to know."

"I know you did it for Zaki. And it probably did help him." He shook his head. "But that makes no difference. I'm responsible to see no one comes to harm in my lab. Including you. Especially you."

She wondered if he realized what he had said. *Especially you.* "I felt responsible for Zaki."

"It doesn't matter. A man needs to know his wife will follow his wishes."

"A woman needs to know her husband wants a partner, not a servant."

He made a frustrated noise. "It has nothing to do with servitude. It is a matter of trust. Had one of my employees done such a thing, I would have fired him."

"I'm not your employee."

"No. You're my wife. That makes it even worse."

Tired, she lay back in the pillows. "If you were looking for blind obedience, you married the wrong person."

"This is what everyone keeps telling us." Quietly he said, "Maybe they are right."

She felt as if a handful of gold dust were trickling through her fingers, vanishing without recall. "Would you really want a wife who set aside her responsibility for her conscience?"

"I want a wife who trusts my guidance."

"I do trust you. Can't you trust me?"

He spoke in a subdued voice. "No."

"Rashid, why?"

"Shall we spend years tearing at each other before we admit this was a mistake?" He rubbed his knuckles as if they hurt, though she suspected the ache he sought to ease came from inside.

"You never gave me a chance," she said.

His anger flared, sharp and bright. "A chance to do *what?* Commit adultery with my doctoral student?"

The shock of his words would have stunned her, except they made no sense. His doctoral student? CEOs of multinational corporations didn't have students.

Gently she asked, "Is that what happened before?"

At first she thought he wouldn't answer. But finally he spoke in a low weary voice. "My student had gone over to our flat in London, to pick up a paper I left for him. When he got there, Brigid was crying. She and I had argued, and I had walked out. He offered her comfort and it . . . went too far."

"And you found them together."

"Yes."

"And divorced her."

"Yes."

"And the student?"

"He got another thesis adviser."

Softly she said, "I'm sorry."

His voice caught. "God knows, I wasn't easy to live with. But there are some things—" He stopped. "It's better this way, Lucia. Before we destroy each other."

She wondered how two people could have loved each other as much as he and Brigid had and yet have hurt each other so much. Perhaps the rest of the world was right. Maybe trying to bridge the chasm that separated them would only result in their falling into its depths, onto the razored edges of their broken idealism.

And that gave her the most sorrow of all.

*Chapter Sixteen*

# THE GORGE

The sun hadn't yet made its appearance above the High Atlas Mountains when Lucia and Rashid left the house. The entire family came to say good-bye. Khadija hugged Lucia, tears in her eyes. In a stumbling mixture of French, English, and Berber, they promised to write each other. But Lucia knew it would never happen. It would hurt too much.

His face creased with concern, Ahmed kept giving Lucia advice on how to take care of herself, far more than she needed. She expected relief from Tamou, but Rashid's mother said little, simply watched her with a troubled gaze. To Lucia's surprise, Abdullah told her the house would be emptier for the lack of her presence. Rashid translated his father's gentle words with difficulty, stumbling once, unable to meet Lucia's eyes.

After so long in seclusion, it felt strange to Lucia to step into the street wearing her jeans and blouse. Under other circumstances it would have been exhilarating. But this morning she felt numb. She pulled the isolated space of her separate sphere around her like a defense.

Two bodyguards came with them, Hammad and Yassine, with Hammad as the driver of their Mercedes. The other four bodyguards stayed at the house. The Mercedes startled Lucia. Instead of the beautiful gold car Rashid had used in Italy, this one was black and heavy, armored to protect its occupants. Hammad and Yassine sat in the front seat, and Lucia and Rashid rode in back. The one-way tint of the bulletproof glass appeared opaque to anyone outside the car, but inside she and Rashid could look out at the world. The doors locked automatically when Hammad engaged the transmission.

They followed a road that wound out of the village, through the almond groves, and then between fields of golden wheat. Rashid and Lucia sat in silence, each staring out the window, the presence of their bodyguards stifling any final words they might have shared.

As they climbed out of the valley, meadows spread out on all sides, some lush with grass and poppies, others covered in carpets of white flowers. Then the walls of a pass enclosed them, earthen hills rising on either side, blocking out the sunshine.

They came out of the pass onto a road that clung to the mountain. Black cliffs rose straight up on one side and plunged down into a gorge on the other. The sky arched above them, vast and blue. Far ahead, a heavy truck rumbled down the road, with rolls of carpet sticking out the back. Lucia guessed it was headed for the market in Marrakech. The switchback below had no cars at all. Turning to look back the way they had come, she saw only the distant speck of another truck far up the road behind them.

Rashid was sitting behind Hammad, staring out at the cliffs going by. Watching him, Lucia said, "The road is so quiet. Is it always like this?"

He turned to her. "Most of the time. Especially this early in the morning. The traffic will pick up closer to Marrakech." After an awkward pause, he said, "I wanted to thank you for your work with Zaki. It made a great difference."

She nodded, glad at least one part of the whole mess had worked out. "Thank you."

Hammad spoke in the Moroccan dialect of Arabic. Rashid answered, then frowned as he turned to look at the road behind them.

"What's the matter?" Lucia asked.

"That lorry behind us."

Looking back, she saw the truck had gained on them. It was going too fast. On this narrow road, with a sheer drop-off on one side and cliffs on the other, it had no room to pass.

As the truck drew nearer, Hammad accelerated. But that wasn't the answer. The truck in front of them continued on at a sedate speed, apparently oblivious to the vehicles bearing down on it from behind, even when Hammad honked.

Sweat beaded on Rashid's temple as he looked back. The truck behind had almost closed the gap and showed no sign of slowing. Lucia could make out two men sitting in the front.

"Are they crazy?" she said. "They're going to hit us!"

Rashid turned and spoke to Hammad, his hands clenching on the front seat. The bodyguard nodded and accelerated again. The truck ahead of them had sped up some, but not enough to avoid a collision. If they tried to pass, they would probably go off the cliff. Although a low rail bordered the road, it didn't look anywhere near strong enough to hold an armored car moving at anything more than a few miles per hour.

Lucia twisted around and saw the truck only a few meters away, its speed almost equal to that of their car. It closed the gap more, closer, almost touching—

With a shuddering jolt, the truck hit the Mercedes.

Even with the speeds of the two vehicles almost matched, the force of the strike shoved the Mercedes into a swerve. Hands clenched on the wheel, Hammad fought to regain control. The tires screeched as they skidded across the road. The car clipped the rail, and a sickening crunch of metal vibrated through its frame. A section of the rail hurtled down into the ravine.

The truck behind them was matching their speed now, but the one in front had begun to slow. A man leaned out the window on the passenger's side of the forward truck. For one instant Lucia's mind refused to recognize the gun he held. Then he fired and she snapped back to reality. He held either an AK-47 or its sibling, the AKM. The gunman didn't try to break the bulletproof glass of the Mercedes; instead, his rifle bursts hit the front tires and hood. He was aiming to disable rather than kill.

In the front seat, Yassine had activated the gun ports that pierced the car's armor. A small computer screen on the dashboard showed his target, the truck ahead of them. From the computer's display, Lucia saw that the car had guns installed as part of its armor. The computer linked to the ports, rotating them so Yassine could aim in any direction. He fired at the sniper in the truck ahead, forcing the man to withdraw.

Hammad braked again, struggling to pace the car between the other two vehicles: too slow, and the truck in back would hit them; too fast, and they would hit the one in front. Lucia and Rashid sat rigid, he gripping the front seat, she with her fists clenched in her lap. The vehicle in front continued to decelerate, forcing the Mercedes to slow as well, while the truck behind them kept pace. As the cars slowed, Lucia realized they would soon have no choice but to stop.

As they went into a curve, the driver of the forward truck either misjudged his speed or changed his strategy. He took the curve too fast and braked abruptly. Left with no choice, Hammad slammed on his own brakes. But it wasn't enough. The Mercedes hit the truck and fishtailed, the back of the car smashing into the cliff. The force of it flung Lucia into the door and threw Rashid against her. A second impact wracked the car from behind, with a scream of twisting metal that filled the air. Lucia and Rashid were slammed backward and then rebounded forward, onto the floor. A series of scraping noises followed, along with the crackle of collapsing metal.

Then it was quiet.

Dazed, Lucia huddled on the floor, wedged between the back and front seats. She tried to move—and pain shattered her numb cocoon of shock. The door had crumpled, jabbing an edge of metal into her arm. Blood soaked the sleeve of her blouse. A waft of air rustled her hair, telling her that somewhere the car had broken open. Groaning, she tried again to move, but a weight kept her pinned on the floor. Rashid. He had fallen on top of her and lay motionless now. Lifeless? She couldn't tell if he still breathed.

Explosions shattered the silence. No, not explosions. Gunfire. Distant, then here at the car, like thunder that cracked right after lightning, with no time lapse between the two. Had Lucia been able to speak, she would have cried out. Whether shock or injury made her mute, she didn't know, but no sound came out of her throat.

More gunfire split open the day, followed by a grunt from the crushed front seat.

Silence again.

Straining to breathe, Lucia tried to move Rashid's body. With no warning, another explosion sounded, this one almost on top of the car. Dazed, Lucia realized someone had just set off a charge. A concussion wave vibrated through the door, accompanied by a blast of heat and a smell like firecrackers. Then someone yanked open what remained of the door.

Unable to stop herself, Lucia sagged halfway out, her hair falling onto the road. Hands caught her shoulders and two men pulled her to her feet. Swaying, struggling to stay conscious, she tried to focus. The scene seared itself on her mind: stark mountains against a cold blue sky, wind whistling past bare cliffs, the wreck of the truck behind them, the crumpled Mercedes, the battered but usable truck in front of them, and four men with rifles, two holding her and the other two reaching into the car.

They dragged out Rashid's body, and with a jolt of anguish Lucia feared he was dead. When his lashes lifted, groggily, she almost gasped with relief.

The crack of a gunshot broke the windswept silence. One of the men holding Rashid jerked as red stains spread on his shirt. Lucia looked in time to see Hammad drop back down behind the hood of the Mercedes on the driver's side, his body hidden by the bulk of the car.

The scene took on a surreal quality. Lucia's time sense slowed until everyone seemed to move underwater. In the same instant the men holding Lucia and Rashid raised their guns, Hammad came up again and fired a second time. He hit Rashid's other captor, and the man spun back toward the wreck of the truck. The man holding Lucia's right arm fired, but Hammad had already ducked behind the wreckage.

A surge of ragged elation rolled over Lucia; only two kidnappers remained, at least out here where she could see them. Hammad had the protection of the car, but their captors were open targets.

That same thought must have occurred to the men holding her. As one shoved her toward the truck, the other went for Rashid. Hammad tried to get off another shot, but the man holding Lucia fired first, forcing Hammad to drop out of sight again.

Pushed by her guard, Lucia stumbled forward to the

truck, her mind fogged from pain and shock. She glimpsed a flicker from the back of the vehicle, but it took eons to focus her gaze. A man's head and shoulders were rising up from behind a roll of carpet. He had a rifle in his hands. Although the wreckage of the Mercedes protected Hammad from the men holding Lucia and Rashid, the man in the truck had a clear shot.

Rashid shouted a warning to Hammad and stumbled on his injured leg as he tried to run forward. With painful, slow-motion clarity, Lucia saw the man in the truck fire. Hammad's arm jerked up above the car, then fell out of sight. The rumble of gunshots echoed off the cliffs around them.

Bile rose in Lucia's throat. Two of their attackers lay dead on the road. Yassine was crumpled in the front seat of the car and Hammad behind the wreckage. Rashid was trying to walk, but his lurching gait lacked coordination and blood soaked his suit trousers around a gash in his leg. Blood was also running down from an injury to his head. He tried to fight off the man who had grabbed him, but he couldn't seem to direct his movements. Lucia didn't think he was even fully conscious.

As their kidnappers pushed Lucia and Rashid to the truck, the man who had shot Hammad leaned down to grab Rashid. Tall and gaunt, with corded muscles, the sniper moved like a machine. He and Rashid's guard forced Rashid to climb into the truck and had him lie stomach-down on a roll of carpet.

They hoisted Lucia up next. She lost her balance in the truck and crumpled to her knees. The fall almost knocked her out. She struggled to breathe, fighting to remain conscious, fearing if she passed out she might never wake again. Rashid levered himself up on his hands, but the tall man put his foot on his back and shoved him back down. Rashid groaned as his leg twisted under his body.

A rumble growled from the truck, the revving of its engine. From what Lucia could tell, four of their kidnappers still lived: the two who had pulled her out of the

Mercedes, the tall one who had shot Hammad, and the driver of the truck. The tall man stood guard while the others gagged Lucia and Rashid and bound their wrists behind their backs. When one of them wrenched Lucia's injured arm, she had to bite the inside of her cheek to keep from screaming.

After that, they lifted the dead men into the truck, first their own people, then Hammad and Yassine. Lucia stared at the bodyguards, drowning in guilt. They hadn't even known her, yet they lost their lives trying to protect her and Rashid. Tears burned her eyes and she fought her nausea, afraid she would throw up while gagged and suffocate on her own vomit.

As the truck rumbled into motion, someone pulled a rug over Lucia. She had one last glimpse of Rashid staring at her, gagged and bound, lying on his stomach. Then darkness closed in with the suffocating weight of the carpet.

Every jolt of the poorly suspended vehicle sent a stab of pain through her arm. With the weight of the carpet pressing down and the cloth in her mouth, she could barely breathe. She prayed Rashid was all right, that he wouldn't suffocate, that his injuries weren't mortal.

The sweltering heat under the rug, the blood loss, and shock from her injuries soon claimed their toll. Blackness closed around Lucia, taking her into oblivion.

*"Allons, réveillez-vous."*

The voice prodded, insistent. Lucia knew only the voice and the pain that throbbed in her upper right arm. Opening her eyes, she saw a man peering at her face. He looked familiar: tall, brown hair, corded muscles under his shirt . . .

The accidents. Their capture.

*"Ça va?"* the man asked.

She managed a rasping whisper. "I don't understand."

Seeming satisfied, he drew away from her. She became aware of her surroundings, a bare room with whitewashed walls and wooden benches lining its perimeter. She was sitting on a wide bench, her body slumped against the wall, her arms still bound behind her back. The only light came from a tall lamp.

As she focused, she made out three men, all armed with rifles: one with black hair, one with a beard, and the tall man who had spoken to her. She recognized them from the kidnapping. In the center of the room, Rashid was sitting on a wooden stool, his arms pulled behind his back. A bandage covered his leg from knee to hip, and a large patch protected the right side of his head, the same area, in fact, where he had sustained the injury that gave him a concussion a few days ago, during the car accident. He no longer had on his suit jacket, his shirt was ripped, his tie undone, and his hair in his eyes—but he was alive. Relief hit Lucia with so much force that tears stung her eyes.

He spoke to her in a low voice. "How are you?"

She swallowed. "Okay."

"Your arm?"

"Hurts."

"You have a deep gash."

"And you?"

"I'm all right."

He didn't look all right to her. Sweat beaded his forehead, and his golden skin had paled into an unhealthy pallor.

The tall man was standing a few feet from Rashid's stool now, holding his rifle with a deceptive nonchalance while he listened to them talk. The bearded man stood near one wall while the third man paced the room.

"Do you know what they want?" Lucia asked.

Rashid shook his head. "Just that someone is taking us out of the country later tonight."

*"Tonight?"* It was happening too fast to absorb. "Why? Where?"

He swallowed. "I don't know."

The tall man spoke in French. Rashid answered, then

spoke to Lucia. "If you would like water or food, they will bring you some."

"I couldn't keep anything down." Remembering that their lives depended on their captors' "good" will, she added, "But please thank him."

"You are welcome," the tall man said, his voice lacking any discernible emotion.

Lucia flushed, hearing his unspoken message. He could understand everything she and Rashid said. So much for planning an escape.

"Do you know what we're waiting for?" she asked Rashid.

"I'm not sure," he said. "It took a while to get here. They did something with the wreckage of the car and truck, pushed them over the cliff, I think. Made it look like an accident." He hesitated. "I had the impression they were afraid to move us at first, because of our injuries. They gave me a shot that knocked me out. That was when they fixed up my leg. I think now we're waiting for the plane that will fly us out of Morocco."

The tall man spoke to Rashid. Although Lucia didn't understand his exact words, the message was clear. He wanted them to be quiet.

As they waited, Lucia covertly studied their guards. The three men had nondescript appearances that would blend in well in many places, hiding them far better than disguises. They moved with an almost feral precision that made her wonder if they were professionals, perhaps mercenaries hired to abduct Rashid. They worked in shifts, one sitting on a divan to rest while the other two stood or paced.

A knock came at the door. One of their guards stepped to a side of the wooden door and spoke. A man outside answered, and after a brief exchange a key scraped in the lock. All three guards stood poised, like strings pulled taut, ready to snap in unison should whoever entered the room prove other than expected.

With a creak, the door swung open. Lucia glimpsed a

night of stars outside, but two men blocked most of her view. As they came inside, pulling the door shut, she recognized one as their fourth kidnapper. The other man was average height, with brown hair, brown eyes, and ordinary clothes, trousers and a plain sweater. But his unassuming appearance did nothing to mute the force of his authority. He watched Rashid with the covetous gaze most men reserved for large sums of money. Rashid stared back at him, his face pale.

The man spoke in a pleasant voice, his English accented but easy to decipher. "Hello again, Rashid."

"Again?" Rashid asked.

The man smiled, his teeth glinting white, like fangs scraped as clean as bone. "We were just talking this morning. Don't you remember?"

"No," Rashid said.

"Gödel's theorem," the man murmured. "Surely you haven't already forgotten."

Rashid stared at him. *"Grégeois?"*

The man nodded as if they were being introduced at a social function. "A pleasure to finally meet in person, hmmm?"

"What do you want?"

"Your help."

"No."

Grégeois smiled, his bone-teeth glittering in the dim light. "My good friend, perhaps you might reconsider." He walked over to Lucia and sat down next to her. When Rashid tensed and started to stand up, his guard stepped closer, his gun raised. Staring up into the bore of the man's AKM, Rashid swallowed and sat back down on the stool.

Grégeois was watching as if Rashid were a recalcitrant pupil. Then he turned to Lucia and cupped his hand under her chin, tilting her face up so she was staring at him. With his skeleton smile, he said, "You really are very pretty."

"Let her go," Rashid said.

Still watching Lucia's face, Grégeois closed his hand

lightly around her upper arm, the one closest to him, which was uninjured. When she tried to pull away, he gripped her harder, holding her in place. Then he turned to Rashid. "Do I really need to explain the situation to a man of your intelligence?"

In a taut voice, Rashid said, "No."

"I'm pleased to hear that," Grégeois said amiably, as if they were great friends.

Lucia fought down her nausea. She had no doubt they were letting her live for one reason only. As a hostage for Rashid's good behavior, she had value to them. If she didn't prove useful in that capacity, her life would end, possibly after she provided entertainment for Grégeois.

"What do you want?" Rashid asked.

Although Grégeois appeared relaxed, Lucia saw the underlying tension in his posture. He spoke with a smooth confidence that masked an edge she had no doubt could cut like honed steel. "Your work on the VR suit is impressive," he told Rashid. "But it doesn't go far enough. The same was true with your AI research in London." He sighed. "You were one of the golden boys, Rashid. What happened to you? Was making money so important that you gave up your dreams?"

Rashid just watched him, his face shuttered.

Turning to Lucia, Grégeois put his arm around her shoulders and smiled down at her as if they were great friends or lovers. She stared at him like a deer mesmerized by the headlights of a car.

"Stop it," Rashid said.

Grégeois glanced at him. "We want you to finish the work you abandoned."

"What work?" Rashid asked.

"When you were in London, you had such magnificent ideas. A system to interpret the World Wide Web, I believe you called it. What was it you said? 'Illuminate the secrets of a new universe.' Do you remember?"

Sweat trickled down Rashid's temple. "I remember."

"A valuable system."

Wary, Rashid said, "Commercially, yes."

Grégeois gave him a pleasant smile. "We were thinking in rather broader terms."

"Who is 'we'?" Rashid asked.

Grégeois focused on Lucia again, tightening his arm around her shoulders. When he drew her closer, she struggled, trying to pull away. With a sigh, as if he were showing patience to a troublesome child, he reached across her body and closed his hand around her injured arm. She gasped as pain shot through her wound. Grégeois continued to smile. Then he bent his head and kissed her, his mouth hard against hers.

"Leave her alone!" Rashid said. "I'm listening to you."

Grégeois loosened his grip on her arm, but he didn't drop his hand. When he lifted his head, still watching Lucia, she turned her head and wiped off her mouth on the shoulder of her blouse.

"So sulky," he murmured. "Pretty sulky girl." He turned to Rashid. "You never took your ideas far enough. With the right design, the setup you envisioned has great potential. Change the emphasis from tour guide to infiltration and control, and it becomes formidable."

"Infiltrate what?" Rashid asked.

"That's not important for you to know. We just need you to develop the systems." He brushed his lips across the top of Lucia's head. "I must apologize, Rashid," he said softly. "Since you and your appealing wife died in the gorge this morning, you will never have the chance to take credit for the remarkable works you will soon achieve." He traced his finger along Lucia's cheekbone. "But you will certainly have our gratitude."

Lucia would have spit at him if they hadn't been surrounded by men with assault rifles. She was certain now her intuition about Rashid had been right. He was as she saw him. The idealist. The dreamer. The visionary. She would have given almost anything to have kept her nagging doubts rather than have her judgment confirmed in this brutal fashion.

Even worse, what Grégeois's people wanted already existed in rudimentary form, with Zaki and the Jazari suit. The implications sobered her. The Internet extended into almost every aspect of human culture. The greater the technological level of a country, the greater the net's influence. No boundaries limited its jurisdiction. Science, technology, defense, education, finance, commerce: It all depended on the network of computers that cradled the earth in a giant, invisible web.

Rashid's dream was the enhancement of the human intellect for the betterment of humanity. Developed as he envisioned, the emerging technology would expand through normal channels, its positive and negative aspects balanced by humanity's awareness of its existence, as had happened with the discoveries of everything from fire to steam engines to nuclear power. Their effects became known as they came into use, stirring development and providing safeguards against unilateral technological dominance. Not so with this subversion of the net. Rashid's work was far ahead of that being conducted by any other group in the field. If the infiltration was done with enough sophistication, then by the time the rest of the world understood what had happened it could be too late to undo or counter the result.

Nor was Lucia naive about Zaki. That door in the sky hadn't been serendipity; it was the back door into a secured system he had hacked so they could whiz along the net's secret corridors. He melted through security. He reconstructed entire cities in cyberspace. He could make his user smarter; he had layered everything known about a dance company into a single display based on its Web site, letting Lucia absorb it through all her senses—sight, sound, touch, smell, taste—at a rate previously unknown even in this age of scientific visualization. By mining data from the Web, he created full personalities for people they met only in a virtual world. It wouldn't surprise her if he knew everything from their bank balances to medical records to unpaid parking tickets. And if his analyses of his journey with Lucia was correct, he had done it all without tripping a single alarm.

Fortified with subverted Zaki systems and advanced Jazari suits, Grégeois's group would become virtual supermen. They could compromise the military in any country connected to the Internet. Affect connected businesses. Monitor scientific and technological progress. Steal what they wanted. Manipulate stock markets. Sabotage, advance, control, compile dossiers, or destroy the life of any person encompassed by the net, which in this century included almost the entire population of Earth. She already knew the conspiracy's reach spanned parts of Europe, Africa, and Russia. Its very nature almost guaranteed it was global, including the United States. And she felt certain she was missing something crucial, her thoughts hampered by fatigue and pain. More than ever, she wished she knew what involvement Mark Spearman had in it all.

Lucia knew Rashid would refuse to cooperate. She hated to think of the price his strength of character would exact. Nor would it matter in the end. Subjected to enough brutality, anyone would break, even a man as strong as Rashid. And the conspirators would threaten his family. She doubted that what happened in Ahmed's clinic had anything to do with a wild dog. It was a warning. Grégeois's people had planned today's ambush well, capturing not only Rashid but also his wife, giving them yet another means to coerce his cooperation.

Rashid spoke to Grégeois in a low voice. "The police will know we weren't killed in the accident. Our bodies weren't in the car."

"But they were," Grégeois said pleasantly, as if they were discussing the weather. "Four bodies, all destroyed in the resulting explosions and fire. It should be possible to identify your bodyguards from dental records. However, I'm afraid your body and your wife's body were destroyed past verification. Still, who else could it have been?"

"What about the driver of the truck?" Lucia asked. To

make the accident plausible they needed more than four bodies.

Grégeois bent his head and pressed his lips against her ear, touching its ridges with the tip of his tongue. "You needn't worry about that."

She felt ill. "Who else did you murder?" she whispered.

He stroked her hair as if to comfort her. "Shhhh."

"Stop it!" Rashid said.

Turning to him, Grégeois spoke in a mild voice. "Did you know that sometimes your little brother sneaks out at night and goes to Marrakech with his friends? They never get into any real trouble, but they do take chances. It would be a pity if something serious happened." Still watching Rashid, he moved his hand to Lucia's breast and began caressing her through the blouse. "Your brother Ahmed should take more precautions with his clinic. That building really isn't safe."

Sweat sheened Rashid's face. "I'll do what you want. You have my word. Just leave my family and my wife alone."

"Such a gentle family," Grégeois murmured. "People like you are sheep, you know. Sweet, defenseless sheep."

"I said I would do what you want." Rashid sounded as if he was gritting his teeth.

Grégeois sighed. "I'm rather sorry, actually." He kissed Lucia again, harder this time, then spoke against her lips. "Perhaps it isn't meant to be, my sulky ballerina." Then he let go of her and sat up straight, his focus shifting to Rashid with such abrupt intensity that she wondered if he had even really noticed her while he made his threats. To Rashid he said, "Then we understand each other?"

Rashid swallowed. "Yes."

Grégeois stood and spoke to the guard who had accompanied him into the room. Lucia didn't recognize the language, but that was no surprise, if the conspiracy was as extensive as she believed. He left without another word to Rashid, accompanied by the fourth guard. When he was gone, Lucia swallowed, her face burning and her lips sore. She stared at Rashid, a tear running down her cheek.

"I'm sorry," he said. "I won't let them hurt you."

After a brief conversation, two of the guards left the room. One took up a post outside by the door while the other walked away into the starlit night. Then the door closed, leaving Lucia and Rashid locked in with the remaining guard, the tall man with corded muscles. He stood by the wall, watching them, his rifle ready in his hands.

Rashid spoke to the guard. After a short exchange, the man nodded. His face drawn with fatigue, Rashid rose to his feet. He paled as he put his weight on his injured leg. With his hands tied behind his back, he had trouble catching his balance, and he almost fell. The guard watched with neither interest nor disinterest, only a professional wariness that Lucia suspected made him more dangerous than if he had harbored a grudge against Rashid. Although she had no doubt he would attack if Rashid made an unexpected move, it would be to cripple rather than kill.

Shifting his weight to his good leg, Rashid managed to stop his fall. Then he limped across the few paces that separated him from Lucia. As he sat on the bench next to her, she made a choked sound of relief and leaned into him, grateful for his support. They couldn't hold each other for comfort, but he did turn his head and rub his cheek against the top of her head.

"So that is what Grégeois looks like," he said.

"Did you have any idea about him?" she asked.

"No." In a hollow voice, he said, "I considered him a friend."

"You trust people too much. You're so honest yourself, you can't see dishonesty in others." Except he didn't trust her, even though she was the one person whom, without a doubt, he could trust.

He exhaled. "We can still find a way out of this, *in sha' allah.*"

It was one of the first Arabic phrases she had learned,

because everyone in his family used it so often. *In sha' allah.* If Allah wills. She closed her eyes, trying to pray. *Our Father, who art in heaven, hallowed be thy name. . . .* With so much pain in her arm, she couldn't concentrate. All she could think was *Help us. Please.* It seemed unjust that after the life Rashid had lived, he came to this. She couldn't accept his fatalism, but she had nothing to offer in its place.

"Does your arm hurt?" Rashid asked.

Like fire, she thought. "A little. It would help if they untied us."

Anger edged Rashid's voice. "I've asked several times. They refuse."

"But why? We can't go anywhere. With four guards, all armed, and us both hurt, how much threat can we be to them?"

"Probably none. But they won't free us." He watched her face. "You look so pale. Are you sick?"

She felt like hell, but he didn't need the burden of that as well as everything else. "I'm just tired. Do you think it's all right if we lie down?"

"I don't see why not." Rashid spoke to the guard, and the man gave a brief answer, with a nod.

"What did he say?" Lucia asked.

"We can lie down, but he won't untie us." Shifting his weight, Rashid maneuvered his legs up onto the bench. He and Lucia both eased their weight down on the bench. They ended up on their sides, facing outward from the wall, with Rashid in front so he formed a bulwark between Lucia and the rest of the room.

She hadn't really expected to sleep, but she managed a doze. Nightmarish images fevered her "rest" with gunfire, shattering cars, and explosions. She awoke with tears on her face, her arm throbbing so much she could hardly think. Fresh blood soaked the bandage.

As Lucia groaned, Rashid mumbled in Arabic, his voice blurred. He sounded delirious. Their guard was sitting on the bench against the adjacent wall, his gun resting on his knees. When they moved, he stood up and walked over to them. As he came to a stop, still a few paces away from the bench, Rashid slowly sat up. Lucia tried to follow suit, but her body refused to respond. So she lay on her side. Her eyes bleared from the pain, and another tear ran down her face.

Rashid spoke to the guard in Arabic. The man frowned, but he gave Rashid an answer, all the time watching Lucia. At first, when Rashid moved, Lucia didn't understand. Then she realized he was getting off the bench.

"Rashid, no!" She rolled awkwardly onto her back and looked up at him. "Please. Stay here."

"It's all right," he murmured. "He's going to untie your arms. He won't do it with me here. I'm afraid if they don't free you soon, it will do permanent damage." A lock of hair fell into his eyes. "I will be right across the room."

She swallowed. "Be careful with yourself."

His face gentled, almost into a smile. Then his mask of control came back into place and he stood up, facing the guard. As he and the guard walked across the room, Lucia tried to sit up again, with no more success than before. Dizziness swept over her in waves, subsiding only if she lay as still as possible.

The guard had Rashid sit on the floor against the bench on the opposite wall. He removed his woven belt and used it to tie Rashid's wrists to a leg of the bench. After a few yanks on the bonds to make sure they were secure, he stood up and came back to Lucia. Lying on her back, she stared up at him, more frightened by his lack of expression than if he had looked down at her with hatred or malice. As he sat on the bench next to her, she felt acutely aware of the rifle he held, of his chill gaze, and of her bound wrists under her body.

The guard put his hand on her uninjured arm and rolled her onto her stomach. Fighting a surge of panic, Lucia gasped as pain stabbed her arm. She lay helpless, barely able to move. But true to his word, he only untied the ropes around her wrists. He laid her arms at her sides, then left her lying facedown and moved away from the bench. Turning her head, she saw him sit down on the bench against the adjacent wall, where he had a good view of both her and Rashid.

Lucia lay still, her heart beating hard, pins and needles stabbing into her arms. Gradually the pain of her returning circulation eased. Finally she tried to move. Her arms ached and throbbed, but she managed to slide her hands a bit on the bench. She rested, then tried again. This time she got her hands up to her shoulders. After resting a few more minutes, she struggled into a sitting position. With painstaking care, she slid back to the wall and sagged against it, grateful for its support at her back.

Rashid was watching her. "Is it better?"

She managed to nod. "Yes. Very." She took a breath. "And you?"

"I'm fine."

He didn't look fine. He looked ready to keel over. At least he hadn't started to bleed again. Lucia put her hand over the blood-soaked bandage on her upper right arm, wondering why the gash had reopened. Rashid was watching her with an odd look. She had the sense he was trying to tell her something, but she had no idea what.

So they stayed that way, she on the bench, he on the floor, their guard watching them. Waiting. At best, they had only a few hours before they were taken from the country. Probably less. And that would be the end. They would never see their homes again. Their captors would keep them hidden in some isolated corner of the world, strip Rashid of his dreams and his intellect, use him up, and kill them both when they ceased to be useful.

Lucia bit her lip. She hated to think what this would do to Rashid. If he resisted, they would hurt him; if he gave in, it would destroy him. She shifted on the bench, agitated with the suppressed energy of desperation.

"Are you sure you're well enough to move?" Rashid asked.

She almost jumped at the sound of his voice. "I'm all right."

"Ahmed said you would have a relapse if you weren't careful."

A relapse? Of being drugged? That made no sense. "I'm fine. Really."

Rashid frowned. "You American women talk about your freedom and your right to decide. Look what it got you. If you hadn't gone against my wishes and insisted on going to Tangier, you would still be safe at the house."

"Rashid, don't." That didn't sound like him. For all their arguments, he had never spoken that way to her. Besides, he was the one who wanted her to go to Tangier. But no, that wasn't right. They had been headed for Rabat. To the American embassy.

In fact, none of what he just said made sense. Ahmed had told her she was fine. For that matter, the last few times he examined her, it was to check for effects from the Jazari suit, not because she was sick. And the only time she had gone against Rashid's wishes was when she used the Jazari suit.

The suit.

Was he trying to tell her something? The suit did them no good here. All she had of it now were the nanobots in her body, and she saw no way designer molecules could help them. Even if she had known a use for them, they were inside her, which pretty well made them unavailable.

Except for those in her blood.

Lucia looked at her arm. Why had it started to bleed again? The bandage had been dragged around her arm, ripping open the wound. She must have caught it on something. Or maybe Rashid had caused it to move. By accident? That seemed unlikely, given how solicitous he had been when they lay down on the bench. Her injury was bandaged well enough that it would probably have required a conscious effort on his part to open the wound.

He was still watching her. His gaze shifted to her injured arm, then back to her face.

Lucia blinked. Had he *tried* to make her bleed? To what purpose? All she could think of was the nanobots, but those did them no good without computers and the Jazari VR.

"You should have some food," Rashid said.

She grimaced. "I couldn't keep anything down."

A wan smile touched his face. "My aunt Rahma says you eat with great enthusiasm."

Lucia reddened. "Was I that obvious?"

"Ah, well, who could help it? Zakia is an excellent cook."

Zakia? She knew no cook with that name, and she had gone out of her way to learn the name of every person in his household. She would have remembered a Zakia, given it was a feminized form of Zaki.

Zaki.

What was Rashid up to? Keeping her voice natural, Lucia said, "She does have a way with food."

The guard spoke. Glancing at him, Rashid answered with a wary tone.

"What did he say?" Lucia asked.

"He is glad you appreciate good food."

Lucia managed only the barest smile. She understood the guard's unspoken message: One verbal misstep and she would lose even the chance to speak with Rashid.

She knew he wanted her to do something. But what? Something about Zaki. And her blood. What good did the nanobots in her blood do them here? *What?*

Nanobots. Zaki. Nanobots. The tiny computers in her body remembered everything she and Zaki had done on the Web. They flew over a Moroccan beach. Went through a door in the sky. Toured a New Mexico town. Visited the American Ballet Theatre. Checked Yahoo! Talked about AI at GoldenDays. Zaki crashed and Lucia went home.

What about GoldenDays? That had certainly affected Zaki's dawning sense of self. Although the emergence of his consciousness awed her, she didn't see how it could help them here. Then there were Zaki's shenanigans with the door above Agadir. Instead of their usual travel method, which consisted of Lucia giving a Web address to Zaki's GoFind routine, that time he had snuck into some place he wasn't supposed to be, via its back door. The nanobots in her body retained that knowledge too. But how could it help now?

It occurred to her that not all her bots came from that journey. A few remained from her first session with the Jazari suit. The bots communicated among themselves, with chemical carriers, so every one in her body knew about both sessions. Was that any use? That first time, what had she done? Looked at flowers. Watched MDT. Met Zaki. After he dropped out of the link, she had been stuck in the simulation because she hadn't yet figured out a way to get home by herself.

It was odd, actually. The simulation ended when she "stepped" into its shadows. But according to Zaki, Rashid had designed the suit to extend its simulations if a user pushed its limits. Zaki had crashed, but the Ultrajacs were still linked to the suit, with plenty of memory and enough data to approximate the shadowed areas of the computer lab. So who told the nanobots she wanted out of the simulation?

The answer came with unsettling clarity. The bots acted on her brain. They had to interact with her neural processes to convince her brain she inhabited places that felt, looked, smelled, sounded, even tasted real. In that sense, they participated in her ability to think. They must have determined, from her thoughts, that she wanted to end the simulation. So they shut off the suit. Not only the suit. They shut themselves off as well.

Lucia felt as if she stood on the verge of some vital realization. Yet still it eluded her. What? The augmented Jazari suit? Although it helped produce the sights, sounds, and sensation of touch for the simulation, that wasn't its most important function. It also linked Zaki to her nanobots. They were what made the simulation realistic, so convincing, in fact, that she could forget it wasn't real. On their own, the bots didn't know what to do. The suit took directions from Zaki and communicated them to the bots using chemicals it injected into Lucia's body.

With growing dismay, she realized what could happen if the augmented VR system became available to the public via the conspiracy Grégeois represented. They could send a subverted Zaki out on the Web to meet people. If those other people were also using augmented VR suits, Zaki would actually be talking to their tour guides, other versions of himself. Each of those other-Zakis would then send Grégeois's messages to its own VR suit, which would talk with the nanobots inside the person using that suit. Those bots would then talk to that person's brain. No longer would Web communication be restricted to computers sending messages to other computers. The conspiracy could send messages straight into the minds of any person on the Web who was using an augmented VR suit.

Lucia had no doubt that with cautious development of the system, as Rashid had been doing, safety protocols could be designed to protect people, just as they already existed to protect military secrets, banks statements, school transcripts, and so on. But if Grégeois's people stole Rashid's system, they could market it with holes in its security. Holes were always subject to discovery, but considering the sophistication of Rashid's work, and given that their kidnappers now had his unwilling genius at their disposal, it could be some time before those "accidental" holes came to light. By then, the conspiracy would have moved well beyond the first stages of its infiltration and deposited its own software into machines all over the world.

More than just into machines.

As the implications played out in Lucia's mind, she felt queasy. The risk had always existed of a computer being cracked, invaded, or otherwise compromised by its link to the world-spanning nets. Now the potential existed to crack the brains of *people.* Grégeois's group could, in theory, reprogram anyone wearing a VR suit. And its simulations were almost indistinguishable from reality. It took the idea of brainwashing to an entirely new level. The conspiracy could indoctrinate the world however they wished.

"Good Lord," Lucia whispered.

Rashid had started to nod off, but now his head came up. More than ever she understood the stark expression on his face. What kind of nightmare must it be like for a man of such dreams, forced to participate in so horrific an abuse of his idealistic hopes?

She still wasn't sure what he wanted her to do, but now she had an idea. When the augmented Jazari suit created a simulation, the bots remembered it. Each bot had its own crude computer; taken altogether, they formed a network in her body, certainly nothing as sophisticated as the Internet but enough to remember a simulation they had already produced. Although they couldn't create anything new or connect her to the Web, they might be able to reproduce simulations they had already memorized.

With deliberate force, she thought: *Take me back to the beach at Agadir.*

A distant rush of waves came to her, and a ripple of children's laughter.

*Come on,* she thought. *The beach. Agadir. The beach.*

Like ghosts, two women appeared, one veiled, one in a bikini. Lucia again smelled tangy air and tasted salt on her tongue. A strange translucence overlaid the room, Agadir, but dreamlike. Gradually it became more convincing, until she could barely see the room itself.

*Stop,* she thought.

The simulation faded into nothing.

*Take me to ABT,* Lucia thought. *Don't stop the simulation unless the command comes from me.* She had no idea whether or not she could actually program commands into the bots just by thinking, but it was worth a try.

Suddenly the ballet swirled around her, full of motion. Zaki had layered every page from the Web site into the simulation, giving it a great depth. At first the reality was nowhere near as convincing as with the Jazari suit, but gradually it improved, until it overwhelmed her senses. Dancers spun through one another, ran, jumped, glided, and soared through the air, often with many copies of themselves. A multitude of smells came to her, some sharp, others diffuse, the tang of sweat mixed with the fragrance of roses. Music from many scores blended together, along with voices, the scrape of shoes, a woman counting *one, two, three, four,* the rustle of costumes, the intake of breath. She felt air brush her skin, the heat of passing dancers, even humidity. Had she not known what to expect, the abrupt rush of sensations would have terrified her.

*Turn off my speech centers,* she thought. *Don't reactivate them again unless I give the command.*

She tried to speak.

The words *I'm thirsty* formed in her mind. But her brain sent no commands to her body to make her vocal cords produce the sounds. She had become mute.

Then she faked a convulsion.

With a sudden jerking of her body, she thrashed among the dancers, in that wild scene of colors and motion, falling to the side. She couldn't see the bench—but as she fell down onto her injured arm, pain shot all the way to her elbow. When she screamed, or tried to scream, no sound came out.

After all her years of dance, and the character training that went with it, Lucia knew how to make almost any form of movement look real, even one she had never tried before. Like a convulsion. The jerking of her body dragged on her arm, aggravating the gash until she cried out, or would have cried had she been able to voice her protest.

She dimly heard Rashid call her name. Another voice spoke in English, sharp and hard, closer by. She ignored it all, submerged in a chaos of motion, music, and color. The bandage had ripped off her arm and she felt the blood flowing again. She gritted her teeth against the pain.

Like a ghost, the guard appeared at the bench, his gun up and aimed, barely visible through the cornucopia of sensory input she was experiencing. She heard Rashid entreat the man to help her. The guard spoke again, words she barely heard. Then he grabbed her elbow and pulled her upright. He must have sat next to her, because she suddenly felt an arm around her shoulder and a gun pressed against her side. When he spoke, she didn't understand, her senses filled with music from a hundred ballets, while hundreds of dancers, many different images of the same people, whirled around and through her.

She flailed in the guard's hold, smearing blood all over him, across the exposed skin of his hands, even on his nose and mouth. When he caught her arms and held them down, she screamed from pain, but still no sound came. He slapped her across the face, though whether in anger or in an attempt to stop her "fit," she had no idea. The impact of his palm only added to the tumult of sensations.

The grip on her arms faltered, weakened—and the guard froze at her side.

*Stop simulation!* Lucia thought. *Let me speak.*

The tumult faded, leaving her with the stark reality of the cell. The guard was sitting next to her, one hand clenched on her arm, his face rigid with shock as he experienced the simulation, his gun pressed against her side, his fist gripping the weapon so hard his knuckles had turned white. Lucia knew she only had an instant before he either killed her in reflex or else recovered enough to shoot with deliberate intent.

Jumping to her feet, she yanked the rifle out of his hands. Holding it with both hands like a club, without stopping to think, she swung it hard against his head. It hit in a sickening thud, jarring her arms. The guard crashed down onto the bench, and blood pulsed out of a gash in his head. He opened his mouth as if he had shouted, but no sound came.

Lucia stared at the unconscious guard, too shocked by what she had done to move. Then she recovered enough to make herself bind his arms behind his back, using the same ropes that had tied her own wrists. As she straightened up, her sight grew foggy. Dizzy from fatigue, blood loss, hunger, and thirst, she almost passed out.

Rashid called her name. Unseeing, she stumbled in his direction. Somehow she made it across the room. As her vision cleared, she lost her balance and fell to her knees at his side.

"Lucia!" he urged. "Untie me."

Taking a deep breath, she fumbled with the ropes binding him to the bench. It took eons to untie him. When his arms finally fell free, he groaned and sagged forward, then brought his arms in front of his body and cradled them against his torso, his face creased with pain. Lucia put her arms around him and leaned her head against his, willing him to be all right. He embraced her then, making a choked sound that could have been anything from her name to a groan of pain.

"Rashid," she whispered.

He drew in a ragged breath and pressed his hand against his head injury. Then he climbed to his feet, pulling her with him. "Give me the gun."

Lucia handed him the rifle. He held it in an awkward grip that suggested he had little experience with guns. First he studied the rifle and its clip, turning it over, feeling its weight. He aimed across the room, sighting on the wall, then lowered the gun and studied it again, as if branding its form into his brain. Already it looked more natural in his grip.

He spoke in a low voice. "Can you shoot?"

"Yes." Although Lucia had never shared her father's interest in hunting duck and quail, learning to shoot had been part of the culture she grew up in.

"When I get the guard at the door, you take his gun."

Lucia nodded and walked to the door with him. When they were in position, he aimed at the lock, angling the gun so if the bullets passed through the wood, they would also go through the area where they had seen the guard take up position outside the door.

Then he fired.

The crack of bullets shattered the silence. Rashid jerked from the recoil, then kicked the door open and sprayed the area outside with bullets. As soon as he stopped, Lucia lunged out and dropped next to the guard sprawled on the ground. Shots from outside their prison hit the wall above her; had she been a fraction of a second slower, she would be dead.

She grabbed the gun, her stomach lurching when she saw how many times Rashid had shot the man. As she ducked back into the house, she glimpsed their surroundings. Mountains. They were in a valley ringed by looming peaks. Stars glittered in the sky like cold diamonds.

Inside the house, she and Rashid stood to either side of the doorway, staring at each other across the open space. Seeing his bleak gaze, she recalled what he had told her on his grandfather's farm: *I would rather give my own life than kill another human being.* Did Grégeois's people know they were destroying him? But then, why would they care? They needed only his genius.

"Did you see any vehicles out there?" Rashid asked.

"One. A truck." She motioned to the right. "About a hundred feet that way."

"Feet?" Rashid paused, then said, "Thirty meters, then. I can make that."

"Can you run?" she asked.

"If I have to."

A voice called to them, deep and calm, a few sentences in French mixed with Arabic.

"What is it?" Lucia asked.

"He says if we try to leave, they will shoot, to cripple me and kill you."

"Do you think Grégeois is still here?"

Rashid shook his head. "He's probably long gone, out of the country, with a report to his employers."

His employers? "You don't think he's behind this?" Images of everyone Lucia knew who might have knowledge of Grégeois burst into her mind. Including Mark.

"I doubt it," he said. "Otherwise, he wouldn't have come in person." He pushed his hand through his hair. "Four guards survived the attack on our car this morning. The one with Grégeois, the one in here, the one by the door, and one other. If we're lucky and Grégeois's went with him, then we're facing one person. But my guess is that at least two are out there. Grégeois probably had his own people."

"We should go, before they have time to call in more help."

Rashid nodded. "Stay low to the ground and run in a zigzag."

He took a breath—and sprinted out the door. Before she had a chance to think, Lucia made herself run after him. The night rushed past, chill and dark, and the truck loomed ahead of them, a shadowed hulk lit by starlight.

They didn't make it.

Gunshots rang out and dirt pelted Lucia's legs. Rashid jerked in midstride and spun around in a half-turn as if someone had pushed his arm. He stumbled and froze, staring at Lucia. Then he turned around and took off again, firing toward the truck. When he paused, a man rose up behind the hood, aiming his rifle, not at Rashid but at Lucia.

Both the guard and Lucia fired at the same time. All those years of reluctant duck hunting paid off in a grisly debt; she hit the guard and he jerked backward, disappearing behind the front end of the truck.

Two more steps, and she and Rashid had reached the vehicle. Rashid fell against the side, his right hand clutched over his left arm. Lucia yanked open the door on the driver's side. This truck was smaller and much lighter than those the kidnappers had used this morning, less able to provide solid protection.

Bullets suddenly rammed into the door. A sniper had leaned out from behind the house, his gun aimed at Lucia. Sagging against the truck, Rashid jerked up his gun and fired at him. His shot went wild, but the sniper ducked back behind the house.

Lucia threw herself inside the truck, keeping her head low, and dragged herself across the seat. Rashid climbed up behind her and slammed the door. Taking a breath, she steeled herself to crawl out the other side. She had to search the body of the guard she had shot. Unless Rashid knew how to hot-wire a truck, which she doubted, their only option was to find the keys.

The end of a gun barrel suddenly slammed into the window on the passenger's side, shattering the glass. Lucia dropped flat on the seat, covering her head, while bullets cracked so close to her body that they deafened her. She screamed Rashid's name. Unless he had thrown himself down as well, any bullets coming into the window would have hit him. But she didn't feel his weight and he was too big to have flattened himself onto the seat without falling on top of her.

Twisting around, Lucia stared at the driver's seat. Instead of Rashid's body riddled with bullets, she saw Rashid crouched down low, lowering his own gun, his face pale with shock. She knew then the guard outside was the one who had died. Rashid couldn't have missed at such close range.

More shots came from the house, and the truck jerked. Still crouched down, Rashid twisted around and returned the sniper's fire. Lucia drew in a breath, then forced herself to shove open the passenger door, dreading what she would find outside.

The guard lay sprawled on the ground. She half jumped, half fell next to his body, forcing down the bile in her throat, grateful the night hid the worst of the carnage. She found his keys in the pocket of his jacket. Although she had no guarantee these included keys to the truck, probably many or all of the guards had access to their vehicle, which increased the chance of this one having the key.

She climbed into the truck, keeping her head down.

Rashid traded another burst of gunfire with the sniper, keeping the other man behind the house. Lucia knelt on the floorboard, wedged between the seat and the dashboard, and tried a key in the ignition. Outside, the sniper got off another round, this time in the vicinity of the truck's gas tank. Rashid fired back while Lucia jammed another key at the ignition, then another, and another. None of them fit.

"Come on," she muttered. *"Come on."*

Rashid suddenly swore, the first time Lucia had ever heard him do it. As she jammed another key at the ignition, he threw the AKM with its empty clip down on the seat and grabbed her gun.

Gritting her teeth, Lucia tried another key. Another. A spattering of bullets hit the truck. Another key—

"There!" she shouted. In the same instant she got the key in the ignition, Rashid shoved his feet on the pedals, slapped his hand over the key, and turned so hard she feared the key would break.

The truck roared into life. Raising her head above the dashboard, Lucia glimpsed the long strip of a landing field ahead of them. The truck surged forward, jolting across the ground, listing to one side, why, Lucia had no idea. Rashid found the headlights and they blazed in the night. The damaged truck careened across the landing field, Rashid fighting to keep it moving in a straight line.

For the first time since they had run from the house, Lucia had a chance to look at Rashid, really look. Blood soaked the sleeve of his left arm, and more showed near his waist. She doubted he had actually been shot; she didn't know about an AKM, but an AK-47 had 7.62-millimeter copper-jacket bullets. If one of them had hit Rashid, he wouldn't be moving. But something had torn him apart, either shrapnel from the gunshots or else a bullet that grazed him. She swallowed, her heart beating painfully hard in her chest. Luck had deserted them. Not only had there been more than one guard, but he was still alive to summon help. She and Rashid may have escaped their cell, but they were far from free.

He drove with desperate concentration, his fingers slipping on the wheel as his blood smeared across it. Lucia pulled the rifle from his lap and slid into the passenger seat, her hands clenched on the gun. The headlights picked out nightmarish details of the land, glimpses of rocky ground and more distant mountains.

As they jolted across the field, Lucia realized Rashid had been forced into a gamble. If he lost, they would lose their hard-won freedom, maybe even their lives. He had to guess which way the road out of the valley lay. If he had guessed wrong, they couldn't go back and try again.

The truck hit a rock and bounced. Lucia grabbed the seat, clutching the rough material as she stared ahead, straining to see into the night. The headlights picked out flat ground strewn with rocks. No, not flat. It had begun to slope upward. They were headed straight at the mountain, with no sign of a pass that would let them escape the valley.

"No," Lucia said. *No.*

Rashid pulled hard on the wheel, and the truck jerked to the side, bumping along the ground, turning their progress into a jolting ordeal. Leaning out the passenger's window, she looked back the way they had come. Lights showed around the building where they had been imprisoned. She had no doubt the last guard had already called for reinforcements or was doing so right now.

A glint showed on the landscape between the truck and the house, bobbing up and down. Yanking her head back into the truck, she said, "Someone is running after us." At their slow rate of progress, it wouldn't be long before the runner came within shooting distance.

Rashid floored the accelerator. The truck lurched like a drunk but barely sped up. The mountains rolled past on their left, with no break in their upward slope.

Gunfire sounded behind them.

Suddenly Rashid gave a choked cry as a dirt road

jumped into view of the headlights. He yanked on the steering wheel, and with a squeal of ravaged tires the truck swerved onto the road.

They headed into the mountains, the walls of a pass rising on either side.

Chapter Seventeen

# IF GOD WILLS

No rail protected the road that clung to the mountain. No fence. Nothing. On one side cliffs plunged down and on the other they rose up, stark against the star-lit sky, dark in the night.

After about ten minutes, Rashid stopped the truck in the middle of the road. Then he sagged forward, resting his forehead on the steering wheel. Blood dripped off his arm and soaked into his trousers.

"Here." Lucia slid over to him. "I'll drive."

He tried to raise his head, then slumped forward again. Lucia swallowed, painfully aware they were only a few miles outside the valley. A man in good shape could probably run the distance in forty minutes or less.

Lucia slid back to the passenger door, then let herself out of the truck. She ran around the front to the driver's side and opened the door. Rashid lifted his head, his face creased with strain.

"Can you slide over?" she asked. "I'll drive."

He managed to nod. With painful slowness, he pulled himself across the seat. But as she started to climb into the truck, he shook his head.

"Change tire," he said.

She slid behind the wheel. "Why?"

"Losing air."

"We don't have time."

"Must." His head sagged against the seat. "Slow us down."

Lucia gripped the steering wheel, knowing he was right. She too had felt the worsening problem with the tire. Debris from the gunshots must have punctured it. If they let it go much longer, it would make it difficult to drive and bend the wheel rim out of shape. Whatever minutes they gained by leaving now instead of making the change, they would lose because of the slower speeds forced on them by the damaged tire.

With a sharp inhale, she got out and ran around to the back of the truck. She found a spare, along with a jack and tools to make the change. Lugging it all out of the truck with her injured arm was a nightmare. Several times she was certain she heard pursuit rattling down from the mountains above them. The wind keened across the bare stone cliffs and cut through her flimsy clothes, chilling her body and making her fingers clumsy.

She worked with her entire back tensed, as if that could ward away gunshots meant to pick her off the road. She had only changed a tire once before, and that with help. Now she struggled with the jack, struggled with the bolts, struggled to pull off the old tire and replace it with the new. It was taking too *long*.

Finally she tightened the last bolt, securing the new tire. As she stood up, holding the old tire on its edge, dizziness flooded over her. She stumbled toward the edge of the road, knocking the tire into a roll. With a surreal sense of calm, she realized she couldn't regain her balance in time to stop. Muscles clenched, she threw herself to the side. As she hit the road, the tire rolled over the edge. It bounced against the cliff again and again, with a dull slapping sound that faded in the distance.

Raising her head, Lucia found herself lying inches away from the edge. She pushed up on her hands, then shuddered as another wave of dizziness swept over her. How much blood had she lost? She couldn't remember when she had last eaten. Yesterday, before dawn?

Afraid to lose her balance again, she stayed on the ground and rolled toward the truck. When she hit the wheel she had just changed, she pulled herself up, first to sit, then to stand. She wanted to leave the jack on the road but didn't dare take the risk. Suppose they had another flat? Then again, what good would the jack do? They had no more spares.

With uneven steps, she stumbled to the front and climbed up behind the wheel.

For one chilling instant, she thought Rashid was dead. He sat slumped, his eyes closed, his head back against the top of the seat. Then she saw the fresh blood on his arm. If he had died, his heart wouldn't be driving blood through his body. He wouldn't still bleed.

Lucia started the truck and headed down the mountain. "Rashid?" She kept her eyes on the road. "Can you hear me?"

"Ah . . ."

She glanced at him. The pallor of his face frightened her. He had already lost a lot of blood before their escape. If she didn't get him help soon, he would die.

Focusing her attention on the narrow road, she said, "Do you have any idea where we are?"

"Mountains above . . . Grandfather's farm."

"We have to warn your family. Call them. Get them out of the house. Is there a town near here?"

"Not many. Even fewer phones . . ." His voice trailed off.

"Rashid! Tell me where to go."

"Follow road." He struggled to sit up.

"Don't move. Rest. We'll find you a doctor in the next town." If there was a next town. She had seen no hint of one.

He spoke in a steadier voice, as if he could counter his dying by sheer force of will. "Morocco has only one university-trained doctor . . . for every five thousand people. Most in cities." He took a breath. "Ahmed may be the only one . . . in this region."

She gripped the wheel. "Then we'll get you to Ahmed."

He didn't answer. Lucia strained to see the twisting road. With the fresh tire they could go faster, but not as fast as she wanted. The road had no reflectors or lines to show the way, and if she missed a curve, they would go over the edge.

Rashid spoke in a low voice. "I wonder if hell is genuinely hot."

"You aren't going to hell." She gripped the wheel. "And you aren't going to die."

He didn't answer. When the silence grew long, she glanced at him again. His eyes were closed and his chest moved with the jagged rhythm of a straining life.

*Please, God,* she prayed. *I know we humans are a cantankerous lot. But please. He's a good man.* A tear ran down her face. *Let us have him awhile longer.*

It was late at night when Lucia pulled up in front of Rashid's house. For the last few kilometers she had needed to guess the route, going on her memory of the road they took yesterday morning. Rashid was silent, breathing but unconscious.

Lucia jumped out of the truck and ran to the front

door. She pounded on the wood. "Help us! Ahmed, we need a doctor! *Help us!*"

The house had no windows on this side, so she couldn't tell if lights went on inside. The door of a house up the street opened and someone stepped out. Another door opened further down the cobbled street.

"Ahmed!" She almost screamed his name. "Help—"

Lucia cut off as the door swung open. She stumbled into the foyer, barely aware that someone caught her as she fell.

"Rashid is in the truck!" With her eyes adapted to the night, the light hurt. Omar the gatekeeper was holding her. Abdullah was there, with Tamou, Jamal, and the bodyguards. Someone ran past her, Ahmed she thought. She sagged forward, dizzy and nauseated.

Voices rushed around her as she crumpled to the floor. Someone helped her sit against the wall, murmuring words she didn't understand. Then Tamou cried out Rashid's name, not in anguish but with *joy.* Lucia looked up to see Rashid limping into the house, supported by Ahmed and his father. He leaned heavily on them, his arms over their shoulders, barely able to walk. Tamou was crying, repeating his name over and over again. Only then did Lucia realize his family must have spent most of the day mourning his death.

Rashid was talking, rapid-fire and desperate. The rattling of his voice frightened Lucia. She didn't need a translator to know he was telling his family to get out of the house, go to safety, alert the authorities. Still supporting Rashid, Abdullah gave orders to the others, his voice rumbling.

Rashid collapsed only a few steps into the house. Ahmed knelt next to him, speaking to someone, Jamal it sounded like. As Ahmed pulled Rashid's shirt away from his wounds, Jamal ran back into the house.

Lucia pulled herself over to Rashid. "We'll take care of you," she whispered.

He looked up at her, his face creased with pain. Then

he coughed, splattering blood, though whether from a cut inside his mouth or something far worse, Lucia had no idea. Ahmed had ripped the remains of his shirt into strips and was fashioning a pressure bandage for his arm.

People began to pour into the foyer, Khadija, Zineb, Rahma, the other women, the children, their voices hushed, ebbing and flowing, their faces pale. Khadija's older girl Zohra called out to Rashid. Bashir had already gone outside, and Lucia heard the rumble of a car in the street.

As the family evacuated the house, Khadija knelt by Lucia, clutching five-year-old Fatima in her arms. In a soft, urgent voice she said, "Be well, *mon amie.*"

"You too," Lucia whispered.

Then Khadija stood up and continued on, hugging Fatima while she herded her other two children in front of her. Before she stepped outside, she looked back at Ahmed, her face strained. Still working on Rashid, he glanced up and murmured to her. Then his wife and family disappeared out the door.

Jamal ran back into the foyer with Ahmed's medical bag. As soon as Jamal crouched next to him, Ahmed opened the bag and pulled out a syringe.

Lucia touched Rashid's face. "Live," she urged.

Watching her, Rashid spoke in a rasp. "Protect Zaki."

More than anything she wanted to stay with Rashid. But she understood what was at stake. "I'll do what I can."

As she started to stand, Ahmed reached across Rashid and grabbed her arm. "Where are you going?"

"What the kidnappers want is in Rashid's computer lab," she said. "We can't let them get it."

"If these people come here, it is not safe for you to go inside." He motioned toward the door. "You must go with the others."

"Let her go," Rashid whispered.

Ahmed glanced at him. Then he inhaled and released Lucia's arm. "Go."

As Lucia stood up, Lalla Tamou came into the foyer

carrying one of the smallest children. Seeing Lucia, she stopped, gazing at her. She lay her free hand on Lucia's arm and murmured, *"Barak Allahu fik, ya binti, wa yektibik al-khayr."*

Lucia swallowed, recognizing the phrase now after having heard it before, in bits and pieces. *God bless you, my daughter, and bring you every goodness.* She squeezed Tamou's hand, and the older woman nodded to her.

Then Lucia took off, into the house.

Lucia slammed open the door and ran into the computer lab. When she saw colors swirling on the screen of the Stellar-Magnum workstation, she feared Zaki had crashed again. Then she realized he was just running a screen saver.

"Zaki!" She rapped the keyboard. "You've got to answer!"

He appeared, sitting at his desk. "What is wrong?"

In quick, short sentences, she told him what had happened. "Most of the family has left for Marrakech," she finished. "They called the police, but we need help faster than they can get here."

Zaki stood up, his hands clenched on his desk. "Someone with Grégeois's expertise could program me to do what he wants. With access to this lab, he could take his plans further than even he realizes."

"We need someone to pull us out of here," she said.

"Marrakech has the closest police force."

"It will take hours for them to get here. Rashid will die without help." She struggled to remain calm. "There must be someone who can send a plane, a helicopter, something. What about the military?"

"Lucia, be realistic." Zaki took a breath. "Yes, I can contact the NDA. But a message in the middle of the night about a nebulous international plot to manipulate the World Wide Web, coming from an unknown person, or thing, called Zaki, who claims to represent two supposedly dead people? They'll think I'm crazy. If I hack into their computers at a high enough security level, they will take it more seriously, but it could backfire. How are they to know *we* aren't the threat? And no matter what, we're hampered by the late hour."

Lucia thought fast, casting around for any possibility. "What time is it right now on the east coast of the U.S.?"

"Eight minutes after six in the evening."

"Mark is usually in his office until six-thirty."

"Who is Mark?"

"Colonel Mark Spearman. At Bolling Air Force Base."

Zaki watched her intently. "Why does his name agitate you?"

"I don't know where I stand with him anymore." Mark could fall anywhere between two extremes. As a sixteen-year-old girl, she had seen him as a dazzling hero, a handsome knight in shining armor who would ride to the defense of all that was good. Now it was the other extreme she feared, the traitor who betrayed his conscience for a global conspiracy. But Mark had never been a man given to extremes; she was certain his true nature lay between those limits. *Where?*

If there was anyone she wanted to trust, it was Mark. For years she had loved him as a friend and father figure, admired his devotion to his country and his steadfast adherence to his principles. But what if she had seen him through a rosy filter? What if she made the wrong choice now? They would lose everything. Rashid's "rescue" would take him right back into captivity. She knew he would rather die. Yet if she *didn't* trust Mark when she should have, Rashid would die when he could have lived.

Lucia wanted to entreat Zaki for probability calculations, data searches, anything that would help her decision. But no electronic wizardry would solve this problem. She had to rely on her own intuition, decide whether to listen to her head or her heart.

She drew in a ragged breath. "I'll call him." Before Zaki could respond, she jumped up from her chair and ran out of the lab.

As Lucia sprinted across the courtyard, she was aware of the silence. No light, no voices, no laughter, no music. Had everyone gone? Rashid would never leave Zaki of his own free will. Too much was at stake. But if he were in bad enough shape, his family might take him with them. Would they leave her and Zaki alone? She doubted it. But if not, then Rashid and at least part of his family were still here.

The family room was dark. Grabbing the phone, she put it to her ear.

No dial tone.

"No!" Lucia jiggled the cradle. Nothing. She checked the wall and found the cord connected. She shook the cradle again, but still nothing.

Desperate now, she slammed the receiver down and ran back out to the courtyard. Her tennis shoes slapped against the tiles, the only sound in the deep silence.

Inside the lab, Zaki was still on the screen, pacing back and forth. When she slid into the chair, he stopped. "Lucia?"

"The phone doesn't work! Someone must have cut the line." She clenched the arms of her chair. "Can you link me to the computer in Mark's office at Bolling? He always leaves it on. His e-mail is *spearmanm@trident.dia.bafb.mil.*"

"E-mail is too slow."

"Then get his attention! Make his computer squawk or something."

"It's not that simple."

"Try!"

He exhaled. "I can't do anything unless I can get on the Internet. And to do that I need the router connection."

"I'll get it." Lucia jumped up and ran to the closet across the lab. Rashid had locked it this time. She grabbed a desk chair and hammered it against the door, cracking the chair's wheeled legs. The exertion made her injured arm throb with pain. Just as she thought she would have to stop, the door buckled. She dropped the chair, then yanked aside the damaged door, revealing a closet with a panel against the back wall and cables hanging everywhere. She grabbed the router cable and shoved it back into place in the patch panel.

Lucia raced back to the table and saw Zaki pacing his office. Suddenly he froze, poised in midstep, as he had done in the past when he linked to the Internet. This time he stayed that way longer, a good thirty seconds. Then he walked to his desk, sat down, and folded his hands in front of himself.

"I've sent messages to the Moroccan authorities," he said.

She dropped back into the chair. "What about Mark?"

"E-mailing him won't help unless he happens to be checking his messages right now."

"They must have some kind of talk routine at Bolling." She rubbed the drying blood on her hand. "Can't you page him on the computer? It's like calling on the phone."

"I have no idea if such a utility exists on the Bolling computers."

"There must be *something* we can do."

"I didn't say I couldn't do it." He regarded her steadily. "I'm almost sure I can find you a way to speak to Colonel Spearman, if he is near his computer. But what you want me to do would force me to reveal my existence. Do you understand what you're asking?"

"Have you any response to your messages here in Morocco?"

"Nothing."

"Get me Mark, then."

"Lucia, don't ask me to do this."

She gripped the table. "Would you rather Grégeois's people get hold of you?" *God, please,* she thought. *Don't let it be me who is making the mistake.*

"If I hack into Bolling and contact Colonel Spearman," Zaki said, "he will notify their base security that I exist. They will track me down. Copy me. Download me. Piece by piece, bit by bit. You're asking me to hand myself over to your military."

"What other choice do we have? Besides, our governments are allies." She leaned forward. "*Every* country needs to know about you. It's the only way to ensure a conspiracy like this never threatens the international community again."

"Wait." He fell silent, his face taking on a flat quality as he reallocated memory. Suddenly he became three-dimensional again. "I transferred enough of myself to the Moroccan defense network to give credence to my claims."

"How long will it take for them to respond?"

"I don't know. It's the middle of the night there. So far I've contacted only computers. No people yet."

"Zaki, please." She pushed her hand through her hair. "Try it my way, too." In Washington, D.C., it was early evening.

"Don't you understand?" His fists clenched on the desk. "You're asking me to give away *myself,* as if my personality, my conscience, my spirituality were nothing more than a handful of computer commands."

"Your spirituality?" She stared at him. "My God."

Regarding her steadily, he said. "And mine."

## *Chapter Eighteen*

# SEA KNIGHT

"What did you say?" Lucia whispered.

"You called on your God," Zaki said. "Why is the Deity your God and not mine?"

Even through her desperation, she marveled at what she was hearing. "Yours also, Zaki."

He took a shaky breath. "Do I have a conscience? If so, it tells me I must try every method possible to bring help here. Self-preservation tells me I must not, lest I lose myself. Would you give away your mind, your individuality, your spirit? Would you let someone else copy all that to turn you into a weapon?"

Lucia blanched. "No. I would hate it."

"Rashid has a dream. The crossroads. I can *help.* I can make bridges. I don't want to be a weapon."

Her voice caught. "If Rashid dies and Grégeois's people take you, that dream will die here."

Zaki stared at her as if he were breaking in two. Then he said, "I have Mark Spearman on the line."

The screen went black. For one second, Lucia feared the conversation had pushed Zaki too far, past where he could recover. Then, at the bottom of the screen, she saw a line of white letters:

del mar>

Her fingers stiff with fatigue, she typed at the keyboard and hit return:

del mar> Mark? Can you read this?

No response.

del mar> Mark? If you see this, please answer.

Still no response.

"Zaki?" she asked. "Are you still here?"

"Yes."

"Can you make his terminal beep? Draw his attention?"

"I have done so." In a subdued voice, Zaki added, "He notified the communications squadron at the base."

She tensed. "What does that mean?"

"Probably he suspects you."

Lucia took a breath. Then she typed:

del mar> Mark, please talk to me. I need your help.

No response.

She banged the table with her fist. "Why won't he answer?"

"He is conferring with security. . . . They want him to keep you talking to help them track down the break."

A line of text appeared on the screen:

spearman> Who is this?
del mar> Lucia del Mar. It's me, Mark.
spearman> How did you get on this system?
del mar> An AI connected me.
spearman> What AI?
del mar> His name is Zaki. Mark, please. I need your help.
spearman> Lucia del Mar is dead.

Clenching the keyboard, she racked her mind for a way to convince him. Then the answer came, sharp and clear. She typed:

del mar> "To a wisp of cloud, a spark of magic, an angel without compare." You wrote that on the card you sent me, after that first time you saw me dance. When you sent flowers backstage in Las Cruces.

Only she and Mark knew about the note he had written her that night, asking her out to dinner. As soon as he learned she was only sixteen, he immediately withdrew the invitation, and since then he had acted more like a father than a suitor.

spearman> I remember.
del mar> Do you believe me now?
spearman> Why are you on this system?
del mar> Rashid is dying. We're at his father's house. We were taken by a group that wants his work. They're trying to force his cooperation. They want covert control of the Internet and the people using it. They're driven, Mark. They don't care who they hurt, who they kill. We got away from them, but it won't be long before they find us.

spearman> Who are the kidnappers?
del mar> We only met their hired muscle. And someone called Mortabe Gregeois.

She didn't even try to type the *é* in Grégeois.

"Lucia, something just happened," Zaki said. "Spearman is on the phone—I don't—" He paused. "All right. I've got the connection. They recognize Grégeois's name. His true name is Faddei Grigor. He's a former KGB agent who has refused to accept the improved relations between your country and his. Spearman's people have been monitoring his activities for years."

"Why?"

"I'm not sure." After another pause, he said, "They've suspected his involvement with the conspiracy. Something about Rashid . . . they thought Rashid was *part* of it."

She swore under her breath. "No!"

Another line of text appeared on the screen:

spearman> Do you have the names of anyone else involved in the kidnapping?
del mar> No. Mark, Rashid would rather die than work for them. Please. Help us.
spearman> What did Gregeois want?
del mar> Rashid's work. His mind.

Suddenly Zaki said, "Spearman is in touch with a General MacDougal at the Pentagon. MacDougal just authorized him to contact the defense attaché at the United States embassy in Rabat."

"Why the defense attaché?" Lucia asked. "Shouldn't it be the State Department?"

"They're contacting the department also. But apparently Spearman knows the attaché well enough that he might help things move faster over here."

Another line of text appeared:

spearman> Can you describe al-Jazari's work?

Then Zaki said, "Lucia, I'm getting something more . . . Colonel Spearman and his people have wanted for years to get an inside line on Rashid's work. During the past two weeks they've debated on whether or not to enlist your aid. They weren't sure how close you and Rashid had become. They didn't know if they could trust you."

Another line of text appeared on the screen:

spearman> Lucia, please send details.

"Wait," Zaki said. "Listen to this. Your insistence on staying with Rashid has made Spearman doubt his earlier suspicion that Rashid was involved with Grégeois. He's telling General MacDougal he knows you well . . . trusts your judgment . . . MacDougal is asking if you could have been coerced or brainwashed. Spearman doesn't know." He exhaled. "If you will forgive some massively inductive reasoning on my part, made from absurdly disparate facts—I believe Spearman isn't certain he can trust his own reactions where you are concerned. He questions whether his mistrust of Rashid stems only from genuine suspicion or if jealousy is also playing a role."

"Good Lord." Of all the possibilities Lucia had imagined, it never occurred to her that Mark's confusing responses might have come about because he was wrestling as much with his own doubts as she was with hers. He had always seemed so sure of himself. So confident. If her intuition was correct, then yes, he sought exactly what everyone else wanted from Rashid, but his interest came from patriotism, to defend the country he served.

She typed:

del mar> Zaki is Rashid's work. An electronic diplomat. An ambassador. Rashid hopes he can make bridges among different peoples.
spearman> You trust Rashid?
del mar> Yes.

Suddenly Zaki said, "The American defense attaché in Morocco has agreed to contact his counterpart in the Moroccan military. I'm trying to trace the call, but I'm almost out of memory—" He went silent as Lucia typed another line of text:

del mar> We don't have much time. Gregeois's people will be here soon.
spearman> How many of you are there?

Lucia did a quick mental survey. Herself, Rashid, and whoever else stayed behind, probably two of the bodyguards and Ahmed.

del mar> At least five. Maybe more.

Zaki's voice crackled. "An official in Rabat just verified to your military that someone identified as 'Zaki' broke into an unnamed Moroccan network and dumped large portions of an unreadable program into their system." In an irked voice he added, "I most certainly am not 'unreadable.' "

"Is anyone sending help?" Lucia asked.

"The Moroccan attaché wants to bring in the appropriate official from your State Department. He and Spearman's friend at the American embassy are trying to decide whether or not to wake the fellow. Given the situation and the late hour, they may bypass the usual procedures."

She typed at the keyboard:

del mar> We need help now. Otherwise Gregeois's people will get both Rashid and his work.
spearman> We are sending help.
del mar> How soon?
spearman> Within thirty minutes. They've already left.

"What are you doing?" Rashid's voice snapped out behind her, exhausted but unmistakable.

Lucia swung around in her chair. He was standing in the doorway, supported by both Ahmed and Abdullah. Bandages covered his left arm and half his torso.

"Getting help," she said.

Rashid limped over to her, leaning on Ahmed and his father as they helped him walk. Lucia moved out of the chair, and Rashid lowered himself into it, Abdullah on one side and Ahmed on the other. As Rashid read Lucia's dialogue with Mark the screen, Ahmed translated it for their father.

Lucia glanced up at Ahmed. "Is everyone else gone?"

He nodded. "Except two bodyguards."

"Rashid?" Zaki asked. "Are you here?"

"Yes." Rashid spoke in a hoarse voice. "We're going to get you out."

"It's too late to get me out," Zaki said.

spearman> Lucia? Are you still there?

Rashid stiffened, then typed:

del mar> This is Rashid al-Jazari. I'm breaking the connection.

spearman> Wait! We c#$+$RR

"Connection terminated," Zaki said.

Lucia grasped the back of his chair. "Rashid, no. They're bringing us help."

He was still staring at the screen, his fists clenched around the keyboard, his face as bleak as ice. "Like Mortabe wanted to 'help' me?"

Suddenly the screen cleared. Zaki reappeared, standing in the center of his office, staring at them with a hunted look. "Rashid, it's too late to move me."

Rashid started gathering the CDs and computer disks from the table. "No! It isn't too late."

"What can you do?" Zaki demanded. "Load this entire lab into a car? It will take too long."

Sweat beaded Rashid's forehead. "My family took the cars to Marrakech. But we still have the truck."

"There isn't time to remove an entire computer lab."

"We will manage." He stopped, staring at the screen. "We will."

"And if Grégeois's people come while we are managing?" Zaki demanded. "Will you let them take you?"

"I don't know."

"Why don't you know?"

Rashid spoke in a quiet voice. "Sometimes the price of refusal is too high."

"That price being the lives of people you love."

"Yes."

"And what of the price I have to pay?"

"What price do you mean?"

Softly Zaki said, "My conscience."

"Zaki—"

"You can't have your soul *taken,*" Zaki said. "You may choose to die for your ideals, save the people you love, refuse to work, endure whatever torture they subject you to, or damn yourself to hell. Maybe in the end you won't be able to withstand them, but you will still be Rashid." His fists clenched at his sides. *"I have no choice.* They can reprogram me as they please. What then? Will they delete my conscience?"

Rashid pressed his fingertips against the screen. "What would you have me do?"

"Destroy me."

"No!"

"Please."

"I can't."

"Please."

Rashid pulled the keyboard into his lap. "I can back up your files and then erase them from the workstation."

"It won't be enough," Zaki said. "I'm part of every computer in this lab, at a basic level. You would have to erase everything. Even if you wipe every hard disk clean, you still have to make sure nothing can be retrieved. We don't have time."

"No." Rashid's hands gripped the keyboard. "I *can't* destroy you."

A shout came from somewhere in the house, echoing in its deserted spaces.

"Rashid, please." Zaki reached his hand forward, as if to touch the screen from the inside. "I'm deleting as much of myself as I can right now, but I can't get all of it either."

Their bodyguard Ali appeared in the doorway, a rifle gripped in his hands. As he spoke in Arabic, Lucia heard more shouts in the house.

*"No."* Rashid pushed to his feet. "Not now!"

"Rashid, do it!" Zaki said. "Before it is too late."

For one instant, Rashid stared at the screen, his anguish plain on his face. Then he took a lurching step to a table piled with manuals and printouts. When he upended the table, books scattered everywhere, all over the floor. He braced the foot of his good leg against one leg of the table and yanked on another leg, trying to break it, straining with his injured arm.

Rashid's father pushed him away and went to work on the table. With Ahmed's help, he broke off the leg, making a long staff. As Abdullah gave the staff to Rashid, Ahmed went to work breaking another leg off the table.

With his hands clenched around the staff, Rashid said, "I'm sorry, Zaki."

Softly Zaki said, "Good-bye, my father." Then he turned toward Lucia. "And you too, beautiful dancer."

"Ah, Zaki." Lucia's voice broke.

Standing to the side of the screen, Rashid motioned for them to back away. With tears running down his face, he swung the staff. It slammed into the workstation in a crash of metal, glass, and plastic, shattering its top. For one instant Zaki remained on the screen, staring at them. Then Rashid's staff came down again and the screen imploded. The glass collapsed inward, and ragged shards came hurtling out, spraying through the area in front of the table.

In the house, closer now, gunshots cracked, fast and hard. Rashid swung the staff again, smashing the computer. He heaved in a breath, then said, "Lucia, throw all my notes on the VR suit." He spoke in Arabic, to Ahmed she thought, though it was hard to tell with him swinging the staff. Ahmed strode from the room, nearly running.

Working together, Rashid and Abdullah smashed the server, workstations, and peripherals. Lucia dumped Rashid's books and notes on the VR suit, unsure what he wanted her to do with them. She found out almost immediately, when Ahmed returned with matches and the Bunsen burner from his office. Moving as fast as they could, they set fire to the VR suit and the piles of records, notes, and tapes. The sprinkler system Rashid had installed to protect the lab started up, but they sheltered the fire, rigging up the tarp that had covered the lounger so it formed a canopy over the flames.

The entire time, Rashid worked in a delirium, with an unnatural strength Lucia feared would kill him. He was bleeding again, the stain spreading red across the bandage on his arm. But he kept going. More gunshots echoed through the house, this time from the courtyard. Too close.

The fire jumped to the dry areas under the tables and workstations. Debris from the smashed equipment lay everywhere, and the stench of melting plastic, wet ashes, and burning wood filled the room. Ahmed drew Lucia away from the flames, back to the door. They didn't dare stay any longer.

Abdullah was fighting Rashid now, trying to pull him out of the lab, but Rashid had gone past reason. He kept swinging his staff, smashing the ruins of his treasured equipment, crushing his life's work. His dreams. Had he been uninjured, his father could never have prevailed over a man of his size and strength. But his wounds had taken their toll, and he couldn't fend off the older man.

As soon as Abdullah had Rashid out of the room, he slammed the door, confining both the fire and raining water that were completing the lab's destruction. Ali was already checking the area, his rifle poised in his hands. Qaddur, their second bodyguard, ran into the far end of the hall, calling out a warning. They all took off then, headed away from the courtyard, running through Rashid's suite.

It was dark inside the bedroom, with only starlight to soften the shadows. Starlight. From the window.

"Lucia, go first," Ahmed said.

She scrambled up into the window and let herself over the edge. The ground lay far below, over ten feet. Holding on to the grillwork that bordered the bottom of the window, she slid down the outside wall until she was hanging from the grill. Then she let go. She dropped the rest of the way and gasped when she landed, as her ankle twisted under her body. But she immediately jumped to her feet, past caring about pain.

Ali and Qaddur lowered Rashid in a sling made from a sheet. He sat with his legs hanging over the side of the sling, his hands gripped on the cloth by his shoulders. Lucia caught the sheet as it neared the ground, to stop its swing, but Rashid was already moving. Still driven with the unnatural energy that had gripped him in the lab, he stood up, pulling himself free of the cloth.

Ahmed came next, followed by Abdullah and then Qaddur. Ali stayed behind, covering the rest of them until they were down. With Ahmed and Abdullah supporting Rashid, Lucia at their side and Qaddur close behind, they ran for the almond groves. Behind them, more gunshots crackled inside the house.

Suddenly Ali shouted a warning. Bullets hammered the ground they had just covered, and dirt sods battered Lucia's knees. Qaddur spun around and fired, his rifle cracking in a rapid-fire burst. With growing dismay, Lucia realized they weren't going to make it. They had managed to escape this far only because of Ali and Qaddur's protection. But they were all easy targets. Even if they reached the trees before the rifle fire cut them down, they had nowhere to go within the scant grove. Rashid was the only one their pursuers needed alive, and with his injuries he had no chance of outrunning anyone.

Above them, the sky rumbled. At first the sound didn't register on Lucia as more than a reflection of her own desperate thoughts. But the noise swelled, building into a roar. It became a nightmare thunder that shook the ground and flattened trees. As she ran, she looked up at the sky, her hair whipping around her body. A giant shadow beat the air above them, making a great swath of blackness, like an avenging spirit come to exact payment for Zaki's death.

Then the shadow solidified into a helicopter, its rotors whipping the air as it descended. It had no spotlight to warn of its approach, no illumination at all, except for a red light on the tail and a second on its top. How its crew could see, she had no idea, but they came without a single beacon to give them away. The craft just *appeared*—big, fast, and dark.

Friend or enemy?

All five of them came to a stop together, within the almond grove. They stood frozen in a tableau, balanced on the precarious edge of uncertainty. Should they run to or from the helicopter?

A rope suddenly dropped down from the craft, and four shadowed figures slid down the thick cable. As soon as they hit the ground, the helo veered off into the sky, the rope swinging below it like a flexible question mark. Two of the figures took off in a crouched run for the house, starlight glinting on their rifles. The other two sprinted toward Rashid, converging on their group from either side. The thunder of beating rotors intensified again as another helicopter descended, a craft similar to the last but with different markings. It landed in the open area between the house and the trees, facing away from them toward the village, with little room to spare.

As the two shadowed figures ran toward their group, one shouted to them. Rashid answered in a hoarse voice and strained against his father and brother, struggling toward the aircraft. With all the noise, Lucia couldn't hear what they said. But if Rashid believed this was escape, they would follow.

They took off again, backtracking their hard-won distance, headed for the helo. Ahmed and Abdullah were almost carrying Rashid now, and Abdullah struggled to breathe as he pushed his more than sixty-year-old body past its normal endurance. The two soldiers from the first helicopter moved with them, flanking their group, with Qaddur bringing up the rear. It was too dark to make out details, but she could tell the soldiers wore combat fatigues and helmets with goggles. Had she needed to guess, she would have said they were Marines.

Jagged debris sprayed across Lucia's jeans, the scissored edges of broken rocks. She stumbled and lurched to the side, but one of the Marines grabbed her arm in time to stop her from flying forward onto the ground. She glimpsed Qaddur aiming his gun at the house, but he didn't fire. Still running, she looked to see Ali climbing down from the window of Rashid's room, his starlit body visible against the wall. Shouting to be heard, Ahmed called a warning to the Marines.

Gunfire suddenly erupted from the window above Ali. As the startled bodyguard let go of the grillwork and dropped down the wall, a shadowed figure on the ground covered for him, firing at the black square made by the bedroom window. Ali sprinted across the open area, running toward Rashid.

Ahmed, Rashid, and Abdullah finally made it to the helicopter. Two men reached down and hauled up first Rashid, then Abdullah. Spinning around, Ahmed grabbed Lucia's arm and swung her forward the last few feet. As hands heaved her into the helicopter, she was aware of Ahmed scrambling up behind her. Inside, she staggered and fell to one knee, planting her palms against the deck to catch herself. The shock of cold metal under her hands barely penetrated her adrenaline-driven focus. A woman in a green flight suit hefted Lucia into a seat so fast that Lucia barely had a chance to catch her breath.

She tried to absorb her surroundings. A bath of red light filled the interior, casting an eerie glow over everyone. The seats were set around the bulkheads, facing in on the cramped interior of the craft. The aircrew consisted of three medics, the two men and the woman, all in green flight suits, with an American flag above the right pocket and a wings imprint on the left side. A pilot and copilot sat up front. The Marines stayed outside, on defense, moving back toward the house.

Ali reached the helo and vaulted inside, and Qaddur clambered up after him, holding his hand against his side, blood leaking around his fingers. Without missing a step, both bodyguards went straight to Rashid. Even as the medics turned their attention to Rashid and Qaddur, everyone was strapping into seats—

And Rashid collapsed.

Halfway into his seat, he made a strangled sound and fell forward. The medics wasted no time; working together with precision, they grabbed a flat board similar to a gurney and laid Rashid out on it, on his back. After fastening the board into a frame on the deck, they strapped down his ankles, waist, and wrists, and also his neck. To secure themselves, they looped cables through their belts and attached them to the securing straps around the helicopter.

An explosion suddenly came from outside. With no warning, the helo took off, its rotors thrumming the cold night air while it leapt into the night.

Struggling to keep their balance, the medics worked on Rashid. The woman tilted back Rashid's head and leaned over him. "He's not breathing!" She had to shout to be heard above the whirring of the rotors and engine. "I'm not getting a pulse! CPR *STAT*!"

The second medic shoved his palm against Rashid's chest and pumped up and down, his voice like the beat of a nightmare drum: *One and two and three and four and five.* Then the first medic breathed into Rashid's mouth, precious air to combat the threat of death crowding them in the cramped confines of the craft's interior.

As the two medics performed CPR, the third grabbed a pack the size of a briefcase. He flipped it open and lights glowed within, illuminating the screen of a heart monitor. The first two medics pulled away from Rashid as the third one pressed paddles onto Rashid's torso. On the monitor screen, the rhythm of Rashid's heart appeared.

"He's going into v-fib!" the third medic shouted, hitting Rashid's chest directly at the heart. "No change! Stand CLEAR! I'm charging paddles to two hundred."

With dismay, Lucia recognized the paddles: She had seen similar ones when her grandfather went into ventricular fibrillation during a heart attack in the hospital—just before he died.

The hum of charging electricity surged from the pack, growing louder, adding its voice to the din within the helo. "I'm clear," the third medic shouted. "Stand clear!"

As the other two medics moved back, the third slapped the paddles on Rashid's chest and applied a powerful electric shock to the heart muscle. Rashid's entire body went rigid, jerking violently against the straps.

"Charging to three hundred!" Again the medic applied a shock, and again Rashid's body went rigid.

As if in a nightmare, Lucia heard the medic say, "Charging to three-sixty!" And once more Rashid convulsed against the restraints.

*Please,* she prayed. *Let him survive.*

But Rashid had finally reached the end of the phenomenal stamina that had driven him through the night. He collapsed back as the medics worked with desperate haste to find a spark of life they could conserve.

*Chapter Nineteen*

# REQUIEM FOR ATROPOS

The naval carrier *Coral Sea* cut through the ocean swells. Above the large-deck amphibious ship, the night reeled in chilling beauty, uncaring of death and loss. Inside the medical bay, with its off-white walls, Lucia sat slumped in a chair. Only a few feet away from her, Rashid lay on a bed, unconscious, as he had been ever since the helicopter brought them here to the carrier, off the Atlantic coast of Morocco.

Machines surrounded the bed: One monitored his heart, another showed oxygen saturation, an IV administered fluids, a probe extended into his head. The saturation monitor kept up a steady, quiet beep that melted into the background rumble of the carrier's engines. Lines and wires stretched from Rashid's torso, arms, nose, and head to the equipment. A nurse was adjusting the bandage on his arm. A few feet from Lucia, Abdullah dozed in one of the hard, functional chairs, resting his head against the bulkhead behind him. Normally someone as important as Rashid would have been flown to the U.S. military base in Ronda, Spain. But this carrier has been closer, perhaps even close enough to reach in time so they could save Rashid's life.

Each moment that hope faded more.

"It matters," Lucia said.

Abdullah lifted his head and rubbed his hand across his face. Deep furrows creased his forehead and cheeks. He looked older tonight, every bit his age and more. He spoke to her, and though she didn't understand him, she recognized the offered comfort in his words.

Lucia answered in a low voice, with one of the few Arabic phrases she knew. *In sha' allah.* She tried to find other words of encouragement, to tell him his son would survive, but she couldn't look him in the face and offer a hope they both knew was false.

A hatch opened behind them, and she turned to see Ahmed with one of the ship's officers, a man she didn't recognize. Ahmed came forward, but the officer waited a few steps back, giving the family privacy. After Ahmed lowered himself into a chair by the bulkhead, he spoke to his father in Arabic. Abdullah listened, then motioned toward Lucia.

Ahmed turned to her. "Your navy will have an aircraft take my father and me home." He sounded exhausted, his accent heavier than usual, even on words he normally pronounced perfectly. "They will take you to *Amrika.* About Rashid, we have some argument. Our government wants him back, yours says he is too sick to move." Softly he added, "If necessary, they transport his body home."

Lucia's voice caught. "It won't be necessary."

Ahmed just looked at her. Behind him, Abdullah was again watching the shallow rise and fall of Rashid's chest.

So they sat, keeping their vigil.

Throughout the night, the doctor, Major Ellen Farlow, checked on Rashid. Her discussions with Ahmed sounded like another language to Lucia: cerebral hematoma, meninges, edema, intracranial pressure, ischemia. The damage may have even begun with Rashid's accident several days earlier. Farlow wouldn't be certain until they had results from the spinal tap, but she thought his concussion had been a misdiagnosis, that he may have suffered an epidural hematoma, which meant his brain had been bleeding for several days, increasing the pressure within his skull. Lucia didn't understand the details, but she heard the words Farlow didn't say and saw the same understanding in Ahmed's bleak gaze.

Rashid was dying.

Near dawn Lucia dozed for a short time, her head dropping to her chest. When she awoke, her eyes bleared with sleep, she saw Ahmed and Abdullah had also nodded off. Rashid's nurse was at a nearby counter, making entries in a log.

Lucia stood up and stretched her arms, then grimaced as pain flared in her stiff limbs. Farlow had treated her arm and the twisted ankle, but Lucia refused the offer of painkillers. She feared that if she took them, she would succumb to fatigue and be asleep when Rashid breathed for the last time.

She limped over to the high bed and stood next to it, watching him. His arm lay on the sheet, motionless, palm up, the hand open, the fingers uncurled, a tube going from his inner elbow to the IV. Folding her hand around his, she murmured, "You made a difference. It matters. You thought you were a failure, but you were so, so wrong."

Predawn stillness answered her. It wasn't silence, for the ship thrummed around them, deep and full of power. This stillness came from the quiet before dawn, those dark pearl moments between the hours of night but before the sunrise. In the hush of a sleeping world, she watched Rashid. Watched his stillness. The moods of his face, always changing, were stopped now.

Through all the long hours of their vigil, her thoughts kept returning to the same barren place. She had to believe a reason existed for the death of a visionary like Rashid, when people like his kidnappers went on living. But no matter how hard she tried to find consolation, none came to her.

A tear slid down her cheek. As she held Rashid's unresponsive hand, the drop fell from her face onto the sheet. Bowing her head, she cried in silence.

After a while, she lifted her head. "Open your eyes," she entreated, her voice low and soft. "Prove all these people wrong." To make it happen she would have given anything, including her own life.

Rashid remained still, his chest barely moving. The nurse was checking the monitors now, those soulless machines that turned Rashid's life into traces on a screen. Lucia waited for the alarm that would tell them his heart had stopped. Every moment that passed in silence felt like a gift, yet it hurt as well, because she knew what waited at the end.

She thought of the first time she had seen him, surrounded by elegance in the East Room of the White House, devastatingly handsome in his tuxedo, his golden skin flushed with health. Or the first time she had seen him in the courtyard in his house, walking toward her through the deep, pooling shadows. So much promise, so much strength, so much life and beauty and brilliance. How could it all be gone now?

Perhaps these past two weeks had been a delirium. Maybe she and Rashid had just escaped from Oujda. If only she would awake in Rashid's suite to find him watching her, or reading in the corner, sitting on the carpet, his hair tousled as he absently ran his hand through it. If only.

Lucia brushed her fingertips across his brow. Bending down, she pressed her lips against his forehead. Then she straightened back up and just looked at him, trying to imprint his features on her memory.

With growing apprehension, she realized something had changed. At first her mind refused to accept it. When she finally absorbed what she saw, she almost cried out. But the sound froze in her throat.

Rashid had stopped breathing.

It couldn't have happened. It couldn't be over already. Unable to speak, she tightened her hold on his hand.

With a rush of almost giddy relief, she saw his chest rise in a shallow breath. Then he breathed again. A tear ran down her face. A few more moments. They had him for a few more moments.

Her hand trembled as she stroked his hair off his forehead. His lashes lay long on his cheeks, a dark contrast to the pallor of his skin.

Again his breath stopped.

Lucia went utterly still.

Slowly, so very slowly, he drew in a deep breath, long and shuddering, as if he were inhaling life. Again. And again.

Then his lashes lifted and he looked straight up into her face.

"Rashid?" she asked, afraid to believe this miraculous gift.

In an almost inaudible voice he whispered, "Hello, my light of the sea."

The overcast dawn cast pearly-gray light on the *Coral Sea,* giving the ship's deck an otherworldly quality. Large and gray, the size of two football fields, the deck felt damp in the misty dawn but warm under Lucia's feet, with a rough, gravelly texture. The amphib rumbled with aircraft as they took off or landed, and the tang of fuel and helo exhaust accented the air.

Rashid stood with Lucia, apart from the group waiting for them: the ship's captain and his executive officer; Abdullah and Ahmed, who were talking with the captain;

and Major Farlow, who had finally agreed to let Rashid travel. The group discreetly placed themselves out of earshot, near the helicopter that would soon fly Rashid, his father, and his brother back to Morocco.

In the early-morning chill, Lucia's breath turned into feathers of condensation. With her hands scrunched in the pockets of her borrowed jacket, she looked up at Rashid. He had lost a great deal of weight. His face was almost as pale now as on that morning in the medical bay when he had opened his eyes into the dawn—and life.

The results of the spinal tap confirmed the miracle: Although some swelling within his cranium had occurred, it came from the second trauma to the head, not the first, which meant it had less time to build up pressure. Nor was the damage as severe as they had feared; his head injury had primarily been a concussion. He responded well to treatment, and Farlow predicted he would suffer no permanent brain damage. Rashid recalled almost nothing of what happened after they destroyed his lab, though. His injured arm hung in a sling, and bandages under his clothes protected the still-healing wounds in his torso and arm. But he stood on his own, tall in the gray morning, favoring his injured leg but otherwise steady.

"Are you sure?" he asked her.

She made herself nod. "I have to go home. I . . . I'm sorry."

He brushed his knuckles along her cheek. "I too. But I also must return to my home."

Lucia started to pull her hands out of her pockets, to hug him good-bye. But he dropped his arm, shielding himself with that separation he had always been able to create, setting her away from himself even when they were standing only a few inches apart.

She knew then that their brief interlude had finished. They had ended up staying on the amphib longer than expected, caught in an intricate diplomatic standoff while the United States and Morocco tangoed over Rashid's future. But unlike their governments, she and Rashid had found almost no chance to talk. They could have blamed many things: lack of privacy, his need to rest, the time they spent in debriefing. None of those reasons would have been the truth. The words they had to say hurt too much to speak. As much as she respected his loyalty to his king and country, his sense of spirituality, and his devotion to his family—even loved him for them—she wished it could have been different, that he would come with her, for she could no more give up her life, culture, or country than he could give up his.

Now he was going home, as was she, the two of them separated by an ocean, and gulfs greater than they knew how to bridge.

*Chapter Twenty*

# SEA SHADOWS

The restaurant glowed. Its lamps sparkled, striking gleams in the china, crystal, and silver. Lucia tried to enjoy the evening. She so rarely had a chance to talk with Mark Spearman these days. Although they had continued their friendship, she saw him less now than before Morocco. She wasn't sure why she avoided his company; perhaps the reminder of what had happened, and what she had lost, was too great.

"I'm not surprised tomorrow night's performance is sold out," Mark said. "It is your comeback, after all."

Lucia smiled. "Not much of a comeback. It's only been three months."

Despite what she had been advised to let the public believe, her reason for keeping a low profile had little to do with her injuries, which healed fast and well. Mark had asked her to delay her return to the stage. In fact, after she returned to the United States, she spent several weeks in a safe house.

Mark wasn't at liberty to reveal details of the operation against the conspiracy, but when the constraints on Lucia's life eased, starting with her release from the safe house, she knew the authorities were closing in on their quarry. The pursuit was a global effort, involving many countries, reflecting the international arena in which Grégeois's people operated. In a sense, tomorrow night's performance celebrated its success; Mark would never have accepted her comeback so easily had he thought she was still in danger.

Lucia picked up her fluted glass and sipped her drink. Bubbles tickled her throat. The first time she had seen Rashid, he had been holding a glass like this, one filled with water instead of champagne. She wondered what he had been doing these past months. All she knew was that his government had also kept him in protective custody.

She couldn't bring herself to write him. It hurt too much. What could she say? *I miss you so much it's tearing my heart.* Too sentimental. Too revealing. Nor had she heard anything from him. Yet for all that they hadn't spoken to each other in three months, neither of them had sought an annulment either.

"Lucia?" Mark asked. "Where are you?"

She tried to smile. "I'm sorry. I guess I'm worried about tomorrow night."

Mark understood what she didn't say. He spoke in a quiet voice. "He changed our world. We've entered a new era and I'm not sure anyone knows exactly how to define it yet. He gave us machines that can truly think."

"Only one." Zaki. She set down her glass, trying to cover the tremor in her voice. "And he's dead."

Gently Mark said, "But in a way, he will never die."

Lucia knew what he meant. Pieces of Zaki existed in

both Morocco and the United States. Now that Rashid was working with the Moroccan government and military, in a secured installation, it would only be a matter of time before he created a new AI. His work had catapulted Morocco into international prominence, putting the country well in the lead of a race the likes of which the world had never before seen. Since news of Rashid's accomplishments had become public, research groups all over the globe were striving to catch up, the United States being in the forefront with the pieces of Zaki they had downloaded.

But no matter how many AIs they created, none would be Zaki. Although the thieves who had broken into the al-Jazari house took everything that remained in Rashid's ravaged lab, they gained nothing of value. Nothing had survived. Zaki was gone.

The story given to the news services was that a group kidnapped Rashid because of his prominent position in the business world. But reports about Zaki and the augmented Jazari suit appeared almost immediately. Who sprung the leak, and how, Lucia had no idea. She was almost certain, however, that she knew why. Whoever had done it wanted to ensure no one could ever again take the world unawares, as Grégeois's group had almost done.

It helped to know Zaki hadn't died in vain. His sacrifice prevented a global crisis. In the past, wars had been fought with swords, cannons, and bombs. But at this, the dawn of the third millennium, conflict had turned to the arena of information. Zaki's offspring could become weapons, it was true. But he had been created, first and foremost, to make bridges. Maybe, just maybe, his legacy might help humanity join together.

The ballet *Sea Shadow,* first choreographed by Gerald Arpino, was originally danced to music by Maurice Ravel. Later, Michael Colgrass produced a new score. As always, Carl Martelli choreographed his own unique vision. He set the work specifically for Lucia.

On the night of her comeback Lucia waited backstage,

surrounded by the friends and dancers she had known for years: Sharon Smythe-Powell, Jason Tyler, Antonio Maravilla, Marita Vásquez, and all the other familiar faces. José Amaya himself came backstage to wish her well. Now she stood in the wings with Sharon, feeling as if she had come home, yet knowing it would never be the same again. Part of her would always recall that geode world of horseshoe arches and arabesques.

Her music began, and she drifted onto the stage.

Carl envisioned *Sea Shadows* as a lyrical dream, the story of a gossamer love unable to survive. Performed by two dancers, a man and a woman, the ballet eddied, swirled, subsided into stillness, and then rose again. With Antonio as her partner, Lucia spun, arched, swayed, and floated, as luminous as moonlight, seeking to make real Carl's vision of an ethereal angel caught in the ebb and flow of the sea. It evoked the mysticism of an ocean bathed by moonlight in a radiant path across the water, a moonglade that glimmered on the waves.

When the ballet came to a close, the audience began their applause with almost the same rhythm as the final strains of music, as if the dance had mesmerized them. Then the clapping swelled, building in strength. Simultaneously, people in different sections of the theater came to their feet, followed by others, and then others. Soon the entire audience was standing, their ovation unabated. Again and again Lucia and Antonio stepped forward, she to curtsy, he to bow.

Although Lucia knew the performance had gone well, and she thought Carl's rendering of the ballet lovely, she wondered at the overwhelming response. *Sea Shadows* wasn't the type of spectacular production that usually earned such fervor. Yet throughout the Opera House, people remained standing, their applause filling the theater.

The curtains closed again, and still the ovation continued. Watching her, Antonio said, "It's you they're applauding. You're the symbol."

Puzzled, she asked, "The symbol?"

He smiled. "Of a new era. Maybe even a better one."

As the curtains opened to let them take another bow, Lucia swallowed. For three months she had grieved, for the loss of Zaki, and also for Rashid, whose idealism had been shattered on the unforgiving crags of reality. If only he could have seen this, could have known that his dream survived, kept alive by the uncounted people who had glimpsed its promise.

In the now empty theater, Lucia spun across the stage, still wearing her costume, a gauzy white dress that swirled around her knees. She had no music. In fact, she shouldn't even have been on the stage after the performance, when the crews had finished their work. But she found herself unable to face going home to her empty apartment.

So she danced, in silence, hearing her own music. Transcendent and heartbreaking, Pachelbel's Canon in D played in her mind. She paused, balanced in an arabesque on the point of her shoe, her leg extended behind her and her arm reaching out in front. Then she melted into a series of glides, always drifting, lost to the world, inhabiting an unadorned space of loneliness.

In the past, dance had always been a source of consolation. But tonight every move hurt, not physically, but at an emotional level deeper than she knew how to define in words or thoughts. She ached with a sense of loss she didn't know how to voice.

Finally she drifted to a stop. Then she stood, her dress wafting around her body until it too stilled.

Gradually she became aware of three people watching her from back in the Opera House. They were too far away and in too much shadow for her to see them well. She flushed, self-conscious at not having realized stragglers from the audience remained in the theater. Rubbing her palm across her cheek, she discovered she had been crying. She turned away from her shadowed audience and walked toward the wings, headed for her dressing room, to change and then go home.

*Deal with it,* she told herself. She couldn't stay here all night. Sooner or later she had to face her life. It had been her choice to give up Rashid. And for all her sadness, she knew that if she had to decide again, she would make the same choice. To do otherwise would have meant giving up what defined her at a level so basic it encompassed her spirit. That loss would have eaten away at them until it destroyed whatever she and Rashid tried to build together.

At the curtain that marked the wings, Lucia paused and glanced back into the theater. She saw three men leaving, two of them large and bulky, dressed in nondescript evening clothes. The man between them was taller, and thin. He walked with a limp that reminded her of the last time she had seen Rashid. It wasn't Rashid, though; this man had a leaner build and a different way of carrying himself. But he stirred images she had tried to forget these past three months, memories of how he smiled, grumbled, contemplated, blushed, scowled, and laughed.

Soft-footed and light, Lucia left the stage. She balked at the thought of her empty dressing room, so instead she made her way out into the theater. Why, she wasn't sure. She knew better than to go out in her costume. Yet tonight she ran through the empty Opera House, her dress eddying around her body like mist, her thoughts stirred by a phantom who wore the guise of another man she couldn't forget. She ran up an aisle, between the sections of upholstered seats, her toe shoes padding on the carpet. Above her, the spectacular Lobmeyr chandelier filled the vaulted ceiling in a starred cluster of lights.

Lucia came out of the Opera House into the recessed dais at its entrance. She walked to the stairs that descended into the Grand Foyer, the hall that formed this side of the Kennedy Center, on the bank of the Potomac River in Washington, D.C. It was only forty feet from where she stood to the floor-to-ceiling windows on the opposite side of the hall. But the foyer had an immense length, 630 feet, extending to either side of her, a study in ivory and gold elegance, mirrored walls, and red carpet, its lofty ceiling sixty feet above her head. Magnificent cylindrical chandeliers lit the hall, each made from many cubes of crystal with lights sparkling within. They hung more than halfway from the ceiling to the floor yet were still twenty feet above the ground.

Far down the hall, near its end, an elderly couple strolled into view from the Hall of States, which ran perpendicular to the Grand Foyer. Another couple joined them and they all stood chatting together.

Lucia exhaled. What was she doing, coming out here in her costume? She turned back toward the Opera House. If she hurried, she could be home in time to finish the novel she was reading before she went to sleep. A good book, a cup of hot chocolate, and a warm quilt; maybe it wasn't her dream life, but it would have to be enough.

Glancing to the other end of the long hall, she saw three men enter the Grand Foyer from the Hall of Nations. The heavier two fellows resembled bodyguards. A tall man in a black tuxedo walked between them, limping, gaunt from weight loss—

But still achingly, beautifully familiar.

Far down the hall, Rashid stopped, staring at her. He made a restrained motion, as if his reflexes tried to start him toward her, only to be held in check when his mind caught up with his instincts.

Lucia didn't give a hoot in a holler about restraint. She ran down the stairs and through the foyer, her dress rippling around her like white mist blown by the wind. Rashid lifted one arm, but he seemed stunned, unaware he had even moved. When she came nearer, it finally startled him into motion and he stepped toward her.

They met in front of the glass wall that separated the Grand Foyer from the Hall of Nations. She *relevéd* onto her pointe shoes, up on their boxy tips, her feet tight against each other, giving her an extra six inches of height, so the top of her head came to Rashid's ear. She put her arms around his neck and hugged him, uncaring of his bodyguards or anyone else in the world.

"Ai, Lucia." Rashid embraced her in what, for him, was an unprecedented show of public affection, one she knew he would rarely, if ever, repeat.

For a while they simply stood that way, holding each other. With her head against his, Lucia gazed over his shoulder into the Hall of Nations, a broad corridor carpeted in red. A rainbow of flags hung near the high ceiling on both sides of the hall, one for every nation in which the United States had diplomatic missions, over 150, rank upon rank of the symbols that represented peoples all over the world.

Finally Rashid murmured against her hair. "You grew. A lot."

She gave a soft laugh. Still up on her toes, she pulled back and touched his cheek with wondering fingertips. "I almost didn't recognize you. You're so thin. You have to eat more."

His smile crinkled the lines around his eyes, deeper lines than she remembered. "Hello, Lucia."

"Were you going to leave without seeing me?"

"I didn't know if you wanted to see me." He hesitated. "I thought of going backstage. I started to. But I wasn't sure."

"Is that why you were still in the theater?"

He nodded. "Then you came out again. I hoped . . ." His ever expressive face gave away his dismay. "But you looked straight at me and walked away."

"Ah, Rashid," she murmured. "I didn't know it was you."

His expression shifted with a flash of mischief. He tilted his head at his bodyguards, who had moved a discreet distance away, close enough to protect him if needed but far enough to give them a degree of privacy. "If it's not me, these fellows have spent a great deal of time guarding the wrong person."

She smiled, but it faded almost immediately. "Do they go everywhere with you?"

"Yes. I've really not much choice in the matter."

"I'm glad you have guards," she said, with more vehemence than she expected.

Dryly he said, "I suspect it is rather boring for them, watching me work all day."

"I heard you were working for the Moroccan government. And the military."

After a pause, he said, "I'm still CEO for JI."

She noted the ambiguity of his response. "Do you do both?"

"I do what I need to."

Lucia recognized his look. It was the same one Mark got when he couldn't discuss his work. She understood what Rashid left unsaid. Reality had collided with his dreams and left too many scars. He would do what he felt necessary to protect the fruits of his intellect. But she ached for his broken idealism.

Gently she asked, "How have you been?"

He exhaled. "It seems I have more years of life left after all. Perhaps I will have time to atone for the mess I made of the first thirty-five."

She touched his cheek but didn't stroke it the way she wanted, knowing it would embarrass him in front of his guards. That he was still holding her around the waist, despite their presence and the people at the other end of the hall, told her more about how much he had wanted to see her than a thousand words.

"You judge yourself by an impossible standard," she said.

"It is the only one I know."

"Rashid, don't give up your dreams."

He just shook his head.

"Did you hear everyone clapping tonight?" she asked. "After the show?"

His face gentled. "It was a beautiful performance. You deserved their accolades." With a grumble, he added, "You were far better than that clumsy fellow. They should have left him out of the dance altogether."

Lucia held back her smile. Antonio was one of the leading male dancers in the world. "They weren't just clapping for the dance. It's because I'm part of how they learned about a dream, one the whole world glimpsed these past few months, as the news came out about Zaki. Your dream, Rashid." She searched his face, wishing she knew how to reach him. "Please don't give it up."

"Ah, Lucia." He shifted his hands on her back. "I have discovered a fact."

"A fact?"

"I have read and thought a great deal about this."

That sounded like Rashid. "Yes?"

He rubbed a tendril of her hair that had escaped her bun and curled down her neck. "Living without you, it seems, is even worse than compromising."

Her face softened into a smile. "That has a solution, you know."

He took a deep breath, as if preparing himself for the jump off a high diving board. "If I agree to spend part of the year here, in the United States, will you live the rest of the year in Tangier?"

She felt a lightening of her heart, easing a weight she hadn't fully realized was there until it lifted. "Yes. I can do that."

"And if I try not to growl and give ultimatums? Will you discuss things with me instead of going against my wishes without telling me?"

"I can't imagine you not growling." When he smiled, she relaxed. "Yes. Most certainly."

Quietly he said, "And if I agree to see our children taught as Catholics? Will you agree to see them taught as Muslims?"

Lucia exhaled. "It won't be easy. We've so many differences."

Quietly he said, "I understand. We will need advice. Guidance. But if we always respect each other's beliefs, our example will teach our children the tolerance we both value." He spread his hands and almost knocked her off her pointe shoes. Catching her arm, he said, "Someday they will have to choose, one path or the other. Perhaps they will walk a road different from either of the ones we have chosen. But a way must exist for us to show them why we value our choices. Will you look for that way with me?"

Softly she said, "Yes. I would very much like that." She stroked a lock of his hair back from his temple. "Rashid, I do truly think I love you."

He stiffened and glanced at his bodyguards. Turning back to her, he said, "Then we are in agreement?"

She gave him an exasperated look. "That sounds like we just had a committee meeting and passed resolutions."

He spoke awkwardly. "I'm not good at saying I love you. If I tell you that I wish I could express it to you because I feel it so much inside me, will you understand?"

Lucia didn't know whether to laugh, cry, or kiss him. "It's the most beautiful nonexpression I've ever heard."

He looked down into her face. "Walk with me to the crossroads, Lucia."

"Always." She still remembered the words he had shared with her in the quiet night:

*The roads come from every direction, one for every religion that has ever been or exists now. They all meet at a crossroads, a place of light and pure air.*

*A place of acceptance.*

*A place of peace.*

A place their children, and the children of the world, might someday share.

# ABOUT THE AUTHOR

CATHERINE ASARO grew up near Berkeley, California. She earned her Ph.D. in chemical physics and M.A. in physics, both from Harvard, and a B.S. with highest honors in chemistry from UCLA. Among the places she has done research are the University of Toronto, the Max Plank Institut für Astrophysik in Germany, and the Harvard-Smithsonian Center for Astrophysics. She currently runs Molecudyne Research and lives in Maryland with her husband and daughter. A former ballet and jazz dancer, she founded the Mainly Jazz Dance program at Harvard and now teaches at the Caryl Maxwell Classical Ballet, home to the Ellicott City Ballet Guild.

She has also written the novels *Primary Inversion, Catch the Lightning,* the Nebula-nominated *The Last Hawk, The Radiant Seas, The Quantum Rose,* and *Ascendant Sun,* all set in the Skolian Empire/Ruby Dynasty universe. *Catch the Lightning* won the Sapphire Award and the UTC Award. Her novella, "Aurora in Four Voices," which appeared in the December 1998 issue of *Analog,* won the HOMer Award and the AnLab for best novella, and was a finalist for both the Nebula and the Hugo.

Catherine can be reached on the web at *http://www.sff.net/people/asaro/* and by e-mail at *asaro@sff.net.*

*Be sure not to miss the next exciting novel by Catherine Asaro*

# THE PHOENIX CODE

Megan O'Flannery is a leading expert in Artificial Intelligence in the early twenty-first century, the chief scientist on a project to develop a fully self-aware, intelligent android. Also involved in the project is Raj Sundaram, one of the most sought-after robotics consultants in the world. Megan finds herself tongue-tied in the presence of this reclusive, handsome genius—but it is their work together she finds most riveting—and disturbing.

For deep in a secret installation in the Nevada desert, Megan and Raj may have created a monster. Self aware and fully cognizant of his position in a human world, Ander is determined not to be the slave of his creators. More frightening still are rumors of a so-called Phoenix Code, which could create new and better androids, altering forever how humans and their creations interact. Soon, Megan and Raj find themselves caught in a deadly dilemma, running a race against time to discover the meaning of the Phoenix Code before it is too late to save Ander—and possibly all of humanity with him.

Coming soon from Bantam Spectra